The Garden Where Four Rivers Flow

The Garden Where Four Rivers Flow

The Angel's Song

Uriel Hart

Copyright © 2022 Uriel Hart

The moral right of the author has been asserted.

Apart from any fair dealing for the purposes of research or private study, or criticism or review, as permitted under the Copyright, Designs and Patents Act 1988, this publication may only be reproduced, stored or transmitted, in any form or by any means, with the prior permission in writing of the publishers, or in the case of reprographic reproduction in accordance with the terms of licences issued by the Copyright Licensing Agency. Enquiries concerning reproduction outside those terms should be sent to the publishers.

This is a work of fiction. Names, characters, businesses, places, events and incidents are either the products of the author's imagination or used in a fictitious manner. Any resemblance to actual persons, living or dead, or actual events is purely coincidental.

Matador
Unit E2 Airfield Business Park,
Harrison Road, Market Harborough,
Leicestershire. LE16 7UL
Tel: 0116 2792299
Email: books@troubador.co.uk
Web: www.troubador.co.uk/matador
Twitter: @matadorbooks

ISBN 978 1803132 433

British Library Cataloguing in Publication Data.
A catalogue record for this book is available from the British Library.

Printed and bound in the UK by TJ Books LTD, Padstow, Cornwall
Typeset in 11pt Adobe Garamond Pro by Troubador Publishing Ltd, Leicester, UK

Matador is an imprint of Troubador Publishing Ltd

For the New Children, both old and young

Here stands the angel of the golden gateway,
a gateway that shines brighter than a thousand suns,
come from the garden where four rivers flow,
in search of his long-lost but not forgotten love.
This angel who once sang at the beginning of the all,
who shall sing once more at the end of all things.
So be wary you few who would come to this place,
who would walk through this gateway,
who would drink of these waters,
where three ways meet and time stands still,
for only the true heart may bear the rapture of the fair kind.
Yes, be wary of this book which is not a book,
whose words are writ in fiery tongue,
this nugget of gold from the alchemist's cauldron.
Yet if still so willing, be you wild, wise and tender,
be you silent and still,
and listen to the angel's song.
And listen to the angel's song.

Contents

The Golden Gateway	1
After Today and Before Tomorrow	18
Neshama	28
Red Star Rising	41
Master of the Hidden Craft	57
Mother of a Million	69
The Silver Thread	85
Nocturne	98
The Valley of Gehenna	108
She Rides a White Horse	124
Loom of Ariadna	136
The Narrow Gate	143
The Quickening	157
Where Three Ways Meet	164
When Beauty Smiles	178
The Spiral Staircase	186
Machowl	197
Weeping Fire	210

One Stitch Unsewn	218
The Watchman's Horn	226
Hungry Ghosts	238
Endless Echoes	252
Yuriko, the Lily and the Covetous King	264
Thrice Blessed	277
A Bruised Reed	291
The Pale Shadow	300
Quintessence	312
Wind Dancer	320
The Sacrifice That Is No Sacrifice	328

The Golden Gateway

Be still.
Be still now, our children.
Be still now, our joy,
our hope, our love, our light.
Take rest from your labours, from your sport and play,
safe held in our arms in the last light of day.
Come now, be heedful, hear the voice of the angel,
and listen to the David's song.
And listen to the David's song.

There once was a carpenter who lived in a clearing by the side of a mountain. And by the side of this clearing, by the side of this mountain, there stood a great forest of cedars. A mighty assembly were they, tall and majestic, all garbed in ancient coils of knotted bark and sea-green moss, vestments more wondrous than the robes of King Solomon. Like sentinels they stood, the vast girth of their trunks pulsating with power and vitality, their branches held high in endless prayer. To hear the voice of these cedars filled some with dread and some with joy, a sound of wind and waterfalls and crackling fire. Of demons that muttered. Of angels that whispered. Intoxicating too was the sublime scent of its fragrance, perfuming the distant valleys, pastures and plains, as alluring as the Queen of Sheba in all her splendour. Varied and many were the tales of those few, those few who dared enter the dark forest depths. Mysterious strangers unexpectedly met, drifting down pathways like morning mist. Shafts of iridescent light, dancing and shimmering high above the treetops, rainbows emanating from a source unseen. Tales of how the forest gave rise to strange thoughts and uncanny visions, stirred long-forgotten memories, both sad and ecstatic, of things somehow sacred and set apart. And as the eyes of many fell upon this unearthly gathering, rippling like waves upon an emerald ocean, some wondered whether it was not the wind that caused the trees to dance, but the trees that did cause the wind to be.

As for the age of these trees, none truly knew for sure. There were some who said they were a hundred years old. There were some who said they were a thousand years old. There were some who said they were as old as the mountain, and some that they had stood here since the beginning of the All. The Davids, the storytellers of the tribe, would sing to the children of this forest's great beauty, exquisitely fashioned by some unseen hand, filled with a presence that caused tongues to be stilled and spirits to soar. And it was said that hidden somewhere in the dark forest depths, lay a grove no map could either trace nor find, for only the true heart could come upon it. An enchanted place, a magic place, at whose centre there stood a golden gateway, whose light burnt brighter than a thousand suns. The children would listen, their eyes glazed in wonder, their mouths hung wide open, bursting with curiosity and overflowing with questions, yet heedful of not breaking the storyteller's spell. From whence had it come? To where did it lead? What manner of miracle shone beyond its twin pillars? And as they quietened their thoughts, sat as still as they were able, the words of the Davids sounded out ever more clearly. For this was the gateway to the heavenly garden as spoken of in the holy scriptures. The Garden of Eden. The Garden of Paradise. The Garden of Great Delight. The Garden Where Four Rivers Flow. This garden from whence we all once did stray.

How this carpenter loved the forest, this great family of cedars. He loved them as his family for they were his family. He loved to smell their fragrance upon the wind, to hear the music of their leaves, to see their roots delve deep into the earth, his mother, their branches reach high to his father, the sky. As a boy he had climbed them, always content to be held in their clasp, unyielding as a mother holding a newborn babe.

"Look. Look how high I have climbed. Look at me all you winged ones, for behold, I can fly with you. Look at me, my friends, in the village far below. Look at me if you can, for I am as invisible as the wind. I am as tall as a mountain. As high as the clouds. I can sail upon the moon. I can reach out to the sun and clasp the stars in my hands."

His eyes would grow wide in awe and great delight, huge distances and limitless panoramas spreading out before him, far to the mountains, across the valleys and wide-open plains, all the way to the city and sea. And sometimes when he rested, enveloped in silence, he wondered if the great artist had seen such a vision when beholding earth and heaven upon the seventh day. For ever as such are the thoughts of our children.

When he was sick, his mother would make medicine from their leaves and bark and he knew wellness would return like spring after winter. Like dusk after dawn. Its taste was sweet and fragrant upon his tongue, upon his lips, for the ancient trees also loved his family, his tribe and circle, and so gave freely to them of their bodies. They loved to feel the tickle of the young walking ones upon their branches, to hear the songs of the old ones as they walked towards the shining beyond. Deeply they felt a timeless kinship, these trees of remembrance, forbidden to be felled by the axe of any man, except by the hand of the one they had chosen.

Here this carpenter lived with his wife in their abode of stone and cedar, and with her he knew great happiness. Through many seasons their love was forged and tempered, through lightning and thunder and arching rainbows, through the heat and the chill, the light and the dark. She loved to bathe in the merry green fire dance of his gaze and to look upon the lines etched upon his face. Some spoke of the times they had shared: of how they had laughed and smiled when they were still young, chasing the leaping salmon where the two rivers meet, of secret kisses beneath a high summer moon, of fierce arguments and frowns transformed as if by magic into shining smiles. Sometimes she would laugh with him, saying, "Oh, my love, my sweet man of green, filling my hearth with the scent of your mistress. How fortunate you are not wed to a jealous wife, for truly I know you share your good heart with another. Do you not know I see another has captured your heart? That I see the way you look at her, the tender touch with which you hold her, how you gaze upon her as she dances in the mist and twilight, the dawn and in the glow of a moonlit night? Shall I ever have to share you, my beloved husband, my willing servant and master?"

When still young he feared he would lose his love, for who could live with one so consumed with their craft? But now he saw the slight curve in her beautiful mouth, curved in an inward smile and felt only peace. For how he loved to carve the wood the trees had gladly given. These trees that taught him the inner mysteries of their very being and essence, that he might carve in knowing. And his craft was exceedingly beautiful and he did make for many: for his family and tribe, for rich and poor, for priests and princes, for kings and queens. But cradles and canopies were all alike to this good carpenter and he imbued each with the song of his spirit, of his own kind heart.

One day, as he returned home early from the forest with wood and leaves sprinkled upon his back, he saw the distant form of his wife. It was a special evening heralding a night set apart. The Passover night. As ever, his steady footsteps quickened for the sight of her, eager to once more reside in the balm of her good company. He loved to share with her the thoughts and happenings of his time in the forest and the forge, to hear of the time she had spent apart from him. To break bread with her, to laugh a little and feel her touch upon his dusty, muddy skin. No longer was it strange how she always seemed to know when he was coming, and it was his delight to see her face turn towards him and see her lovely smiles. But this day she did not turn, nor did he hear his name cast from her lips. Only instead, the faint sound of sobbing. His heart leapt up like a startled deer and he felt sorrow. He threw down his sack of precious cargo and ran to her.

"Why are you crying, my love? What has happened? Are you hurt? Has any harm befallen you?"

His wife turned to face him, brushing away the tears trickling down her cheeks, her eyes still reddened and filled with sadness. She smiled for her husband and stood up to greet him.

"I am sorry, Heshel. I did not realise you were there. It is nothing. Please, do not be troubled, my husband. No harm has befallen me. No harm. I am crying because I have been watching a butterfly that came to rest upon my dress."

Though somewhat relieved, still he wondered what had caused such apparent grief in her.

"Speak to me of this butterfly, Rebekah. For many are the times I have seen your dress adorned with butterflies and wondered why they come to thus settle upon you? Yet never before have they been the cause of such sorrow."

She looked at Heshel. To feel such sorrow yet behold such a face.

"Aaaah… my love… this butterfly, if a butterfly it was? Such a beautiful creature to behold. Wondrous." She fingered the air as if weaving upon a loom, her eyes shining with a liquid lustre. "Yet I could not fathom how a butterfly had come so early in the growing season. Where had it come from? Such strange thoughts arose in me, my Heshel. So strange I was unsure if they were even my own. I wondered if it was the first of its kind, for in all my days in the forest, I have never seen such a butterfly. Or perhaps not the first, but the last. Or maybe it was the only one of its kind. How would it feel to be so, I wondered? Such feelings this butterfly stirred in me. Such feelings. I marvelled at the shapes and textures of its wings and wished I could weave such beauty. It was coloured with a violet such as I have never seen before. Bright, bright violet. Maybe it was the same butterfly that flew forth from the Garden of Paradise of whom the Davids have sung?"

She looked at Heshel. Her heart felt gladness to apprehend the light of understanding in her husband's eyes.

"As I watched over it, I realised it was watching me too, maybe even wondering about me as I wondered about it. I watched it trembling upon the hem of my dress. So fragile. So very beautiful, yet so alone. And then I knew. Yes, I knew this butterfly had found its final resting place. How strange this place should be upon me. I watched its last shiver before departing this good earth and wished I had the power to breathe new life into it. But I could not. So instead, I sang to it. I sang to it with all my heart until it became still. Still, as all things must one day be stilled."

She paused for a moment in deep reflection.

"As even our love must one day be stilled, my good carpenter."

She sobbed once more. He looked into her eyes, filled with so many questions he knew he could not answer.

"Am I not silly to cry at such things?"

The carpenter felt great love for her sweet and tender spirit and sensed there was even more to her tears than this. Even more to her sorrow. More than she could admit to him or even to herself. For in the passing of the butterfly, she had felt a long-held hope die within her. He looked at her, his beloved wife, whose tears he could not assuage. Was she not too a beautiful and fragile butterfly, trembling upon the hem of his robes? She said no more of this that evening but went and cooked a delicious feast. And they did somehow find laughter, a laughter which echoed from their dwelling all the way to the forest.

But he knew her as well as the wood he carved. That night at the Passover, in the shelter of the great hall, Heshel gazed at his beloved amidst the good company of their tribe. He saw her smiling as the children sought the hidden affikonan, the unleavened bread, laughing and squealing in the excitement of the chase. He saw her heart tremble, watching their eyes shine like owls in the night, each one patiently awaiting the spirit of Elijah to come and drink red wine from the silent cup. He felt her listen to the youngest of the tribe, nervously and proudly reciting the Kiddish, the blessing and prayer. Her eyes danced in the firelight in great delight. Yet he also glimpsed her secret sorrow.

As sudden and swift as a hawk on the hunt, the spirit of understanding came upon him. He knew Rebekah had arrived at the certainty that this child would never be the offspring of her body. He remembered how he had once seen her with her hands clasped together, pointing to the sky as if in prayer. How he had seen her touching her belly and heard her crying out. Over time, the fear had grown that she could never be with child, for she held within her a barren womb. The two of them had spoken of this many times. She felt she had failed him, that she was not a whole woman and their union could never be complete. And his sorrow was that he had failed his bride for his seed was bad, that he was not a whole man and their union could never be complete. But of this, he remained silent, knowing there was no greater pain than the sorrow of a mother. Many times he had told her that she and his trees were all he needed. Yet the wound still grew. His pain grew deeper, for there was nothing he could do to give his love what her womb cried out for. So this time he said nothing, instead only holding her in his strong, gentle arms. He just held her.

That night as she slept, he slipped out of the cabin and ran to the forest in great despair.

"Great trees, my ancient kin and kind. Oh, please help this sad and sorry man. If it is in your power, whisper to me so I may know how to make my love with child. What leaves may I use? What bark must I brew? What must I do? Is there anything this simple carpenter can do to bring joy to the heart of his bride?"

Yet he heard nothing. No reply. No response to his cries. The little remaining strength ebbed away from his work-hardened body and he fell to the ground like a struck-down cedar. He fell for a thousand years into an abyss that sucked him in. Never had he felt so alone or devoid of hope. For his own life he cared not, but only for the grief that filled his sweet, brave maiden. The world went dark and his vision blurred into nothingness. Only silence and nothingness.

"This must be death," he thought, before thought too retreated. No longer could he smell the fragrant aroma of his beloved cedars, nor taste the pine and cypress-scented air. His hand reached out in the throes of death. And something took hold of it. Something held it firm.

"Is this what death feels like?"

"I am not death, Heshel. Do you not remember me?" spoke a familiar voice.

He slowly opened his eyes. Before him he saw a whispering willow, the very same willow he had once known in his youth. And therein, the flame-haired spirit: the Lady of the Forest.

"Did you think I had forgotten you, the one who set me free to follow my dreams? No, this could never be, my beloved carpenter. This could never be. And now has come the moment, for it is my honour to help you as you once helped me."

With infinite tenderness, she held his hand.

"Blessed walking one, our ancient kin and kind. Heshel, son of the fisherman, son of the healer. The young man who once came to soothe my sorrow and quench my longing. Heshel, he of whom the stories are told by the old cedars to the tender saplings. Our Heshel. Never alone or abandoned, nor out of reach of our protection. Did you not know that your sorrow is our sorrow too?"

To hear her voice again. To feel her touch. From somewhere deep inside, his anguish flowed out with the force of a fast-flowing river. This proud carpenter, not given to tears yet not strong enough to stem the torrent of his grieving heart. But this wound he had kept hidden from everyone now lay open and exposed, seen by the eyes of this Lady of the Forest. Seen by her beautiful eyes that blazed with mercy. He felt his wounded heart being touched by her hands. No, not her hands. Her very soul. A touch as delicate as a spider's web. Probing and soothing his aching heart. A wind from the east, fragrant with wisdom and kindness, as soft as the brush of a butterfly's wings.

"Heshel, Heshel, our kin and kind. Walk once more amongst us as you did when you were still but a boy. Come to me. Come to we. May you know that this very evening, this very night, you and your love have been betrayed by your laughter. Your laughter which did wind its way to us, to bear witness to your heart's secret anguish. Secret even from each other. And we did know anguish too, for ever as such is love."

He felt wrapped in linen, in a warming wind. Held in her arms, once more. How he had missed her. Oh, how he had missed her. Falling, falling, as he had once fallen, long, long ago. Neither alone nor forsaken. And was he not too but a butterfly, trembling upon the sleeve of her emerald robes?

"Listen to me. Listen to we. Listen with your all. For this night shall be as no other night. Listen and see, mortal one. Listen and see and stand upon me. Climb upon my branches as you did as a boy, and look upon this star-filled sky. For on this night set apart, there are glad tidings written there for you and you only. And glad are we, our friend and redeemer. Yes, glad are we."

He climbed his way upwards, feeling just as he had when he was a little boy. And when he had climbed as high as he could, he saw, shining brightly through the veil of rustling leaves, the seven stars that were holy to his tribe. For a moment, the Lady of the Forest ceased her sweet communion, only swaying and dancing in ecstatic silence. The motion of stillness. Memories awoke of how he had once been rocked in his mother's arms. He closed his eyes and heard the sound of leaves that chimed like temple bells. A mighty and majestic stillness. A pregnant void. A voice. The silence that speaks. Nothing and everything. Everywhere yet nowhere. Full yet empty. A heart must burst beyond its boundaries to know this love. Listen. Listen. He heard her singing only for him, the birds and the wolves falling silent to hear her, to hear the sweet song of their beloved lady. Who dares break the sanctity of this silence? Only she. For she had more to say to this mortal one, held firmly in her grasp of branch and hand.

"Do you hear it, our good carpenter? Do you hear the song of these seven sisters? Let us lend you our ears, our love, that you may hear them sing of the Blue Star Spirit. A spirit most high and seldom come."

Never had Heshel listened with such intensity. And as he listened as if with new ears, he thought he caught sight of a bright blue star, cradled amidst the seven stars.

"Listen with your all now," continued the flame-haired spirit. "Listen closely, for this high spirit yearns to walk in your world. Yet it has been decreed that this may only come to pass by the choice of a mortal one. A choice that has been given to you, our Heshel. To you and you only, do not ask us why. A choice to be made here where three ways meet."

Heshel felt an unexpected and animal fear. He felt like Atlas with the weight of the world upon his shoulders. Who was he to make such a choice? Just a man. A simple man. A simple carpenter who made his home by the side of a forest. Neither Solomon, a priest, or a king, but just a carpenter.

All this the Lady of the Forest heard. She looked at him, her beautiful eyes wide, wide open, her ruby-red lips slightly ajar and breathing in deeply, her hand clasped upon her heart. Astonishment and concern written all over her face.

"Why… you are Heshel. Our Heshel. Heshel of whom the stories are told. Heshel of the strong arm and mighty axe, whose blow split asunder the sealed gateway between the worlds, for not even the dark magic of the Pale Shadow could withstand the might of Heshel's blow. Heshel, whose axe is the lightning and the thunder. Whose sharp blade is but a lover's kiss. Whose eyes see far. Far and wide. Which see into our world. Into our realm. Heshel, the mighty one. Heshel of the true and steadfast heart. Heshel, master of the many crafts. Heshel, friend, servant and mortal king of the Fair Kind."

She saw Heshel struck as if by the blow of a mighty axe, to hear the weight and import of her words. She smiled at him with eyes filled with kindness and understanding. The smile of a friend, a look that spoke of unbreakable allegiance.

"So, our Heshel, know that if you should so come to choose, a child shall be conceived before this night gives way to morning's first light. But if this should come to be, you must know this child shall one day be called to make a sacrifice, just as other hearts have made oath here where three ways meet. And if this conception should come to pass, you must promise you will not intercede, even if you see your precious wife's heart seem to be breaking. Only your faith in us, the rooted ones, shall be your salvation if this moment comes. If you cannot so choose, your path shall still be a good and blessed one. So, our good carpenter, be still and choose. Choose well and be well."

The carpenter did just as the Lady of the Forest asked and gave himself over to the spirit of stillness and prayer.

And then, after a moment or maybe a lifetime, he gave of his answer.

"Beloved willow, my holy lady and my salvation, I know well that I must choose this night. And this must be my choice alone, for as such has my holy lady spoken. Yet I am a carpenter with no axe, no blade, no tools. I am a rabbi without books, a fisherman without a rod, a weaver without threads. Please, my lady, please help this lost carpenter one more time, for I do not know how I can make this choice on behalf of my beloved? I know that to be with child would bring her the greatest joy, yet I also know this joy will bring her great sorrow. It cannot be my right to make such a choice on her behalf for she should be free to choose herself? If it be right and proper, please help me. Please guide me for my strength is faltering."

He felt this lady, this dazzling spirit, easing her way even closer towards him. Her eyes looking endlessly into his. A beauty beyond compare. Her skin upon his skin, her heart upon his heart and even everywhere else within.

"My good carpenter, how I have always swollen with happiness to feel your touch upon me. Through you, I have come to know the secret wonders of the walking ones. Through you, I have come to know your pains, your delights, your conflicts and kindness, your anger and tenderness, your deepest dreams and visions. And through you, I have come to know the innermost heart of the walking ones. Listen to this old tree one more time, for only this can I say to you this night. Listen, you who are sufficient. You are correct when you say it is not your right to make such a choice for another walking one. But you are not two spirits but one spirit, for your love has made you as such. As these two bodies shall make one body, if you shall so come to choose. Not two decisions but one decision, for you are hers and she is yours. Now, tomorrow, forever and always."

The branches of the cedars moved just a little, yet this little moving was sufficient to reveal to the carpenter the infinite ocean of stars sparkling brightly above. And now he could see more clearly, the brightest, bluest star he had ever seen, flickering brightly amidst the seven sisters as they danced in procession, each one holding a candle, an illuminating light. This, Heshel saw with the eyes of his heart. And with the ears of his spirit, he heard their song. As the blue star descended and came ever closer, he began to feel within his breast a second heart. A father's heart, for as such was the love he felt for this star, this soul. And so too did this spirit feel such a love for him. All of this, the Lady of the Forest gladly witnessed. All was now clear. All was now right. The heart of this good carpenter broke into the song of his decision, with all of the leaves of the forest rustling in happiness to witness his word.

"Then so it has been chosen and so shall it be. You and your love shall know joy this night. Love each other beneath our canopy of leaves and stars and know the quickening. Make your hearts as strong as the rafters of Solomon's temple and the beams of the ark. And on this morning of his coming, for a son he shall be, we desire you to sow a circle of seven cedars. Upon the eve of his seventh birthday, you shall bring him to this circle, for this shall be his school and his temple. Here he shall learn what he needs to know, to do that which he needs to do. But of this choice you must remain silent that this magic be kept strong."

With this, she smiled upon him as only she can smile. And, before she departed and he went on his way, she spoke to him one final time, whispering, whispering, as only a lover should ever whisper.

"In every joy, a secret sorrow. In every sorrow, a secret joy."

And then she was gone, the air still tingling with the symphony of her presence. The good carpenter quickly returned to his wife, the forest still shimmering and swaying with joy. Quickly, quickly, he runs. So quickly he seems to take flight, no longer feeling the earth beneath his feet. Racing, racing. His heart is racing and galloping and pounding. Swift as a stallion through the corridors of watchful trees. So swiftly he runs that he whips up a wind. The robes and the train of a homecoming king. And all the while he sees but one thing. The face of her. The face of Rebekah. His Rebekah. This weaver of magic and mystery, whose threads were wrapped all through and around his heart. Inseparably woven together.

Ahead he saw their dwelling, nestling in the clearing by the side of the forest. Closer still, he now could see a light flickering through the window, where within she awaited. He opened the door, careful not to disturb her sleep, walking to the side of the bed with the ease of a good dream coming. He saw her stirring. He saw her move and turn to look at him, as she often did in the play of the night. Her hands reached out now to touch her husband's skin. But he was not there. She opened her eyes to discern a familiar form, gazing at her from amidst the shadows.

"Is that you, Heshel? Why are you not in bed? Where have you been?"

He struggled to speak, yet speak he must. Like the youngest reciting the Kiddish for the very first time.

"Wherever I roam, my Rebekah, I shall always remain at your side."

His voice faltered, choking and brimming over with feeling for her. He took her hand and tenderly stroked it. Her fair skin was as pale as marble, as luminescent as a harvest moon. Her beautiful eyes still glazed with sleep.

Her delightful mouth, yawning, breathing in deeply. As she stretched and sat up, he eased in beside her and cradled her in his arms. He saw curiosity aroused and dawning in her eyes as she wiped the sleep away. In these eyes, he saw the rising sun. He saw the pearly moon gleaming. Heshel held Rebekah's hand in his. He held it as if his life depended on it. He felt it trembling. He knelt down beside her like a priest before the altar. How wild he looked. How wild and handsome. Wild like the wind. As wild and strong as a wind from the north. As warm, soft and gentle as a wind from the south. A fire burning by her side and burning for her only.

"Come with me, my darling wife," said Heshel in half-whispered words, in a voice that for a moment was no longer his own. "Let us two depart, Rebekah. Let us go to the forest and make our bed there, for there is magic abroad this night."

"I feel it too, Heshel. I see your coat sparkling as if showered in magic dust. I see your eyes blazing with a joy I would know. Let us not wait a moment more lest it fly away. I will come with you, my beloved. I will gladly come with you, my handsome one. Lead me by the hand, my husband and true friend. Lead me, good master. Lead me to the place from whence you have come. Lead me to the pitcher from whose waters your thirst has been quenched. Lead me to the waterfall in which you have bathed, in which you have been freed from heartache and despair."

All this they then sealed with a kiss. Yes, this they sealed with a kiss. Hand in hand, they walked into the forest. Hand in hand and heart in heart. And, as they did so, Rebekah thought she caught a fleeting glimpse of a violet butterfly darting this way and that, fluttering beside her all the while. Over the arching, violet bridge that spans this world and that, Rebekah and Heshel did walk. Then, when, and now.

Now, when and then. Upon this night that was as no other night, these two did know each other as they had never known each other before. She, the Eve and he, the Adam. And in the crescendo of their love, they heard the sound of laughter and saw a blue and blinding, liquid light. Of this, they never spoke again, a robe of silence most befitting. Back to their house they went not saying a word, still tingling and on fire with new-found hope. That very night Rebekah dreamt her womb was filled with shafts of blinding rainbow light and felt a stirring within. She felt filled with glory for glorious she was. So glorious that the unseen world crowded closely all around, just to behold the blessed sight of this weaver, this daughter of Ariadna. And with the dawning of a new day, an immense and vibrant rainbow arched above the forest. Into this, the good carpenter went, that he may sow the seeds of the seven cedars, just in the manner the trees had shown him. In a spirit of prayer he dug the soil, carefully planting each precious seed until they formed a circle. And when he had finished, he bowed his heart and quietly uttered these few words:

"Always and forever."

And gladness filled the glade.

After Today and Before Tomorrow

It happened one morning, many moons earlier in the season of singing. His seventeenth birthday had been fast approaching, time to put on the mantle of manhood. Time to follow the path mapped out for him, to commit himself wholly to the rabbi's calling. Yet the burden of his father's expectation weighed so heavily upon him, that Heshel sometimes wished he had not been born a man at all. Better to have been born not with feet, but roots. Not flesh, but bark. Neither hair nor arms, but leaves and branches. For his heart cried out to be that for which it felt fashioned. The heart of a carpenter. Just a simple carpenter, and nothing more. But now he must leave such childish indulgence behind him, or so he had been told one time too many. Only in the depths of the forest could he find refuge, here where time seemed somehow stilled. Where it all made sense. Where it all felt right. Once more to be amongst his brethren, to feel his heart begin to sing, a red-breasted robin set free from the cage. Yet he knew this joy would all too soon come to pass. And though not even the trees could hold back the tide of his calling, today, upon this fairest of spring mornings, he would drink in of this magic, one final time.

As he walked towards the forest, Heshel caught sight of little Zakiya at play in the field. He paused for a moment, watching her head bobbing upon the red ocean of poppies.

"Zakiya. *Zakiya.*"

Yet she did not hear, for though she was near, she was far, far away. And where she was, she heard only the wild wind whispering above the surface of the meadows, the contented cooing of a thousand turtle doves. A wistful smile stole across Heshel's face, to see this delightful vision of youthful abandon. It awoke memories of how he too had once run through this same poppy field. How he had felt himself to be riding upon the wings of a great red dragon, a fabulous beast that could belch out huge plumes of fire, scorching the earth should he command it to do so. And though he knew the time for such childish whimsy would soon be over, for just a brief moment, he too heard the sound of a thousand turtle doves cooing.

Onwards he travelled with growing heartache. For him, and him only, the cedars stood waiting. This walking one whose passion they would not so easily yield. A wistful wind leapt forwards from a twist of their boughs, brushing his skin, blowing back his hair. Deep beneath his feet, thick roots hummed out in tender contralto. Heshel felt stricken by an all-consuming grief, overwhelmed by the full consequence of his allotted fate. For he had decided that if he could not follow the carpenter's path, he would never set foot in the forest again. How could he, when all that would walk there would be a hollow shell? A hungry, homeless ghost, perpetually tortured by the sight of his forever lost love. Better to forget. Better to fall into a dreamless sleep than to suffer the anguish of this neverending half-life. To be condemned to hang yet never die. This, the price wagered for his heart's sole transgression. Fated like Prometheus, who dared steal fire from heaven.

In dirge-like spirits and with heavy footsteps, his vision become bleary with barely held-back tears, he crossed over the threshold into the forest of Elnazar. As he did so, he did not notice the lovelorn glance of Rebekah fall upon him, nor did he hear her plaintive sighs. All this, the forest did also feel, for his sorrow was their sorrow too. Closer they came, though rooted to the spot, each one a priest bestowing absolution. To feel their breath on his skin, to hear once more their holy whispers, to wander again amongst the trees of remembrance, Heshel felt subsumed into a lighter spirit. He began rummaging for stray chunks of fallen wood, tossed and scattered around the roots of the trees, sifting through them to find the choicest finds. Carefully he selected them, block by block and piece by piece, placing them inside his trusted sack, to carry them home upon his broad shoulders, there to carve and fashion however he should please.

"Release me."

What was this? An unfamiliar voice? A barely audible whisper that spoke of distress. Yet whether near or far, Heshel could not tell. He felt a chill spread through his blood. He knew well that for all its beauty, this forest was also a ferocious and deadly place, a place all too easy to find oneself lost in. Here lingered not only the sweet fragrance of the trees but also the scent of death, decay and of the bloody kill. He stopped and listened to the surrounding silence, broken only by the occasional sound of bird call or the scuffle of some unseen presence amidst the brush and bracken. He looked all around but still saw no-one. Maybe he had imagined it? Such things were commonly known to happen in the forest.

Strange sounds and sights. Voices fashioned by the wind as it rushed across the treetops and played like pipes through hollowed branches. This was surely what the voice must have been? Heshel decided to continue on his way. But after only just a few more paces, he heard the voice once more.

"*Help me,*" it called out in a piercing cry, a cry Heshel now knew was not the voice of the wind.

"Who is there?" he called out in rising panic. "What has happened? Where are you? Are you hurt or in danger?"

No reply. Only a dreadful silence in the now ominous atmosphere. How quickly everything could change here. How swiftly anything could shift its shape and form. Fear reared up in the dire and dismal half-light. Creeping shadows slithering closer, glimpsed darting here and there from the corners of his eyes. Maybe there was a hungry wolf or a bear on the prowl? If he strayed upon it as it made ready to devour its victim, it might attack him instead, an attack that would be brutal and swift. Or perhaps it was a person who was trapped in the bogs? Had not these bogs taken the lives of a good few before? If not a bog, then maybe an unknown and dangerous assailant was abroad, having left their victim bound and captive, at the mercy of the forest? This lawless one could be watching him right now, making ready to mete him harm. Instinct told him to leave without delay. But this Heshel was a dutiful young man who did not lack a fighting spirit. He could not abandon whomever had called out for his aid. He must compose himself. He took a few deep breaths and called upon the counsel of reason, just as the rabbi had taught him. He determined it was most likely someone unfamiliar to the ways of this forest, someone who had become entangled in the thick shrubs or roots. A traveller. He took a few deep breaths before moving towards what he thought to be the direction of the voice.

"Please, *please*, release me."

"I am coming. Where are you? You must help me for I cannot see you."

"Here I am. Yes, here I am. Just around the very next corner. Please, I implore you, have no fear. I hold no desire to alarm you in any fashion, nor any wish to cause you harm. My only desire is that you will step closer, so I may see your face once more. You must come to me as I am unable to walk towards you, for I have not been fashioned in such a way."

The unseen person must surely be injured, this one who spoke in unfamiliar tongue? Maybe even delirious? He moved closer.

"Thank you, young walking one. Thank you for heeding my call. Here I am. Yes, here I am. It is I who have called you. I, who am the abiding spirit of this tree."

Heshel's thoughts were now in complete disarray. He was by nature a pragmatic young man, but now he felt himself to be falling into the gaping mouth of madness.

"It cannot be that trees can talk," he reasoned.

"Can you say this for sure?" came the reply in a velvety voice. A woman's voice. "Perhaps the rule of reason holds no sway here, son of the fisherman, son of the healer."

"How can you hear my unspoken thoughts, whomever you are? How do you know whose son I am?"

"Because I have learned to listen with my all. Can you say the same, young walking one?"

"I do not understand any of this at all."

"Time may remedy this lacking, if you should so will it to be."

It must have been one of his friends playing a trick on him. So further gave counsel the voice of reason, still as yet unwilling to loosen its obdurate grasp.

"Please come out now from behind the trees where you are hiding. Show your true face to me and end your sport."

"There is no concealment here, Heshel. Only revealing. Revealing and nothing more. Ah… if you would only see a little further. For here I am. Yes, here I am, standing and waiting in readiness for you, and for you only."

Though Heshel could not see her, he heard such longing in her voice. He must find her. He felt nothing else mattered. Not even his life. Yet despite all his effort, find her, he could not. He tried to step forward but remained rooted to the spot. What magic is this? Memories came to him of stories sung by the Davids, of spirits of the forest that could cast a spell upon a mortal one, leading them into the realms of madness. To be lost in limbo, in an endless maze. But these were only tales for children. Yes, these were only fantasies.

"Tales for children? Fantasies? Do you truly take me to be formed from only the substance of your imagination? Say it is not so, our Heshel. But if so it is, then pause to consider whether it is your kind and not we who are the written stories."

Heshel could feel the rule of reason being forced to relinquish its grip. Or reason as he had for so long understood it to be.

"Please forgive me. I am sorry. I did not wish to cause you offence. And I am sorry that I cannot find my way to you."

"Only the true heart may find the way that leads to me. There is no other path."

Such sorrow in her voice, filled with a yearning he knew only too well.

I wish my heart were true, for then I could find you, he sighed in unspoken words. But he could not hide from she who heard each and every forest whisper, who heard the sound of each leaf and blade of grass.

"Come closer. Yes, come closer, but only if this should truly be your true desire. Take three steps closer and let the forest take the measure of your heart."

This voice he felt compelled to follow. Just three more steps to everywhere and nowhere. With renewed determination, he walked around the next forest turning. And, as he did so, he saw a most extraordinary sight. Stretching out seemingly endlessly before him, the longest corridor of evenly spaced-out cypresses he had ever seen, converging into a nexus of vibrant, fiery green light.

"Do you not know, young wandering one, I have spoken to you many times before this hour? That through many of your passing seasons, I have watched you as you have walked unseeing amongst us? Do you not know that each time I have called out to you? Yes, I have called out to you but you did not hear. But all this changed on the day you unknowingly strayed upon me and came to rest against my bark. What a shock it was to feel you, you who wear the robes of transience and mortality. A shock and a joy, as if something wondrous had made its abode deep within me. Yet I also felt a pain, sharper than a beetle boring into my bough. Ever since that moment, I have desired to follow you upon feet of flesh. I have desired to walk down this corridor of cypresses and into the world of the walking ones. And if my desire could only come to pass, then I would know the wonders of which I have heard the birds singing."

"I think... I think I understand."

Whether he thought them or said them, these words he spoke. Sudden birdsong broke out all around. Heshel walked still closer towards this light, seeing something dancing behind a veil of green mist.

"Come closer to me, Heshel, and I will tell you the more. Yes, come closer, and I shall tell the telling. Of how today I heard the sound of your footsteps approaching. What joy I felt to hear those footsteps which I have come to know so well. And I felt this may be my last chance to call to you, for you might never come this way again. I chose to give voice to my longing even though my desire is forbidden in the realm from whence I come. But how shall I live if I am forbidden to follow the dictates of my own true heart? Is it not better the lightning should strike me down than to continue to live this half-life?"

The words of the voice could have been the unspoken words of his own heart and soul. How beautiful, this voice. What manner of being could give utterance to such beauty, a beauty he hungered to know.

"So, Heshel of the Fierce Kind, does it lay within your gift to release me into your world? If it does, will you do so? Will you release me that I may wander into the world beyond the glade?"

Heshel felt each word resonating in his flesh and bone. Closer and closer, brighter and brighter, as if walking through the spray of a tumbling waterfall. And then, he awoke. And then, he saw. There, right before him, a most beautiful willow, a willow he had never noticed before. As tall as an elephant, shooting out strands of brightest green, its lithe and sinewy trunk glistening and wet with dew. He reached out a hand to touch her trunk, to touch her bark, to feel the textures of her wondrous, emerald gown. To sift his fingers through her beautiful leaves. Her touch was electric. It caused the hairs on his body to stand on end. His muscle to twitch. The scales to be removed from his eyes. And there, residing in the bough of the willow, he saw a small, winged figure amidst the folds and veins of wood. She was very beautiful, her red hair flaming like fire.

"I can see you, I can see you. I see your body, your wings, I can even see your face. But what am I to do? I do not know how to release you. I do not know how to cut you out, for surely you are formed from spirit and not of bark. No axe nor blade I possess can set you free. What shall I do, spirit of the tree? What shall I do?"

"If it is true your heart would release me, then you must know it is only a rare magic that can unlock this door. Go home and find the one who holds this key, the one who can teach you how to release me. Then, if you so desire it, return to me. Go home and find the one of whom I have heard the squirrels speaking. The one from far away. Go home and I shall wait for your return. I know well how to wait. And if this be your truest will and desire, then you must return when a year and day has passed in your world. A year and a day, not a moment less nor a moment more. For on this day and this day only, the door to our world will be open for you, but thereafter, shall be forever sealed. Ask me not why it is so, but so it is."

With a heart filled with longing only to serve her, Heshel gave his reply.

"I will go home, beautiful spirit. I will look for the one who can show me how to release you and then I will come back. I promise I will return."

"Then I shall await that gladsome day, Heshel. And because you were moved just by pity for my cries, I shall tell you the more of who I am. I am the Lady of the Forest. And the ways of our kind I shall teach you, good carpenter to be, if you so choose it."

"Beautiful spirit, I do so choose."

"Very well, Heshel. Then one more word shall I say to you before I must depart. If that moment should come to be, if you should come to find me waiting at the open door, then gladly shall we reveal to you the mysteries of our bodies, that you might carve an ark worthy of a king. A drop of our green fire shall run through your veins and your works shall be living, for therein shall we make our abode. But of all this, you must hold your silence."

And with these words, the Lady of the Forest was gone, leaving Heshel rooted like a tree amidst the silence. Silence, silence, all now silent, her last whispered word now become a wind. Silence. Completed. No more words to be spoken. No time to linger, to gaze upon the glory of her face and flame. Time to depart. Time to return. Return to time from that which is timeless. Once more to the world of all known and familiar. Return though you feel your heart might break. Right now, right now, this very moment. Return by the way from whence you came. Home to your hearth and home to your kindred, there to seek the one from far away. Seek and find and find and seek, this one of whom the squirrels are speaking. And here, and here, this lady shall be waiting, waiting for you here where three ways meet.

Neshama

Little Zakiya had been the first to see him. There she had been at the edge of the forest, chattering happily away to herself, a little light feather floating on a carefree breeze, her nostrils filled with the sweetly perfumed air, her ears echoing with the sound of the birds in song. No longer the chill of a winter wind upon her cheeks but instead, a mellow heat that stroked her skin like warm, wet kisses from a mother's lips. Above her, a busy song thrush wheeled in flight, its beak stuffed to the brim with moss and twigs.

I must hurry and collect sticks to make myself a nest, she thought to herself.

Look over there, a drove of hares scurrying across the exposed and open grasslands, halting for a moment to survey the terrain, long ears pricked up and bodies taut. If only she could fondle even one in her arms. Suddenly she stopped and gasped with excitement to behold ahead in the distance, a field filled with a thousand or more red butterflies. What a vision it was. What a game she could play. She would run towards them until they exploded into flight and turned the bright blue sky into vibrant blood red. Excitedly she ran as fast as her small legs would carry her. But as she got closer they did not flutter away, for they were not butterflies at all. Rather, they were a vast expanse of poppies stretching out endlessly all around. Red beyond red. A red such as she had never seen before. Her eyes opened wider and wider to see it the more. The teeming earth beneath her feet tingled with possibilities, as numberless as the flowers that formed this rippling red ocean, made more vivid still against the veil of azure-blue sky. Bright, rich, ruby-red, as if red snow had fallen upon the land. As if sheaves of corn had been transformed into a lake of wine with just one wave of the magician's hand. Or maybe a giant had passed this way, a giant so tall that his head reached the clouds, who had shed but one drop of his blood upon the earth.

"I'll pick this one and that one. Oh, and that one too. Thank you poppy for letting me pick you."

Soon her basket was overflowing with the choicest flowers. For a moment she rested from her harvesting and peered into her basket. It looked so full. Her fingers swam beneath the surface of a multitude of petals, fishing for the stem of what seemed to be the largest poppy of all. "Ha, ha," she giggled to herself, "I have found the poppy queen."

To gaze upon it caused her to stare in near disbelief, to see the wondrous form she could distinguish at the centre of every single flower. There, engraved like a precious stone in a ruby-red ring, a many-spoked and golden star. To see it nestling there, she now understood a little better what her mother had once told her: that she was like a poppy, vibrant and bright, full of life and passion, at whose centre there lived a star come down from the heavens, therein to make its temporary abode. She held it still closer to her face, blowing upon its delicate petals, watching them flutter like butterfly wings. What magic this breath, this little wind inside her.

In her mind's eye, she saw all the flowers entwined into a beautiful garland to place upon her mother's head. Her young heart trembled to think of the look of surprise and delight on her mother's face when she would gift her this crown.

Her basket now full, Zakiya made ready to leave. As she gathered her things she felt hungry, despite having eaten all of her bread and cheese. Even the goat's milk was gone. Suddenly she sensed she was not alone. She saw a movement in the corner of her eye. She turned around to see no further than a hundred or so footsteps, the form of a man in a nearby clearing. She froze. He was dressed in strange attire and was making camp, a tent that was black and textured as if made from hair. So black was the tent, it looked as if it could not possibly belong in the scene before her. It looked wrong. The man was holding a bulging sack in one hand. Nearby, a huge white horse was contentedly grazing. So white was this horse as the sun reflected upon its immaculate sheen, that it also looked somehow wrong and out of place. Zakiya felt a sick feeling in her belly. Her heart raced to see him stop his labour as if he too were sensing an unseen presence. He stood with an eerie stillness, his hands resting upon his hips, gazing upwards towards the summit of the red mountain, deep in thought. His appearance was so strange she thought he might be a spirit from the forest. Maybe even one of the hungry ghosts spoken of in the ancient stories? His tent was surely made from human hair. His sack surely bulging with a dead body he had dragged back to his camp, to cut off its hair to add to his home, to cook its flesh in the pot she saw hanging above a fire. Maybe he would not even cook the body but consume it raw. What if he saw her? What if right now he was sniffing the air like a ravenous wolf to catch hold of her scent? If she was not careful, he might catch her and gobble her up. He was a ghost. She just knew it. How else was it she had not seen him there before? He must have been invisible. She had to leave right now. With a sudden burst of energy, she ran and she ran, not once looking back, most of the poppies falling out of her basket, scattering upon the ground and leaving a trail behind her. Past the edge of the forest and across the fields, across the brim of the hill until she saw the village of Elnazar coming fast into view. What relief to see its sanctuary. As she ran, Deborah the baker caught sight of the frightened child.

"What is the matter, Zakiya? What has happened? Are you hurt?"

Zakiya stared at Deborah, her cheeks flushed red and a wild look in her eyes.

"There is a ghost in the field."

"A ghost? Why, there are no ghosts, sweet child. These are only stories."

But Zakiya was not so easily appeased.

"There is a ghost in the field. A hungry ghost. He lives in a house made of human hair and he cooks people to eat."

Deborah crouched down on her haunches and took Zakiya's hand. She smiled kindly at the little girl.

"Calm yourself, Zakiya. You are safe now. Your imagination has just got the better of you, that is all. Tush, the storytellers should not tell such tales to small children." She calmly stroked Zakiya's cold and shaking hand. "The truth is you have probably just come across a traveller. Think about it, my darling. Why would a ghost need a home to live in or flesh to eat?"

But still Zakiya remained unpacified.

"I do not know. But there is a ghost. There is. He looks like a man but I know he is not."

Zakiya snapped her hand away and ran off. On seeing her running, Deborah felt a sudden dread rise up inside her, a feeling that sucked all the air out from her lungs, leaving her gasping and reeling. As if there had been an avalanche inside her.

Rebekah. Rebekah, now her only thought. *Where is my Rebekah?* Her daughter had gone roaming alone in the forest earlier that morning and had not yet returned. All manner of fears now arose in mother Deborah, overwhelming her like a torrent and sweeping her away. What if this man, for a man he surely was, had brought harm upon her girl? She had heard tales of kidnap and murder, of men who had become wild monsters, of avaricious slave traders who would stalk in the shadows, picking their prey as easily as Deborah could pluck a daisy from the grasslands. With no other thought than the safety of her daughter, she ran off to the fields. As she approached ever closer, she saw something glinting upon the ground. Specks of bright red.

Oh my God! thought Deborah, with mounting fear. Blood. It was blood. "Rebekah. *Where are you?*" Quickly she arrived at the trail of blood, only to find it was not blood at all. It was a trail of poppies. No time to stop. She ran and ran as fast as she could until she came to the poppy field.

"I must calm myself down. I must be calm. Rebekah is unharmed and I have let myself be carried away by the imaginings of a child."

She tried to draw in a few deep and soothing breaths. But instead of calm, the ghastly, nameless dread grew stronger, a claw reaching deep into the keep of her belly, ready to scoop out long-forgotten memories and expose them to the shock of the violent light. Memories, blurred phantom-like images of a day long since past. A day of falling rocks and frantic cries. Ashen faces twisted in horror, giving voice to words she could not bear to hear. Words that could shatter a heart into a million pieces. She could not bear it. Run,

run away into the merciful mists of oblivion. She swooned, with only the sea of poppies to break her fall. Her body fell to the ground like a rag in the wind, there to rest awhile in the dreamless void.

How long she had lain in nothingness she did not know, but slowly, she found herself to be once more. She felt something take hold of her.

"Simeon? Is that you?"

How her heart wished it were so. Once more to breathe in his familiar scent, the smell of clay and limestone, of fire and red wine. And whether she was alive or departed, she did not know for sure.

"Have no fear, my dear, for all will be well."

A voice. The voice of a man. Deep and gentle. Most pleasing to hear and with a calming cadence. But oh, my heart, it is not his voice. Not the voice of him who was once my husband. She felt a cloth upon her brow, cool, wet, and reviving, slowly being stroked across her cheeks and chin and neck. Am I ready to awaken? I do not know. Slowly she opened her eyes. A light so bright and dazzling. She squinted until gradually, a form took shape. This light, a revelation, revealing him to her for the very first time. Surely this must be the spirit of Elijah, come to take her home? How handsome he appeared, she could not help herself from thinking. How strange she should have such a thought. Yet handsome he was: his beard of blazing silver and eyes of burning blackness, his radiant smile that could calm a cobra.

"Take a sip of this, if you are able."

The feel of cold metal against her lips.

"You have fainted but suffered no injury."

The taste of water upon her tongue, this tongue that another used to kiss in another life once lived. Cool and reviving, this nectar easing its way down her dry, scratchy throat. She felt as if she were tasting this heavenly unguent for the very first time. It felt fresh and cleansing as it streamed deeply within her, flowing into her all.

"Slowly, my dear. Slowly, there is no rush."

She heard the rustle of fabric. She heard the distant sound of wind blowing through the trees. She saw his skin, as dark as oil and ash, as moist and lustrous as the flesh of an eel.

"You are not the first woman to faint upon seeing me."

So spoke the stranger, bent down at her side and leaning over, his eyebrows quizzically raised in playful arches, a dancing glint and sheen in the darkness of his eyes. Close by she caught sight of a white horse's face. It whinnied loudly as if in knowing laughter, before returning to grazing with a disdainful toss of its mane, nonchalantly munching upon the delicious grass.

"Thank you, my friend, I love you too." So spoke man to beast.

The horse banged its hooves upon the earth. Deborah felt waves of vibrations coming through the ground and tickling her back. All seemingly conspired to force out a giggle. Why was she giggling like a little girl? Perhaps it was not water but wine? How like the appearance of an awakening queen, the man thought to himself. How strange he should have such a thought. Her skin as pale as alabaster. Her long mustard-coloured hair with some streaks of silver, tied neatly in a bunch at the back like knots of dough. Intimations of a diligent and dutiful woman. How pleasing the form of those sensuous lips, now slightly curling in the hint of a smile. Such a face he could gaze at forever, never growing tired of exploring each fold and contour. But now her eyes were open wide and looking deeply into his, probing his face and measuring his heart. Eyes that held two shining citrine crystals. Her senses returning, she felt more fully the man's hand holding hers. It felt warm. It felt like flesh. It felt filled with blood pulsing beneath its skin. Now, it seemed she was completely awake. But with this revival, her terror returned. A vision of Zakiya's face. Talk of hungry ghosts and thoughts of slave traders. Her body leapt up as if with a will of its own. She stood swaying as unsteadily as a newborn colt.

"*Rebekah*," she cried out with all the force she could muster. "*Rebekah, where are you?*"

She pushed the man's hand away and took several faltering steps backwards.

"Let go of me. I must find my daughter."

"Please calm yourself, my dear. Give yourself a moment to recover. Just a few moments. Then, I give you my pledge, we will find your lost daughter. Fear not, for I am highly skilled in the art of finding lost things."

The way he looked at her spoke of genuine concern. She reached out her hand in instinct towards him so that she could take a few more sips of water and be more fully revived. He smiled and nodded in accord, handing over his pitcher. She smelt it first. It looked like water and smelt like water. She drank for she was so very thirsty. Never before had she felt such thirst. She poured a little water onto the palm of her hand and wiped it across her face, then poured some more upon her head. She felt it coursing through her hair and down her back.

"Please, if you will, tell me what your daughter looks like?"

She hurried to describe her daughter in as much detail as she could. As she did so, she saw the furrows upon his brow start to melt away.

"Why, I surely saw this same girl earlier entering the forest." He pointed towards the small clearing into which he had seen her go. "She sat right there, gazing intently at something I could not see. Her hands were fingering the air as if weaving upon a loom." Weaving upon a loom? Four words that gave rise to a surge of hope. "Her eyes were filled with such awe I could not help but wonder, what manner of mystery had so caught her attention? I wanted to approach her but dared not disturb her from her deep contemplation. So I waited until she departed, only to find she had been gazing at a spider's web."

A spider's web? What more proof was needed? Only her Rebekah would sit and stare at a cobweb for so long. He had surely seen her. Yes, he had surely seen her. Yet though he had seen her, this did not mean that all was well. Her thoughts assumed the form of her dear friend, Yitshak, the butcher. She felt his fierce, guardian spirit come upon her. She heard his word. Be wary. Be discerning. Observe, gather, assess and act. Be wary of strangers who disarm with laughter. Be wary of those whose ways are unfamiliar, who live beneath the hand of a different rule. Clever indeed is the thief who steals in disguise into the heart of the temple. Be cunning, be patient, be watchful and heedful, before taking the measure of a human heart.

In such a spirit, Deborah looked at this stranger dressed in unfamiliar attire. Just because he had seen her daughter was not sufficient proof he was not a slave trader. Maybe he had taken her Rebekah and was holding her captive? Even now he might be scheming to take this young woman's mother as well. She looked at the tent erected in the near distance, made of black hair just as Zakiya had described. Here, right before her, was Zakiya's hungry ghost. She must be careful now. There would be no time to go for help. She stared at him with all the intensity of a wolf on the hunt. A mother wolf.

She stared and stared, not only with her eyes but also her heart. She felt full of suspicions. She felt braced to defend herself. Yet, for all this, she also held the strangest feeling. How familiar he seemed, this man whose eyes shone as brightly as burning coal. Familiar in the manner of a long-lost friend. Had she not felt the true touch of care and kindness when she had felt his skin upon hers? She composed herself as best she could.

"Please, tell me, sir, what is your name?"

"My name is Azar."

"Where are you from and what is your trade?"

"I am a blacksmith and a carpenter from the village of Asnavant."

"Asnavant? I have not heard of Asnavant. It must be very far away. What is your purpose for coming to Elnazar?"

She saw him go silent, bringing the weight of consideration down to bear upon his words. *Why did he do so?* Deborah thought to herself. *Why not just answer straight away? What did he have to hide?* She questioned him in a voice that was a cutting blade.

"Have you come here to steal our children?"

She saw him wince as if struck by a forceful blow.

"May the gods strike me down right now if I hold even the tiniest portion of such vile intent in my heart. But you are welcome to search my tent if you believe I would commit such a heinous crime."

She saw hurt and abhorrence in his eyes, eyes that held a familiar expression, the look of care in a father's eyes. To see such feeling, she felt a pang of remorse for having spoken to him so. Yet she knew it was not beyond the scope of a deceiver to call forth such feelings of sympathy. So Yitshak the butcher would have counselled.

"What proof can you give me your account is true?"

"There is no sufficient proof. Only an adept thief would seek to persuade you otherwise. But perhaps, if you were willing to give me the gift of time, you could then take the measure of my word?"

She liked the tone of his reply though she knew not why.

"I want to believe you, but how can I know you are speaking truly?"

He now said nothing. Instead, he simply looked at her directly, eye to eye, holding her gaze with a look that was neither forceful or mesmerising, but kind, still and open. She felt solace enter her spirit, the muscles in her body starting to relax and let go their grip. This testimony she trusted, the testimony of her own muscle and sinew, her own blood and bone.

"I am sorry. I fear I have spoken with too much force and harshness."

"No need to apologise, my dear. No need at all. I can see you have suffered a terrible shock. Believe me, my line of questioning would have been just the same if I were standing in your shoes. What could be worse than fearing that harm has befallen your child?"

"Thank you for your understanding. I have no need to search through your tent. Thank you, Azar of Asnavant, for bringing me such welcome tidings of my daughter. And thank you for watching over me and tending to me. I am in your debt."

"It is an honour to do so, daughter of Elnazar. And please, do not speak of debt. It is my honour to have watched over you."

"Tell me, is there any way I can return your help in kind?"

"Perhaps you would take some tea with me before you leave? Not only will it help restore you for your journey home, but I would also be grateful for your company. I have been alone for too long."

"Yes, I would like that."

"I would also be grateful if you told me your name."

"Oh, please forgive me for my rudeness. My name is Deborah."

"Deborah," repeated Azar, sounding out slowly every part of her name. She liked the way it sounded when spoken by him. She felt a playful spirit whip up inside her.

"But what assurance do I have you will not gobble me up? Maybe you are indeed a hungry ghost? You must tell me first what is your tent made of and what is in your sack."

"Why, my tent is made from goat's hair and my sack is filled with cedarwood to build a dwelling. What else would it be made of?"

"Never mind," replied Deborah, smiling.

"Perhaps you would like to first check what I am cooking in my pot and what is in my sack?"

"Maybe I will."

She went to take a look. It smelt delicious. She saw that it was soup. She looked in his sack. Chunks of wood and nothing more.

"These chunks of wood. Did you cut them from the trees of the forest?"

"Oh no, I knew not to use my axe upon these holy trees. I used only the wood the trees have gladly given."

"How did you come to this knowledge?"

"My wife gave me good counsel about the trees of remembrance."

Why did she feel a pang of sadness to know he had a wife?

"And how did she know?"

"Well, Deborah, this is a little harder to explain. Zara is guardian of a book that holds the power to reveal many hidden things."

"Speak to me of this book."

"So many questions," said Azar, with the broadest of smiles. "It seems it is not only water you thirst for. Please, if you will, I will answer all your questions in good time. But I really would like to have some tea. Would you mind? The turn of events has quite unsettled me. And it is the custom of my tribe that no guest should ever leave without being fed. Yes?"

He extended his hand towards her in invitation. Gladly, she accepted and entered therein.

Red Star Rising

"Welcome, Deborah. Welcome to my home. To my house of hair."

As she walked through the entrance flap, the otherworldly sight that met her filled the baker with wonder. For though furnished with only the most basic of things, to enter the tent was to step into a miniature palace, an Aladdin's cave, a world of vibrant colour and delicious, unfamiliar scents. It was cool, round and surprisingly spacious, lined with fabrics of many different shades, held up in the middle by a tall, single pole, elaborately painted with fruits and leaves. All was soothing to the senses, neat, elegant and harmonious, aesthetically pleasing: the cushions and pillows, the small, wooden chest, the carpets, the quilts, the pots and the pans. Momentarily, Deborah felt transported by the strangest sensation. As if everything was breathing. As if everything was dancing. The pile of books on the beautifully carved table. The mats made from goat's hair and dyed with henna. The long, gleaming sword, sending out dazzling shafts of reflected sunlight. The large, hanging tapestries. The dizzying melange of pictures and patterns.

"Please, Deborah, sit and make yourself comfortable. My home is your home."

Azar gestured towards an immaculately embroidered rug. Deborah kicked off her shoes and sat herself down.

"Rebekah would love to see this craft. Did you make this rug, Azar?"

"Oh no, I have no such gift. Zara made it. Now tell me please, Deborah, what tea is your preference? I have a wide selection of leaves and flowers from which to brew. Or maybe some coffee? See, I have the choicest beans."

He picked up a jar and tipped some beans onto his palm, placing them beneath her nostrils so she could savour the scent.

"Delicious, no?"

"Mmmm... beautiful. I have never smelt such coffee before. But please, if you will, I would like you to choose on your guest's behalf. Surprise me, Azar."

"I think you have perhaps already had enough surprises for one day. So, I shall prepare you a brew to both calm and restore you. And me too, for that matter. There, the physician has made his diagnosis."

"Very well, good master. I entrust myself to your good counsel and shall drink of your medicine."

She stretched out her legs, then proceeded to collect some cushions to make herself comfortable. Azar glanced at her curiously as he ground down some seeds.

"My, how like a busy beaver you are. Are you making yourself a nest? Or perhaps a dam?"

She laughed out heartily.

"I am afraid this old back has become too accustomed to sitting on chairs."

"I am sorry for my oversight. It is our custom to stay close to the earth. Let me prepare you something more fitting. You will find me resourceful and skilled at improvisation."

"Oh no, I will not think of it. I will do as you do in your home. I am in your world now. I would like to conduct myself according to your customs. I wish to learn of your ways." She clasped her hands together like a little child pleading. "Please, Azar. Please, teach me. You will find me to be a most attentive student."

"I do not doubt it. So I will gladly teach you, young lady, but only upon one condition. That you will promise to reciprocate in kind."

"Agreed."

So, amidst this slow dance of reciprocation, they whiled away hours sipping tea and chewing dates, Azar delighting in speaking of his ancestors: the wayfinders, the stargazers, the sons and daughters of Asnavant. The Black Stone Tribe. He spoke a little of their beginnings, of their long journey home to the foothills of the holy mountain; of their dreams, their struggles, their sacred stories. The foods that pleasured them. The songs that uplifted them. The games they loved to watch their children play. And as day became evening, Azar entertained Deborah with both formality and ease, dancing attendance as if she were a queen. How long had it been since the widow of the stonemason had last felt such attention lavished upon her? How good it felt to be thus sitting, talking and laughing, just in the manner old friends talk and laugh. Sharing with each other ever more intimate things. And amidst all this conversation, Deborah found Azar to be not only a blacksmith but also the fire priest of his tribe. The Baal-Azar. Yet of all the many things he told her, his face never lit up more than when he spoke of his wife.

"They used to think that she was a Jinn, you know."

"A Jinn? What is a Jinn?"

"A spirit that makes its abode in the mountains." He paused and looked thoughtful. "And in a manner of speaking, they were right. Yet Zara is far beyond the scope of words to describe."

Deborah had not often heard a man speak of his wife with such reverent words.

"It seems you have a most uncommon wife. It must have been a matter of great import that has caused you to be so far away from her."

"Indeed it was, Deborah. I was summoned."

"Summoned? Who summoned you here, Azar? I have heard no word of such a thing?"

"I heard the call of the red mountain."

"The red mountain? Mount Horeb? The mountain of the Prophet?"

"Yes. The mountain spoke to me in the form of a dream. And as I suspect you will enquire about the substance of this vision, I must tell you it is not our custom to share such sacred things with those who stand outside our circle."

"Oh," exclaimed Deborah, feeling momentarily rebuffed and unexpectedly hurt, before quickly collecting herself, as was her way. Azar looked closely at this woman. He saw the streaks of silver in her hair. They spoke to him of suffering. He saw the lines around her eyes and mouth. They spoke of beauty perceived in wide-eyed wonder. Of kind words spoken. This woman who did not stand outside his circle.

"Please forgive me, Deborah. I have spoken in error. Do not ask me how or why, but somehow you have come to unseal my tongue."

"Unseal your tongue?" she swiftly retorted. "Why, who in the world dare seal the tongue of the blacksmith of Asnavant? And if you do not mind me saying, I am fast forming the conviction it would be easier to stem the flow of the River Jordan than to silence this fire priest."

Azar regarded Deborah with surprise on his face, trying to take the measure of her words, before bursting without restraint into uproarious laughter.

"Ha, ha, ha," roared the magi in great delight. "By the word of Vata, I am uncertain as to whether you have made me compliment or insult? Still, I trust this good woman takes my meaning well enough. So, this river shall flow and this tongue shall tell. I shall speak of a vision that came to a young son of a fire priest, to turn his familiar world upside down. But first, let us go outside and sit in sight of the holy mountain. Such things should be done in their proper place."

Deborah nodded solemnly in silent assent. He took her hand. She gave it gladly. How content she felt to be led by the hand of fire priest.

"Come, let us make our seat upon this rock. This little piece of the mountain has been a good friend to this stranger since his first coming to Mount Horeb. That's it. Come a little closer. Sit by my side. Do not be shy."

She felt the brush of his tunic against her arm. She felt a thrill to feel it. She saw him take off his sandals, close his eyes and breathe in deeply.

"Ah, Deborah, is not the air exquisitely perfumed this evening?"

He stretched out his arms, palms faced upwards towards the sky.

"A moment to collect myself, please."

He shuffled his feet, his toes and heels digging into the earth. The feeling beginning. His skin starting to itch. She saw him shudder. Behind the veil of his eyelids, she watched his eyeballs, moving, pulsating, as if searching for something. The air sparked electric, a coming storm. His flesh transmigrating, a robe to be worn. A tabernacle in which something other fast assumed form. He began to speak. His voice was loud. Loud, crisp and clear above the ocean-deep silence.

"In truth, even now I still shudder to think of it. Touch my hand, if you will. Can you feel it tremble? Yes, my body still testifies to the aftershock of what I can only describe as a holy terror. I can assure you this vision was no pretty picture. It was an earthquake. It was a tidal wave sweeping me away from everything familiar."

He took a deep breath to regain his composure. How remarkable, he mused, that even after more years than he cared to remember, to give himself over to this memory still filled him with the awe.

"I was fifteen years old, still just a boy on the edge of manhood. Not that I saw myself as such, of course. It was then I encountered a most unusual young woman. It happened when I was selling trinkets from my stall in the market place of Estakhr. At first she had seemed to be no different from any other young woman out shopping with her parents. She had stopped to examine a piece of my jewellery. If memory serves me correctly, it was a most exquisite piece. A malachite necklace. And just like every good trader, I had been trying my utmost to seal a deal. But I became distracted by the sight of her ruby-red cloak and headdress, her golden tiara inscribed with strange symbols. My hand came to accidentally brush against hers. Now, in my homeland, such an act is deemed to be a crime. A transgression of God's law. Only a properly betrothed woman is ever permitted to be touched by a man outside of her immediate family. Not even the hand of a priest is permitted to touch such a virgin. I felt a sudden terror. I braced myself for her father to scold me, or perhaps even beat me. Or maybe, even worse, he might report me to the temple priest. I would lose my livelihood. I would be whipped in the main square as an example to others. I might even be imprisoned should the priest be ill-disposed towards me that day. Moments passed that seemed like days, waiting to learn of my fate. But they remained still and silent. I felt a growing relief that no rebuke had been forthcoming. Yet how in error I was to believe the danger had passed. For then it happened. The woman looked into my eyes with a forbidden intimacy. Her eyes were filled with knowing, devoid of the slightest trace of fear. She stopped me in my tracks. She utterly bamboozled me. I felt her spirit probing me and was helpless to defend myself. I would have screamed but had no voice to."

He looked at Deborah, trying to ascertain her reaction to all he was saying.

"Have I perhaps been too forward? I have not spoken of this to anyone else but my Zara. Perhaps you take my words to be no more than the ravings of a madman?"

"If it be madness, Azar, then so too could be said of all of our prophets and seers, with their strange words and visions. No, your words fill me with nothing but wonder. Your story intrigues me. It holds my attention a willing captive."

He bowed his head in appreciation.

"Very well. I will continue. But please understand, what follows is hard to explain." He pointed to a spot in the centre of his forehead. "With just one finger, she touched me here. I saw an explosion of indigo light as if something had been switched on inside my mind. So great was the shock, it jolted me straight out of my body, taking me to a place existing quite outside of time. I found myself standing at some other nearby vantage point, as if what I had thought to be 'me' had been split entirely in two. And the 'me' that was there, saw itself to be attached to this body by one single, silver thread. I saw my own face, every bit as clearly as I now see yours, the face of a somewhat brazen and callow young trader. I saw too, my frozen, dumbstruck expression. Yet I felt no contempt. I felt only love. Then as quickly as it came, the vision left me. I found myself returned to my body and not content to be so. And when I regained what remained of my senses, the young woman was gone. Disappeared. Nowhere to be seen."

Was that a tiny jewel-like tear that glistened in the corner of his eye?

"What was I to do, Deborah? The experience had left me with no stomach for barter. I was shocked and bemused. I was unsure as to whether I had only imagined the whole encounter? Perhaps I had fainted? Perhaps it had been no more than a delirium, a mirage in the desert, brought on by the heat of the midday sun? So I packed up my stall and made my way home, all the while thinking of this wondrous young woman. I felt a longing I could not fathom. I was filled with regret. If only I had been able to stay alert and awake. Perhaps then she might have taken me with her, for one such as she could have come only from the highest heaven? But she was a rare and beautiful bird that had taken to flight, flown far away, surely never to return."

He glanced to the sky with faraway eyes, following the flight of an invisible flock.

"That very same night, the dreams began. Again, please understand, I had been a boy who had no interest in such things. Visions were for the children, the possessed and the holy." He sighed, his sad eyes facing downwards. "How I must have vexed and perturbed my father, for though I was deemed to succeed him as the fire priest of Asnavant, I showed not even the slightest of priestly proclivity. But this all changed when I dreamt of the holy red mountain. It was a red such as I had never before seen in nature. It stood so high it touched the vaults of heaven. Its peaks pierced a sky which wept blood and fire to feel it. It was ancient beyond the ability of a mortal to measure. I felt… I felt as if it was alive. As if it was aware of me and trying to tell me something. But I did not then have ears to hear. And when I awoke, if asleep I had been, my sheets were soaked in sweat. I was greatly disturbed, for never before had I witnessed a greater glory. It was a vision surely not of this world."

Though she tried to conceal it, Deborah was taken aback and even a little afraid, to behold those eyes so ablaze in exaltation.

"Night after night, the vision returned. Night after night, setting me on fire. My familiar mind had departed. My thoughts were no longer my own. What madness was this, that I found myself desiring to become a holy man? What had she done to me? What spell had she woven? Perhaps she was a conjurer or a poisoner? A Jinn strayed far from the mountain? Maybe a saint, or even an angel? All I knew for certain was that I had no choice but to find her. So I hunted for her. I hunted in the market and the villages beyond. I searched in the foothills and upon the mountain peaks. I searched in the wilderness. I searched for her even in the depths of my dreaming. But nowhere could I find her. For she is she who is not to be found. No, instead I found only failure and grew sick from its taste. And, all the while, I burned with this fire from within, with all the ardour and agony of the lovestruck. Me, who knew nothing of the ways of love. I teetered above an abyss of madness. Poor young boy, who did not yet know that the divine is neither a prize to be won, nor to be courted through guile or wilful ways. She is a lover to be wooed. A goddess to be served. But time has been kind and brought me to a higher understanding. I have been blessed by a lady who taught me how to tend this fire. I have been blessed by a priest who gave me good counsel. Who gifted me faith, that I may wait for the summons of the holy red mountain, even should it be in a life yet to come."

He took Deborah's hands in his, turning to directly face her, his expression, ecstatic.

"How very fortunate this man has been. What mercy he has received. For this heart has come to open like a thousand-petalled flower. Yes, my sweet Zara spoke truly when she called me her lone scarlet crowfoot. Her flower of the eventide. Her late in blossoming, winter rose."

The sky blazed and flickered with the embers of dusk. The sun soon to set.

"Just listen to me talking. The night is fast coming. I must complete my obligation to you. Would you permit me to ride you home?"

"Gladly. But I find myself unready to depart. This mother worries for the welfare of this burning boy. Speak to me of his plight. What fate befell him? Have mercy upon me, magi from the mountain. Do not condemn me to a sleepless night, disturbed by the clamour of so many unasked questions. Please, complete your testimony. Tell me beneath the cover of this majestic twilight, of how this seed has come to full flower. Of the propitious wind that has carried you here, to watch over me in my hour of need."

Her words reminded him of his mother when he had been but a small child: a voice of gentle authority, persuading him to finish all the food on his plate.

"How am I to refuse you? Your wish shall be my command. But first I shall bring you a hide to keep you warm. There is a chill in the air and I see you shiver."

"Thank you, Azar, but I feel no need. It is not the wind that causes me to shiver. And this rock of Horeb warms me well enough, as so too does your story."

"Then I will speak of the advent of the Red Moon of Daena." She clapped like a child, then caught herself doing so. *What magic is this, that this man restores me in joy?*

"This is our ancestral name for when the moon turns blood red. By what name are such manifestations known by your tribe?"

"We name such moons the Cup of Salvation. A time which calls us to be ready for the Prophet's return."

"The Prophet's return? Do you speak of Elijah? Elijah the Prophet? Elijah, the fire priest? Elijah, the Lampstand of the Silver Shining?"

"The Lampstand of the Silver Shining? Why do you say so when only our rabbi thus names the Prophet? By what means have you become familiar with his hidden name?"

She paused in reflection as if searching for understanding. Azar watched her with pleasure, to see the bright light of insight illuminate her face.

"You have learnt this from Zara's book, have you not? Please, fire priest, speak to me of this book as you promised you would."

"Well, it is true I did bind myself to you in pledge. And it is true you have honoured your part of our infernal pact. I cannot deny your having graced me with your presence, nor having broken bread with me. An act, by the way, for which you have my eternal gratitude. The tide runs against me. The river flows ready to sweep me away. Poor magi, against whom all things now seemingly conspire, demanding I complete my part of the bargain. Very well, Deborah. But of this book I may share little, for it is not my story to tell. Zara calls this book her golden gateway. The Book of Love.

The Book of Us. It holds the power to reveal many hidden things. It speaks of that which is, and what once has been. It speaks of things still yet to come. And from time to time she lets me stray upon it, yet only in the wilderness. From its pages I have learnt much of sacred lore: the lore of not one tribe but the lore of many. I have learnt how to read from the book of nature. I have come to understand, in small measure, the language of the stars. For each thing, a pattern. For each thing, a cycle. For each thing, a movement, a rhythm, a signature and song. It was there that I learnt of the Red Moon of Daena, a rare and portentous sign in the heavens. A celestial alignment of which our prophets have long spoken, heralding the time of the return of Daena. Is your tribe familiar with her name?"

"No, Azar, we have not been so blessed."

He smiled inside, to hear her thus answer.

"How to speak of her, Deborah of Elnazar? Is mortal tongue so fashioned, that it should utter her high and thrice blessed name? For she is she who is both end and beginning. The Scarlet Lady of Merciful Countenance. The red dragon whose breath can set the earth on fire, whose wings shake the world and move the stars from their orbit. And in the Book of Love, I saw her coming. I saw the moon become darkened, occluded in shadow, her face turned red as if beneath a veil. Upon her head, she wore a crown of stars. I saw Meissa bent down before the rod of the fisherman; the bennu bird take flight from the crucible of ash. Al Dabaran, the red star, shining uncommonly brightly behind Parvin, the company of sacred sisters."

Though spoken with utmost gravity, yet still a twinkle in his eye.

"No trifling matter, I assure you. I cannot tell you, Deborah, how many sleepless nights I have spent before all this came to pass. For who would have thought it, that I should be deigned fire priest on watch and duty? And though many pretended otherwise, none truly knew what this vision might bring. No, not even Merhdad the stargazer, blessed be his name. So I did what it behoves a fire priest to do. I made myself ready. Three nights of fasting and wakefulness, of making penitence and prayer. I washed my robes in the waters of the mountain stream. I brought them to cleanliness by lavender and sage. I tightened my sash and, with faith, girded my spirit. I gathered my tools, each one vital and essential, ready to perform my priestly obligation. Ready for the rising of this Red Moon of Daena. Ready to make ritual, to make petition on behalf of our tribe. Ah, who knows the burden of the fire priest, for always upon their shoulders, the fate of the tribe. The fate of our children."

He stood for a moment and paced around.

"Would you care for some more tea?"

"No thank you. But please, Azar, take some time to refresh yourself."

"Very well, Deborah. A moment, please."

He sipped some water and lit a pipe.

"Is the smoke too overpowering?"

"Its fragrance is pleasing."

"I am glad. Its scent reminds me of home and brings me comfort. It helps settle my nerves. Good. I am refreshed and ready to continue my account."

He sat back down, close at her side.

"At last, it was time to go to the high mountain altar. To begin my ascent. Never had I been more prepared, yet never more anxious. And then it began. With each step I took, I felt I was followed. I knew, without doubt, there was none who dare intrude on the fire priest at ceremony. If not my kin, then what? A Jinn, a stray goat, or perhaps the wind through the rocks? I quickened my pace for time was pressing, whilst all the while, I felt a growing presence. Louder and louder, clearer and clearer, my name being whispered in familiar voice. So I stopped. I turned. Imagine my astonishment when I saw it to be Zara, hopping deftly across the rocks, her white robes stained in red moonlight as if daubed in blood.

'Listen to me, fire priest. Listen to me, Magi, for my time is brief. You must go a new way. You must tread a new path, a path only revealed by the bright light of faith. So go now, my love, my true friend and kind master. Walk you with swiftness. Walk you in safety. To the foothills, to the foothills, for your lady is waiting.'

"Before I could utter a word, she was gone. I did not understand. I could not comprehend. Zara knew me to be bound by my priestly obligation. Her words unleashed a plague of doubts and fears. What was I to do? Which way to turn? What path to follow? What choice to make? By now the sands of time were fast running out. The moon was rising, redder, vaster, than I had ever witnessed before. I felt despair, for such was my overwhelming sense of failure, I could have easily cast myself over the edge of a cliff. But then, it happened. My little miracle. I felt my heart begin to sing. Singing like an angel above my shoulder. Singing of my faith in my shepherd girl. My brightest blessing. I awoke as if from a fitful dream. I ran like a madman to the place where all paths converge. And it was then I saw her, a star descending like fire from heaven. Closer and closer, a shadowy figure, all draped in robes of bright ruby-red. Oh, Deborah, how my heart burst in rapture to see her once more, as real as real could ever be. My lady of Estakhr, utterly unchanged and radiantly smiling. Reunited after so many years spent waiting in the wilderness. She spoke no words.

She had no need to. I knelt before her. I felt her breath upon my neck. I felt her hands upon my crown. I heard a mighty wind arising, the whole universe making ready to speak. And the word came upon me: the word of Jabal Musa, the mountain of Moses.

"Listen. Listen. Listen. Listen.
To the Voice of the Silence.
To the Voice of the Flame.
The Prophecy fulfilled.
The Word uttered, proclaimed.
For when the red star rises and the blue star descends,
when these two have come to be as one,
when goat lies with leopard and wolf with the lamb,
salvation shall spring forth from the Rock of Horeb."

Azar paused, his words still reverberating. Can silence echo? If so, now it did. He stood up, took a few steps and shook his hands like a heron flapping its rain-soaked wings.

"So now that I have brought you to understanding of my reason for being here, I have a request to make of you. Do you consider it possible that your tribe will grant me favour to build myself a dwelling until I have fulfilled my calling at Horeb?"

He dramatically whisked off his turban and ruffled up hair, hair that was still surprisingly black, in sharp contrast to the blazing silver of his beard.

"If not, why, I shall have to live as a mountain hermit and clothe myself in robes of black goat's hair."

Deborah could not help but laugh. How quickly the terrain shifted in the presence of this visitor.

"Like Elijah? Perhaps that is not a good idea. Imagine if the children should stumble across such a sight. No, Azar, I shall gladly put forward your request. I will advocate with all my heart upon your behalf."

"Thank you. I could not have a more persuasive ally."

Soon they were riding as fast as the wind, Deborah shouting out directions whilst holding tightly around Azar's waist. Along the edge of the field of poppies, around the edge of the cedar forest. Across the wide open plains, across the brow of the hill, in sight of where the two rivers meet. And when they arrived at their destination, Deborah's arms lingered a few moments too long. He turned round to face her and made his goodbyes.

"Perhaps Zakiya was right?" she said thoughtfully. "Perhaps you are a ghost? And if you are not, then maybe it is me that has been a ghost? For now, I see a part of me has been dead for too long. So thank you, fire priest, for delivering this woman safely home."

Master of the Hidden Craft

Not master of you,
but Master of the Hidden Craft am I.
Of the seeing heart and ancient dance.
The willing servant of the secret flame that is never hidden.
And most beautiful are they who master this craft,
for they shall forever blaze in ecstasy upon the first
altar of love.

"Mother, where have you been? I have been worried about you. Why are you crying?"

So many competing feelings, Rebekah felt. Each one a wave. Each one a wind. So many feelings she could not tell which one was true. Perhaps all of them? Perhaps none of them? Relief and joy, anger and laughter, fear and curiosity and others too. Yet all of these voices were somehow stilled by the wonder of the vision that now appeared before her. There, upon the back of the largest, whitest stallion she had ever seen, she saw her mother riding into Elnazar, her arms wrapped around the waist of an unusually dressed man, her eyes moist and sparkling in the fast-fading evening light.

"I am so sorry, my darling," called out Deborah. As the horse ever so regally cantered towards Rebekah, Deborah turned to snatch a glance behind her, wondering if he would still be there? Had he been no more than the best of dreams? Had he melted away like snow in the sunshine? But she felt her heart smile, to see, to see that still there, he was.

"Please forgive me, my darling daughter, for having caused you such concern."

Rebekah gazed at this man, garbed in an emerald-green kaftan, a bright orange turban upon his head, his powerful hands upon the reins, a bright ruby-red ring upon his finger. She saw finely crafted sandals upon his feet, his confident, upright and noble gait as he sat in the saddle like a king on a throne. As if he had stepped right out of the pages of the ancient stories. As if she were beholding Melchizedek himself. How strange to have such thoughts.

"Let me introduce you to Azar."

"I am honoured to meet you, Rebekah," said Azar, offering his hand in greeting. "I see that this daughter shares a mother's beauty."

As she took Azar's hand, Rebekah noticed the slight flush of her mother's cheeks.

"Why did you run off in search of me? You knew I was going to the forest. Why did it take you so long to return?"

Deborah was not sure how to answer. She only knew she had been swept away by the mighty winds of change, that the spectre of the past had pushed her into an abyss, finding herself broken yet still alive.

"I cannot quite explain. Please give me time. I will tell you everything, every last detail. I promise. But for now, I can only say this: that something in me which was buried in the dark, has been brought into the light by some hidden hand. For when I ran to search for you in the poppy fields, I found not only Azar, but also myself. Does this sound strange? Can you understand this, my precious daughter? Maybe I have lost my reason due to my fear of some terrible harm having befallen you. Or maybe I became intoxicated by the scent of the poppies? I am not sure. Yet somehow, when I was with Azar, it was as if… as if time itself stopped."

The horse suddenly brayed and snorted, thudding its hooves upon the ground.

"Manners! Manners!" exclaimed Azar. "Apologies, Deborah. Please forgive the interruption. Oh, Jamil, a little patience would not go amiss, my fine and loyal friend." He affectionately stroked the horse's mane and turned to Rebekah. "I think he likes you. No, let me rephrase that. I am certain he likes you. You are honoured. Believe me, I speak the truth when I tell you Jamil does not take kindly to just anyone. Far from it, in fact."

"And what if Jamil should not take kindly to you?" asked Deborah.

"Well, let us just say that the fruits of Jamil's disaffection help gardens to prosper."

As if in agreement, the horse shook his tail like the sweep of a broom.

"Yes, this magnificent stallion has very refined taste and is *very* choosy. So, I had better introduce Jamil to you without further delay."

Azar winked knowingly at Rebekah.

"He likes such formalities. He is a horse of royal pedigree who was reared in the White Palace of Marib. We were brought together by the grace of a queen."

Jamil turned to Rebekah and curtsied before her. She had never seen a horse move in such a manner. Jamil's ears pricked up and he opened his mouth, seeming to smile with a toothy grin.

"Oh my," exclaimed Rebekah as she stroked his nose, "what a handsome fellow you are. But please forgive my rudeness, Azar and Jamil, but we must make haste. Yitshak is getting ready to ride out in search of you, Mother. Even as we speak, he is assembling the hunting party."

"Then I see the time has come for me to depart," said Azar. "You have pressing matters to attend to and I must also make haste. The sun will soon be setting and I must make my observances. It is time for the ghost of Asnavant to disappear."

But Deborah did not want to let him go. This he felt, betrayed as she was by the word of her hands, hands that still firmly gripped his own.

"Please, fire priest, will you grace our table and have supper with us tomorrow? I would like to reciprocate your hospitality. I also hope to have an answer to your request."

"Thank you for your invitation. I would be honoured. I would love to come. I am already looking forward to that hour, Deborah and Rebekah of Elnazar. Come on, Jamil, time for us to ride like the wind."

Mother and daughter listened to the thunder of hooves as Jamil galloped away. And as soon as they had disappeared beyond the brow of the distant hill, Deborah made haste to Yitshak's stables. There, in the courtyard, she caught sight of him, furiously pacing around and blasting out instructions to the other men, the very epitome of strength and leadership. Yitshak the hunter. Yitshak the warrior, the butcher, her steadfast friend. Husband to Sarah and father of Zakiya. His thick, black curly hair, as dark as a raven. His eyes yet blacker still. Piercing. Assessing. On fire with vigour yet as still and ready as a crouching leopard. Well used to watching and taking the measure of both enemy and prey. Tall and broad-shouldered with huge, powerful hands. Fearsome. Not one you would do well to antagonise. Leave medicine and mercy to the women. Leave learning and judgement to the rabbi. His sworn duty only the burden of protecting and feeding his own. He and his band of brothers, together fashioning an impenetrable wall of fire around the borders of Elnazar. And the deep scar carved beneath his left eye and the lesions on his arms were testaments to his pledge.

"Yitshak. *Yitshak*," cried Deborah as she raced towards him.

He sprang off his horse and ran to meet her. She felt the heavy thud of his long leather boots as they pounded upon the ground. She saw the tassels of his coat flapping like the wings of a raven. He came to her, embracing her like a tender hurricane, holding her and kissing her upon her cheeks. How relieved he was to see the widow of Simeon, this woman he had made oath to protect and to provide for through all the remaining days of his life. As such he had promised Simeon's departing spirit, this man who had been Yitshak's brother in blood and dearest friend. And nothing on earth, nor even beyond, could break the vow of Yitshak, this fiercest of men.

"Deborah. Deborah. Where have you been? Thank the Lord that you are safely home. I thought… I thought…"

So unlike Yitshak to stammer or falter, for every act of this ablest of hunters was steady and sure. A proud man whom it became to remain strong and calm in the face of adversity, in whom the enemy should never, ever be able to discern even the slightest trace of weakness.

"I am so sorry for causing you alarm, Yitshak. Please forgive me, my mighty man."

"All that matters is that you are safe and well."

He gestured to the other men to dismount.

"Let us go inside. You must tell me precisely what happened and of this hungry ghost."

On seeing Deborah entering the house, Sarah ran to her and gave her a hug. The wife of the butcher had also spent the afternoon worrying about her precious friend.

"Come, sit down," she said to Deborah, leading her to the kitchen table, a sisterly arm laid upon her shoulder, warm smiles upon her round and freckled face. "Let me pour us all some wine. I think we could all do with some medicine to calm us. Does Rebekah know that you are safely home?"

"Of course she does," snapped Yitshak, his nerves still on edge. He looked at his wife with a guilty look upon his face. "I am sorry, Sarah. Let me take my medicine."

"Well, Yitshak, you are excused, for it has been a trying day." She turned to Deborah. "He has been worried about you, more than my proud hunter will ever admit."

"*Mother Deborah!*" Bursting into the kitchen came Zakiya, her rest having been disturbed by the sound of voices talking downstairs. "I thought the ghost had eaten you."

"As you can see, my darling, I am very much alive. He has not eaten me, I am pleased to say. Look. Not even a nibble. You can sleep well, Zakiya, for he is not a hungry ghost. He is a man just like your father. And just like your father, he is a good man."

"So now, back to bed, my little poppy."

"But I am wide awake."

"Very well. Come, Zakiya. Let us check the horses and make sure they are settled for the night. I think your father and Deborah need some time alone."

Sarah lit some candles and stoked the fire before leaving with Zakiya. Carefully, with accuracy and focus, Deborah proceeded to tell Yitshak all that had happened, for it was not Yitshak's nature to have patience with idle chat. Deborah knew well that this warrior had need of making swift assessment. This was his way. His nature.

"Azar, you say." He could not conceal a slight hint of scorn in his voice.

"This stranger has frightened my daughter. There must be good reason for her to take him for a ghost? She is not unaccustomed to encountering travellers."

"His appearance is a little unusual, it is true. He is from very far away."

She recounted all that she had learned of Azar.

"From Asnavant? A Persian? A fire priest? A magi? I must be honest with you, Deborah. I do not like this. I do not like the smell of it at all. I have heard stories of these magi and their enchantments, that they are idolators and practitioners of the magical arts and are not to be trusted. How can you be certain he has not beguiled you?"

"Because my heart tells me otherwise. I only know that when I awoke, I did not know him to be either a priest or a Persian. I just saw the face of a man who was kind and concerned. A man who was helping me in my time of need."

She took Yitshak's hand in her own.

"Please, Yitshak. Please just meet with him. Please do this for me, for my heart tells me you two shall become the best of friends."

The best of friends? With a fire priest? Yitshak felt momentarily overcome with feeling. He would never want to have another best friend. That place belonged to Simeon. It would always belong to Simeon. But neither did he wish to cause Deborah any more hurt. Had she not already had her fill of suffering? If only he could have spared her the pain of that terrible day, when the earth had shaken and

Simeon had been buried beneath a river of stone, crushed and irreparably broken, never to return. The butcher had been there in the limestone quarry at Deborah's side. He had seen her run to her husband, lifting stones and boulders with the strength of three in her efforts to unearth him. But all she had found was his face now turned to ash. Yitshak had watched her hold his head against her breast, that she might warm and restore him as best a wife could, that her love might chase away even the chill grasp of death.

"Simeon," she had screamed out. "Simeon, do not leave me. Do not leave me, my husband."

She had called out with her all to his departing spirit, that he might hear her cries and find his way home. But the hand upon her shoulder was not his, but Yitshak's.

"He is gone, Deborah. He is gone."

The villagers would speak admiringly of the strength of Deborah, of her praiseworthy fortitude in meeting this terrible adversity. But they did not know, for she would not let them know, that beneath the widow's veil, she cried a little every night. No, they did not know, for she would not let them know, how deep ran the bitter tears of her desolation. This anguish, this agony, she would not, could not, permit anyone to come near to. Not even the good counsel of the rabbi. Nobody. Not even God, such was the perpetual sting of sorrow lodged deep within her heart. No, no more hurt did Yitshak want this widow to feel.

"Do you really want this man to stay here, Deborah? Please help me understand, for I am only a simple butcher."

"Oh, Yitshak, my dear friend, there is nothing simple about you. You are clever and cunning. How else would you be able to protect us all so well, our beloved and loyal servant? But in answer to your question, I can only say this.

I believe Azar to be a holy man. And I have no proof of this other than the testimony of my heart."

"A holy man, you say. I know this is something you would not say without good reason. I see too you are confident he poses no threat. Very well, Deborah. Let us go and discuss this matter with Rabbi Ishmael. Only a portion of this matter falls under my jurisdiction. The rest falls under the rabbi's judgement. Though it is clear the land upon which he wishes to build his dwelling is beyond our territory, the foothills of the mountain is holy ground. Let this matter be weighed by the wisdom of the rabbi. Let us go to him now without further delay."

"As you please, Yitshak."

It was only a short walk to the rabbi's home where Ishmael sat in the firelight, reading the Torah with his now fast-failing eyes, teasing his worn-out fingers through his long, white beard, massaging the crown of his near-hairless head. Contentedly he chewed on a morsel of his beloved cake, baked, spiced and seasoned by Deborah's hand, whilst feeding his soul with the manna of the holy scriptures. Yet though sitting by the fire as if in the garden of great delight, he sensed something coming.

"Oy, yoi, yoi. Who is that banging upon my door? Only the thunder and Yitshak can knock in such a manner."

"Coming. Coming," he called out in a raspy voice, prising himself painfully from the comfort of his armchair, then slowly opening the creaky door.

"Deborah. Yitshak. Yes, come in. Come in. Sit yourselves down and tell me what brings you both here at this late hour."

Ishmael listened attentively to their accounts of what had transpired that day, then signalled for them to join with him in the spirit of prayer. In silence, holding the holy scriptures close to his heart, with body stilled and eyes firmly sealed, he sought the guidance of the Most Holy One. And though often he feared the vision would not come, the Shekinah always gave of her grace to this most devoted of servants.

With his inner eye now opened, he saw many squirrels rushing around in a great commotion, loudly chattering and busy gathering. He saw a stone fall from the sky onto the still surface of the lake, sending out large ripples in every direction. He saw a great forest of trees, cedars and sycamores, acacias and cypresses, oaks and willows and many more. How diverse these trees, yet also how much the same. And amidst all these, a tree so high it seemed to touch the sky. Tall as a mountain and set apart. Its leaves and bark were as red as blood, a tree such as he had never seen before. He opened his eyes and breathed in deeply.

"So many tribes. So many different ways. So many trees of a different genus. Yet are we not all one family? Do not all trees belong to the great family of trees? Many trees, yet one tree only. Many trees from many seeds. And the seed of this man's coming has been a calling. A vision. An instinct, if you prefer. Is this beyond the scope of El Shaddai's power? Are we ready to conclude he has not heard the voice of the holy mountain? Can we be certain this seed was not blown to Elnazar by the breath of the Shekinah, and sown in this soil for some higher purpose? From what Deborah has told us, I am not in a position to do so."

"But Rabbi, is it not also true some trees yield a bitter harvest? That to eat of their fruit would be to bring us harm? Are not some fruits forbidden, and forbidden for good reason? We must choose. We must discriminate. We must not absolve ourselves of our responsibilities. We cannot merely cast our future into the hands of fate."

"You speak truly and persuasively, Yitshak, just as a hunter should speak. This is good, for such debate is the mother of truth. So let me ask you, my brother, is it not also true that sometimes the most bitter of fruits and deadly poisons have become the most potent medicines in the healer's hands? How should we discriminate without full and prior knowledge? How shall we decide which fruit is a balm and which is a bane? The question seems to be whether or not we should suspend our judgements and give this man a chance to prove himself. For is it not also said that the proof of a thing is the thing itself?"

"A chance, Rabbi? Proof? Can we afford such a luxury? Can we risk the well-being of our children in such a manner for the sake of one Persian?"

"Can we risk ignoring a portent from the Most Holy One?"

"What portent?"

"The word of the red mountain."

All this was hard for Yitshak, the hunter. He did not inhabit a world where mountains speak. He was not one for dreams or portents or fleeting visions. Yet he also had the utmost respect and trust in his rabbi and would never wish to give any offence.

"But Rabbi, this man worships different gods. How can we be sure the rumours are not true and that they steal children to sacrifice to their mountain gods?"

"Conjecture and rumour and nothing else. If our fate was subject to only conjecture and rumour, Yitshak, then we would all be dead and buried by now. For are we not also conjurers and murderers in the eyes of many?"

"Why give him a chance to remain here? Why take even the slightest risk for this man who is nothing to us? We have not one scrap of evidence that his word is true."

But Ishmael had also closely watched Deborah as she had spoken of Azar. He had seen her light up from a source somewhere deep within her, as bright as the light of the everlasting candle in the sanctum of the synagogue. He saw smiles upon her face, smiles he had not seen for all too many years. He had heard the enthusiasm in her voice and seen her hands held together as if in prayer. His seeing bore witness to the spirit of resurrection that danced in her eyes.

"Aaaaaaaaaaaah... Yitshak, my noble friend. Evidence. Evidence indeed. You say he is nothing to us. Yes, you are quite right. Or I should say that you *were* right until this morning. But look at your sister's face. Look at Deborah. Look carefully at her, our protector, and ask her why we should give this man from far away a chance."

Yitshak looked at the baker's face. How wonderful to see her dear face light up like this. He did not want to ask her why.

"The testimony of Deborah's heart is enough, is it not, Yitshak?"

Yitshak bowed his head in silent affirmation. As for Deborah, all she knew was she was a different woman from this morning. As if she had lived a lifetime in one day. That a poppy had somehow been seeded in her heart's fallow field. The brightest, reddest poppy.

Mother of a Million

Azar sat gazing at the holy mountain, daubed red by the hand of the setting sun. This sun, this magician, this priest of priests, turning vast white clouds into nuggets of gold. The teal-blue sky seeped with vibrant vermilion as if pierced and stained by the sharp, craggy peaks. Bright, bright red, just like the poppy fields in which he had first found Deborah. He thought of her face. Her broken, beautiful face, flickering and flaming with salvation smiles. How fortunate to have been blown to the stone mason's wife, upon this most preternaturally beautiful of days. Blown to safe harbour, so far away from home.

Home. How he missed his home. The place where she was. But now was the time to commune with his bride, to fly to each other through the crack between the worlds just as they had promised, the one to the other. Both his eyes and her eyes looking upon this same celestial fire, ready to soar through this same golden gateway. Where she was, he was. What he felt, she felt, no matter the distance that stood between them. Such love he felt for his shepherd girl. He closed his eyes. He saw her face. He smelt her perfume. He felt her touch. The sound of her voice as she pronounced his name. "Zara," he whispered. "My Zara." Such blessings. Blessings this day and blessings then. The day when he had first been blown to her, there in the foothills of Mount Asnavant.

He had been exploring by a stream in a snake-shaped gulley when he caught sight of a person at the side of a huge boulder. Carefully, quietly, he hopped from rock to rock, trying to remain concealed from this unexpected intruder. But the crack of one traitorous twig had betrayed his presence. A head turned towards him. The face of a woman. She was wrapped in woollen clothes from head to toe, her features shaded by a hat and scarf. She began pacing towards him. She held a crook. The attire of a shepherdess.

"What have we here?" bellowed out a sharp, powerful voice. "What is a child doing out alone in this remotest of places? Are you lost, boy?"

Though somewhat frightened, he found his voice. For this Azar was a proud and fearless boy. The son of the fire priest. Not one who should be frightened by a simple shepherdess who dared name him child.

"I am not lost. I am Azar, the son of the fire priest. I often come to walk here."

"Why so, Azar? What do you expect to find in this barren place?"

"I expect to find adventure. Perhaps a new hill to climb. Or maybe some undiscovered cave to explore."

"Yes. Go on…" said the woman. "I know the ways of children well for I am mother to many. I know there must be more to your being here than that."

Azar had the strangest feeling it would be best not to lie to this shepherdess.

"I like to watch the smoke rising when my father attends the high altar. I watch him although he does not know I am there. It is forbidden for anyone to be within sight of the sacred rituals."

"Then *why* are you there?" she barked like a dog.

Azar was startled by her ferocity. In other circumstances, he might have felt anger for having been rebuked in such a manner. Who was she to thus question the son of a fire priest? But now he felt as if he were trespassing on another's ground. Some inner knowing told him this was her territory. Her domain. It was he who was the intruder. The trespasser.

"I cannot say for sure. I know I transgress to be here and I shall endure the anger of the mountain god for having not heeded my father's commands. But something calls me here. I love to watch the dancing fire. I love to hear the song of the fire priest. My will is no longer my own."

"Then perhaps you are possessed?" the woman said in a voice that crackled and sparked. "Do you not know that it is not only I who am here with you? There are many, many more besides. Did your father, the fire priest, not tell you this? Oh yes, my child, there are many who make their abode in the foothills of this mountain. Very many indeed. And believe me when I tell you, they are not all as merciful as me. You should have listened to your father. Instead, your wilfulness has placed you in great danger."

Azar felt alarmed to hear her words. He clasped the ring upon his finger, given by a priest to bestow protection upon him. The woman saw this. She seemed to mock him.

"No magician's ring will protect you here, for you are far beyond the reach of even his power. Yes, my child, this place is under the rule of another."

His mother had warned him. She had warned him of the spirits that inhabit the mountain, but his stubbornness and pride had caused him to not take heed of her words.

"And yet," the woman continued like a storm cloud retreating, "and yet, what strange twist of fate should have caused our two paths to cross this day? I have taken a liking to you, young mountain goat. Yes, I have taken a liking to you. You are nothing if not proud and brave. But let me ask you, do you know the name of this mountain god in whose honour the fire upon the high altar burns?"

"I do not. I am not yet of age to know the holy name of the mountain god. Not until I am ready to succeed my father and attend the high altar, shall I know this."

She saw courage and defiance in his face. She saw too, the tremble in his lips and his skin grown wan.

"Why are you so certain you shall know this? You speak true but without full knowledge. The mountain god is not bound by the injunctions of mortal ones. The mountain god chooses the one she will. You may be hidden from your father's sight but here you are seen by a million eyes. A million eyes that are one."

Azar was astonished to hear the words of the shepherdess. Where had she acquired her learning? What was the source of the authority with which she spoke?

"You have taken me to be a shepherdess, yet have I said I am as such?"

"I see your clothes and see your crook. The attire of a shepherdess. And who else but a shepherdess would be walking here in this valley?"

"Who else indeed. Beware presumption, Azar, for it is a treacherous guide. Perhaps I have become something else, for even a shepherdess can learn to read. Even a shepherdess can find the sacred books if her heart so desires. Yet I am a shepherdess with neither sheep or goats. A very lonely shepherdess I must be."

"Forgive me for my presumption. But please tell me,

where have you come from and where are you travelling to, for there is no other village except our own in these valleys?"

"You are mistaken. I tell you now that my family have made our home on the other side of this mountain and have lived here for these last seven seasons. And I look after my flocks whilst my husband is away, for he lives the life of a camel trader. How my daughter and I miss him when he is gone."

"I am sorry. But where are your sheep? Are they lost? Would you like me to help you to find them?"

"Thank you for your kind offer but there is nothing that is lost this day, Azar. Nothing lost but only that which has been found. But if you wish to see them, they are just around the corner. And perhaps, one day, you will visit our home that lies close to the source of this stream." She lifted her finely fashioned shepherd's crook and pointed with it to give him directions. "I can see you are a fine young man and my family would be honoured to give hospitality to a son of the fire priest. And perhaps in exchange, you may ask the mountain gods to bless our harvest when you come of age."

Azar looked at the woman. Her features had become clearer as he had unknowingly stepped ever closer to where she stood. Her face was swarthy and handsome. She appeared younger than the picture he had formed of her. Her nose was long and slightly hooked, a shepherd's crook, long, alert and proud, occasionally sniffing the chill air of these high regions. Her chin was strong, jutting out like a mountain crag and marked by a small scar. As for her eyes, they were framed by delicate eyebrows such as he had not expected to see. And her eyes were dark and bright and young, with long, arching lashes. Her clothes spoke of scarcity and yet she had the bearing of a queen. The queen of the mountain. His spellbound eyes followed the shape traced in the air by her crook and he saw a path.

"I would like to visit you and see your home."

"I am glad. Gladder than you can possibly know. For I am mother to a single daughter. A daughter whom I try to ensure wants for nothing. A daughter of whom no mother could be prouder. But it is my pain to see she has no other children for company, ever since the day my sister departed. And children need other children, do they not? Maybe you would like to be with her sometimes? I think you will not find her to be lacking in beauty."

Azar imagined what this daughter might look like. He looked at the woman and reasoned she would be most fair. He felt a longing to find her. The shepherdess closely scrutinised him as he spoke.

"Yes, I would like to meet her. Maybe we can play amongst the stones and in the nearby caves? Perhaps she will tell me about your family and your ways, for I love to learn."

"I will look forward to that day. My daughter shall surely find you most handsome. And in honour of your coming, we shall prepare for you some of our choicest foods that you may have the pleasure of new tastes. For though we have little, the delicacies we make are unrivalled. As fine as fayre laid before a king."

Just to hear her speak was to have visions of a delicious feast, surpassing any he had ever known before. He could almost smell and taste the food.

"But listen, Azar. I must also warn you. There is further reason why my daughter does not enjoy the company of others. There are none who will visit us in our mountain home. There is much to fear here. Here, there are not only goats or sheep, not only lone wolves or lions that have strayed far from the forests and plains. No, here in these mountains, the Jinn make their abode."

"The Jinn?"

"The Jinn. And most fearful are the Jinn. They are more dangerous than a lone wolf or a stray lion for they feed upon the souls of mortal ones. They are the ravenous ones. Their hunger is never appeased. They strike their prey without mercy. Do you not know that to see a Jinn is to court death? I see that you have not noticed the piles of bones left upon the rocks. I see it in your eyes. Look upon them now."

Azar wished he could hide his eyes from her penetrating scrutiny.

"Yes, these bones were once travellers, just like you, who made their way through this pass, never to return. Some were left for dead. Some were taken into the mountain. And those few who survived were forever lost in madness, for it is said the Jinn will unceasingly follow those who come into their abode, pursuing them until they take possession of their thoughts, their bodies, their very souls. I have warned you, son of the fire priest. It is up to you if you take my words to be only the ramblings of a simple shepherdess, unschooled in the knowledge of the holy books."

Azar felt a chill spread through his body. He had always thought himself to be under the protection of the mountain god. But now, he was not so sure. He felt presences creeping up behind him. He saw shadows moving. He turned around quickly to see if someone or something was making ready to attack. Nothing. He turned to once more face the woman but she was gone, as if the earth had swallowed her whole. He looked all around. She was nowhere to be seen. It was surely not possible for her to have moved so quickly? She must be hiding behind the rocks. But why would she do such a thing? He was now close to terror. Perhaps all these rocks had once been people, people who had strayed upon the Jinn and been turned to stone. He prayed to the mountain god for protection. What else could he do?

"The mountain gods will not protect you here. And do you know why? We will tell you. Because you have broken the law. You have transgressed the obligations of your tribe. You have accepted our invitation. And now you shall make payment for your oversight and make good your debt. You shall pay the price. It makes no difference to us whether you are man or boy, for you shall make a delicious dish. You shall be an unrivalled delicacy. As fine as fayre laid before a king."

Was it the wind? Or was it the sound of countless, invisible nostrils, sharply sucking in the chill air, smelling him in anticipation of feasting? For the ravenous ones hungered and were hunting him. There was no escape. His fate was sealed, his last remaining choice only how he would meet his end. Should he run away as fast as he was able, or stand his ground and die in battle? But wait. Had not the shepherdess shown him a path? Maybe if he followed that path and made his way to her home, there was still a hope he might find refuge? He walked quickly now, making his way around a huge, black boulder where he came upon a small, still pool. At its side there stood an acacia tree.

"Sit here in this place. Compose yourself. Take charge of your fears and find your courage, you who have been called. Be still. Drink in of this beauty and know."

A voice. But not the voice of the shepherdess. He sat himself down and gazed at the water. So still, the water. So clear, this mirror, this window to the sky. And so clear was the reflection of the acacia tree, who could say which was real and which one the illusion? Two trees that were one tree. Two worlds conjoined. Hung between two worlds as if by a thread. He felt a desire spreading through him, to strip off his clothing and dive into this water. Into this beauty.

"Aaaaaeeeeeeeeeeee…" The sharp, rousing cry of a hawk cracking the stillness open. And now the acacia began to sway.

"Look upon me, you seeker of beauty. Look. Listen. Still your chatter. Shepherd your flock and tend your altar, for the ground upon which you walk is holy ground. Gaze upon that which you have unknowingly sought for. Come closer to me, Azar, young one of the wandering desert tribe. Here, where earth meets sky. Overcome your fear. Touch my robes of rock and flame. Breathe in of my kisses, for I do desire thee. I do desire this small and proud goat from the valley of whom my children have whispered. Wily as a wind around my hips. Listen. Listen, for I am the voice that has spoken to your ancestors for countless generations. But only few have found me, for only by the path of love can I be found. Look upon me now, Azar, for you shall never stumble upon this place again."

Azar wanted to cry out. Yet how strangely soft, gentle and melodious had been the voice that had spoken. Crackling as the lightning crackles. A familiar voice, not so different from the voice of the shepherdess. Her voice was a dance. Her voice was a silken robe, cool, smooth and teasing upon his skin. The cutting sharpness of a steel blade, the cry of a solitary owl in the depths of night. Her voice was beauty uttered.

He lifted his head and opened his eyes, eyes that he could not recall closing. Where had been the acacia tree and the crystal clear pool, was only she. A tall woman stood before him upon a rock, a rock so black that it shone with a blinding light. Where the rock ended and she began, Azar could not tell. She wore a robe that shone with the dazzling brightness of a winter moon. Around her waist, she wore a sash of blue that was a summer sky. Her bare feet were clasped upon stone, the talons of a hawk. Her fingers were long and delicate. Her neck, a tower bearing an altar of fire. Her eyes focused upon him with the same burning intensity as the desert sun. His body trembled violently. It knew he was prey. Those eyes spoke of his end. And yet despite all this, the strangest thing: his heart was singing. He steeled his spirit to behold her face, circumvented and crowned with tongues of flame, dancing into the infinity laid bare all around. He felt frozen recesses within him start to thaw. Ferocious. Glorious. Azar fell to the ground and prostrated himself. He knew not what else to do.

"Gaze upon me," she commanded. "Gaze upon me, child of mine, child of my spirit. Gaze upon me, the Lady of the Mountain, the Mistress of the Flame. The one for whom your ancestors have walked the corridors of death and silence to know. The one who is feared more than death itself. To you, I shall reveal my hidden name. To you, I shall reveal my hidden form and glory. Be still. Be silent. Listen and see. Hear and apprehend. For Al'Uzza am I."

To hear her name. To hear her name uttered. It resounded, it echoed, as if through subterranean caverns of memory.

"Al'Uzza am I. The mother of eternity and the eternal ones. And into my hidden temple you have wandered, yet by no stray step. For true and steady is the tread of the risen heart. Come into my temple and into my heart of hearts. My goat, my priest. My son I would have tend my high altar, where earth meets sky and sky meets earth, forever bound in a promise and sealed with a kiss. Come forward, my awaited one. Come, take one step towards me, you for whom my heart has ached. Come, gaze upon me. Gaze upon Al'Uzza, mother of the many and mother of the one. I, whose heart flames like fire upon the mountain summit, giving birth to all that is a shining newness."

Azar heard her every uttered word with his all. And all the while he heard singing, as if from a chorus of a million voices. Whether it was the Jinn or the angels no longer mattered. To hear was sufficient.

"Hear and listen. Hear the sky and earth singing with gladness, this hour, this moment. Look and see and apprehend. Look into my eyes, into my hidden heart."

He did as the Lady of the Mountain asked. All around he heard the sound of birdsong, a sound like a swarm of bees, of waves roaring and crashing as they break upon the shore. Her eyes were not eyes but molten flame, blazing in a light beyond light, blazing with the fury of an erupting mountain, bleeding and spitting liquid fire into the valleys below. Lightning flash, rumbling of the awakening mountain. Crash, crash, crash. Splitting and spitting. Crashing, crushing, exploding, deadly. Blood and bones, licks and lashes of fire. Bang, bang, bang, louder than the death knell of a thousand drums, announcing the bloodstained warrior's coming onslaught. No shelter from the cutting thrust of this lightning, as deadly as a snake, as deadly as the blade of an assailant's sword. Thirsty for blood. A full moon stained red, swooning, hovering above the mountain's jagged peak. As jagged and sharp as teeth poised for the slaughter. Her voice, a thunder crash from which there was no refuge. Her voice, a storm, a raging wind. Her voice, an army of waves, lashing the cliff's ravaged and pock-marked face. "Holy, holy, holy," sang the birds, sang the bees, sang the waves. "Holy, holy, holy," roared the mountain, in a cacophony of falling rocks. "Holy, holy, holy," crackled the spiralling, twisting, forked lightning.

"Have mercy upon me," Azar cried out. "Have mercy, for I cannot bear the glory of your presence."

He fell to the ground as if pierced by a lance. He fell upon a pyre of skulls like a sacrificial ram, like a carcass in sight of swooping vultures. How swiftly had this beauty turned into this savage vision. He waited to feel his body set alight on the pyre, to feel the beaks of ravenous vultures, a dreadful pecking upon his back. The cut, thrust and peck of their merciless talons. Braced was he, to feel the weight of the executioner's sword hack upon his neck. He tried to ready himself for death as best he could. But, instead of agony, he heard these words.

"Have no fear, my child, for I mean you no harm. No ill. No hurt. Only shelter you shall find here. Only protection. Shelter and protection beneath my wings, beneath my robes. It is I that the priests do honour in their loyal and true unknowing. It is my altar they do tend in their unseeing. This sun, this moon, my eye that sees all. This the priests know, but also do not know."

Something vast and everywhere, moving closer. A vibration so strong he risked being shaken off the edge of the earth. Her voice that is everything.

"But Azar shall be crowned in knowing if he should so choose. Here, where the mightiest kings and most feared rulers stand naked before me, stripped of their prowess and power, divested of all their mortal wealth and plunder. Be wary, for the eternal vengeance of a mother's curse shall fall upon the loathsome touch of any that should meet harm upon my children. They shall burn in my being, bound to walk forever through the hall of mirrors that is but a speck of dust in my hands. For as is the substance of fire, so too am I. The fire that is both death and life. The fire that brought forth all that is and, so too, shall bring all to end."

He should have swooned in the utmost terror. But he did not.

"You feel it and know it, do you not, my Azar? That I am not your end but your beginning. So be strong, my child, my very own, for I desire you to serve at my altar. Look upon me. Look deeply through the eyes of your heart. Feel my touch and receive my blessing."

Azar gasped for air. There was no refuge. Alone. Alone with the mountain god. Alone with the queen of the Jinn. Bereft of all strength, this foolish boy who should have listened to the word of the shepherdess. This foolish boy, who should have taken heed of the ancient stories. Here, amidst the dreadful and rapturous intercourse of earth and sky. Yet, as he felt the sharpness of the stones upon which he had fallen, digging and cutting into his vaporous body, he felt a touch upon the base of his spine. Neither gentle nor cruel but, instead, arousing. Awakening. Awakening and arousing, as if a snake were winding its way up his back. As if he, himself, were a mountain pass. Winding, slithering and probing. He was helpless to halt its progress, yet neither did he want to. His will not his own, yet never more so. Slowly, ever so slowly, he felt consumed by a delicious longing to which this snake held the key. Does the mouse know ecstasy in the snake's crushing embrace? Winding and weaving, burning and flaming. To feel her touch upon him. Upon his body. Upon his skin. Upon his spirit. Rising, rising, slithering and turning. Moving all around, treading softly up the steps of his staircase spine. He felt it moving, felt his body stiffening yet quickening. Uncoiling. The blossom bursts from the bud. Panting, panting, a dragon belching a waterfall of flames. Licking, licking. Sweat as sweet as the priest's anointing oils. Was this death or was this life? His skin, peeling away from his mortal frame. Melting, burning, deadly, delicious. He, a mountain, with larvae sprouting from his innermost recesses, pushing relentlessly and steadily onwards, slowly, delightfully throughout his veins. Chunks of clotted blood transforming into rivers of fire. This delicious dying.

Whether he was boy or mountain, he did not know. But mountain or boy, now opened an eye. He saw bare feet upon a black rock. Arousing, flaming, stiffening. A mountain girding itself for eruption. He saw her toes tapping, long and strong, beautiful and delicate. All the while, this snake moving relentlessly within. He felt it seeking and searching, winding towards the citadel of his hidden heart. Brighter, brighter, brighter he blazed, beyond his wit to bear. And as he thus burned, he felt passion such as he had never known before. A secret knowledge buried deep within. The longing to behold only her unveiled face. Fire meeting fire, most beautiful desire. As one in matrimony, these blessed three. Spirit, heart and mind, bound tightly, tightly, like Celtic knots. The binding that shall set free. Mind, heart and spirit. Snake, cord and thread. Pledge carved eternal upon the ageless oak. This body desiring only her hand laid upon him. To feel trickling all over, the resurrecting waters of her anointing sweat. To hear, to hear, the deep wind of her whispers.

"Help me, for I am overcome. My heart is not big enough to bear this vision. Have mercy upon this foolish boy."

"Fear not, for your heart is sufficient. Your heart big enough. But no foolish boy are you, my child. No longer a boy but one who stands ready to become my anointed priest. My chosen. My own. For I am she who would have you tend her altar. You, my goat amongst the sheep. My servant of the flame, if you so will it to be. And, if you so will it, then take this as my gift. Take this as my initiation."

"I do. I *will*."

These few words he gasped. These words he screamed until the vaults of the heavens were filled with his cries.

"Gaze upon me, you who are chosen. You, who are mine and of our kind."

He felt a smile behind her words. An eye that winked. A soft hand upon his back. No longer a boy. No longer a man or even a mountain, but only a shining newness.

"Lady of the Mountain. Mistress of the Flame. Al'Uzza. I see you. I behold you. Glory of glories. And I know I stand before my queen and master."

"Then know this, Azar. I am mother of a million. A million and more. As numberless as the stars are my offspring. A million mouths I must feed. A million stomachs I must fill. For I am mother of the Burning Ones. Yet there is one who would snuff out the light of my children. The ravenous one. The cruel and wrathful one, obscuring the light with the cloak of his pale shadow. Desirous of forever sealing the golden gateway. By his merciless hand much hurt shall come. My priest shall be slain beneath his accursed blade. My priestess shall be nailed upon the barren and bitter cross. My name will be as dust and replaced by another. My children shall hunger. And should there no longer be one to tend my altar, the Burning Ones shall forever depart from this world. The balance will be broken. The trees shall start to wither and die. The birds fall stricken and dead from the sky. The sea shall spew out her poisoned offspring and the mortal ones shall consume their own children alive."

Azar felt his face turn as if to ash. He felt his blood grow cold. But his heart felt so on fire with love for her, it made oath to find and slay this ravenous one. She felt his oath, a firefly darting into her ocean of flame.

"Then remember me, Azar, for I shall soon be forgotten."

"I will carve every word upon the rock of my soul and give the rest of my days over to understanding."

Azar saw himself, an old man, standing robed in purple, silken robes. He saw himself before a golden cauldron that was a blazing fire. He saw his eyes filled with devotion. All around, a swarm of fireflies. And, for a moment, his young heart felt an unfamiliar peace.

"You have spoken well, as I knew you would. So, my young and wily mountain goat, tend my altar and feed my children. Compose yourself, you who have been called. Still your chatter and shepherd your flock. Take charge of your fears, my priest to be. Be silent. Be still, for Al'Uzza has spoken."

And then she was gone. He took out a knife and spilt some drops of his blood upon the ground, then stood watching it trickle into the dry and sun-parched earth.

The Silver Thread

Deborah watched and waited to see if he would come. She felt anxious that he would not. She felt anxious that he would. Why am I behaving like a giddy young girl? What is the matter with me? What enchantment is this? One time too many stepping out onto the porch, scanning the horizon to see if she could see him. Why did she feel a pang of disappointment when she could not? Pull yourself together, Deborah. Stop this silliness. Act your age now. Conduct yourself in a manner becoming a widow. But she found herself unable to do so, helpless to resist the magic of the magi. For she could not deny the joy she felt to see him, this fast-moving white orb on the brim of the hill. He is coming. He is coming. The way she felt with the second coming of summer. And when Azar arrived and dismounted, when they had exchanged pleasant and cordial greetings, she felt her skin grow hot, her gladness betrayed in the scent of her sweat. Yet for the sake of propriety, all this she did her best to hide.

"Good evening, Azar."

"Good evening, Deborah. I feared I would be late. But Jamil has a knack of getting me to my destination on time.

And where is Rebekah? Is she not joining us?"

"Rebekah sends her apologies. In all the worry and excitement of yesterday, she quite forgot she had a prior engagement. She has gone to see her best friend, Hannah. Our tribe will soon gather to celebrate the coming of spring. Our time to perform the sacred dance. And our young women have pressing matters to attend to. Matters of the heart, to be discussed with friends and not with mothers."

"Indeed. Indeed. I understand. Please tell Rebekah I hope to have the pleasure of her acquaintance another time. A dance, you say. I love to dance."

He twirled around, his tunic billowing like an opening flower.

"Careful, Azar. Why, you will make yourself dizzy."

"Far from it. When I dance in this fashion, I am never more clear or well balanced."

"Interesting. I have never heard anyone else say so. Though I think for myself, I prefer to dance in the old-fashioned way."

"Maybe you will show me how you dance one day?"

That night, Azar watched Deborah, chewing upon the delicious bread she had brought to the table. He looked at the creases around her eyes. They spoke of smiles and laughter. They spoke of the deepest sorrow. He looked at her mouth. The mouth of a sensual woman. Lips that had loved to bestow kisses upon her beloved, well used to giving shape to tender words. Her big hazel eyes with specks of yellow, each one a chalice that had held both bitterness and beauty. Fortunate those hands that had stroked their way through her tawny hair, now laced with strands of silver. Deborah looked at Azar. She followed the motion of his jaw as he chewed. Every movement of this man was vigorous and robust yet also delicate and filled with grace.

She smiled inside as a mother smiles, to hear his barely audible purr of pleasure. She felt an unexpected happiness to feed this man. Upon his swarthy, lustrous skin, the slightest glint of sweet-smelling oils. She looked at his combed silver beard, the blackness of his long eyelashes. Strange, how he appeared both old and young. She sensed this was a man who knew what it was to dance in utmost joy. She sensed this was a man who knew what it was to suffer, for all this she felt in the whispers of her womb. Gladly she would bake for him.

"When you have finished, let us go sit on the porch. I have some good news to share with you, Azar of Asnavant."

After Azar had savoured the last morsel of Deborah's delight, they went to the bench in full view of the garden, abundant with flowers and vegetables, brimming over with vibrant colour and fragrant odours. Overseeing all this, lingering beneath the shelter of a small willow tree, a stone angel stood alertly with wings wide open, its eyes gazing forever towards her door. A few stray poppies clustered around its base, seeded not by Deborah's hand but by the hand of the wind.

"I have spoken with Rabbi Ishmael and Yitshak," she said barely able to restrain her excitement. "Neither is in opposition to your building your dwelling. I must admit I was worried about what Yitshak might say, for he is fierce and unyielding in his protection of Elnazar. But my dear friend, Yitshak, has declared you are at liberty to build your home wherever it pleases you, for this region is beyond the boundaries of our territory. As for Rabbi Ishmael, he said only this: that whether you may remain or whether you must leave, falls under the rule and providence of Horeb, and of Horeb alone."

Azar solemnly nodded.

"Your rabbi speaks wisely. I think I would enjoy speaking with him. Please tell him I am happy to bow before his ruling. And please say the same to Yitshak. He sounds like a formidable protector. Not one to have as an enemy."

"Most certainly not."

"I suspect his blessing was not quite so easily won. Do I see the hand of the baker at work in his decision?"

"You would have to ask Yitshak. And I am glad to tell you your chance will come tomorrow night, for he has invited you to share bread at his table. He likes to keep his enemy close at hand. But I am sure when he meets you his concerns will be appeased. What answer shall I give him?"

"I think you have already made that decision, have you not? So please tell Yitshak I would be honoured to break bread with the guardian of Elnazar. I also hope to break bread with Rabbi Ishmael one day. They are both warriors. One who fights with the sword, the other with the word of the holy book. And yet I suspect that neither warrior would dare incur the wrath of Deborah by obstructing her will."

"Why, I am glad you fear my wrath, for I have made another decision. I have decided it is only proper you receive assistance to build your dwelling."

A lesser man would have taken offence. But not so, Azar, for his heart recognised the authority with which Deborah now spoke. And though Azar was fearless in the battle and would willingly look evil straight in the eye, he would always gladly submit to the spirit of kindness.

"I know just the young man to do this. I will send Heshel to you tomorrow morning. I am sure he would love to work at your side. Rebekah has seen him many times in the forest working with wood, although he does not know my daughter has strayed upon his secret passion. She tells me it is as if he transforms into a different person."

"I will look forward to meeting this passionate young man. And as for your daughter, she sounds as if she is a spirit of the forest. A spirit who seems to be as invisible as the wind. Who may say for sure she is not watching us now?"

As he spoke, Azar's attention was caught by a brisk movement close by. There, perched upon the right wing of the stone angel, he saw a dove.

"Or maybe the forest has taught her to be a shapeshifter? Look, there she is in feathered form, listening to our every word."

Deborah followed the direction of his pointing finger and looked at the statue. Azar watched her face, waiting to see her smile. But instead, he saw only a look of puzzlement. Of sudden vulnerability. He looked again but saw no bird. It must have been a trick of the white meleke limestone.

"It seems I am falling under the spell of this forest."

"You would not be the first."

Azar stood up, feeling compelled to draw closer to the statue. So alive and real was the appearance of the angel, it appeared ready to draw in breath and take to flight. In its left hand, he saw the angel held a sword. And, in its right hand, it held an open book.

"May I touch it, Deborah?"

She blinked her eyes in affirmation, though feeling uncertain.

"Magnificent," he said, his fingers feeling their way across its cool surface. As Deborah watched him, her world slowed down. Here, at the side of the statue, was her special place. Her sanctuary. It was here she would come to sit and rest when her daily labours were ended, her daughter sound asleep. She would lean on the angel, her fingers feeling their way across the cold stone surface in whose grooves she could still feel the trace of her husband's touch.

So too, his heart. Maybe if she followed its trail, she could somehow find her way to where he now was? How she longed to feel the strong, steady hand of the stonemason once more upon her.

Now, like a rattle, the willow rustled. The scattering of poppies bowed their heads down. Azar moved his fingers over the angel's wings, as large as an eagle's and adorned with hundreds of feathers. He touched the sword in its left hand and the book in its right. He touched its face and felt its heart as if he were a physician seeking a pulse. Well and intimately his body knew stone, but this was unlike any stone he had felt before. It breathed. It vibrated. He sensed a wave of whispers sweeping towards him from some distant place. Unseen by Deborah, he inwardly braced himself. He felt them enter inside him through the gateway of his hands, ascending towards his place of inner seeing. Little by little, until they came before a golden gateway. "Enter," proclaimed the voice of Azar's spirit. And with this word, a vision exploded into view.

Azar found himself in a limestone quarry. Before him lay a man, his body bloodied and broken beneath a covering of rocks. He knew it to be Simeon, the stonemason. Such pity Azar felt to witness his agony. He could hear his groans and, even too, his final, mortal thoughts. Aching was the stonemason's heart, knowing he could never give his beloved daughter her birthday gift, fashioned from the substance of his heart and soul. Simeon slowly and painfully adjusted his position, his gaze now turning towards Azar, as if something were looking back at him from the other side of the mirror. Each one became cognisant of the other's presence. No past, no future, just the mutual shock of the departed beholding the still yet living. And which one was living and which one was dead, neither one quite knew for sure.

"Spirit," said Simeon, straining to speak, his blood-filled lungs short of breath. "Though I cannot discern whether you are a demon or an angel, I know you are death come to take me away."

Of its own volition, Azar's heart spoke in reply, whilst tears mingled with blood upon Simeon's fractured face.

"Have no fear, Simeon, beloved spouse of the baker and father of the weaver, for only love is here."

A groan, a laboured breath, straining to give form to words despite the searing pain from shafts of shattered ribs.

"Are you made of spirit or flesh or stone?" asked the broken man upon a pyre of skulls.

"Spirit knows spirit as love knows love."

"Then if this is so," spoke Simeon, sensing his remaining time was all too brief, "then promise me, spirit, you will find my Rebekah and give her my present, that has now become my parting gift. I beg you to find it and place it in her hands. Please tell her she will find her father there always in this temple of stone. Tell her that when she holds it close, she will feel my touch upon her as I will feel hers. Will you do this for me?"

Azar placed his hands upon his heart and bowed.

"Thank you, spirit," whispered Simeon. Azar now heard Simeon's thoughts turn to Deborah. The pain of his flesh was as nothing to the pain in his heart to leave her. Who would comfort her? Who would protect her? A mighty wind, a wind that spoke, swept across the quarry as if emanating from the wings of the angel in flight. Simeon felt its warmth upon his skin. He felt its pledge.

"I shall comfort her and I shall watch over her. I shall find her even if she should be lost in the Valley Of Gehenna."

The sheen of death fell across Simeon's eyes like a veil. But with this departing, a light, more bright than the brightest fire Azar had ever witnessed, filled the eyes of the stonemason in silent glory. And a wind passed through the stonemason's lips, a wind that was a word. One final, mortal word that was a million words spoken. A word now spoken by Azar.

"Deeeeebbbbbb… ooorrrrrrr… aaaaaaaaaaaaaaaaaaaah."

As if from a place that was far, far away, Azar now heard another voice.

"Oh my God, Azar," cried out Deborah. "What is happening? Your voice… your voice. It sounded just like his. Just like my Simeon's. Oh, my God."

Anguish in her liver and her kidneys, her heart and her womb. And with this agony came the shock of realisation. She realised, right there and then, that this anguish, this grief, was all she had left of him. The only means by which she could hold onto him. Let him go that he may come closer, whispered the wind. But she would not, could not, let go. For if she did, he would then be gone and lost forever, never to return. She would not let go of his hand as he hung above the abyss of death, its greedy mouth gaping in readiness to swallow her husband whole. She would not let him go. She would never let go of her love. She would not fail him. She could not fail him. But this she now knew to be a sweet deceit, for she had already failed him. She had betrayed her love by not being there at his side as he released his last mortal breath. His wife should have been there. She should have been there to hold his hand and mop his brow. There to soothe him and comfort him, to tell him how much she loved him. But Simeon's wife had not been there and instead he had died alone and in pain. A voice, this time not the wind, interrupted the declaration of her guilt.

"My dear, sweet darling, in whose breast there beats

the heart of an angel. Let the light of truth now cause the shadows of misapprehension to flee. Be still and know your love was not lacking, nor was he alone in his hour of need. Hear and see now, this very moment, as spirit sees and hears. Not alone at all was he, but held firmly in the unyielding arms of love. Never was the baker more with the stonemason. Never, for Simeon felt the spirit of Deborah all around and inside him. Above and below, in his heart, mind and soul. Only you, my darling. Only you. So be still and know. See and hear now, that when came the appointed hour of his soul's departing, it was your name upon his lips. Your name only, his last uttered word, spoken not in pain but rapture."

She could not bear to hear Azar thus speak, yet she yearned to drink in more of his word. Waters that may bring the desert rose to bloom. And as he spoke, wave after wave of understanding came upon Deborah, searching its way into her scarred and tortured heart. She saw clear as clear can be, she had hidden her anguish in order to protect Rebekah. She had hidden her pain so she could be strong and present, that she may not add to her daughter's grief. She had frozen her feelings until they had become as still as stone. And by instinct alone, she had known the only way she could hide her anguish from her little girl, was to hide it even from herself. All of this, a mother's duty.

"Why are you making me feel these things? I shall break apart."

"You shall not break for your true and loyal heart is strong."

"I am not strong. If I were strong I would believe what you are telling me. But I think you are a kind and gentle man whose only wish is to mitigate a widow's grief."

"Oh, Deborah, our pain is not always a wise and faithful

counsellor. Yet tell me, if you will, what proof can I offer you to give credence to my word?"

She could not answer for she did not know.

"Did you know what gift your husband was making for Rebekah?"

"No," said Deborah in surprise at the turn of his words. "It was a secret he kept even from me."

"I tell you in truth, I have seen your husband as clearly as I now see you. Maybe even clearer. If I am deceiving you in any measure, may the Most Holy One strike me down right now."

She knew these were words a priest would not say lightly. She heard his voice, speaking without any trace of doubt or apology but with only conviction and authority.

"Simeon showed me his gift and also where he left it. I will go to the quarry and find it. I will return it to where it rightly belongs."

"What are you, Azar, to know such a thing? How can this possibly be?" Deborah shook with feeling, desperate to believe his every word. And a part of her did believe him, for his was not the face of a liar. His tongue, not fashioned to give shape to deceiving or appeasing words.

"I am a man just like any other man. A man more similar to you than you realise. For my journey to Elnazar has been at a price. I have known too what it is to lose one's dearest love. I have been purged by a grief such as I have never known before. Yet this market pedlar has never secured a better bargain, such is the understanding this passage has brought forth in him. Let me show you something, my dear, that will help elucidate my meaning."

Azar reached for something beneath the folds of his tunic.

"Ah, there you are," he said, producing a silver locket hung on a chain. "My love also left me a message, just as your husband did in the form of this magnificent stone angel."

He snapped the locket open. With the utmost care, he took out a rolled-up piece of parchment. Slowly he unrolled it.

"Zara gave it to me on the day I left her. She wanted me to take something precious of hers. A lock of her hair or even a diamond ring just would not do, for it had to be a something threaded to her heart by a silver thread. Before I could ask her to explain what she meant by this, she committed an act that completely disarmed me."

"What did she do?" asked Deborah, unable to guess what might have so shocked this magi. This epitome of composure.

"As I have told you, Zara is guardian of a special book. A holy book unknown to any priesthood, and which is utterly unique. There are no words to describe how precious this book is to Zara. Even to me, she only speaks of it rarely. Once she told me it had been written in the tongue of angels, that every word contained is made of living fire, only to be read by the eyes of the heart. It was this book she brought before me. She closed her eyes and thumbed through the pages, uttering words I could not quite hear. And when she stopped upon one page, she stroked it with reverence and then tore it out. I was horrified. 'Zara,' I shouted, 'what have you done?'

"Her act aroused many feelings in me. Was this not an act of blasphemy? Would she not incur the wrath of the gods? Had she no fear to do such a thing? And, more important than all these feelings, I could not believe she would damage this book that was so precious to her. Would not such an act break her heart?

"'Oh, my Zara, you have irreparably damaged it. Why? Why have you done such a thing?'"

Azar went silent for a moment.

"Though I am magi, I sometimes think my magic is as nothing when measured against the magic of this girl from the other side of the mountain. She is bound by no earthly law, but only by a higher rule and reason. Only in this light can her acts be understood. And this is what she revealed to me."

"'Azar, my husband, do you truly believe this book to be more precious than my love for you? Oh no, my beloved. Nothing is more precious and this you must now fully know. And this you need also understand. It is an illusion, and nothing more than an illusion, that this book is broken. For this is a book which is not a book. It is a piece of magic, a fragment of eternity, brought into being by love itself. And just as this book is, so too is our love. A love that may never be rent apart. Tell me, Magi, whose hand shall split the fire of the high mountain altar? Whose hand shall split the wave or part the wind? No, this can never be. The fire of our passion has made us two as one. Always and forever. For ever, as such, is the nature of love. Forever undividable. Sealed by the kiss of eternity, its pledge to love.'"

"To hear her word, I asked that she teach me more.'

"'Oh, I shall not teach you, my master. I shall only remind you of that which your pain has caused you to momentarily forget, just as it always behoves a doting wife to do. No, I shall not teach you, but only ask of you to take on your journey, this piece of my heart. And when the time is ripe, it will surely do according unto its own will, and find its way home. Somehow. Somewhere. Sometime. Please, let go of this fear that the book is broken, for in truth, it lacks for nothing. Love has made it the more complete. No page is missing but rather, a new page written. And as this book is, so shall be our love. Let us not grieve for our seeming separation. The leaf falls from the tree to be blown far away by the will of the wind. Yet is it not so that the tree shall remain? Our bodies, the leaves. Our love, the tree. If a tree shall fare well, then shall not our love fare well, even though we may be separated by a thousand miles, or even death itself? Say it is not so, fire priest.'

"It is so, my beloved, it is surely so."

Azar looked at Deborah with unabated tenderness.

"Even now, I have only come to a slow realisation of the reality of her words. I tell you truly, Deborah of Elnazar, I still believed I had betrayed Zara by embarking on my pilgrimage. I feared I would never see her sweet face again, and that only death awaited me on my path to Horeb. But, miracle of miracles, with each step that took me farther from my Zara, I found myself walking inextricably one step closer. And now I see her face everywhere. I feel her touch upon me always. I smell the fragrance of her skin. I hear her voice speaking in the whispering wind."

He looked at Deborah with the eyes of another. Eyes that barely looked human at all, peering deeply into some unseen world.

"Though all may fade into nothingness, yet always shall your Simeon remain. For death is not a cruel and splitting thorn, but a vellum that binds and seals forever the pages of the Book of Love. So the shepherd girl has taught me."

These words in another's mouth might have been meaningless but not when uttered by this Persian priest.

"Speak to me more, Azar, of your love. Speak to me of the first time you met this girl from the other side of the mountain. Tell me how you came to find this precious gem. Speak, for your words restore me."

Nocturne

The first time he saw her was in the cool of an evening breeze. The first time he saw her was in the light of a new moon, whilst wandering alone in the foothills of Mount Asnavant. Amidst these regions, amongst these many crags and boulders, these crevices and cracks, it was all too easy to trip and fall, risking serious injury. And to be injured and alone in the mountains was to be at risk of death. He felt all of his body filling up with an animal alertness. He liked, no, he relished, this sense of adventure, of balancing upon the edge of the gaping abyss. But Azar knew it was time for him to leave, as soon darkness would be ascending, the danger too great. He stood ready to move with the swift, sure-footed tread of a mountain goat. Yet he paused for just a moment, to look one more time at the mountain's freckled face, all scattered with tufts and clumps of bright green moss, hanging bat-like upon the rocky scarp. Fond memories came to mind of his young cousin's face, beaming in greeting through the folds of her headdress.

And then, and then, and then he saw her. This girl from the other side of the mountain. A figure draped in robes of glistening whiteness, stained with the red hues of the setting sun. He gasped to see this figure, holding a book that shone like gold. No face could he discern, for it was veiled within a snowy white headdress. The figure stopped as if having been startled, then turned to face him. Azar's mind raced. He felt sure this was the figure of a woman. Was it the shepherdess, her daughter, or even perhaps, the Lady of the Mountain? He glimpsed eyes of shining blackness, large, wide and open, mouth slightly ajar, revealing teeth as bright as pearls. He saw the slight curves of eyebrows, arched in surprise. He saw her turn and walk quickly away.

"Stop. Please stop," cried out Azar.

But she carried on moving and, as she moved, Azar noticed she appeared to be limping. Was she injured? Had some harm befallen her? He knew better than to follow in pursuit. He cried out once more, though unsure what to say.

"Please stop and talk with me."

Still, the robed figure continued moving away, smaller and smaller, further and further, merging into the distant horizon. But those eyes, what feelings they had sparked in him. He must try one more time to halt her passage.

"Please stop, daughter of Al'Uzza."

The figure seemed to hesitate.

"Please stop. My name is Azar. I am just a boy who lives on the other side of the mountain. I mean you no harm. Has not your mother spoken to you of me?"

The figure suddenly stopped. And, as she stopped, the whole world seemed to stop.

"Thank you, spirit. Thank you for stopping. Please, speak with me, if you will."

He saw her eyes looking startled, afraid, yet filled with curiosity.

"Who are you? Why do you speak to me thus? Why do

you call me spirit?"

Her melodious voice sent tingles throughout his body.

"Are you not a spirit? Are you not the daughter and priestess of Al'Uzza?"

The girl looked at him. She sensed danger, knowing her life now hinged upon her every word, even her every silent thought. For surely this was not a boy, but rather one of the spirits who walk the earth, between the gap of night and day. Just as her mother had once told her.

"Answer me, spirit. How have you come to know her name?"

"I am not a spirit. I am just a boy from a village on the other side of the mountain. A boy to whom she has spoken. It was she who told me her name."

Azar saw thoughts racing through those black and lustrous eyes.

"Your name is Azar?"

"Yes."

She paused for a moment, then bowed in greeting, as was the custom of her tribe.

"Please tell me your name, daughter of Al'Uzza."

"Why do you call me so, boy from the other side of the mountain?"

"Am I wrong to do so? I thought I heard a whisper, telling me you were as such. Please forgive me if I have caused you offence, for I am only a foolish boy."

Was it a smile he saw dart across her beautiful face? With this smile, the girl grew a little bolder.

"Perhaps, Azar, you should be more careful about which whispers you pay heed to. But do not worry, for as you can see, I am also not lacking in foolishness. Why else would I be out at this late hour in this remote place, perhaps conversing with one of the Jinn?"

"I am not one of the Jinn. And are you not her priestess, for you are robed like a priestess?"

Her body relaxed and she laughed out loud. He felt faint upon hearing the delightful cadence of her laugh.

"You clearly have a strong imagination to think such things. But these mountains summon forth all manner of imaginings and visions. Is it not so, Azar?"

He nodded in affirmation of her words.

"But I am not a priestess. I am a shepherdess."

"But I have seen many a shepherdess. They do not walk the mountains in white robes. Nor do they hold books in their hand instead of a crook."

"Well, Azar, perhaps you have never met a shepherdess quite like me. And, since you have not thought to ask, my name is Zara."

Zara. Zara. Her name was Zara. And on hearing her name, he recalled the words of the shepherdess: "Beware presumption, for it is a treacherous guide."

"Forgive me, Zara. Forgive me for my presumption. Truly, in this place, nothing is ever what it appears to be. Not so long ago I met a shepherdess out here. Your words remind me of her words. And the best of good counsel she kindly gave me."

"What did this shepherdess look like?" asked Zara, her face full of feeling he could not fathom. Azar described her carefully, in the minutest detail.

"When did you see her?" she asked in a trembling voice.

"A little over thirteen moons ago."

"Thirteen moons? That is not possible. For surely the shepherdess you met was my mother and she has been dead for many years. What you say cannot be true. Why are you lying to me? Why are you seeking to torment me, cruel spirit?"

But Zara knew, yes she knew, that his words were true. She fell to her knees and gave in to her grief. And though this Azar was a proud and wilful boy, his heart was kind. He took a few steps towards her and sat himself down at her side, placing an arm tentatively across her shoulder. He felt no rebuke. He looked at her white robes now wet with tears. How startling its whiteness against the blackness of her skin, as black as obsidian. He listened to the sound of her sobbing, until, when every last tear had been shed, she raised her sad face and looked at him.

"I am sorry for my words, Azar. Thank you for not leaving me here alone in my sorrow. Please, tell me everything about your meeting with the shepherdess, for it seems you have met my mother's spirit walking abroad in these mountains. These mountains she knew and loved so well."

Azar told her everything. And, as he did so, they each felt a hand upon them.

"Oh, my mother. My mother. How I miss you. I have missed you even more than I knew. Yet now I know you still guide your flock from beyond the veil. That though you are far, you are always near, just as you always promised me you would be."

She knelt upon a rock and began to pray. She felt the hem of her mother's shawl brush across her skin and breathed in her familiar aroma. Azar could smell it, too.

"No simple and unschooled shepherdess was my mother, though most took her to be so. But no-one was more resourceful and determined than she. I tell you truly, Azar, she was unstoppable. Even death, so it now seems, bows down before the will of the shepherdess."

Zara held up the golden book for Azar to see.

"It was my mother who placed this book in my young and unknowing hands. A holy book she found somewhere just for me, although she was forbidden to do so by the command of the priests. But she paid no heed to their admonishments. No bit did she keep in her mouth from their rules and laws. She only knew her daughter hungered for scriptures that spoke of holy things. That I hungered to read. That I thirsted to learn. Such books, the priests told her, are not meant to be read by a simple and untutored daughter of a shepherdess. The likes of us were not meant to read. No, only those whom they deemed to be called to the priesthood should be schooled in this art. I had thought my hunger was a burden to her. I tried to hide it. I was only a lame and useless shepherd girl. But she saw my secret passion. And when I went to bed crying, she would rock me in her arms and tell me I was not a burden but a blessing. A tear shed by the great mother of mercy."

She looked at Azar. She looked for mercy.

"That is what she told me. I was not a curse as my father so often called me. No, I was her brightest blessing. Oh, how I wish it were so."

A breeze wrapped itself around them, warm and caressing. "Soooooooooooooo..." it whispered, but they did not yet hear.

"I tell you, Azar, there were many times my mother asked the priests to teach me to read. Those unholy priests. But though they always refused her, they were no match for my mother. Nothing on earth would stop her from feeding her daughter. Nothing and no-one. She must surely have been an angel, for such was the might of her indomitable spirit. And somehow, somewhere, she found a tutor who was willing to help me. A man who was dressed in purple robes. It was he who gave my mother this golden book."

Azar shuddered to hear word of this priest. And he shuddered to recall the words of the shepherdess, repeating them aloud like a litany for Zara to hear.

"Even a shepherdess can find the sacred books if her heart so desires."

"Yes. Yes. That is what she said to me. What a love my mother has for me. What a love. For our life is hard, Azar. It was my duty to become a shepherdess as she was a shepherdess. I was meant to take over my mother's burden. But from the hour of my birth, my body betrayed me. The gods were cruel, or so I once thought."

She looked at the mountain, a half-smile on her face.

"I was born with an infirmity that was not apparent until I took my first steps. In time it was revealed I was lame in one leg. Oh, I could walk, I could play, I could even run in a fashion, but my infirmity robbed me of the sure-footed tread needed to guide the flock. I lacked the balance and the speed of foot. My parents prayed that time would rectify my lacking. They beseeched the gods to heal me, but the gods did not seem to hear. As I grew older, I would fall asleep in anguish, for I came to believe I was born from bad seed. But I made my bed not only with sadness but also fear, the fear my father would abandon me. I feared he would take me and leave me in some remote place, to be devoured by the wolves that their burden be eased. One less mouth to feed. Yes, he would abandon me, just as I had seen him abandon his camels when their bodies had become broken by their labours. What use was I? What use could a lame shepherd girl be?"

Azar listened to her story with an aching heart. To think she might have been left to the wild wolves, this bright-eyed, clever, softly spoken girl. This priestess.

"I will speak to you truly, Azar. I will speak to you as I have spoken to no-one else, boy from the other side of the mountain. For your eyes are kind and speak of wisdom. I grew to hate myself. I cursed my destiny for having been born like this. I hated the burden I was. I hated the way my father looked at me. Those cold, angry eyes."

As she spoke to Azar, Zara glimpsed her father's eyes, her father's face, covering Azar's face like gauze. She saw his mouth, dry and tight, spitting out curses, muttering cruel words. As fast as it had come, it faded away to leave only Azar, looking at her in a way no man had ever looked at her before. A look she had only seen in her mother's eyes. As for Azar, he had feelings such as he had never felt before. He only knew he desired to place a kiss upon her cheek and wipe away her tears.

"No father should ever look at their daughter in such a way. Never, ever, Zara, daughter of the shepherdess."

She wanted to rest her head upon his shoulder. To fall asleep and dream good dreams.

"How strange I should find myself unburdening my heart to a boy from the other side of the mountain. Yes, you are right. No father should ever look at their daughter in this way. I wish I had known this when I was still young. It was not that I lacked a fighting spirit. I was able to bear the pain of my infirmity, and even the scorn and the laughter from the cruel and unkind. But I could not bear the way he looked at me, a look which crippled my heart and soul. The pain of my leg was as nothing to this. He burnt this pain into me just as in the manner he branded his camels. I saw in his eyes the shame he felt for me. And when the tribes gathered for trading, all of the other fathers would boast of their children's auspicious futures. But not so, my father."

She suddenly stood up, a ferocious look in her eyes, such as Azar had only witnessed in a wounded, cornered animal.

"Do not think I seek your pity with my words. I do not need the pity of any man."

Yet pity he felt, to see those hurt-filled eyes.

"Please forgive me for my outburst. Perhaps I should refrain from speaking further?"

"No, please continue. I want to hear."

"Very well. Thank you, Azar. I will carry on. You must know that my pain became so great, I came to believe it would be better if I stole away in the night and threw my life upon the mercy of the mountains. Or maybe even throw myself over the edge of the cliff, so I could end this sorry life. But intrepid was my mother, and strong enough for the both of us. She had no care for what my father thought. 'Do not worry, my precious,' she would often tell me. 'Do not be sad, my solitary flower that grows amidst the cruel mountains, amidst the cracks and crags. For the gods have chosen another path for you to follow. Believe me, my daughter and my blessing, the day shall surely come when you will blossom beyond the compare of anything. *Of anything*! If it is not sheep and goats you must tend, then you shall be a shepherdess in a fashion known only to the gods themselves. So, sleep soundly, my desert rose, and await their call.'

"Then, one blessed day, my mother brought me a book whose cover shone with gold. I had never seen a book before. The way she held it and touched it, caused me to think it had been given to her by the gods themselves. Oh, my mother. As strong as a mountain lioness are you. As mighty as a mountain. As wondrous as an angel. How could I not have known that even death would be as nothing to your might? How could I not have known you would never forsake me?"

She looked at Azar. She looked at his face and felt only gladness.

"I decided I would dedicate this life and even lives beyond, to the study of this holy book. I would offer my life to the gods of the mountain. I would become a holy woman.

I would give myself to study, prayer and fasting. From that day onwards, even my father could see the change in me. He started to treat me differently. I think he even came to fear me. When he put food upon my plate, he no longer tossed it as if giving scraps to the dogs. No, he would place it before me with respect. And our fortunes changed and abundance came to our home. Life was no longer a cup of bitter gall but was good. Laughter came to our home. Life was good, if only for a short while. Good until the day my mother left, never to return. Or so I thought, until this evening."

The two looked into each other's eyes. Each shared a thought that neither gave voice to. The thought, the certainty, that the shepherdess had returned. That she had never strayed so far away. And neither needed to say it was she who had brought them together in the foothills of the mountain. In the cool of an evening breeze.

The Valley of Gehenna

"Good day, Heshel. May I have a moment of your time?"

Heshel was on his way to school, a little bit late, as he often was.

"Yes, of course, mother Deborah."

As Heshel came closer, towering tall over Deborah, she was surprised to feel herself flushing, just as she had once done in the first flame of her youth.

"How you have grown," she said nervously, letting out a girlish giggle. Come, gather yourself, you foolish woman. Cool your blood and act your age. But this woman was not foolish at all, and true was the voice of the red river inside her. For was it not most crystal clear to all the mothers, that this son, that this Heshel, had shed the mantle of boyhood to become a tall and handsome, assured young man? A mother's leonine pride surged like a wave through her blood and marrow.

"Should you be late for school, then please let Rabbi know I am the cause of your delay. I am sure he will understand and have no need of further explanation. A pressing matter has arisen of which you form a part."

"I will tell Rabbi Ishmael."

"Very good. Now tell me, Heshel, have you heard what happened to Zakiya in the poppy fields?"

"I heard she was frightened by a hungry ghost."

His face assumed a remorseful expression.

"Poor little Zakiya. I am afraid it was not a ghost who scared her but me. It was not my intention. I only wanted to say hello. She must have glimpsed me on my way into the forest."

"So you did not see him?"

"See who?"

"I must tell you, Heshel, it was not a ghost Zakiya saw, nor was it you."

"Of course it was me. There was no-one else."

"Can you be sure of this? Did you know Rebekah was also there, that she saw you ambling through the forest?"

"Oh," he mumbled, feeling like a child whose guilty secret had been exposed. "Then it was Rebekah who frightened her?"

"No, not Rebekah. It was a man who has come from far away."

He felt a chill. He felt a thrill. He felt the weave of destiny spinning and spiralling, doing according unto its will.

"Have my words unsettled you? You look a little pale."

"I am fine. Please continue, mother Deborah."

But though he tried his best to appear calm, he felt desperate to hear more.

"His name is Azar. He is a blacksmith from Asnavant, and also a carpenter. A craft that is close to your own heart, is it not? And above all this, he happens to be a magi from a high and holy mountain. I had the great good fortune of spending the afternoon in conversation with him. I hope you will have the same opportunity. You will then understand why he has travelled so far to come to Horeb."

She drew closer to Heshel, her eyes filled with a bright and mellow light.

"I tell you truly, Heshel, this good man helped me in my hour of greatest need. He watched over me as if he were my very own guardian angel. I do not know what fate would have befallen me without his intervention. And now I wish to reciprocate in kind. He too is in need, although I suspect he would be too proud to say so. But though I would gladly give him all I have, I do not have the skills he requires. Yet there is someone very close at hand who does possess the talent. You, Heshel. You hold these skills in abundance. This I know, for a little bird has told me so. So now I would ask you, even though I know it is a lot to ask, would you please consider helping Azar build himself a dwelling? I do understand your time is precious and given to your studies, but I cannot bear to think of him exposed to the elements. He is not young in age and you know well the elements can be cruel and inclement at the foot of the mountain. As for Rabbi, he has already given this matter his blessing. As has Yitshak."

Had she been too forceful in making her request? She knew well she held a nature that could not help but take charge, such was the power of her strong and resolute will.

"The choice is yours, of course. Take some time to think about it. But I know there is no-one else who would make him a better apprentice. Truly, Heshel, my heart tells me you two are a match made in heaven."

Heshel gazed upon Deborah in surprise. How long had it been since he had last seen mother Deborah talk in such a fashion, so alive, so animated, her arms a whirlwind of gesticulation? Her eyes, twinkling and dancing like a morning star. Take some time to think about it? As if time itself, were hers to give. But how long need he consider her heartfelt request? A second, a minute, an hour or a day? No, for swift came the answer of his heart's true desire.

"I will gladly help him."

"Are you sure? I did not expect such an immediate answer."

"I am certain. I cannot thank you enough, mother Deborah, for brokering this good fortune on my behalf."

"Wonderful. Then it is settled. I will go without delay to inform your father of the situation and seek his blessing."

"I do not think my father's blessing will be so easily won."

"We will see. I am sure Jared will understand. I can be very persuasive when I want to, you know. Leave it in my hands and come to my house when school is over. I will tell you exactly where to find Azar. Maybe you could even visit him this afternoon? I have some things I would like you to take him."

"As you wish, mother Deborah."

All that day, Heshel could think of nothing else. This did not escape the keen eye of the rabbi. Ishmael saw clearly that Heshel was far, far away, yet he called no attention to this absence, nor gave him rebuke. And when school was over, which was not soon enough, Heshel ran to the house of Deborah, knocking a little too loudly upon her door. But it was not Deborah who answered. Instead, before him stood the weaver, eyes wide open and mouth slightly ajar, as coy and fragile as a whispering willow.

"Oh, hello Heshel."

"Good day, Rebekah. Is your mother home?"

She felt overcome with nervousness. If only she could have engaged him in further conversation. She would have loved to do so. But she feared he would take her to be nothing more than a silly girl. And her heart ached to know it was not her company that had brought the son of the fisherman to her door. It was not her he wanted. She gestured to Heshel for him to follow, muttering inaudible accusations at herself with every dispirited step. Why had she become afflicted with muteness? Why could she not just flow with the grace of a swan on the lake? Her mind filled up with thoughts of all she lacked, she delivered Heshel to her mother and then, quiet and disheartened, retreated from the kitchen. She, who was as invisible to him as the wind.

"Hello, Heshel. Just a moment. I have almost finished." She stopped filling a large basket and looked at Heshel. She saw eyes filled with both hope and consternation.

"My father? Is it agreed? What did he say?"

"It is agreed. Your father said he would not obstruct the rabbi's wishes."

"But did he gladly give his blessings?"

"I will not lie to you. There are few things father Jared does with a glad heart these days. But we must be patient with him. He has suffered a great loss."

"So everybody keeps telling me. But look at you. Who has suffered greater pain than you, mother Deborah? Yet you overflow with the spirit of kindness."

Heshel could not disguise his anger. Deborah was silent. This woman, who was always so adept with words, now uncertain as to what might be best to say. And Heshel felt regret, for he feared her silence spoke of having caused her hurt.

"I am sorry for my outburst. Please forgive me. I should not have spoken to you in such anger."

"Do not be troubled by this, our Heshel. There is nothing to forgive. Nothing at all. I do understand. It is better to give voice to such feelings. You might be surprised to know what angry words have poured out from the mouth of this woman who overflows with the spirit of kindness. I too have railed at what life has taken from me. I cannot lie. But let us two not be angry today. Please, for today is a good day. A blessed day, you shall see. For today you shall make the acquaintance of a fire priest from Asnavant. The Baal-Azar."

"The Baal-Azar?"

"Yes, that is what they call him. It is an honorary title, for amongst his tribe he is known to be a high master of his craft."

"A high master? Perhaps it would be better if you chose someone else? I am not sure I am worthy of this task."

"You are worthy and sufficient, Heshel. Please trust me in this. This mother holds no doubt about it. Now, I would be grateful if you take him this bread, wine and cheese. Do not forget to pass on my best wishes to him. And make sure your ears are ready, for how he loves to talk." She passed the basket over to him, her arms shaking and straining to hold its weight. "Have I put too much in it? Is it too heavy? Oh, of course, it is not. What was I thinking? I am sorry if I have caused you offence. Just look at those broad shoulders you have. Elnazar will soon have another mighty man in its midsts. And before I forget, I have also put some food in there for your supper. It is wrapped in blue linen with a spider woven on it." Deborah mused fondly to herself for a moment. "Rebekah wove it for me when she was just a little girl. Please take care not to lose it."

"I will be attentive and guard it carefully. Thank you for your kind consideration, mother Deborah."

"You are most welcome. Now, off you go."

The earth is dreaming, the soil is teeming, overflowing with promise and possibility. Magic everywhere, within and without, around every corner, down each nook and cranny. Everything a symphony, everywhere a song, fields of bustling violet hollyhocks, bowing and bending, bees buzzing busily across endless yellow fields of shortpod mustard. The path now revealed. All seems right and as meant to be. Today, today, the day now come. Salutations to joy and farewell to sorrow. After today and before tomorrow.

Soon Heshel was approaching the tent made from goat hair, just as mother Deborah had described. Close by, a speck of white. Surely Jamil, the magnificent stallion? And there by the tent, stood the form of a man. This must be him. The magi from the mountain. The fire priest turned to face him, sentient of his coming, laying down his axe and offering the carpenter an outstretched hand. As if destiny itself were coming to greet him.

"Good day to you, Baal-Azar. I am sorry if I have disturbed your work. My name is Heshel. I believe you are expecting me?"

"Indeed I am. Come closer. Come closer. I will not bite. Why, you are just as mother Deborah described. I am honoured to make your acquaintance, Heshel, son of the healer, son of the fisherman." He took Heshel's hands in the manner customary to his tribe. "Deborah speaks very highly of you, young man."

As they exchanged greeting, Heshel could feel the strength in Azar's hands, as could Azar feel the strength in Heshel's.

"Mmmmm… what have we here?" said Azar, peering over Heshel's shoulder and into the basket.

"Oh, look, she has gifted me some of her goat's cheese. It smells delicious. Some wine too? And, my oh my, look at this bread. What craft has gone into its making. I have never seen such bread as this. Come. Come. Please enter my home and let us two share some bread and wine. What better way to begin to know each other?"

Heshel looked at the Baal. He saw a large man, tall and powerfully built, with dark skin and gleaming eyes, dressed in a copper-coloured tunic stitched with intriguing patterns. His movements were assured and executed with a measured force. His voice, deep, clear and cutting, rhythmic, musical, and even hypnotic. Hypnotic too were his gestures, the movement of his hands painting pictures upon the skin of the air. Everything he did, he did with great gusto. His loudness was louder, his quietness was quieter, as if the great artist had painted him in more vivid colours. As he invited him to sit, Azar noticed Heshel's attention caught by a small wooden table, highly polished and beautifully carved. Its legs were elegant and fashioned in silver, gazelle-like and inlaid with multi-coloured precious stones.

"Acacia," said Azar. "Does it please you?"

"Very much so. May I make closer inspection?"

"Of course. Please, make yourself at home."

Azar watched the manner in which this young man touched the wood. The touch of a lover.

"Deborah informs me that you are a carpenter."

"Oh no, Baal-Azar. It is true I love to work with wood but I am unschooled in this art."

"I see," said Azar. "Yet I think Deborah is not referring to mere technique. Still, first things first, I must not get ahead of myself. Would you be so kind as to call me Azar? Really, we two have no need for such formalities. I am the Baal only in the presence of lesser mortals. Maybe a merchant? Or perhaps, a king?" He winked like a raven. "But no such titles are needed between you and me. We shall meet on level ground. Azar is what my friends and family call me, and I hope you and I shall be the best of friends."

"Thank you, Azar."

"See, that did not hurt at all. The gods have taken no great offence."

He glanced upwards to the clouds as if seeking affirmation.

"So, you love to work with wood. Deborah tells me you like spending much time alone in the forest. What draws you to be such a frequent visitor?"

"I find myself content there. I prefer to walk amongst the trees than to be sat in the school."

"Perhaps the forest is your school? There are many schools in which we can learn, no? And who better than the sacred trees themselves to teach the carpenter's craft."

"My mother would have said the same."

"Your mother sounds like someone I would have loved to meet. Deborah tells me she was a master healer?"

"There are many who would have said so."

"Blessed be the healer and the healer's craft. And what of the craft of your father? He is a fisherman, I hear?"

His trade is bitterness. His harvest is heartache. So thought Heshel, but did not say.

"His labour fills our tables with plenty."

"Blessed be the fisherman," said Azar, patting his belly and smiling broadly.

"And what of you, Heshel? What is your calling?"

"I am studying to be a rabbi."

"A rabbi? That is a rare and high calling."

"I do not know about callings. It is my father's wish. And the rabbi believes me to be a very promising candidate."

"And what was your mother's wish for you?"

"To be happy. To follow the path of my heart."

"Which is?"

"It no longer matters. All that matters is my duty."

"Would your mother have agreed?"

"She is no longer here to voice her opinion."

"Maybe she is not as distant as you believe her to be. And well do I understand the call of duty. Let me tell you something. Even before the hour of my birth, I was deemed to succeed my father and become fire priest of my tribe."

"And are you not a fire priest?"

"I tend the altar of a different fire. I have answered a different calling. A calling not bound by mortal law. We shall perhaps speak of this further another time. But today, here in sight of the holy mountain, will you bear testimony to your heart's true desire?"

"Forgive me, Azar. I have no wish to cause offence. But my desire is no longer of any consequence."

"Why, Heshel, it is of every consequence. Are not our talents our most sacred gifts, bestowed upon us by the will of the Most Holy One?"

"I believe the rabbi would say so."

"Then speak to me of your talents. Tell me what you believe to be your true calling."

"I often find myself wishing to be a carpenter."

"A carpenter, you say? Blessed be the craft of the carpenter. The craft of the carpenter is a subject that rests close to my heart. Let us discuss this further but in the proper setting. Let us go to the forest. Let the cedars of Elnazar bear witness to our words. And when we arrive, I would ask you to act as my teacher and guide. Who better than Heshel, the son of mother Rafaella, to initiate me into the forest's ancient lore?"

Him? A teacher? Who was he to teach anything to anybody, let alone a high master? He, who could not even obey the wishes of his father. Yet though plagued by such doubts, Heshel felt a dark mood lifting.

"I would be honoured, Azar. I will do my best to be an able guide. Come, follow me, master. I shall take you to a very special place, though to get there I must first warn you, we will have to cross the marshlands. It is the only way. We will have to tread carefully for the terrain is treacherous. I am sure the swamps would like to know the taste of a fire priest."

"Indeed," said Azar, a wry smile creeping across his face. "Then let us hope that I am neither too hot for the marshes to digest, nor too corpulent a morsel. I would not wish to upset them. Anyway, I will have you know I can be as light and nimble as a goat when I wish to be. Oh, please, Heshel, why do you look quite so surprised?"

But surprised Heshel was, and soon even more so, to see how lightly the fire priest was able to move, hopping and bobbing over clusters of saw grass, weaving nimbly as a sprite past the green-coated wetlands. And all the while, with his full and undivided attention, Azar followed the path Heshel traced out before him as if closely following the steps of a dance. Watching for each turn of an ankle, the weight and span of heel and toe. For the ablest of students was the master Azar.

"We are almost there. Can you see them just ahead, at the edge of the forest?"

There, right before them, a dense grove of olives, an assembly of gnarled and knotted trees, echoing with the brusque cawing of an unkindness of ravens. Like an intricate canopy were their entwined, spindly branches, clasped together like the hands of a grandmother in prayer. Weathered and witchy, the twist of their boughs, crouched down on their haunches as if straining to hear. Their bark, all blistered with hollows and wrinkles. Their leaves rustling and shaking, a medicine rattle. And down the triangular corridor formed by their outstretched branches, was a dark, gaping opening, where lurking in the thick and murky half-light, what seemed to be some sort of crouching creature. As if Cerberus himself were guarding this gateway.

"My mother often used to bring me here," Heshel said in hushed tones. "She called it the Gathering Place of the Medicine Moon Mothers. The Grove of the Grandmothers. The Women at the Crossroads. The Guardian Protectors of the Maiden's Sheath. She would come here often in search of their counsel, yet only when the moon was in her fullness. Her fullness, for the harvest. Her waxing, for the seeding. Her waning, for many occluded and mysterious things. This grove, she would tell me, is a very special place, for it is a sanctum that stands alone and set apart. A gateway between two worlds. And when my mother brought me here, she would always smile and fill the grove with her laughter. She would take my hand and look deep into my eyes, singing, 'Come now, the children, to show us the way'."

Whilst Heshel spoke, Azar saw the carpenter's eyes glaze over with a sheen of mellow light.

"It was here where Yitshak first found my mother. She was distressed and alone, unable to remember the place from where she had come. She only knew she had been seeking the Raven King, whose exploits she had heard of in the ancient stories. But, instead, she had heard the sound of wedding bells, a sound she could not help but follow."

Heshel knelt on the grass, scooping up in his hands some soil and leaves.

"I love this place. We would spend the day collecting all sorts of leaves and mushrooms, flowers and bark, with which to make her medicine. This is why I carved this seat for her. I have hoped that one day I will find her sitting waiting for me. But that day has not come."

Wherefore such deep wells of remorse in the eyes of this carpenter?

"Would you care to examine it? I fashioned it from a fallen oak who sacrificed its life giving shelter to our children, struck down by lightning in a violent storm."

"I would be honoured to see the marriage of your craft with this most noble of oaks."

As they stepped forward to do so, the ravens fell silent, then took to the air with a loud volley of caws, aghast and agitated, desirous of knowing who dare interrupt their congress. Fierce was their sharp scrutiny when coming to land, their heads leaning forward, shuffling along branches from one leg to the other, an incredulous shrugging of their flapping wings. And amidst all their commotion, Azar came to see this crouching creature was no many-headed hound of Hades, but an immaculately carved bench with seven seats.

"Beautiful," said Azar, gently tracing his fingers across it. "I see you are not as unschooled as you believe yourself to be. Would you mind if I sit upon it?"

"Please do."

Azar eased himself into one of the seats and laughed.

"What was I thinking? For a moment I thought I was still a young man. But now I see this seat is not carved for one of such ample proportions."

"Perhaps this seat? Yitshak is able to comfortably sit there."

"Yes. Indeed. A much better fit. I am proud to be seated on the butcher's throne. This is truly a wonderful piece of work. Does your father know of this talent?"

"He has never seen it. He would never come here. He hates the forest and everything of it. He believes it to be treacherous and deceiving. An abode of demons."

"How has he come to believe such a thing?"

"He believes the forest stole my mother from him. He believes the forest bewitched her and caused her to lose her reason. And he believes the same punishment should be meted out to the forest as is meted out to every witch, just as commanded in the holy scriptures. But he dare not say this, not even to the rabbi. He only spits out his venomous anger to me."

"And what do you believe, Heshel?"

"I believe my mother had to leave us. She heard the voice of the forest summoning her to return. She was a mermaid who would die if she did not return to the sea."

"I understand such a calling."

"How I wish I had understood. But I was too young. Too selfish. What did I care about some strange call from the forest? I only knew I would lose her. There was no end to my incessant pleading. No end to my crying. I begged her to stay or take me with her. She did not belong to the forest. She was my mother. Mine. Oh, Azar, what anguish I must have caused her. But her own life was as nothing to her love for me. She feared what fate would befall me, to know such sorrow and bitterness at such a still tender age. So she chose to remain with me in Elnazar, even though she knew it would surely spell her end. At first, I rejoiced at my victory. But that feeling was fleeting. There was nowhere to hide from the knowledge that if she did not return to the forest, my mother would soon fade and wither. What else could I do but let her go? I will never forget how she looked at me when I spoke of my decision. No mother could be prouder, she told me, than she was of her little prince of the forest. And she promised she would watch over me until I was ready to join her in the other world. But now I know I will never be ready. And we will never be reunited."

"Why do you say so?"

"Because I have failed her. Every day, I fail her. I made her a promise I have been unable to keep. She knew my father would not understand why she had to leave, for his pain would be too great. Yet she asked me to try and never forget that my father is a good man and he would always hold the key to her heart. I made oath I would do so. But with each passing day, it becomes harder to believe my father has any good left in him. What blasphemies he has uttered. What vile curses he has made. He lied about my mother. He has sullied her good name and branded her memory. He has proclaimed my mother to be an adulteress, that she betrayed him for a man from another tribe. Even grandfather Yitshak, who has all the composure of the ablest hunter, struggled to resist meting out vengeance for staining her reputation with such filthy words."

Heshel looked deep into the passageway, talking as if his mother would hear his confession.

"I cannot forgive him. I will never forgive him. I can barely stomach the sight of him. I only obey his wishes in honour of my mother's memory. It is the only way I may hold onto her. It is all that remains of my promise. What am I to do, Azar? What am I to do?"

"From such poison seeds can only come a bitter harvest. May I pray on behalf of your father, for I suspect it is not you who are lost but him. It seems as if your father's soul has lost its way. I fear he has become a vacant house into which something other has entered."

"I would be most grateful if you would do so."

How good it felt to thus unburden his heart. Heshel felt as if a weight were lifting. A dense fog clearing. For a moment, all that was green turned a little greener. All that was red, a little redder, just as it had when standing at this gateway with mother Rafaella. Azar gazed upwards to the darkening sky.

"The twilight is fast coming. Has the time come for us to return?"

"Would you like to walk a while longer in this hallowed place? We still have some time before night sets in."

"I would like that very much."

The air is shimmering and tingling with the song of the winged ones, of the mourning wheatear and the desert lark, the song thrush, the swallow and the winter wren. So many possibilities, so many hopes and dreams, each one standing like an angel in full array. Before tomorrow and after today.

She Rides a White Horse

Spring became summer, the days became longer, the land throbbed and baked beneath the burning sun. Frogs sought refuge in the shade of the bulrush, oxen sweltered beneath the yoke of the plough. Crickets clicked and jackdaws jabbered, flutters of butterflies and clusters of bees, flitted and hummed in the violet fields. Amidst the branches of the fruit-laden orchards, flocks of yellowhammers trilled towards the bright cerulean sky. And when the balmy night came, the land was bathed in an emerald sheen, calling both lover and the lovelorn, to come and bathe in this magic, to come and roam in the wild.

The month of Menachem Av had come, and with it the day of Rebekah's fifteenth birthday. Azar would soon be arriving to join in celebration, the fire priest having become a regular guest. Happy was the magi to be invited into their circle. Honoured to share bread and wine at their table. Home no longer felt quite so far away, for though a man well accustomed to walking in solitude, he loved to bask in the good company of family. Yet he remained heedful of his conduct, watching and listening, observing and learning the ways of this new tribe, always attentive to the sensibilities of the baker's young daughter.

As for Rebekah, she was shocked to find how divided she felt when Azar came. There was a part of her that craved for his coming. In his presence, even the beams of the house seemed to creak with laughter. She rejoiced to see radiant smiles light up her mother's face. A brighter spirit permeated the home, like spring after the longest, coldest, most barren of winters. She felt helpless to resist the spell of his wondrous stories. She became entranced to hear him speak of his craft. She liked how she felt when he talked to her only. With him, she felt a little older. A little wiser. Yet despite all this, there was a part of her that wanted to scold him, to scream at him, to shake her fist in blind fury and drive him away from the hearth. Each time Azar was invited to sit on that chair by the table, she was reminded of what had been taken from her. That chair. That chair, that had once been his chair. Her father's chair. That chair, that was still his chair. It should have been Simeon, not Azar, lighting the sabbath candles. It gnawed away at her somewhere deep inside, some part of her as restless as the unquiet dead. Those smiles, those smiles upon her mother's face, smiles that rightly belonged to Simeon. Not to this thief, this usurper, this magpie in their midst.

"Oh, Ariadna, why do I feel this way?" asked Rebekah, leaning against the bough of a weeping willow. A tiny spider crawled over the back of her hand and onto her palm. How easily she could crush it if she had a mind to. But why would she even think such a heinous thing?

"Azar has brought only laughter and light to our home. He has brought smiles to my mother. I find myself loving to hear his stories and to learn of his craft. And yet I feel such a hatred for him. What shall I do, queen of the spiders? What shall I do? He does not deserve this. But I cannot tell him or my mother how I feel. I cannot. I would surely ruin it all for her."

Those eyes. Everywhere. Those ears. Everywhere. These words, somewhere, everywhere and nowhere.

"Weave, my daughter," sang in reply, the queen of the spiders. "Weave. Weave it out and weave it in. All of your happiness and all your despair. Let it pour into each and every silver thread, in the manner that the passion of your craft dictates. And by these means, all shall be well and right."

"Will it, Ariadna? Will it truly?"

Rebekah saw the little spider start to move backwards and forwards as if uncertain which way to go. Time to place it back upon the grass.

"Yes, all shall be well. Has the queen of the spiders ever lied to you, my weaving daughter? So go now, for your loom awaits you."

The little spider scuttled quickly away. And, as it did so, an idea flashed before Rebekah's inner eye. She thought to weave a dress for her mother. A spring dress. A dress worthy of the great goddess, Persephone, to wear on her return from the darkness of Hades, walking once more through the flowering fields. She would gift it to Deborah on the day of her own birthday. What a surprise it would be! She imagined the baker putting on this dress for the very first time, a thought that filled Rebekah with the greatest gladness. Her blood became hot, her heart fluorescent, her fingertips tingling with the call of her craft. Time to weave. To weave it in and weave it out. So weave, our seamstress. And when your work shall be complete, your vision made manifest, when you have poured out your despair and your happiness and left one stitch unsewn, then you shall bring to your mother, this art, this heart, this piece of your soul.

"Mother, have you a moment?" asked Rebekah, as Deborah worked in the kitchen. "There is something I would like to show you."

"Yes, of course. Everything is prepared. I shall just close the pot and let the stew simmer."

Rebekah took Deborah's hand and led her to her mother's bedroom. There, laid upon the bed, the most splendid of dresses. It was laced with intricate patterns formed from a plethora of threads, entwined into knots and spirals and flowers and stars. Emerald and purple took centre stage in this symphony of colour, a dress that was not a dress, but a woven song.

"Oh my, it is so beautiful. Who is it for?"

"Who is it for? Why, for you, of course."

"For me? I thought it might be for Hannah. It is surely a dress made for a young woman. A dress for the dance."

"Yes and no, Mother. Yes, it is a dress that is made to dance. But no, I have not made it for Hannah. I have made it for you. It is for you to dance in. I want to see you dance again like you used to. Could you try it on now? I need to see if it fits you properly."

"Right now? But what about our guest? Azar will be arriving soon and I must be dressed appropriately."

Her mother looked uncertain. Vulnerable. She, who was always so strong and decisive, now looked like a little lost girl.

"There is plenty of time. Please, Mother. Do this as a gift for me. You know you dare not refuse me on my birthday. Be quick and I will go and watch over our supper. I can hardly wait to see you in it."

Without waiting for any more words, without taking no for an answer, Rebekah walked out of the room, leaving

Deborah alone with this dress that would grace a queen. What pride she felt to see the majesty of her daughter's craft. She traced her hands through its folds before, ever so carefully, putting it on. No words could describe what she felt to feel its touch upon her skin.

"Do I do it justice, Rebekah?"

Her daughter's eyes spoke of astonishment. And in those beautiful eyes that were a moon and sun, Deborah saw both grief and joy. Suddenly there came an unexpected sound. Thump, thump, thump. The sound of hooves approaching. It cannot be. He has arrived. He is here. So unlike Azar to arrive so early. No time to change. What best to do? A momentary silence, then a gentle rapping. Maybe she could just let Rebekah answer? That would give her time. And yet, and yet, there was that in her which did not wish to take it off. Was it her own will, she wondered, or the will of the dress? She only knew she felt like the first coming of spring. Without further thought, she opened the door. There stood Azar, a bouquet of flowers held in his hands. He appeared somewhat taken aback at the sight of her. To see her was to see a queen in all her pomp and majesty, a glorious denizen from some other world. And the master in him could not help but marvel. Marvelling to behold the craft of the dressmaker.

"Beautiful," he muttered to himself.

"Why, thank you," responded Deborah, twirling around like a young girl at a dance, a mischievous glint in her eyes. "Rebekah made this spring dress for me," she said, as proud as any mother could possibly be. Azar caught sight of Rebekah, watching, listening, lingering in the shadows.

"My oh my, Rebekah, what a gift you have. And to think I have been jabbering all this time about my craft. I feel so embarrassed."

"But I love to hear you jabber," said Rebekah.

"Indeed. Well, before I jaaaaaa... beeerrrrrr... some more, I must pass on a message to you. Jamil would like to take you for a ride as his birthday gift to you. Would you like that? This is not something he offers to just anyone."

Jamil whinnied in agreement.

"Yes, I would like that very much."

"Do we have time, Deborah?"

"Yes, Azar. You have time, now you have arrived here so early. So, off you both go."

"Sorry if I caught you both off guard, but Jamil has a way of getting to places at just the right time. We will not be late coming back, will we, Jamil?"

Azar took Rebekah by the hand and they went outside.

"I am a little nervous of horses. I know it is silly but I just cannot help it."

"Well, Rebekah, let us see if Jamil can remedy this."

On seeing them coming, Jamil snorted and came cantering towards Rebekah, stopping abruptly, banging one hoof on the ground.

"Oh, I fear he does not like me."

"Hmmmmmm... I suspect quite the opposite. Do not be alarmed. This is just his way of saying hello. He is probably just as nervous as you. He is a very sensitive horse, you know. Come closer and put out your hand."

She stretched out her hand towards Jamil. Her heart raced as his enormous head moved towards her, the hot breath from his nostrils like fire on her skin. A big tongue appeared, followed by a row of surprisingly shiny white teeth. The stallion proceeded to lick her hand and rub his forehead against her palm.

"Well, well, well, I think he has taken quite a shine to you. Is this not so, Jamil, my winged one?"

To Rebekah's further surprise, Jamil knelt down upon one knee, bowing his head as if inviting her to mount.

"How are you to refuse this cordial invitation? Oh, Jamil. Are you not a most uncommon horse? I have known no horse swifter. I am sure, Rebekah, there is magic in his hooves. I sometimes even wonder if he has invisible wings. Yes," continued Azar, stroking his beard, "now I come to think of it, you two are, in some ways, quite alike. Come, let me help you mount our noble friend. That's it. Place your feet in the stirrups. Get yourself comfortable. It is fortunate, Jamil, that Rebekah is as light as a feather," said Azar as he mounted. "Now, Rebekah, hold on to me tight. Good. Are you ready?"

"Ready," came back the meek yet thrilled reply.

"Then let us go. Away, Jamil."

As Jamil galloped off, Rebekah felt a surge of tremendous power resonating deeply throughout her bones. She held on tightly as the wind whipped up her hair. Azar chortled to feel her clasp, straining to reach around the large girth of his body.

"Do you know, my girl," he bellowed, "that you have it in you to raise such a wind? I will show you, if you like?"

She tried to answer, but her voice was unintelligible, as she bobbed up and down on the soft, leather saddle. Faster, faster and faster still, the world blurring into nothingness, dissolving into silence, until after what could only have been the briefest of moments, they found themselves standing still at the side of the forest.

"How can this be? We only set off a moment ago!"

Azar smiled and fondly stroked Jamil's ears.

"He is a rogue, is he not? A rogue and a thief, for I am sure he is able to steal time itself. And maybe, one day, you will ride with Jamil all by yourself. Now, do not be bashful,

Jamil. You know you would like that. It would make a nice change from carrying my not so inconsiderable weight, would it not?"

Rebekah laughed.

"Thank you, Azar. Thank you, Jamil. That was wonderful. And yes, one day soon we shall go for a ride together."

"Good. It is settled. Happy, Jamil? Yes, you are. Now come, Rebekah. Let us sit on Heshel's bench. I have something for you."

Heshel's bench? Strange how Rebekah had never seen this bench before. Azar helped her dismount, then reached for something hung to the side of the saddle.

"Here you are," he said, placing an object in her hands wrapped in violet silk. It felt heavy and cold. It had a strange shape. "Go ahead and look."

Azar's tone was light, but inside he was nervous. He watched Rebekah unwrap it, her eyes gleaming with curiosity. There, before her, an immaculate stone spider, altogether unlike anything she had seen before.

"It is wonderful."

"I know how much you like spiders."

"And so you made this for me? Thank you, Azar. I shall place it right beside my loom."

"I am so pleased you like it, Rebekah. But I must tell you straight away, it was not me who made this."

"If not you, then who?"

But somehow, a part of Rebekah already knew. She did not want to, but she knew. How quickly things could change in sight of this enchanted forest. She felt her blood go cold, her muscles start to freeze. She felt her breath go shallow. Her already fair skin turned even paler. As pale and pallid as a winter moon.

"No. This cannot be. It cannot be. It looks like the work

of my father's hand. What is happening? Tell me, did he make this?"

Azar just nodded his head.

"But how… but how do you know for sure?"

Azar pointed out the small mark engraved beneath the base of the statue. Her father's mark and seal.

"I do not believe it. Where did you find it?"

"In the quarry."

"In the quarry?"

The quarry. The quarry. The hateful quarry. The treacherous quarry. The murderous stone.

"My father made this spider?"

"Yes, he made it as a gift for your ninth birthday."

Why was he saying this? Why was he speaking of that which should never be spoken?

"My ninth birthday? What do you know of my ninth birthday? Did my mother tell you about it?"

"Please, let me explain, Rebekah."

But his voice was now distant. She felt it all coming back. That terrible day. That day she did not wish to remember. She felt a growing rage. She felt an overwhelming helplessness. Searing pangs of bitter remorse lanced her heart. Nobody, nobody was meant to ever mention that day again. Nobody. Never, ever. Never, for she had sealed it up. She had buried it and laid it to rest, just as her father had been buried beneath a blanket of stone. For so long she had yearned to tell somebody about this agony inside her. And now Azar had opened up this wound deep within her soul. Her head hung down like a wilting rose. She could no longer hold her secret. Her guilt. Her crime.

"It was my fault, Azar," she said, ever so meekly.

"What was your fault, Rebekah?"

"It was my fault."

All went still. The forest listened.

"*It's my fault that my father is dead!*"

There. She had said it. She had let it out. She had screamed out those words for the whole world to hear. She had made her confession, meant only to be heard by the angel of death at the time of her passing. Words that had been a dagger in her heart for all these years. She began to sob.

"It is my fault my mother has become a widow. If it had not been my birthday on the day of the earthquake, then he would never have been in the quarry."

How Azar's heart ached to hear her words.

"Oh, my darling girl. My darling, darling girl. You must leave behind this erroneous thinking. This is the reasoning of a grief-stricken child not yet seasoned by experience. There is no-one to blame, least of all you. Love, and only love led your father to the quarry that day. A father's love for his daughter and nothing else. Who should be blamed? You, for the transgression of turning nine? Simeon, for making a birthday gift for his precious daughter? If not your father, then maybe the boulders that fell upon him? If not the boulders, then maybe the earth that moved? If not the earth, then maybe the winds that blew across the vaults of heaven? No, Rebekah, none of these are to be blamed. Hear me now. Listen, and if you are able, listen with your all. Be still, my child. Compose yourself and silence your sorrow. Just for a moment. Let go of this hurting that he may come closer."

As if he were an angel, she heard his word and felt his judgement. She felt a light switching on inside her head. And this light in her saw the Shekinah come to descend from the heavens. She saw herself as she had been upon that terrible day. She looked so small, so fragile and tiny, as if even the slightest of breezes could snap her in two. Poor weeping willow. Poor child, sat there all alone in her room, her small heart breaking. Poor child, sobbing quietly on her bed so as not to be heard, silently promising never to add to her mother's load. Never to burden her with a daughter's grief. Never, ever. This forgotten promise, to protect her mother at all costs, by burying her own pain away forever. Far, far away. But Azar had brought all of this out into the glare of the merciful light.

Rebekah looked upon her confessor. His face. His face, that was no face at all. Where before had been eyes and ears and nose and mouth, now was only rock and flame. Where had been the kindest of smiles, now only flew a solitary mountain hawk. That roaring laughter, now become a silent symphony. A calming wind. Stiller and stiller she became. Stiller, becalmed, an open door. She felt the stone spider in her hands. She held it tightly. She held it now with all her might. Tightly, in case it should all too soon disappear. In case all this was just a passing dream. Tightly, tenderly, holding onto this little piece of him, holding it close against her chest. This gift, these blessings of the consoling father. She felt the spider starting to vibrate. She felt it pulsing as if coming alive. The warmth of her blood upon its cold and stony flesh. She felt as if its stone form were filled with veins of blood and fire. A river, a river, flowing from her to it and from it to her. Whispers becoming louder. Whispers becoming words. I am ready to listen. I am ready to receive.

"Daughter of my flesh. Daughter of my soul. My beloved. How I have missed you. Oh, how I have missed you. Come to me. Come to me, who shall always be your father. Come now and find the part of me that still remains, forever sealed by love within my craft. Here in this gift. Here in this temple. Here upon this bridge of stone. Hold me close and feel my heart. And wherever you shall be, I shall be there also. Always and forever, my daughter of Ariadna."

"Soooooooooooooo…" whispered the spider and the witnessing stone angel. "Sooooooooooooooo…" sang the chair and the dancing spring dress. "Sooooooooooooo…" spoke the light in her mother's eyes. The sun is rising in the Valley of Gehenna.

Loom of Ariadna

The spider girl. That's what they called her when she was still but a child. Little Rebekah, straying far from the hearth. Little Rebekah, so hard to see, so hard to find, as if turned invisible, as if veiled in mist. Lingering amidst the flowers of the forest and meadows, splashing her feet in the fast-moving streams, gazing at the world in endless fascination. How wondrous to dream here, she would often muse, asleep in this garden of great delight. Her blanket, the poppies, her pillow, the gorse. Her every thought and feeling, a butterfly, flying this way and that. Her tears, a spring shower. Her laughter, the wind. Never less alone than when making her bed there. Look, there is grandfather sun, always shining and smiling. Grandmother moon, always weaving and guiding. The voice of the river, rushing and roaring. The prayer of the mountain. Each cloud, a puff of smoke from the medicine pipe. The song of the birds winging in ecstatic flight. The considering carp and the pondering pike. The hum of the bees buzzing busily around, building cathedrals of honey up high in the treetops. The tremble of the chrysalis. The army of ants, each one as mighty as Atlas. The snails, slowly journeying with all the time in the world, their tiny antennae, searching and probing, their hairless heads bobbing up and down. Where have they come from and where are they going? How do they know which path to follow? So many questions held this girl from the garden. Yet nothing held more wonder than the spiders weaving their webs. Such marvellous patterns, so beautiful and fragile, flickering and shining in the morning dew. She could not help but to reach out and touch them.

"I am so sorry, spider. I have broken the web you have taken so long to weave."

But the spiders forgave her, for they could feel her heart. And they chose to teach her the mystery of fashioning their webs. So dextrous and nimble, as though plucking the strings of the David's harp. And whilst some of the children were alarmed by their movement and would run away, others grew hostile, finding big sticks with which to beat and crush them. But not so Rebekah. She would, ever so carefully, pick up the spiders, hiding them away from the sight of such children. Ha, ha, ha. To feel them in her hands as they tickled her palms, the quick pitter-patter of their eight tiny feet.

"Run quickly, little spider. Run into the forests where you will be safe."

Yet some of the children saw her and mocked her for doing so.

"You are so strange, Rebekah. Why do you love those little ugly monsters so much? Do you not know they are dangerous? Just one sting and you will be dead. Oh, you are just a silly spider girl."

But they did not know that Rebekah was happy and proud to be the spider girl. And she carried the name with a secret pride.

"I am the spider girl. And one day I will weave a robe that Solomon himself would be proud to wear, for my friends, the spiders, will show me how."

So she would say to the listening spiders. And though she could not shoot out filaments of web from her body as did her kin, she found she could weave her webs in a different fashion: from beautiful threads of many colours. Endless hours sat spinning upon her loom, making all manner of garments for her collection of toys. Yet only Deborah and Simeon knew of their daughter's secret passion, for Rebekah wanted no-one else to know.

One day she was out playing with her friends in the forest, chasing each other as children are often wont to do, one playing the part of the terrifying monster, the others, the part of the monster's prey. Rebekah could feel the hot, uneven breath of the creature upon her neck. She ran faster and faster, her blood racing with the thrill of escaping. Occasionally, she glanced behind her, catching sight of this most fearsome beast shooting out flames from its cavernous nostrils. She ran even faster, looking forward and backwards, backwards and forwards. She could see its face so close behind her. And then it happened. A fast-approaching branch. A sharp, searing pain. A stab in the heart until all things faded into nothingness. She awoke in her bed. Had it all just been a bad dream? As her eyes tried to focus, she could just about make out the worried expression on her mother's face. She thought she could see tears flowing down her cheeks.

"Mother, why are you crying?"

"Oh, Rebekah. I am so glad you have awoken. I have been so worried. How do you feel, my darling daughter?"

"I feel fine. But please tell me, Mother, why have you been so worried? Please tell me why are you crying?"

Deborah struggled to find the right words as she held her daughter's hands.

"I am crying for your loss, my most precious one."

"What do you mean? I have not lost anything."

But she had started to become aware of a dressing upon her face. She felt it once, then felt it again. It was covering her left eye.

"What has happened to me? Why am I in bed with a bandage over my eye?"

"Do you not remember, Rebekah? Do you not remember playing in the forest?"

"Yes, Mother. But nothing after the branch."

Her mother carefully explained all that had happened. Of how she had been badly injured and her friends brought her home. How the many who loved her had joined together in prayer, whilst Rafaella watched over her and tended her wound.

"My eye, my eye. I shall never see again. And if I cannot see, then I shall never weave. I will never make a robe Solomon would be proud to wear."

That night, Rebekah dreamt a spider from the forest had heard her cries.

"Young daughter of the earth, why are you crying so loudly that all the trees, birds and flowers hear you from far away?"

"Do not talk to me about the trees for they have stolen my sight. I hate them. I will never forgive them. Oh spider, I shall never see again. I shall never see again. And I shall never weave again."

"Listen now, sweet daughter. You who are of us, and we who are of you. The spiders heard your cries and did call for me. I am Ariadna. The queen of the spiders."

"The queen of the spiders?"

"Yes, my child. And on my loom are woven the webs of destiny itself. The destiny that is a living story and of which all life is a part. Listen to me and listen well. There is seeing and there is seeing. When we spin the webs you love so dearly, when we spin those patterns and shapes, we see them with another eye. An eye hidden deep within every one of us. I am Ariadna, the great weaving one, and I will show you how to see with this eye, if you so should choose. This eye, Rebekah, can see far and wide. It can even catch a glimpse of the great artist's craft. In not seeing, you will see the more. One eye shall be as a sun that sees far without, the other, a moon, seeing far within. Seeing into eternity, and even beyond."

"Can this really be, great queen of the spiders? Can this really be?"

"Only if you so will it, heartbroken child of ours. For in some losses you gain and, in some gains, you lose. Just call me by my name and I shall teach you how to weave a robe of rainbows. A coat that Joseph would yearn to wear. Even King Solomon, in all his splendour."

Her words wove a web around Rebekah's grieving heart. And with this weaving, the girl felt something opening deep within. An eye like a chameleon.

"Dream me new dreams with your chameleon eye. You shall see patterns and colours no longer known to the walking ones. The same colours and patterns once seen in the gardens of Paradise."

An explosion of colours radiated outwards from some inner place, painting a new world to Rebekah's utter amazement. And now, the voice of Ariadna seemed to emanate from everywhere. Here and there and all around.

"Listen to the word of Ariadna, The Weaving One, who was there at the beginning. Who was there in the

Garden Where Four Rivers Flow. Such stories we shall tell you. Wondrous stories you shall weave into many forms. And, before I depart, there is one further thing you must know. There is one greater than Solomon who awaits to be bedecked in your craft. I speak truly when I tell you, your loss shall make you greater. For you shall no more be Rebekah, the one-eyed, but Rebekah, the three-eyed. And these three eyes shall be as one, and the past, present and future shall all be revealed to you. Yes, even time itself shall bow down before the art of the weaver. But you must never speak of what I shall show you, but only weave your visions into the webs of your craft. A craft I shall teach you. Do you believe the word of Ariadna?"

With her inner seeing, Rebekah caught glimpses of sights beyond her furthest imaginings. And, in this seeing, it was as if she had never seen before. She glimpsed a being whose eyes were as infinite as the stars above. Small pools of blackness that blazed with light and knowing. The eyes of Ariadna. Such love she saw in these countless eyes. Such love for her, a mere speck of dust before this rampant eternity.

"I believe every word you have spoken, Oh, thank you, Ariadna, queen of the spiders. Please teach me of all you have spoken."

Rebekah slept in the arms of peace that night, whilst Simeon remained awake and vigilant at her side. As he looked upon his daughter, he became filled with wonder, to see the broadest of smiles forming upon her face. The room became filled with the smell of hyacinths. And when she awoke the next day, all were amazed to behold her joyful spirit. How happy was Rebekah to find it had not just been a passing dream. For she could now see things such as she had never seen before.

"Why are you so happy after your terrible accident?" her friends enquired.

But Rebekah had become just a little bit wiser.

"I am just so happy to be home with my friends and my family. So very happy."

A butterfly flew in through the window and alighted upon her shoulder. A small butterfly with violet wings. And as it did so, she saw she would become widely known as a master seamstress. That people would come seeking the craft of the weaver, this most gifted fashioner of clothes. But her secret passion was always to fashion her tapestries. Into each one, Rebekah would weave stories that somehow lived and breathed, though only being clusters of colourful, intertwining threads. She would weave many such stories, sat upon her loom like a queen on a throne, some of things that once had been, some of things still yet to come, and some she chose should come to be. For she weaved the web as a daughter of Ariadna should weave, and her creation was beautiful and tender and kind. And with her eye that saw nothing, she saw the All. And in her weave and loom and spin and shuttle, she sang her song. Exquisite beyond compare, this raging beauty. Within the threads sprang sparks of fire like blood through veins. And in whatever Rebekah would weave, she always left one stitch unsewn, just as Ariadna had shown her. One stitch unsewn, so that the one who loved her craft could weave therein, a little of their own story. A little of their own song. For only then would her craft be truly complete. Waiting to be completed by the love of another.

"Where did Rebekah find this magic loom?" the villagers would wonder. "It must surely be made of magic, for how else could this girl create such craft?"

"I am Rebekah, the weaver," she would say. But they did not know for how could they know, that deep, deep inside, she was and would always be, the spider girl.

The Narrow Gate

"Master, what is the secret of your craft?"

Seven months had passed since Azar had accepted Heshel as his apprentice. Seven months of stacking wood and stoking the fire, of learning how to make Azar's favoured tea and attending to all manner of errands and duties. Well made had been the dwelling and so too the forge. And, in this time, little by little and almost imperceptibly, Azar began to speak of different things. He spoke of the elements and of the ethers, of the special magic of each passing season, of how to become as the air and as the earth, the water and the fire. Of how to become at one with his art and craft. He taught him how to empty himself and fill himself, to be heedful of inspiration's kiss and call. He tutored Heshel to make tools from inception to realisation, that they may be vital, at one with his will and fashioned by his heart. How to both dedicate and consummate them. How to hold them and touch them, as a lover holds the beloved. To feel their moods, to know their weight and measure, to follow the path of their own innate and unique motion. How to listen to the voice of the wood with his inner ear, to still his mind that his eye may be opened to their inner form, to feel the pulse and current of the dancing wood. All of this and much more. And Heshel began to realise that he was both sometimes the artisan, and sometimes the tool.

Outside, the icy cold of an early winter's evening had come. A chill breeze stole through the slightly ajar door, making barely perceptible ripples in the folds of Azar's emerald-green kaftan. The magi sat with pipe in hand, holding it as if it were an instrument upon which he played silent music. It was carved from briar in the image of a snake, its bowl shaped in the form of a head, its stem slightly curved, its surface carved with ornately patterned scales. Azar packed the chamber with his favourite blend of aromatic herbs and spices, then slowly drew the lip close to his face and set alight the mix. As it changed into glowing cinders, he puckered his lips, wrapping them around the mouthpiece whilst stroking the stem and carefully inhaling. Heshel watched the smoke race from the pipe like a dragon belching out flames, its aroma filling the room. Its touch was warm upon his skin, blowing past him like a high summer wind. The apprentice had become accustomed to the smoke from Azar's pipe and had grown to like its rich, exotic scent, carrying him to far distant places. Even to Asnavant.

As he drew in the smoke, Azar's eyes glowed like embers, his body relaxing as muscles still taut from labour shed their load.

"The secret… of… myyyyyyyyy… craaaaaaaaaaaaftttt?"

His words drifted out slowly, like mountain mist.

"Why do we love secrets so much, I wonder? Secrets. What is the pull of that which is hidden? What is the source of this hunger to know, to make sense of it all? Are the birds, the animals, the fish or the insects preoccupied by such questions? Why is it we search for the hidden knowledge, sometimes even at risk of life itself? Why do we wish to see what lies behind the veil of the Shekinah? Is it merely to satisfy our curiosity? Is curiosity sufficient, that she may be prevailed upon to reveal her naked glory? That she should admit us to the bridal suite?"

Azar watched Heshel stroking and tugging his beard, the brow of his apprentice furrowed in thought.

"I have answered your one question with many questions, have I not? What an evasive master I am. Ah, my friend, some questions are so very easy to ask. But when it comes to the answers… well, that is not always quite so easy. Some questions may take a moment to ask, yet may take a whole lifetime to answer. Or maybe it is a question that can never be answered, for it is the will of the great mystery to remain a mystery. Maybe it is something that lies beyond the reach of the spoken word, or is something only to be communicated through the medium of silence? Perhaps that is why my lips have been sealed and, so too, your ears. This leaves us in something of a quandary, does it not? A fine apprentice and master, we two shall make."

He laughed as only Azar could laugh, with the whole of his body, with neither shame nor reservation.

"Yes, any fool can ask any question. It is so easy to put the question, but not so easy to complete the quest. But you are no fool, Heshel. Far from it, in fact. And I know well you do not idly ask questions. So, consider this, if you will, maybe it is prudent that we first make ourselves ready and worthy to receive such answers. I am not exaggerating when I say I have known many driven to madness through such lack of preparedness and excess of complacency. We must make of ourselves a receptacle, able to bear the impact of such a divine unveiling. Would you pour your most precious vintage wine into a cup that is cracked? Is it not so, the cup must be made to contain the wine? The anvil fashioned to withstand the heat of the furnace? We must prepare ourselves diligently, in heart and mind, in body and soul. We must know ourselves, deeply, truthfully, intimately. No corner must be left unturned in this sacred quest. We must know who it is seeking the hidden knowledge. We must discern our motives and make them pure and single-pointed. Are we seeking a treasure that will bring us untold power and untold riches? Do we desire to take for our own, the most beautiful woman in all the land? To place a ring upon the finger of her unwilling hand? Could it be our wish to be a queen, whose fame, wealth and beauty exceed even the Queen of Sheba? Or a king perhaps, a king who exceeds Solomon in the scope of his wisdom and magic? Who is worshipped by multitudes, who fall before him upon bended knees? Be wary, my student, of anyone who requires that you bow down before them."

Azar extended out his arms and tilted his head backwards, eyes closed, a maniacal grin on his face, bathing in a waterfall of power. Heshel found himself struggling to take in all of Azar's words. And the master was now in full flow, as unstoppable as a river in the rainy season, leaving Heshel with little choice but to sail with him to whatever destination this current might flow.

"A person must be brave to know the unaltered, undistorted truth of themselves. To look directly into the obsidian mirror. There are few who sincerely wish to know. And of those few, some are too easily led astray, seduced by flattering and convenient answers. We are a creature most adept in the art of self-deception. True knowing does not come easily. It comes at a price. A price that she shall determine. But we must not barter with wisdom or withhold her fee, for the selfish heart shall never find the Mistress of the Flame."

Azar's eyes blazed briefly like molten metal. He glanced at Heshel with undisguised affection, to see his apprentice no less attentive than a fledgeling waiting to be fed.

"Have I ever told you of how I once met a high priest of Egypt on my travels? You know I do not like to repeat my stories."

"No, master. You have not. Please speak to me of this."

"Very well. This will serve to illustrate the point I am making. I shall tell you of this strange encounter, though you must understand it is hard to convey. Even now, I am unsure as to whether or not it was all but a dream. But whatever the true nature of the experience, it profoundly changed me as you shall soon come to understand."

Azar put down his pipe and rested his arms upon his lap.

"I shall recount to you the time when I met with the Purple Priest of Isis. Blessed be the day."

Azar breathed in deeply. Heshel could not read the unfamiliar expression on his face.

"Was he a man of flesh and blood or was he a phantom? This question used to vex me. But no longer. All that matters now is the knowledge he revealed. If I was taken to him upon the wings of a dream or through the intoxication of an unripened fig, it does not matter."

Azar studied Heshel, examining his intense and earnest eyes, his handsome, newly bearded face, his skin still barely touched by the hand of time.

"I was younger than you are. Younger, and *far* less humble. Maybe I was like that because everything seemed to come so easily to me. I felt I had been born under a lucky star. By day, I was a boy who only wanted to idle his time away in sport with his friends, to display his skill and prowess before the admiring girls. At night, I was accustomed to sleeping soundly and dreamlessly and that suited me well. But all this changed with the vision of the red mountain. I had first sought my father's counsel as to the meaning of the dream. But he would only answer that this was a message from the gods and it was for me alone to discover its meaning."

Azar looked down to the table, a sad look in his eyes. Even now, he missed the presence of his father.

"I am afraid I did not then have ears to hear him. I was too impetuous. Too reckless. Now I wish I could go back and tell him he was right. I would thank him for his good counsel. But instead, I sought out charmers, healers, magicians and dreamers, storytellers and stargazers, asking each to unlock the dream's meaning for me. I even went to visit the priests of other tribes. Each one gave me a price for their counsel and each gave me an answer. Oh… I heard countless explanations, countless opinions, some given after deep and considered reflection, some tossed towards me like scraps of meat to a hungry dog. But none satisfied me. I felt that no-one really knew. And, all the while, I felt as if there were a raging forest fire burning inside of me."

He paused for a moment, relighting his pipe.

"What could I do, Heshel? What could I do? I could not continue to live like this. My life felt as though it was no longer my own. Maybe I had become possessed? Why was this happening to me? I was not one of those unhinged people who sought visions, nor did I wish to be. I was no stargazer. I was just a simple boy whose eyes were rooted firmly to the things of this world. Yet these dreams caused my eyes to become distracted. I no longer found joy in my sport. My thoughts were elsewhere, my preoccupations altered. People started to notice this change in me. My parents started to fear for my health, perhaps even for my soul. I decided I would have to go and find the red mountain, for if I did not, the vision would surely kill me. I would leave everything behind. I vowed to myself I would never stop until I found this red mountain. You would hardly believe what a stubborn and impulsive young man I was. When I made up my mind, I would not take no for an answer. So I packed my bag and left a letter for my parents, asking them to neither be sad nor to worry, for it was surely the gods that were calling me and they would give me their protection. But now I know that every night I was absent, my mother's pillow was drenched in her tears and my father's heart heavy."

He laughed to himself, a laugh laced with understanding and compassion, yet also tinged with regret.

"Such a foolish boy. And yet, even now, I can see this foolish boy had no other choice. So I hatched my plan. I would go to the city of Estakhr. There, in the market, I would seek the young woman, the harbinger, whose glance had wrought this change inside me. Maybe she was a saint who had blessed me with a sacred vision. Or maybe she was a witch with evil intent, who had cast a spell upon me. I had no idea. I only knew that if I could find her, perhaps she would take pity on me and give me answers. I prayed for the gods to intercede. Me, this boy who was not given to prayer. But, in truth, I had little faith in such things. So being such a very practical young man, I reasoned if fate should not favour me, I would instead procure all the provisions I needed to undertake my quest. I decided I would give myself three days to find her. Now, you might be surprised just how many people there are in the city. Many women from different tribes, of all shapes and sizes, of different shades of skin. Young women who walk many miles to sell their wares, bearing heavy cargoes upon their backs. Old wrinkled women, sat rocking in their chairs with shrewd, shining eyes. Hawkers and hagglers, adept in the art of persuasion. I knew my chances of picking her out would be extremely slim, as likely as a camel passing through the eye of a needle. On the first day I executed the first part of my plan. I would try repeating the conditions of my encounter. I set up a stall in precisely the same place. Perhaps this would lure her like a bee to a flower? But to my great disappointment, it did not. So the next day I went looking for her. Unfortunately, I could not acquire any help in my search for I was unable to describe her. Where should have been a memory was only blankness. Three days passed and my search met with failure.

With overwhelming sadness, I got ready to leave. Then, at the very moment of my departure, I became startled by the sight of a man in the crowd. There was no obvious reason why I should have been so startled, yet startled I was. He seemed no different from all the other customers and traders who filled the busy market, yet somehow I knew him to be a priest. Mind you, not from his clothing, but only by some inner knowing. Maybe it was the way he moved that caught my attention. He seemed to float above the ground. He moved with the gait of a king. I had to speak to him. So I went right up to him, tugged upon his sleeve and asked him who he was. He looked surprised by the approach of this bold and brash young man, but it was not my way to be cautious. I was daring, just as you are daring. Why, who else but you would *dare* ask me the secret of my craft?"

His face suddenly transformed into feigned rage, his eyebrows leaping up and down like a warrior's war dance, deep furrows upon his forehead, bellowing of disapproval and offence. His eyes held the gaze of Heshel, the antlers of two rams locked together in the push and pull of battle. Silently, fiercely, they stared at each other until overpowered by the spirit of laughter.

"By the hand of Heracles, you are a most wilful and resolute soul. The fates have led me to meet my nemesis, for with you I suspect I have been summoned to make reparation for all my youthful and misguided ardour. But that is good, my student. That is good. Better to do so in life than in death. Now, young carpenter, what do you think happened after I had so rudely interrupted this uncommon man? Do you think he ignored me? Or maybe he boxed my ears? No, do not answer. That was a rhetorical question. Stay alert now, please."

He tapped the stem of his pipe three times on the table.

"No, the man did not rebuff my advance. He just stopped and looked at me in an extraordinary manner. I felt a tremendous force behind his gaze, as if by just one glance alone, he held the power to knock me right off my feet. After what had seemed to be a lifetime, he made a gesture with his finger. It seemed to stop the tides of time. I became immediately fearful for I saw he wore the ring of a magician. My mind told me I had made a fatal mistake. Maybe I had caused him grave offence? He was not a priest but a cobra. He was a panther, a panther that was making ready to pounce. He began to mutter strange words. I thought I saw the air itself ripple as he did so. My fear turned to terror. I knew he was pronouncing a curse against which I had no defence. I could only try and run away as fast as I could. Yes, Heshel, I was a quick runner then. Not like now. Even these old cedars could outrun this old man from the mountains."

He stood up and leaned upon his cane, tottering around as if on a boat in a storm. Heshel could not help but laugh at the sight of Azar, cursing the wind like a drunken man.

"Why do you laugh at an old man's afflictions and infirmities, you scoundrel? I would box your ears if I could just steady myself for a moment."

He waved his clenched fist at Heshel, before seating himself once more at the table.

"But there was also that in me which did not wish to run. Some hidden part betrayed me, an intuition that came from my hidden heart. I had the sudden conviction this man could help me, even though I had been warned to stay away from the lowly magician. For such a man could be deadly. Such a man could trap your soul inside a bottle forever. Yet my heart spoke otherwise. And I was consumed by the thirst of a lost man in the desert. In the desert, who cares about the hand in which the water is held? No. I would not run. I would stand my ground, even if it meant my death. I held his gaze and braced myself for the blow. But no blow came. Instead, he spoke to me. Everything in the market seemed to stop. Even the wind seemed to wait upon his word. His voice was not crude and harsh as I had expected, but gentle and understanding, solemn, delicate and noble. Each word he uttered slowly, kindly, and with great consideration.

"'Only a priest may know a priest. A priest such as me.'

"His words were magic, even though I could not grasp their meaning. He looked at the air above me, at something above my head, but I could not fathom what he was looking for. He closed his eyes. I felt their scrutiny as if he had entered inside me. I could not move. And when he finally opened his eyes again, they had become a deep, deep red, just like the red mountain of my dreams."

Azar stopped, letting Heshel feel the weight of the silence that had gathered all around them.

"The priest smiled and invited me to walk with him. I felt a great rush of joy for I knew him to be a messenger of the gods, come to help me find the holy red mountain. We walked away from the crowds until we came to the side of a river, where we stopped beneath the shade of a fig tree.

He turned to face me. He said he would help me as best he could, for the Guardians of the Gateway had whispered to him.

"'It is they who have surely blown our paths together this day. And now you stand before the gate of the Purple Queen. She who is the revealer.'

"As he spoke of her, I saw his body rippling as if gripped by an ecstasy.

"'But to hear her word, boy from the mountains, you must first cross this river, for the answer you seek awaits on the other side. I must warn you first, this is the river of no return. Should you cross over, the world you return to will never be the same as it was. This is the price you must pay for this crossing. This is the price you must pay for this knowledge. So make your choice, seeker of the red mountain. Shall you pay the ferryman?'

"The red mountain. Where else was there for me to go? I was already lost, so what matter if I never returned? Better to die seeking the red mountain than to live with no hope of ever finding it. I gave voice to my decision. The priest ushered me a few steps forward and bathed me in the cool and fresh river water. He poured some liquid on his palm and rubbed it between my eyes. I felt the potion burn my skin. He sang words in his own tongue. And, as he did so, his face seemed to change. He, was no longer he. No, before me, as clearly as I see your face, Heshel, I saw the face of an animal. The face of a jackal. A jackal that challenged me.

"'Why do you wish to see behind the purple veil of Isis? Why do you seek to possess the key to the mystery? Why do you wish to read the words written in fire upon the hidden pages? Tread carefully here, for no robber may live beyond the cloak of Isis, blessed be her name. No robber, no thief, no murderer, no bringer of harm, shall walk behind the veil of the sovereign mistress of magic and mystery. Be wary, for that purple light is a killer. Dare you walk before she who is to be feared more than death itself? She who bears the obsidian mirror?'

"The jackal growled. It bared its teeth, a thousand blades, dripping with blood and coated in a scum of human flesh. It snarled at me with a terrifying fury. I was sure it was making ready to rip me apart and tear the flesh from my bones. I knew without doubt the time of my judgement had come. It was my time to die. The jackal's eyes were now filled with a storm of purple light, so bright I felt it was ready to kill me. In those eyes, I saw my judge and accuser. I saw those eyes looking deeply into my mind and heart. I had no power to keep them out. I felt their scrutiny step across the soil of my soul. But those eyes, that were as fierce and ruthless as a hungry hawk, became suddenly filled with mercy. Mercy for me, this foolish, untutored boy. The face of the jackal disappeared. leaving only the face of the priest, who quietly bade me take his hand. He led me into the river which had now become a raging torrent. Yet, miracle of miracles, we walked across. Whether the waters ran shallow or we had walked upon the water, I did not know. All I knew was we had reached the other side.

"'Hear the words of the Priest of Isis, blessed be her name. He to whom the Guardian of the Gate has whispered. Listen carefully, even though you feel as if your heart is breaking. It is not yet your time. You must return home. You must cast away all thought of seeking for the place of your vision and give yourself fully over to the waiting. Go home, fire priest to be, and await her call. Wait for her to summon you, even should your flesh change to that of an old, old man. Gird your spirit with faith, for our Lady is ever true to her willing servant. Be strong and resolute and you shall find the red mountain, in whatever manner, fashion or form that she so wills it to be. I can say no more than this. But before we depart on our separate ways, and depart we must, I would have it that you take this as my gift. As my initiation.'

"He placed his hand upon my heart.

"'Never forget, young wily goat from the mountains, this is no lesser than the red mountain of your vision.'

"The priest looked upon the ring on his finger. He kissed it before removing it and placing it upon my own."

"'In the long, dark days of your waiting, may it serve as a light to illuminate your path. It has served me well, Azar, and it shall be a faithful servant to you.'

"In the blink of an eye he was gone, as if the river had swallowed him. Gone. Departed. Never to be seen again. At least, by me."

Azar now looked at this ring on his finger. Even now, the sight of it filled him with awe. This ring, crowned with a red ruby at its centre, set amidst a pair of bright, golden wings.

"Here on my finger, the ring has remained ever since that day."

"But master, I have looked at your hands almost every day, yet I have never once seen this ring upon your finger. How can this be?"

"Who can say for sure, Heshel? But this much I believe: that this ring you now see has something of the nature of the Priest of Isis. As was the nature of his substance, so too is the nature of this magic ring. I speak truly when I say this ring has revealed itself only to Zara and Rebekah. And now it has chosen to reveal itself to you. Is there no end to its mysteries?"

Azar looked at Heshel and turned to stoke the fire. He drew in from his pipe and once more filled the room with smoke.

"What is the secret of my craft? Why, there is nothing secret in my craft. There is nothing hidden. There is only that which is waiting to be seen."

The Quickening

The Mistress of the Flame returns in her flowery robe and soon shall come the night of the dance. See the poppy fields ablaze with red, a carpet upon which her feet shall tread. All is growing, all is gathering, the winter now past, the season of singing returned. The blood of the earth courses with hidden fire. Buds are opening, leaves are sprouting, hares are chasing, busy with their labour are the birds and bees. The wheel has turned, our children, and soon shall come the time for us to build our Sukkah, our shepherd's hut. Come, let us roam once more in the forest and fields. Let us build our house from leaves and branches, from mud and stones, from the sweat and toil of our prayerful hearts. And therein we shall house and give honour to the first lamb of spring, one drop of whose blood shall rain blessings on the seeds we shall sow. Come gather, our children, and may your young hearts be glad. For she comes. She comes. Just one kiss shall awaken her king from his slumber, shall kindle the sun into burgeoning heat and light. Yes, she comes, she whose touch awakens and stirs all into new life and being, whose breath gives rise to the quickening. Whose delicious dance and amorous glance shall set, once more, the world aflame. And we, like she, shall feast and dance and sing. All of this but a gift of the dance.

Rebekah sat upon a rock where two rivers meet, her feet dangling in its racing waters. It felt cool and refreshing, tempering the heat she felt coursing through her veins, the fire of the quickening burning inside her.

"Look," the elders would exclaim to behold their fast-transforming children. "Look, the fire of God has awoken in this one."

When Rebekah gazed at herself in the mirror these days, she saw an unfamiliar face looking back at her. Who was this person on the other side of the mirror? A young woman whose eyes were filled with longing and desires, with hopes and dreams and doubts and fears. A young woman who looked so different from all the others. Why could she not just look the same, for who would wish to escort this young woman to the dance? Who would wish to take the hand of this strange spider girl? Who could fall in love with this broken face? She did not know. All she knew was this desire inside her. Her sighs joined the wind as it sculpted water into rows of waves. So clearly could she see how the boys now looked at the girls and the girls at the boys. Furtive glances and flushing cheeks, laughs that were a little louder, hurts that cut a little deeper as sparks of molten light shot out from their eyes. Hard slaps and pushes, barely perceptible touches that tentatively lingered a little while longer. Awkward bodies straining to walk in prowess and grace. Fingers teasing and combing back hair, voices singing like the wind through the treetops, voices bellowing out loudly like rams and bulls. Yet beneath the agitated surface, Rebekah could see the undercurrents, the magnetic pull drawing this one and that one together. She saw it in the manner Jacob looked at Hannah. How she wished the 'he' she desired would so look at her. But he did not. He hardly seemed to notice her at all. She had once asked Ariadna to teach her how to form a web within which she might catch his attention. But the queen of the spiders had told her this was not the way to court love. How silly, she thought to herself, to be longing for him. He, who was over two years older than her. How much older than her, she knew to the exact day. And now, with the dance fast approaching, Rebekah had begun thinking she would have settled for anyone asking her to partner them to the dance, for her fear of humiliation was starting to take hold. With every new coupling, her dismay and desperation grew.

For a moment, she felt like throwing herself into the river and letting it carry her far away to who knew where. She splashed her feet around and kicked up the water. It felt comforting as it lapped upon her soles and between her toes. She felt some measure of solace in its sharp, fresh smell, here at one of her favourite places. She still felt a thrill to see the leaping salmon, the kestrels careering and swooping across this great divide.

"Two rivers meeting," she said out aloud. Two rivers meeting as two lives meet, the one running into the other and becoming as one. Just like Jacob and Hannah. Had it not been only yesterday her dearest friend had come racing to find her, to share with Rebekah her wonderful news, even before she had told her mother or sister? At first, Hannah's excitement had been so great she could hardly make her meaning intelligible. Rebekah had laughed to see her friend in such a state.

"Calm down," she had said. "I cannot understand a word you are saying."

Hannah grabbed both of Rebekah's hands and clasped them tightly as if she were an anchor. She panted rapidly, her eyes darting this way and that, her cheeks all flushed.

"What madness has made you its captive?" asked Rebekah, struggling to force the words out between her laughs. "Whatever it is, it has stolen your tongue. I can better understand the braying of a donkey. What has happened to you?"

"He has asked me to the dance. *He has asked me to the dance!*" Hannah shouted out loudly as if Rebekah had lost her hearing.

"*Who has asked you to the dance?*" shouted back Rebekah in kind.

For a moment, these two childhood friends just sat together, holding hands and gazing into each other's eyes. These two, fiercely loyal, the one to the other. Together, Rebekah and Hannah could and would take on the world. Together, these two would face insurmountable odds, would join together in battle, should anyone ever dare to cause the other harm or hurt. Sisters of spirit, if not in blood. No less alike than the closest twins. How many times had these two laughed and cried, the one with the other, each tear and smile weaving them ever closer together. Their love was a ladder by which they could storm the heavens. But now, holding hands, they both could feel it. Yes, they both could feel it, this touch of change upon their lives. A change to all this. This that had been their first true love.

"I'm sorry, Rebekah. But really, I just cannot believe it. Jacob has asked me to the dance."

Rebekah smiled at Hannah. But beneath her smile, she feared tarnishing this joyous moment with her underlying feelings. No, not for a lack of heartfelt joy for her friend. She did feel joy, for this heart only desired happiness for her Hannah. She only wished the very best for her. And handsome and well-skilled was Jacob. A prize desired by many of the girls. Yet in this joy, Rebekah could also feel the sharpest sorrow, a cold, steel lance piercing the core of her heart. She did not want to, but she could not help it. And so too did Hannah. She too feared causing hurt to her precious friend, this one she would not cause pain to for all the world. But had they not always known this moment would come? Rebekah looked at Hannah. Beautiful Hannah, so strong and smart and daring. With Hannah by her side, the daughter of Ariadna felt vibrant and brave. This Hannah, who saw beauty in Rebekah where the others could not. To Hannah, she was not the girl who was blind in one eye, but instead, a girl who was beautiful and funny. Who was wise and whole. And only with Rebekah did Hannah have no caution in what she said, for their friendship was not bound by any such fears. No secrets nor pretence could divide these two. But change was a river, a river whose course neither could halt nor change, whose flow might come to sweep away such a love. What would remain, they wondered, should this love come to be shared? Would its light start to fade or even be completely extinguished? Neither knew. As Hannah looked at Rebekah, she had never seen her looking more vulnerable and fragile, not even when she had lain injured in her bed. She softly squeezed the weaver's hands, looking pensively at her friend's long and delicate fingers.

"Do not worry, Rebekah. We shall go together to the dance. All together, me and Jacob, and you with the object of your desire. You will see. It shall be a wonderful night."

Rebekah wanted to believe her. She wanted to believe her with all her heart. But now, alone by the river, Rebekah's thoughts were otherwise.

Maybe I am ugly? Maybe they do not ask me to the dance because of my appearance?

As for 'the object of her desire', she knew for sure he would never ask her. Why would he? Heshel was now a man. But she was just a silly girl. Just a silly girl with a broken face. Yet how handsome was Heshel, the son of the fisherman and the healer. So much older than the others he seemed to be. Older and wiser. As aloof and wondrous as the peaks of the mountain. His walk spoke of strength and confidence. She looked admiringly from afar at his tallest of bodies, his broadest of shoulders, his large, roughened hands she knew to be devoted to his craft. How she longed to feel those hands upon her. Sometimes, when she crept up as near to him as his shadow, she could smell the fresh smell of cedar upon his garments, would notice the sawdust upon the soles of his shoes. She saw his dark eyes, filled with an intention and focus quite unlike any of his peers. Rebekah saw something of the wolf in him. She saw in his eyes, a spirit that was wild and roving, was fierce and free. Tall and upright as an elm was Heshel, his face intense and resolute, framed with a full beard that marked his newly come manhood.

How many nights had Rebekah danced alone in her room. She only had to close her eyes, and like curtains parting, the scene would unfold. A full moon kissed the treetops. The air was filled with the scent of cypress trees and orange groves, echoing with the chuntering sound of frogs calling to each other amidst the misty marshes, all beneath a symphony of stars. She could feel her body held firmly in those arms. She could feel their strength, the texture of muscles beneath cloth, his hands upon the nape of her back, his fingers waltzing up and down her spine. Firm and tender, she felt so safe within his arms, as if nothing in the world could harm her now. Wrapped gracefully around her slender, lithe body, she would dance and sway with Heshel, panting with the thrill of it all.

"Rebekah, supper is ready," called out Deborah.

How fragile the magic of this inner seeing. A hummingbird darting between the worlds. Rebekah sighed as the vision faded.

"How foolish I am to imagine such a thing. A foolish girl, besotted with this man who sees only his wood. A man who just wishes to spend his days with Azar learning his craft, who has no thoughts of love. And even if he did, his fancy would be captured by girls who are beautiful and graceful. My dreams only torture me, for is it not cruel to long for something that I can never have? If only the tree had pierced both my eyes so I had never seen Heshel."

Where Three Ways Meet

To be with her. To be with her, to stand in her presence, to bathe in her glory, to be restored by her beauty and reborn in her light. A year and a day had now almost passed, and soon it would be the time for Heshel to return to where three ways meet. He trembled to think of hearing her voice once more, her voice that was a thousand voices. Of seeing her smile, a thousand smiles. Tomorrow, tomorrow, upon morning's first light, to traverse the fields to where the Lady of the Forest would be waiting. The moment now come for his pledge to be honoured, come now the hour for Heshel to fulfil his task. A task he could not, would not, dare not fail. But with each passing day, he had found himself becoming ever more anxious. He tossed and turned in his bed at night, his faith in himself leaking away. Leaking as if there were a hole in his heart. He felt plagued by doubt. He doubted his readiness. He doubted his worthiness. He judged himself to be lacking in knowledge. He had made insufficient progress upon the magical path. He did not know the spells, the prayers, the incantations. And now Heshel knew he had run out of time. If only he could have asked his master for help in this matter, he might then have found some help and perhaps even some solace. But he knew he could not for he was sworn to silence.

"How is it that the hopes of such a beautiful spirit have come to rest upon one such as me? What a cruel twist of fate. Who am I to set her free? Who am I to set anyone free? I, who am myself, a prisoner of doubt. I, who harbour within me, every weakness, every vice, every manner of sin. I, who see only my own failure, reflected every day in my father's eyes."

"What is troubling you, Heshel? You look tired and seem distracted. Why such a heavy heart?"

"I am not sleeping well, master."

"Hmmmmm… I see," said Azar, stroking his beard. "Perhaps you are working too hard? Well, that part, at least, I can rectify. Today we shall take rest from our labours and celebrate."

"Celebrate? But what marks the occasion?"

"Has it escaped your notice we are approaching the first anniversary of the day I first made your acquaintance? Of you becoming my apprentice?"

"It had not escaped my notice."

"I am glad to hear it. And I must tell you, Heshel, I am a most fortunate master. No master could have found a more able and willing apprentice. You have been a most diligent student. You have helped me in building my home. You have blessed me with your good company. Do not worry, I shall not labour the point. I know compliments do not rest easily upon you. But today, I wish to gift you something."

"A gift? For me?"

"Why, of course for you." Azar went to a chest and brought out a box, measuring in length from elbow to fingertip. He handed it to Heshel. "I hope it pleases you."

He carefully opened it. As he did so, a light shot out from the box as if a spirit had been released. Light reflected upon metal, the blade of an exquisite axe. And, nestling at its side, a chisel, every bit its equal.

"Are they not a little like us?"

Heshel could not help but smile.

"They are magnificent."

"Please, test their weight and measure. See if their handles rest soundly in your hand."

Heshel held them. He touched them in the fashion he had been taught. He felt their form and imbibed their spirit. He studied the engravings etched into their handles. Symbols and letters, a language he did not yet understand.

"So, how do they feel?"

"Perfect."

"Only perfect? Oh dear, I was hoping for so much more. Please forgive me, my student, for I have failed in my task. Ah, it is good to see you smile, my friend. May these two be faithful servants in the pursuit of your craft. May they serve to bring to fulfilment, whatever task you might ask of them."

That night Heshel slept peacefully, his tools close by his side. And before even the first fleck of morning light had peeped above the mountain, he was up and ready to set off for the forest. The village was quiet, not even one light flickering through even one window. So early the hour, even the farmer and the rabbi were still sound asleep. All was suffused with a melancholic greyness, murky, chill and damp with drizzle, the sort of chill that could seep, gnaw and claw beneath one's skin and into one's bones. Heshel could barely delineate the cedars through the dankness and gloom, the creeping mists and pockets of dense fog. All looked so much darker than he had expected. He had made no provision for such a half-light. He regretted having brought no torch to light his way. But now he had no choice other than to enter this dimness. This lack of light.

"I have come, Lady of the Forest," he tentatively announced. "I have returned, just as I promised. Please, call to me, that I may find my way to you."

Nothing but silence.

"Here I am. Please help me and guide my way."

No word. No sound. So he listened and he listened and listened some more. But still, no reply. He pressed on deeper into the forest, towards the corridor of cypresses by the way he remembered, whilst the mist gradually turned into impenetrable fog. The many familiar landmarks became only a few, until few became none. Heshel tried to reassure himself. It would not be the first time he had found himself lost in the forest. He would retrace his steps as he had often done before, tracking his boot marks on the mud and grass. But when he looked down, he saw there were none. How could this possibly be? And still, relentlessly, the fog grew thicker.

"What brings you here, young man?"

A voice, raspy and raven-like, cutting through the eerie silence. An old woman peered at him fiercely, her face veiled in a hood that seemed to be made from the mist. Her skin was as knotted and gnarled as the bough of an olive. She had a sack upon her back from which some twigs popped out. Though startled, Heshel felt relief to see her, for time was marching on. This woman was surely familiar with these parts. She would be able to guide him on his way.

"Good day to you. My name is Heshel. I am so glad to find you. I am lost and am looking for a very special willow tree."

"Willow tree. What willow tree?" she snapped at him.

"The old willow tree that stands alone at the end of the corridor of cypresses."

"Oh," exclaimed the old woman. "That willow tree. Yes, I know it well. You are not far from it at all. I will show you the way. But first, you must appease my curiosity. Why is a young man such as you searching for a silly old willow tree in this forest? Surely you have better things to do with your day? I see your clothes, your finely fashioned branch, your blade glistening in your pocket and know you to be a carpenter. Surely you have pressing work to complete? I see your fine and ruddy countenance and know the girls of your village must blush to behold you. Say it is not so. Surely your time could be happier spent in their admiring presence and not spent seeking in these woods for a tree that could furnish you with but little wood for your craft, or little shelter for spending time with the girl of your choosing?"

"I am looking for the willow tree because it was a thing of great beauty to me. And, as I am a carpenter seeking inspiration, I thought I would spend the day musing in her presence."

"Oh, is that all. Well, I think I know the tree you mean. Yes, maybe I will show you the way. But first, you must do something for me. A favour for a favour. You say you are a carpenter. Fashion me a walking stick to make the passage of this old woman through these woods a little easier. I have never come upon a carpenter in these forests, let alone such a handsome one. If your craft pleases me, I will show you the way to that which you seek."

How strange she had never encountered a carpenter before. Still, he would do as the old woman asked. She seemed well pleased and laughed out loudly. He looked around to find fitting wood. When he was satisfied, he began fashioning the stick as the woman watched from the shadows. To make a worthy utensil would take some time, and he had already lost a good portion of the day. But he sensed the woman would not be satisfied with anything other than his very best work, so he laboured hard to make her the finest of canes. All the while she peered at him. As she did so, she took out a dead rabbit from a second small sack, then plucked out its fur, little by little, tuft by tuft. From time to time, the carpenter nervously glanced over towards her. He felt as if she were skinning him alive.

"I do hope I am not distracting you from your labour," she cackled, staring intently at him all the while.

He worked on until the cane was completed, then offered it to her in the hope she would accept it. She studied it closely. She carefully felt its textures. She felt it in her arms and tested it with her weight. She said nothing, but instead, silently nodded her approval.

"Go down this middle path," she said, pointing a spindly finger before her. "Walk straight and true, and you shall find the tree you seek. But before you go, lest you offend me, please eat one of my apples. I see you have been lost a while and must surely be hungry."

She delved deep into her sack and pulled out a choice, red apple. Heshel was mindful not to offend this stranger in an unknown part of the forest. He knew friendly forces could quickly turn against him. So he took her offered apple, bit into it, chewed and swallowed it and politely thanked her. She smiled at him. But her eyes were not smiling, for he glimpsed them as she departed, unexpectedly swiftly for her age. It was a look that was chilling.

The ways of people are many and varied, thought Heshel. *As many and varied as the trees of the forest. I am fortunate to have met this old woman who knows these parts. Now I shall surely find my way to the Lady of the Forest.* But, in truth, he was not so certain.

He walked and walked. But as he walked, the fog became so dense even the sight of his own limbs began to fade. As if he were transforming into a ghost. Surely he had been deceived by the old woman? She was not an old woman at all, but rather a demon in disguise. A demon that had led him deeper into the forest to leave him lost. How had he been so blind? "Forgive me, Lady of the Forest," he cried out. "Forgive me, for I have failed in my undertaking and now shall never find you. I am lost. All hope is gone."

Yet though lost, Heshel knew he would not die in the forest. He knew the fog would lift in time. He knew too he would neither starve or thirst, for he knew the ways of the forest and that it would feed him. But he also knew he would not find his way to the whispering willow in time. The day was fast fading. It was his fault, and his fault only, as he had not been properly prepared. He had entered the realm of the spirits where all is different. He had been impetuous. He should have walked with care. He should have walked like Theseus as he weaved his way to the heart of the labyrinth. His father was right about him. He was right to be disappointed. Every such thought was a sword piercing his heart. Life was cruel and had shown its true face in the old woman. He felt tears in his eyes as he sat himself down, knowing he had no other choice than to wait for the fog to depart. And when he had found his way home, he would have to somehow live with his sorrow and failure.

A sound. A barely audible rustling. Heshel lifted his head and peered into the all-pervasive gloom.

"She is back. She has come to see if I am dead from her poison apple. Perhaps she has come to feast upon my flesh and bones and gloat upon my misfortune."

But it was not her. An auburn hare emerged into view. It nuzzled amongst the leaves and hopped briskly about.

Suddenly it became aware of another presence and froze. Its long ears pricked up and listened. Heshel could see the whites of its eyes. He felt love for this small creature, trembling before him.

"Hello, hare. I am so happy to see you. Please do not be frightened. I will not harm you."

The hare seemed to listen. It looked at Heshel with a puzzled expression, before the tension melted away in its small, robust body. Movement returned to its limbs. And it then did something that brought utter bemusement to Heshel. Slowly, very slowly, it began to walk backwards. Step by step, gazing intently at Heshel all the while. And in the eyes of the hare, Heshel no longer discerned fear but something other. Heshel had watched hares before but had never seen one act in such a manner. Step by step, it retraced its steps until it was once more swallowed up by the fog. Though now departed, the look in its eyes remained with Heshel. How different it had been from the callous look in the old woman's eyes. As mysteriously as the hare had appeared, the look in its eyes now somehow transformed into words.

To break the spell of this magic mirror,
break and crack, break and crack.
To awaken from the dreaming death,
walk my way in perfect trust.
Walk in my skin, backwards to go forwards,
and forwards to go back.

The fog lifted, if only just a little. What could these words mean, he wondered? Were they just the ravings of a broken man or something more? Whatever they were, they were all he had. He gave himself over to the spirit of reflection. Deeper and deeper within himself he went, until just as the hare had emerged from the gloom, an idea revealed itself from somewhere amidst his mind's dense confusion. Maybe it was madness, but he would walk like the hare. He would walk backwards into the fog. And if he should fall into some unseen peril that lurked therein, then that was how it must be. Perhaps one day, his body might be found. Or maybe it would just dissolve, becoming at one with the forest. But he would die looking for this lady. He would die in good faith and not in the vice of despair.

He shut his eyes and backwards, backwards he walked, envisioning the Lady of the Forest as he did so. He pictured her face in the darkness and saw her clearly. Backwards, backwards, eyes held closed. Backwards, backwards, despair shedding like clumps of snakeskin. He felt himself changing, shifting shape and form. His body become smaller, ears sprouting tall and upright upon his head, perceiving minutiae of details beyond anything seen before. He fell on all fours, his skin lined in felt. Intoxicating fragrance of leaves, nuts and grasses, his fine whiskers shivering as he darted around. For how long Heshel roamed in this manner, he did not know. But when he opened his eyes, wherever he was, whatever he was, he was still alive. He had not fallen into an abyss of nothingness. And though the fog was still dense, he saw a flickering. Whether or not Heshel was hare or man, he could see a tiny light veiled within the fog.

It must be a firefly, he thought. *My heart rejoices to see you, firefly. And if you may, please take me to the whispering willow. To the Lady of the Forest, for you I will follow.*

The firefly beckoned him with a brighter flicker, and Heshel followed this trail of light.

"Come with me. Come with me," sang the firefly, darting upwards and downwards. And Heshel followed the path illuminated before him.

"Run with me. Run with me," sang the firefly as it flew ever faster, an arrowhead dipped in flame, flying straight, steady and true, towards the good archer's perceived aim. And Heshel ran like a stallion upon the endless and infinite open plains.

"Fly with me. Fly with me," sang this firefly, a phoenix flying high above the seven worlds. And Heshel flew deep into the unseen and invisible realms upon wings of crimson flame.

As he followed the light of the firefly, he felt himself walking down a corridor where all around were lighted candles, held up high. Whether in the hands of priests or trees, he did not know. But a holy presence emanated therein. And with these lights, the fog burnt away, the forest returning to sight and resounding with song. Round every corner, Heshel saw mysteries he had never had eyes to apprehend before. Every tree and flower, each small creature that darted between the shady bowers, the whispering leaves gliding over the grasses, all spoke to Heshel of the way back to the willow. Soon he was back where he had met the spirit of the tree. Yet it was not how he had remembered it at all. He had not seen the arched bridge from this side to that, disappearing into a mist of green. And in that mist, a waiting form. Had she been standing there all the time, watching and waiting? She, who was just the same as he remembered, yet also somehow changed. The forest echoed with her majesty. Her face was etched with solemnity and strength. Her face was grace chiselled into a mountainside. Sounds of laughter in the breeze. The intoxicating melody of birdsong. Her hair was a flaming hearth fire warming Heshel's heart. The smell of her. The smell of her.

"Most merry meet, mortal one."

The sound of her voice. His heart did inwardly kneel. And inwardly, a dam was rent asunder, from which burst forth a thousand tears. He sobbed, filled with a grief such as he had never known before. The memory of her. How had he lived or breathed without the sight of her? Kindly, melodiously, she spoke once more to him.

"You have returned to me and glad I am. Yes, glad I am."

Heshel was silent. His body sensed that no human voice should intrude upon the holiness of this place. She read the whispers of his mind.

"No stray foot may enter upon this path, for only the true heart may bear the rapture of the Fair Kind. And by only such a heart may this place be found. There is no other way. Here, where three ways meet. And where three ways meet, I have waited for the one, who one day, would come. So, merry meet once more, mortal one. Merry meet, old friend, both lost and found. Merry meet, my long-departed love. How I have longed to hear your voice once more. Please, speak to me, mortal one. I have missed hearing your thoughts, hearing of your journeys in the other world. To my kind, to hear the stories of your world are a thing of wonder. We, who do not wear the robes of transience."

"Thank you. Thank you for opening my eyes once more to your presence. It has been so long. I have sometimes feared it had only ever been a wondrous dream or a passing enchantment."

Heshel glanced at her eyes. They were green fire, a-dancing, a-dancing. They were eyes of enchantment, a-weaving, a-weaving. Beautiful beyond compare. Lustrous and kind, searching into his all.

"If this has only the substance of a dream, Heshel, then let it be a dream shared by only we two. And know this too, our good carpenter, that a year and a day for you is but a fleeting moment for our kind. Yet even since that moment

I beheld you beneath the whispering willow, I have missed you more than you may ever know."

Every word from her lips caused his blood to race. His heart to dance.

"Please tell me, Lady of the Forest, most glorious apparition, by what name may I address you? But only if it may please you, for one such as me to know."

"I would gladly hear my name spoken from your lips. From your tongue that is true. I have many names, Heshel. Many names in many lands. In many worlds and in many times. Yet all my names are but one. And this one name can never be spoken by a mortal one, for the mortal tongue is not so fashioned. But for you, I shall wear a new name. A name that shall be for you and you only, from this moment forth. You shall know me as Glorianna. Glorianna, The Three-faced One."

"Glorianna. Glorianna," sang Heshel. "Even your name is wine upon my lips. You who are hope and salvation to this lost and lonely pilgrim. Yet I do not comprehend how it is that despite all my time in the forest, I have been blind to the sight of this blessed bridge? Maybe my heart is not true but blind? How else is it that I had never seen your glory, great queen of the forest?"

"Well, Heshel, if it is as you say and your heart is not true, then there is only one other way you have come to find me. It can only be that a true heart has fallen in love with you. A rare and seeing heart that has vouched for you."

"I do not know of any such heart that so loves me. But if you say it is so, Glorianna, then so it must be."

"You have spoken well, Heshel. So know this too. You stand where three paths converge and time stands still. And you must now choose which of three paths you shall take. But you must first know there is but one path by which you may set me free."

"Please speak to me of these paths, Glorianna."

"One is the path back from whence you came, back to the life you have always known. And, as every choice has its price, if you must so return, then all this shall be as a fading dream. A dream whose life is but a butterfly day, evaporating like mist into the slumbers of forgetfulness. If you so choose, I can say only this: your life will be a good life. A life thrice blessed."

Heshel looked upon Glorianna and knew this path was not for him.

"Please, speak to me of the other paths."

"The path across the bridge is the path into my world. Few come this way, but of those few many cross over. Mysterious and magical and beautiful beyond the imaginings of the mortal world is this garden. And of those many that cross over this bridge of stone, only few return."

Heshel desired to journey into Glorianna's realm with a passion he had never felt before. Yet he knew too he must return to fulfil his pledge.

"This path appears wondrous yet not for me. Please speak to me of the final path."

"This third path is the hidden path. The secret doorway. The path of the return. There is only one way to discern this passage, but of this way, I am forbidden to speak. Only the seeing heart may come upon it. This path leads also into my world. Few have come this way and fewer still have found the key. For ever as such is the nature of things."

Heshel felt a sudden panic. There was just one path he could travel and he did not know how to find it. He was truly lost and had never felt more alone. But as he looked up at Glorianna and gazed into her eyes, he suddenly perceived a door. His heart soared like a lapwing and flew towards it. He flew and fell. He fell and flew. All this Glorianna saw.

She saw him consumed by the fires of the living death. And as he fell into the endless abyss between the here and there, she unfurled her wings and flew to him. Three tears of joy rolled down her cheeks only to be caught in a goblet, clasped in the beak of an accompanying sparrow hawk. Glorianna laid down his all but motionless body and held his head in her lap, pouring droplets of elixir upon Heshel's tongue.

"Awaken my love and see the world anew. Walk for a while amongst the Fair Kind."

And Heshel did awaken. And of his walks amongst the Fair Kind, we shall speak, perhaps, another day.

When Beauty Smiles

"Only fragments will you remember of your walk in our realm."

"Please, my Lady, do not let me fall into forgetfulness. I could not bear to forget even the smallest of details. What use will this mind be if it cannot remember? What use these eyes, bereft of such beauty? What use these ears if they can no longer hear your voice? How shall this heart find the will to beat should it forget what it is to walk with the Fair Kind? And what of my spirit? What light shall still burn should this spirit hold no remembrance of you? Oh please, my Lady, my queen, my friend, I beg you, do not let me fall into slumber again. Do not let me walk lost and alone in the darkness of my inner blindness."

"Has it come to this, our Heshel, that we should be as beggars? Does not our love share everything gladly? No, grieve not, our love, our mortal king. Harbour no such fears, for we shall always be with you. Always and forever. You, who have drunk from our cup of wonder. You, who shall see the world as if through our eyes. Heshel, who shall peep like a raven through the cracks between the worlds. So be you strong, true and steadfast. Be you a chalice of hope and kindness and return to the world of the mortal ones to fulfil your task. There, where awaits you the greatest of wonders. There, where you must find the whole of your heart. Go now, our carpenter, and leave this place in a spirit of peace and gladness. Follow the flight of the sparrow hawk, the trail of the flickering fireflies, the path of the hare and the bright light of the woodlouse, through the veil of green mist and across the bridge, and do not stop to pause nor turn to look behind. And when shall come the time of your return, you shall remain here forever, if you should still so will it to be."

And then she smiled, before placing a kiss upon each of his eyes.

"There, our Heshel. Our love and our pledge are forever sealed with these kisses."

And then it was over. And then it began. Somehow, he came to find himself walking towards the edge of the forest, the fog now lifted, the day now bright. He could not recall how he had come to be there. He only knew what had felt to be many years, had only been moments. Yet in those few moments, he had come to see the whole world anew.

In such a spirit, the very next evening, whilst sat at Azar's table sipping his tea, Heshel's gaze fell upon a tapestry he had never noticed before. It hung enticingly by the fireplace, a tapestry that was a window into a familiar world. He moved closer, called by the magnetic spell of its beauty and craft.

"It is remarkable, is it not?"

"Hello, Azar. I did not see you there. Yes, it is wonderful."

"Indeed. In truth, I have been a little perplexed as to why you have not commented on it earlier."

"Earlier? What do you mean? You can only have put it there this morning?

"Why, Heshel, it has been there for over a week."

"Over a week? How can that possibly be? What magic is this? Are you just pretending?"

"I am guilty of no such heinous crime. Well, not this time."

"Have I been so distracted? Yes, it could be this. Unless this tapestry was made by the Purple Priest. Is it so? Does it hold the same power as the magician's ring?"

"Well, it does indeed hold magic. But it was not made by the hand of the Purple Priest."

"Then who?"

"Can you not guess?"

"Did a trader pass through the village?"

"No, Heshel. Think of someone much closer to home."

"Please tell me, Azar, for I would dearly like to speak to them."

Yet even whilst speaking, realisation dawned upon Heshel.

"Rebekah?" he said, with astonishment written all over his face.

"You are quite correct. It was indeed fashioned by Rebekah."

"Rebekah? Why, I knew she liked to weave, but it never crossed my mind her craft could be as high as this."

"Beware presumption, Heshel, for it is a treacherous guide. As for Rebekah, what can I say? My dear friend's daughter has a secret passion of which she has become the master. I tell you truly, this girl has a knack of surprising me as no-one else can. Watch out for Rebekah. She wears a cloak of invisibility. She is a creature of the forest who leaves no tracks. She made me this gift in celebration of my coming to Elnazar. Even Deborah did not know her daughter had been labouring long through the night."

But this was not the whole of the story. Deborah had told him with tears in her eyes, that her daughter had come to regard Azar as her second father. That this tapestry was the only means by which Rebekah could show him the measure of her love.

"How shall I speak of my spirit daughter? There are no words, Heshel. No words. A moment... please."

He reached for his pipe and lit it, drawing in slowly.

"Go to her, Heshel. Do not let shyness bar your path. Go to her now and ask her to speak of her craft. Tell her I sent you. She will understand. Now please, my friend, I would welcome some time alone with my thoughts."

"Very well, master. I shall do as you instruct."

His mind ablaze with thoughts of the tapestry, Heshel went to the house of Deborah.

"Heshel. How good to see you. Tell me, how fares my dear friend? Is he well?"

"Indeed he is, Mother Deborah. He is well and robust and, as ever, lost in his craft."

"Is he a good and kind master to you, Heshel, the apprentice?"

"I am blessed to have Azar as my teacher and guide."

"I am glad to hear it. So, has that old rascal sent you on his errands? Have you come to collect the sweetbreads that he so longs to devour? Is this what has brought you to our home this day?"

"No, mother Deborah. This is not what has brought me to your door. May I speak with Rebekah?"

"Rebekah? I am afraid Rebekah is away in the forest just now."

"Tell me where she might be. I will go and find her."

"I think it best if you wait for her here. Is that agreeable to you? We can share some bread and wine before she returns and perhaps share some stories of our dear and mutual friend. I would like that. And when Rebekah comes home, I am sure she would be delighted to speak with you."

"Thank you, mother Deborah. I would love to accept your gracious offer."

But before they could do any of these things, they heard the door burst open.

"*Mother*," Rebekah bellowed, before suddenly catching sight of Heshel. Deborah saw the astonishment in her daughter's eyes, her mouth hanging wide open, her fingers grabbing for the door knob as if to stop herself from falling.

"I have some errands to do," said Deborah. "I shall leave you two alone to talk."

As her mother left the room, Rebekah felt the blood rush to her face. Why was her body betraying her? She did not want him to see her blush. An awkward silence filled the room. Heshel could not help himself from just gazing at Rebekah. He looked at her long, dark, mahogany hair. He had only seen her before with it tied back in a bun, knotted and weaved like Deborah's bread. It cascaded around her face loosely and even wildly, framing it so she appeared like a young lioness. He saw her eyes, one peering intently at him, flushed with the innocent and proud, fragile earnestness of youth. The other, blazing as if illuminated from within. An eye as ancient and still as his beloved cedars. He gazed upon her hands, nervously clasped together. Her fingers were long and slender and filled with grace. They were beautiful. The hands of an artisan. Her neck was long, as beautiful as a swan. How strange he had been so blind for all this time. As once he had been blind to the Lady of the Forest.

"Good day, Rebekah. Are you well?"

"Yes," she answered, a little too politely.

Heshel felt clumsy. He was unsure if she had finished her sentence or was about to say more.

"Your mother certainly bakes delicious bread," he said with all the composure of a drowning man. Why had he said such a ridiculous thing? All this took Rebekah by surprise. She had never seen Heshel flustered in this manner before.

"I would like to speak with you about your tapestry if you will permit me? I have never seen such a work before. It… it speaks to me in a familiar tongue."

Rebekah still could not believe what was happening. She reasoned that she must have fallen asleep upon her bed, ascending, descending to the best of dreams.

"Thank you, Heshel. I would like that."

Her words crept out quietly from her mouth, so distorted by nervousness she barely recognised her own voice. She did not want to answer him with foolish words. She did not want him to take her for just a prattling young girl. She looked into his eyes. Eyes like a wolf. Eyes like a wind. Earnest and kind and true. What beautiful eyes this carpenter had. A deep, deep chestnut brown that danced with flecks of amber and molten flame. And now those eyes were fixed upon her, just as she had long dreamt they would. She liked the way it felt, to bathe in the scrutiny of Azar's apprentice as he stood listening in front of her, hanging upon her every word. Nervousness soon changed into courage, then courage to ease. Into the belly of ease she glided. And when she next spoke, no longer spoke a nervous girl but instead, a composed young woman. A young woman overflowing with a radiant grace.

"Azar calls it the star language. Has Azar discussed this topic with you? No? Well, our master tells me that when I weave, I weave in the star language. In truth, I am not sure I do. I only know I love to weave. And sometimes, I am unsure if it is me that is weaving the tapestries, or if it is the tapestries weaving me? Does this sound strange to you, Heshel, apprentice of the Baal-Azar?"

But it did not sound strange at all. He knew exactly what she meant. He felt joy to hear her giving voice to such thoughts. He watched her mouth giving shape to her words, a mouth as full and ripe as a pomegranate. What beautiful shapes her mouth formed, blushing like ripened tomatoes upon the vine. As soft as a pillow filled with gorse. Gentle curves beside the corner of her lips, together forming the sweetest of smiles, her eyes overflowing with intensity and knowing. Oh, those eyes of Rebekah. How had he never seen this beauty before? He had so many questions, yet now, right now, he only wanted to hear the sound of her speaking. Her voice, deep and melodious, flowing like water from the fountains of paradise. The smell of the forest upon her hair. And it was no young girl who stood before him, but rather, a gracious woman.

"I sometimes feel as such when I am lost in my craft. But please, speak to me of the tapestry you have gifted to Azar. Speak to me of its conception for I have never beheld such beauty and artfulness. It deeply affects me in a way I do not understand. It gives rise to a fever in my blood."

Rebekah could not help but giggle.

"Just listen to me. I am talking foolishly. I should go."

"Oh, please do not. I love to hear your words."

"Really?"

"Yes, really."

"Azar says your tapestry has awoken the poet in me. If he is correct, then believe me when I say your tapestry must hold a powerful magic to have done such a thing."

She wanted to tell him everything. Every small part. Every tiniest of details she wished to lay bare to him. To speak of Ariadna. To speak of her mother with a million eyes. Yet well she knew she must hold her silence. As for Heshel, even as he asked Rebekah about the tapestry, he felt the earth beneath his feet start to melt away. For now, he knew his only remaining desire was to look at her. Spellbound was Heshel. All thoughts of the tapestry now left far behind, his heart dancing and swaying to the rhythm of her word. Swept away by the strangest, most wonderful feeling. So speak true to her now, apprentice to the magi. Be true to your self, or be nothing at all.

"Rebekah, would you do me the honour of being my partner for the dance?"

All went still. All went silent. Had he been too forward, too reckless? Had he given offence? Would his unplanned words scare the weaver away? Rebekah stood frozen, shocked by the unexpectedness of Heshel's request. She must be dreaming. She just had to be. There was no other explanation. This could not be happening. But if she were dreaming, then she wished never to wake.

"Gladly," she replied.

The Spiral Staircase

So brightly shine the stars this night. So close, so many, they seem to be. These shimmering lights of his ancestors' campfires, turning on the axis like spokes on a wheel. A million and more gateways to a supernal shining. A million pinpricks through the veil, and he, the threaded, woven weft. As Azar looked high to the vaults of the heavens, he felt joy to see the star people, this caravan of nomads, traversing the sands of the endless dark desert. He became as one with all of the stargazers, present, past and future, sentient of the echoes of their still-living knowledge, stored in the very molecules of his blood. There, the familiar sight of the milky road and the little cloud. The falling eagle and the neck of the snake, the lion and the tortoise, the goat and the horse. He saw the wolf, the hyena, the hare and the hen. The string of pearls and the curve of the river. He saw Meissa, the shining one, and Errai, the shepherd. Yet tonight, in the direction of the archer's bow, he noticed an unfamiliar form. A bright blue star, easing its way through the throng of star people. It shone with a vibrant, pulsating, lapis lazuli light, a fragment of summer sky in the depth of night. But only the eye of the seasoned observer would have been able to detect it, as if it were loath to call attention to its own incandescent beauty. Dancing like one of the blue-skinned deities painted on the walls of the palace. Dancing like Krishna. Dancing like Kali.

"Master? Is that you?"

A tentative voice breaking the silence.

"Heshel?"

"I am sorry if I startled you."

"No more so than the owls and the wolves. Come closer. I can barely see you. That's it, come closer to me, my young, prowling wolf. Come and sit by my side."

"Have I broken your meditations?"

"No more so than the crickets. But I was neither praying nor given to contemplation. I am stargazing. Would you care to join me?"

"Yes, master."

"Then this is most opportune, for tonight the star people reveal themselves uncommonly clearly. But before you do so, go and find yourself a blanket, as the night is cold."

Having found himself a thick hide of bearskin, Heshel huddled down beside the magi.

"So, Heshel, what has brought you out here at such a late hour? Did your talk with Rebekah go well?"

"It did. She is… she is… remarkable."

"She most certainly is."

"How could I have been blind to her beauty for so long? I have never heard a girl speak as she does."

"She speaks with a wisdom beyond her years."

"How is this so?"

"Only Rebekah knows the source of her knowledge. Who knows, perhaps one day she shall speak to you of such things?"

"I hope so. Her words are filled with such grace and knowing. And her eyes, why, they shine like the moon and sun."

"I understand, my brother. Yet I find myself unaccustomed to my apprentice waxing so lyrically. Only in your craft have I seen you express such poetry. What manner of magic has Rebekah spun upon you? You cannot accuse me of not giving you fair warning."

"I do not know, my teacher. And, in truth, little more do I care. I only know I have asked Rebekah to partner me to the dance. I could not help it. I had no plan to. The words just seemed to flow from my mouth of their own volition."

"Rebekah does have a way of unloosening one's tongue."

"She does. She does."

"And how did she answer? Is she willing to partner you?"

"She is. She will."

"Then I am gladder than words can say."

"Thank you, Azar. Please forgive me for my lack of forbearance. I just had to tell you. I will go now and interrupt you no further."

"Please, do not go just yet, Heshel. Stay a while longer. I would like your company. You never know, it just might be that Rebekah's magic has also caught me in its web. Perhaps you should seize this opportunity and ask what you will of this poor, unguarded magi. Or, as Rebekah might put it, this sleepy, grizzly bear."

"If I stay as you request, will you speak to me of the star language?"

"Oh, so you wish to broker a deal? You wish to haggle in the market place? Be careful, young barterer, that I do not pick your pockets."

He draped his arm affectionately upon Heshel's shoulder.

"The star language, you say. You wish me to speak of the language of our heavenly family. But are the star people not already assembled and ready to speak for themselves? Would it therefore not be more fitting for us to sit in silence, to listen out for their word without need of mediation?"

"But you have not yet taught me how to hear them, master."

"Have I failed you in this, my most able student? No, I think you hear them well enough. Yet it seems you do not recognise that you do so. No matter. Time will surely remedy this. And as for this night, if the star people so wish it, then I shall speak as their proxy. But I would ask that they first please bless us with a sign."

A shooting star sped suddenly across the sky, illuminating the tips of the trees and the mountain crest.

"By the beard of Hatshepsut, what a prodigious omen. The star people must consider my wits to be dulled this night, that they should require me to behold such an unambiguous portent. Very well then, Heshel. Your wish shall be my command. Let us begin. Raise your gaze to the heavens and tell me what you see."

"I see a sky full of stars."

"Anything else?"

"I see infinite space."

"Anything else?"

"A great ocean of blackness with a hint of purple."

"Anything else?"

"I see planets and constellations. Even dust clouds. I see an endless mystery."

"Very good. Very good. But anything more?"

"What else should I be seeing? Please guide me, stargazer. What would I see if I were blessed to see through your eyes?"

"Through my eyes? You clever boy. What a cunning question. You move with all a huntsman's stealth and guile. Yet you must truly have taken me to be sleeping. Be careful, my student, for this bear sleeps with one eye open."

He winked at Heshel in his most ridiculous fashion.

"You would really wish to know? Are you certain? Perhaps you should be a little more careful in what you ask for. Why, young carpenter, right now you would be seeing yourself as I see you. Are you ready for such a revelation?"

But Azar's words had already somehow unlocked a door. In his mind's eye, Heshel glimpsed for just a moment, a most perturbing vision. It was as though he were seeing himself through the eyes of his father. Eyes blinded by fury. Blinded by a speck of ceaseless discontent. He saw a shameless young man marked by the spirit of failure. A face that too closely resembled the face of his mother. A son of questionable allegiance, prattling on endlessly of his foolish dreams. A traitor, bringing into the homestead the sickening stench of the treacherous forest. A wild child gone astray, in need of being set straight by the rule. But then there came suddenly, a most merciful light. Gone now the spectre. Repelled and vanquished. Diminished, departed and chased away. Banished, cast out by the word of the magi.

"What would you see through my eyes? Well, my apprentice, when I gaze at the night sky, I see just as I did when still a little child. I feel as if I am the only person awake in the whole of the world. My thoughts flow more clearly and my heart knows peace. To sit beneath the stars is to be reunited with my ancestors. I become as one with all the other stargazers who have gone before me. Their eyes become my eyes. Their curiosity, my curiosity. Their knowledge, my knowledge. For do not our star family give us knowledge of the seasons and the cycles of time? The knowledge of the wind and rains, of the planting times and the reaping times? Do they not speak of what is, what was once, and what is still yet to be? Are they not even willing to reveal to us the very beginning, the source of all things, if only our eyes could see that far?"

"The source of all things? But how is it possible?"

"By becoming as angels, by seeing as they do. By realising that we are made from the very same substance of which the stars were once conceived."

"Can it really be so, that the stargazers hold the key to future sight?"

"Yes. Such a one was Merhdad, blessed be his name. His word has stood the test of time. Many of his prophecies have already come to pass. It was Merhdad who revealed to my people the Red Star Prophecy, a vision of a golden age that is yet to come. A time of unparalleled change. A time when the door to the gardens of paradise shall once more be unsealed. When all things secret shall be revealed. But no-one holds knowledge of that hour, though many pretend to. No, not even Mehrdad. Perhaps not even the Most Holy One? Now, my hungry young pup, are your questions satiated?"

"Not quite. I fear this whelp thirsts for more milk."

"Then continue with your line of questioning."

"I would hear more of the star people. Are they fashioned like us? Or are they closer in substance to the high spirits and angels?"

"Star people. Angels. Spirits. Just words, my dear, fashioned by the limits of our mortal tongue. For how shall we describe the indescribable? But we must try our best, must we not? Call them higher beings, if you will. They are the walkers between the worlds. Some of these are our ancestors, those who have walked further ahead down the good red road. Then there are those who have never walked amongst us before but have now chosen to do so. Yet each of these share with us the deepest kinship."

"Have you ever encountered such a blessed being, my teacher?"

"I believe the lady of Estakhr was such a being. But let us tread carefully and quietly when speaking of such sacred matters. The high spirits flee from those who talk too loudly. They are butterflies in a lilac meadow. And, just like butterflies, are startled away by the sound of heavy footsteps."

"But how shall I recognise such a being if I should be so blessed to meet one?"

"Tell me, Heshel, how shall you recognise the one for whom your soul does seek? In this question, you will find your answer. And it is not the habit of the star people to draw undue attention to themselves. This is not because they wish to remain hidden, but because only the true heart can bear the rapture of their undiluted presence. Yet even they are revealed to the heart that sees, for they are unable to conceal this one precious thing: the look of divine wonder that shines in their eyes. How shall you recognise them? Why, these blessed ones are the children with the faraway eyes, who carry a wisdom far beyond their earthly years. They are the humble ones, who speak less of 'I' and more of 'we'. They are the dancers upon the rainbow's edge. The gentle and pure ones with a fierce warrior spirit. The kind ones. The shining ones. Ah, my apprentice, how shall I find adequate words to speak of them?"

"Who better to speak of them than the fire priest of Asnavant? And please tell me if you will, what is their purpose in walking amongst us?"

But Azar looked up to the stars and let out a sigh, the sort of sigh that signalled to his apprentice that the time for silence and reflection had now come. And when Heshel departed, Azar remained seated upon the rock until the first light of dawn.

"Master? Is that you?"

A tentative voice, breaking the silence.

"Rebekah? What brings you here at such an early hour, my darling?"

"I hope I did not startle you?"

"Oh no, not at all. I felt your coming."

"Have I no secrets from you?"

"You know well, my young weaver, you hold secrets enough."

He smiled mischievously, beckoning her to come and sit at his side.

"Then tell me truly, does not this wizard already hold foreknowledge of my heart's gladsome news?"

"Indeed. Indeed. But by no covert means. I heard of it from the lips of a carpenter. Oh, my Rebekah, what a handsome pair you two shall make. How happy I am for my daughter and teacher."

"Me? Your teacher? Ha, ha, ha. Tell me, is Heshel a teacher to you as well?"

"He is. Very much so. Does this surprise you? But please refrain from telling him. How else will I command him to do his chores?"

As they sat laughing together, a thoughtful look settled like a butterfly upon Rebekah's face. Her face, a flower questioning the source of the rain.

"Was your hand at work in all this, Azar?"

"No, Rebekah. It is not the duty of a fire priest to play the part of matchmaker."

"Then what has caused this sudden change in him?"

"Perhaps you should ask Heshel. Perhaps the eyes of his heart have opened a little wider?"

"Did you teach him this?"

"You already know this cannot be taught."

"Perhaps not? Yet what is beyond the art of this wondrous grizzly bear, come to us from the far distant mountain? And speaking of grizzly bears and magic mountains, you will never guess what Zakiya asked me the other day."

"Did she ask if a corpulent yet hungry ghost was going to eat her for breakfast?"

"No, Azar. And your form is not corpulent but ample. Please do not speak of yourself in such a deprecatory manner."

"I will heed your word, young master."

"Actually, she asked me what powers the magi possesses."

"How did you answer?"

"I said you are just like a bear from the mountain. You are big and strong yet can move incredibly quickly when you want to. That you are fierce to protect your own and hold a heart as big as the sky."

"Thank you, Rebekah."

"Oh no, but there is more. Zakiya did not give up quite so easily. You know how children are. She asked me again what powers you have."

"How did you escape being stalked by this huntress?"

"I could not. She would not cease from pursuing me. So I just spoke truly. I said that you dive so deeply into the silence you can hear almost everything. I said your eyes see far beyond even the most distant star. Your hands overflow and burn with the magic craft. Your words are steeped in power, for they are wise and true and kind. I said your heart is a holy fire that burns upon the mountain top, giving guidance to the lost and warmth to the lonely. A heart that heals, that can restore breath to the departed. And as for your spirit, only few may glimpse how high this majestic golden eagle soars."

This time Azar was silent and overcome with feeling. He succumbed beneath this blow of love like a struck-down cedar. All of this Rebekah saw. She placed her hands on his hands.

"But this still was not the end of the matter. Still, Zakiya persisted with her questions."

"She reminds me of Heshel. She is also a ravenous raven."

"Indeed. And little poppy wanted to know if your powers allow you to walk on water. I told her I had never seen you do so."

She fixed her large and questioning auburn eyes upon him.

"Can you walk on water, fire priest from Asnavant? Nothing would surprise me as to what you are able to accomplish. For who dare limit the heart of the passionate master?"

"You know it is not my habit to speak of such matters, Rebekah. But just for today, I will answer this question. I will do so because I love you, just as I love the curiosity of our children. How I love to gaze upon this light of our little stars. So yes, I can walk upon the skin of the water. So too may I be borne upon the back of the wind. But only if it should be the will of the water and the wind to let me do so. Do you understand?"

"Yes, I think I understand. I will try and explain this to Zakiya should she ask me again. And, master, there is another most pressing matter I would discuss with you."

"It must be very important to have brought you out so early. Very well, Rebekah, you have my full attention."

"Would you partner my mother to the dance?"

How many times would this daughter of Ariadna catch him unguarded?

"It has been so long since I last saw her dance. I want to see her dance again. Please. Have you not often told me these bodies were made to dance? It is my heart's desire to see you two dance together. There, I have said it. I have lodged my petition."

"How shall I give answer, my spirit daughter? What words can I say? You know my heart would dearly love to. Truly and with my all. But I am not sure if Deborah would feel comfortable to do so."

"Trust your teacher when I say this would bring her only joy. I just know it. I feel this truth running through the bones of my fingers and the threads of my spindle."

"Then I will gladly do as my teacher requests."

That night Azar slept peacefully, cradled like a babe in the arms of mercy. And he dreamt of a vast flock of snow geese flying across the sky. As they came closer, soaring above his head and across the lake, he felt their song explode inside him. The song of his homeland. The incomparable sound of the women of his tribe, trilling, ululating, as was their way when came the nuptial hour. The sound of the zaghareet. The sound of joy. He saw a dusky woman all dressed in white silk, holding aloft a bouquet of white roses, her face beaming with smiles. Standing at her side, Azar saw a man all dressed in black, his finest suit, nervously waiting to take the hand of his bride. To dance with her for the very first time. And the star people smiled to see these two, whose love had formed a bridge between earth and sky, ascending, descending, treading upon the steps of the spiral staircase.

Machowl

Yes, our children, these bodies were made to dance, as all things were made to dance. In the silence, the dance. In the stillness, the dance. Within the mighty thunderclap and the restless mountains. In the atom, the atman, the aten, the dance. In the skip of the lamb and the samba of the snake, the flamenco of the flame, the graceful ballet of the moon and sun. In every heart that beats, the dance. That ant crushed beneath your heel, the dance. Those dancing gods and their many gestures. This death, a midwife dressed in dancing shoes. But why, oh why should we speak at all of the dance, when the dance speaks in silence and in the tongue of all things.

Look. Look. Who is this walking through the forest? It is Rebekah and Heshel, arm in arm, hand in hand, entwined together like Celtic knots, drifting like clouds through the purple twilight. See them coming. See them coming, side by side, dancing with new-found grace in a world transformed. The birds, they sing in unfamiliar harmony. A mellow breeze spirals, twists and jigs, warm and embracing, suffused with the scent of jasmine and lotus blossom. Bright stars are peeping through the treetops, a firefly swarm of gleaming smiles. See. See, these two, a racing stag and tender fawn, gliding to the dance through the chiming woods, waterfalls of words tumbling from their lips, their hearts, their blood, a blazing fire. Hear them talking. Hear them talking. How well they seem to know and understand each other. How familiar the utterance of each other's words.

"Heshel, I shall tell you this evening, something I have shared with no other. Not Azar, not Hannah, nor even my mother. These last two dances I have watched you closely. I have admired every step you made. I could not stop myself from staring at you like a giddy girl. And though I blush to say it, even when I tried my best to look away, my eyes could not resist returning to you, as if my will were no longer my own."

"You felt all this just to see my clumsy dance?"

"Clumsy? How could you say such a thing? There was nothing clumsy about your dance. Truly, a king would be content to dance as you do. I found myself wondering what passion could inspire such movements."

Her lips. Her lips. The shapes they make, the subtlest of movements, each one as red as a ruby, each one a doorway from which comes forth a voice of gentle yet measured authority, springing forth like manna, like vintage wine.

"Forgive me, Rebekah, but I do not understand. I did not dance because of any secret passion. I danced only because it was expected of me. I danced because I did not wish to further disappoint my father. I fear that it was only my body that was dancing and not my soul. I failed to give proper honour to my partners. But how could I dance if my soul was elsewhere?"

Such a deep well of sadness in this carpenter's eyes.

"I think you are very hard upon yourself, Heshel. Why do you judge yourself so sternly?"

She rested her hand upon his chest. How beautiful this hand. Thrills and tingles to feel her gentle touch. Comfort and healing where had been only hurting.

"It was only your body at the dance, you say? Maybe? Maybe? Yet should this be true, and it is not my place to doubt it, then this strong body is filled with its own grace and knowing. Perhaps you do not honour the knowing of your body as much as you should? We must honour these bodies. Does not the rabbi teach that these bodies also hunger to know the Most Holy One? And soul or no soul, you danced with a grace I have seldom seen. Those girls were fortunate to share such a dance with you. It will only remain with them as a cherished memory. Trust me when I say this, for there are some things hidden from the sight of the boys. Some things that only us girls know."

"I will try, Rebekah. And I promise you, this night I shall dance with my all."

"Then I shall be a fortunate girl indeed."

She closed her eyes. How many times had she imagined this, that she, Rebekah, would be walking with Heshel to the dance.

"I must pinch myself to see if I am truly awake. For how can it be that I, Rebekah, have stepped into such a dream as this?"

Echoes, echoes, of another time. Another world. Maybe even, of another life once lived.

"If this has only the substance of a dream, then let it be a dream shared by we two. And dream or no dream, I have never known such a happiness before. How I wish, Rebekah, I had not been blind for so long."

For a moment, her eyes looked far inward in silent reflection. For a moment, her eyes gazed deep into him, shining with a startling prescience.

"For every thing, a time and season. A time to mourn and a season to dance. Yet maybe, I wonder, it was not you who was blind, but me who was invisible? If only I had not stayed so long in hiding. Yet blind or invisible, yet here we two stand."

For a while, they stood still that this dawning, this overture, might never, ever, have need of ending. To cease the wheel of time from turning. She turned to him, a nervous expression on her face.

"I must tell you, Heshel, I have never danced with any man before. I have only danced with the willing wind."

Heshel looked into the eyes of this girl. Why had he never looked into the eyes of any girl before?

"If it is as you say, then I shall be as the wind for you this night. To dance with you tonight can only be perfection. And even if this perfection were to include the ridicule of all those around, then let it be so. I do not care. I only care that I will dance with you this night, if you still wish to."

"Your words are my delight. I will gladly dance with you. But please, do not be as the willing winds, my new-found friend. I wish to feel the touch of your hands upon me. I wish to wear them like robes and feel their craft upon me."

Her hair, a waterfall of auburn tinged with crimson, and desirous was he to go and bathe in those waters. The way this girl spoke. This girl, who was no girl at all, who instead spoke with a knowing as rare as a phoenix. Yet now they both could feel it. They could feel it flicker. They could feel it shimmer. For the wheel of time once more was turning. And there, lingering before them, the great hall coming into sight. The villagers gathering from every direction, each one dressed in their finest apparel, filling the fields with their expectant chatter.

"May blessings rain upon you, Rebekah and Heshel," said Obadiah the cobbler.

"What a handsome pair you make," chortled Martha the midwife. How good to see this Martha, by whose hands many had been delivered into this world. And as Obadiah and Martha each traced the path of the young ones' besotted gazes to their source, they remembered a paradise they too had once strayed upon. A time when they had roamed together through the flower-bedecked fields and open meadowlands, prancing and dancing like lambs in springtime. Hearing as if with new ears. Seeing as if with new eyes. What joy is this, that what had seemed so long ago, is now resurrected by the touch of first true love? Memories came to mind of how they had once gone to the dance with each other. They each saw once more that face, still bright and vivid and miraculously unchanged, neither gone nor forgotten, but still there beneath the folds and furrows of aged flesh. And when Rebekah and Heshel departed, Obadiah and Martha kissed the other passionately upon the lips as they had once done so long ago, holding each other close and tight. Breast upon breast.

Onwards, onwards, as if walking upon the back of the mist and wind, this feeling when she walked with Heshel, when she walked by his side. The way she felt when she walked by the stillness of the lake, shimmering with the last reflected fire of the day. The smell of him. Of leaves and bark, of fire and the fragrant wind, of unguents and oils, unfamiliar, mysterious, delicious and enticing. To feel her hand in his. She felt its seasoned strength as her own rested in its firm and true grasp. His gaze when he looked into her, filled with secret smiles that only these two might know and share. To hear him speak. A flowing, steady stream were his words. She longed to hear him give form to his knowing and seeing. She longed for him, and in this longing, they each felt drawn, the one to the other, upon the wings of an irresistible and invisible force.

Arriving at the wide-open doors of the banqueting hall, they walked through as if entering another world. There, the altar covered in the finest linen, bedecked to bless and pray for the coming harvest. There, the brightly polished silver menorah, the golden cup of Elijah overflowing with the blood of the vine. The choicest array of plates and cups, stacked up as high as the Tower of Babel. Walls abundantly covered with budding vines. Tables heavily laden with fruit, nuts and wine, a scattering of poppies and scarlet crowfoot, the heavy, sweet scent of snow-white lilies, the fragrance of mandrake, the perfume of myrrh. A vibrato of colour and intoxicating smells, the air rippling with music, pulsating with the beat of the frame drum, the hypnotic melodies of the kinnor lyre.

"Rebekah," a voice called out through the throng of expectant people, their chatter as loud and joyous as the hum of gathering bees. The voice of Hannah. Rebekah caught sight of her dearest friend moving purposefully through the crowd, her hand holding firmly onto that of Jacob, pulling him along as if he were as light as a kite.

"Rebekah. Oh, you look wonderful." The look in her eyes became as sharp and focused as a crow upon a worm. "Where did you get that gorgeous dress?"

She threw her eyes up to the heavens in the way only Hannah could, a look that was a herald of good times coming. Those pretty, kind eyes, two goblets filled with humour and precocious knowing. Those blue, blue eyes, those dancing eyes, an ocean in which Rebekah loved oft to swim.

"Silly me. You made it, did you not? Of course, you did. You clever weaver, you. Well, old friend, this time I really think you have surpassed yourself. I do not suppose you would care to swap dresses? How else shall I come to be crowned the queen of the dance?"

She turned her head quickly to Jacob, her eyes full of play.

"No, not here Jacob, you naughty boy," she said in her best rebuking voice.

"What are we to do with them, Rebekah?"

Rebekah saw Jacob's face flush a little, but the heat in his blood was soon quelled by the softest of kisses.

"Why, we shall dance with them, of course," answered Rebekah. "What else are we to do? But please forgive us, Jacob. I must say, you look very handsome. And you must – how shall I put it – you must have the patience of an angel."

"Oh, Rebekah," intervened Hannah, "I do not know what you can possibly mean. And Jacob is most certainly no angel. But yes, he tolerates my excesses as I tolerate his. I cannot deny I talk a bit too much when I get excited, and say things that perhaps lack my best judgement. But look, Jacob. See how Rebekah's ears have closed like the night flowers to protect themselves from my incessant jabber."

"Did you say something?"

"Ha, ha, ha. Anyway, enough of our foolishness. Tell me, are you two looking forward to the dance? I am just praying our feet are not crushed in the stampede."

As she spoke, Hannah turned her eyes towards Heshel. She gasped to do so, a gasp that only Rebekah could see. How manly he looked. How different from the rest of the flock. His full beard slightly sparkling, wet with drops of fragrant oil. His hair, as dark as pitch and as thick as thistles, standing a head higher than most of his peers.

"Can this possibly be Heshel the carpenter?" said Hannah, quickly composing herself. "I think not. You must be an impostor."

"You are correct, Hannah," replied Heshel. "It is not Heshel, the carpenter, for he has surrendered his obsession and laid down his tools."

Heshel glanced at Rebekah and saw her smiles. How beautiful this candlelight dancing in her eyes.

"And how are you, Jacob?" asked Heshel. "Is the music going well? Will you be performing this evening?"

"Yes, Heshel. I will be playing a piece I composed myself."

"I cannot wait to hear it," said Rebekah. "I always love to hear you play the lyre. Your music soothes my soul."

"Really? Thank you for saying so, Rebekah."

"Tell me, does your piece have a theme?"

"I can only say it was inspired by Hannah."

He turned to her with a look of admiration.

"I think that Hannah has become my muse."

Hannah, though still excited and primed to turn everything into laughter and humour, blushed to hear Jacob answer so. And when she looked at Jacob's earnest face, she knew he spoke truly and with the voice of his heart.

"Thank you so much, Jacob. I did not know."

But as the colour on her cheeks faded, a sudden hush fell upon the hall. The rabbi was taking position behind the altar, adjusting his tallit, thumbing his fingers through his beard, resting his fingers on the pages of the Torah. One glance sufficient to herald the Machowl. The circle dance. As if all were becoming a part of some greater being, two circles formed. The inner by the males, the circle of mortality. The outer by the females, the circle of eternity. The rabbi's nod signalled the music to commence. The rhythm of the Baladi, drummed out by three women, accompanied by the melody of the kinnor lyre. Women walking clockwise, the men, in reverse, familiar faces passing, a river of dreams, each dancer looking deeply into the eyes of the other. Faster and faster, whirling and swirling, the young squealing with laughter and bleating like lambs, riding upon this magical merry-go-round. So too the old ones, their aches and infirmities melting miraculously away, their bodies once more robed in the mantle of youth. Quicker and quicker, their heels on the floor like peals of thunder. Around and around and around we go, the known world dissolving into nothingness. An empty void in which they yet somehow remained. Dancing as if this were their first dance. As if it were their last. Life and death and earth and heaven. Time and eternity, woman and man. No longer two circles but only one.

With a wave of his hand, the rabbi commanded the music to cease. Be silent, be still, for the Shekinah has come. Time to pray for the harvest, to pray for the tribe. To pray for each and every thing, each prayer to be robed in a spirit of thankfulness. To cast away sorrow, for she comes, she comes, to make everything born anew. And from the midst of this silence, like a flower from the soil, comes the rhythm of the Masmoudi. Time for the young couples to pair off, to stand the one before the other, their bodies tingling in expectation. So many hours spent rehearsing, each move, each step, danced in the daytime, danced in the dreamtime. Long and lovely evenings that had passed all too quickly, dancing in fields full of flowers in the fast-fading light. Yet it had never been like this. For this, nothing could have prepared. This feeling, as if a million ears were listening. A million eyes watching. With the crescendoing music, they dance and sway, moved by the rhythm of this ancient song, their eyes seeing only the eyes of the other.

How beautiful is she, as if never seen before. How handsome, how unfamiliar, this look on his face, never before so vulnerable and unguarded. Are you the one for whom my soul does seek? Oh, please let me be your fool and king. Come, hold me, admit me, let me be your queen and crown. This feeling. This feeling. Who is he, coming up out of the wilderness like a pillar of smoke? Who is she, this beautiful garden, this well of living waters, flowing like a stream from Lebanon? A rose of Sharon, a lily of the valleys. I thirst for her lips of ruby-red wine, to feel the tease of her hair upon my neck. An apple tree is he, fully laden with fruits for which I hunger. To feel the touch of the other's hand. His shoulder now come to rest upon hers, breast upon breast and cheek upon cheek. Come now to each other. May your feet walk on wind and water, as if turned to wings. Dance our children, dance our young, becoming women and men. Dance and be danced by the yearning and quickening fields. Become you all as those dancing gods with their many gestures.

All of the watchers now encircled around them, transfixed by this beauty, this elegance and grace. The children, filled with awe and admiration, dreaming of when they too would come to dance in this circle. The elders, smiling with pride and wistfulness, remembering when they had once crossed over the threshold. A miracle, as if all were beholding only one woman and man. One man and woman. Dancing. Eternal. And when this dance did appear to have final ending, the children gathered in counsel to perform their solemn duty. To choose the dance that would implore blessings upon the coming harvest. These two who would stand on behalf of every two. Choose well, our children, they had been counselled. But why place such a burden of decision upon such unseasoned shoulders? "Ah," the rabbi would say in reply, "who better to discern the will of the Shekinah than the keen eye of innocence?"

"I think it should be Ruben and Kizzie," first spoke Bethany. "They danced with such energy. It was amazing."

"No, it should be Zachary and Talia," countered Daniel. "Who danced with more elegance than them?"

"What of Hannah and Jacob?" said Amira. "Their dance filled me with happiness. It was so full of joy and smiles."

"What do you say, Zakiya?" asked Bethany. "Which couple do you think should bless the crops?"

Zakiya sat deep in thought, tenderly stroking the petals of the special flower she had found last spring. Oh, little Zakiya, what magic is this known only to you, that when you give your all to the listening, you hear the poppy queen speaking in a small yet powerful voice? Speaking to you of many things? Oh, little Zakiya, how is it that though her leaves have become ever more dry and faded, the poppy queen has yet become ever more beautiful to you? And why, oh why should it be, each time the poppy queen answers but one of your questions, one petal falls and her voice becomes fainter?

"Tell me, poppy queen," asked Zakiya one time, "what is it that sets you apart from the other flowers?"

"I am a flower of the red mountain."

"How is it, poppy queen, I can hear you talking?"

"How is it, young walking one, you are ready and willing to listen?"

"Please tell me, poppy queen, what can I do to stop you from dying?"

"Oh, Zakiya, please do not be sad nor grieve for me. For I am not dying but only dancing. When you are a little older, you shall surely understand the whole of this. And on that day, you shall become Zakiya, the seer of visions. Yes, my child, my most precious petal, you too shall be a poppy queen."

Although all but overcome with grief and sorrow, Zakiya knew in her heart the time had finally come, to ask of the poppy queen her one final question.

"Please tell me, poppy queen, which couple do you choose to bless the crops?"

She felt the flower tingling with joy in her hand. She could hear the whispers of the poppy queen as the choicest flower made her choice.

"Do you remember, Zakiya, the day we first met? The day I picked you? Oh, what a blessed day. How strange that on that beautiful day, I saw these very same two walk past me through the fields to the forest. I found myself wondering if their two paths would cross? I found myself wishing with all my heart they would meet, do not ask me why. And now to see them, my heart is content. So, my darling, let our last moment together be spent beholding them dancing. Their dance shall serve to seal our friendship forever. And happy I am. Yes, happy I am."

"Goodbye, poppy queen," whispered Zakiya, kissing the last petal before it faded.

"Rebekah and Heshel," she tearfully announced to the other children, in a voice that was faltering yet filled with such passion that hearts bowed in unison to the voice of her choosing. Each one, a flower bending to the will of the wind. And when Bethany told the rabbi, he could barely disguise the look of delight on his face.

"Very well," he announced. "It has been decided. Rebekah and Heshel will dance in the fields when the first light of morning comes."

But there was yet one other who had heard the flower of the red mountain speaking. As he had watched Rebekah and Heshel dance, he had seen them become bathed in a blue and liquid, living light. And with this vision, he heard a call.

"Go now, my goat, as wily as a wind around my hips. Go now, my priest, for your task is accomplished. And my daughter awaits you on the other side of the mountain."

All this Deborah saw as she looked upon Azar. She saw his joy and saw his sorrow. She sighed the deepest of sighs, to see the dance of vision shining upon his face, this face she had come to love so well. No slave trader was he. No, not at all. No stealer of children, no stealer of dreams. Never, never, since that terrible day, had she dared dream she would ever know such a passion again. And before the night was over, Deborah approached him and took his hand.

"Please, my dear friend, may I have the pleasure of this dance?"

All of this, the gift of the dance. All this, the gift of the poppy queen.

Weeping Fire

How to leave and say goodbye? What words to say? Though he had never ceased longing to return home to Asnavant and to all that he loved, now his given task was done and he was free to leave, he felt overcome with grief. He had felt such a joy to see Rebekah and Heshel, anointed in the glory of majestic blue light. But now, crying, crying was his heart. Crying to leave all those who he had come to love without limit, to whom his heart was now bound with threads of gold. Crying, crying, are the owls of midnight. Crying are the turtle doves, descending, swooning, from the pale blue sky. Crying are the clouds and the winds that whisper. Crying are the leaves that rustle. Crying are the waters of the lake as they break in sighs upon the stone. Crying are the mountains and so too the stars. Crying is the earthworm as it swims through the soil, to taste but one drop of his bitter tears. So too, the clod of clay beneath the heavy tread of his feet. Why, oh why, must his heart be once more crushed like grain beneath the weight of a millstone? Better to have no heart than to know anguish like this. Fear not, she had said, for your heart is big enough. But as he thought of Deborah,

Rebekah and Heshel, Yitshak and Sarah, Rabbi Ishmael and little Zakiya, Martha and Obadiah, Jacob and Hannah and all the others, he felt his strength falter, his life force draining away as if he had suffered a mortal blow. As weak as Samson beneath the yoke of the Philistines. How his heart had hurt to leave his Zara. How it now stung with sorrow at the time of the return. Breaking. Breaking. This aching desolation. This living death from which there was neither escape nor refuge. Please hold back the hands of time that I may stay here a little while longer, that I may delay the day of departure. Yes, he would speak to them of this tomorrow. And tomorrow again. And maybe tomorrow shall never come and the wheel of time will stop turning? Or maybe he could slip away in the dead of night as if he had never been anything more than a dream, a ghost or a morning mist? But he knew he could not. And though his spirit now seemed somewhere far away, his legs conspired to deliver him to the house of Deborah, walking slowly and painfully, a condemned man walking towards the gallow tree.

Help me, please help me, for there is her door. It comes towards me, and with its coming, so too comes my demise. This door I once walked through to find my hidden family. This door I shall soon exit for the very last time. Please do not betray me, my hand. Please do not sound upon her door for this shall surely seal my end. Feet stand still and walk no further. Spirit now transform me to an effigy of stone, that I may linger here for the rest of my days. Knock, knock, knock, his knuckles betraying his presence, banging like a knell upon her door. Each knock, a blow struck against his breast. Mercy, please make it that she is not there but away to gather grain. Spare me the sight of her beautiful face. But she is not away in the field. Beyond the door, Deborah is waiting, hearing the familiar sound of his knocks. So well she knows them that she discerns their hidden language. Why, she wonders, are they not sounded out with his normal vigour but are instead muted and forlorn? What trouble do these knocks herald? She opens her door to him, still feeling his knocks upon the gate of her heart. This one who would always and forever be granted admittance. He sees the door creaking open and sees the fading daylight fall upon her face. They gaze without words until she breaks the spell of this silence.

"What is wrong, Azar? Why so sad? Come in and speak to me that I may put it right."

So spoke the word of friendship. But not even the baker could put this right. Not even the baker could hold back the flow of time, nor subdue the call of the holy red mountain. All words deserted him. Lead me, baker. Lead me where you will for I am lost and weary. Into the kitchen they went and sat down. She looked at him. And as she looked at him, she remembered seeing his face for the very first time. There in the poppy field. There in the sea of flame. Her body already knew what her mind did not wish to hear.

"Oh, my Azar, I see in your eyes what your mouth dares not say. You are leaving us, are you not?"

A barely perceptible nod of his head.

"When will you go?"

He heard the slight tremble in her voice.

"I shall leave with the coming of the next full moon."

"But that is only two days away. So soon? Do you have to leave with such speed?"

"The stars are fortuitous that day. And I fear if I stay longer, I shall never be able to leave."

A long silence followed. And in this silence, Deborah gave herself over to practicalities, for she was also not ready to feel this hurt. This dutiful woman.

"Then we shall have to work hard that you may be ready and have ample provisions for your journey."

"I am grateful, my friend."

Deborah looked downwards and sighed. A sigh so deep. A wind that worried.

"I do not like to think of you all alone out there in the wilderness, all by yourself for such a long time. What dangers will you face? What if you get lost or are injured?"

It was her unspoken wish to be there with him, right by his side. But she knew she could not.

"Thank you for your care. How fortunate I am to feel such care. But truly, I will not be alone, nor without protection. I will have Malka to give me company. I shall have the sun to warm me and its light to uplift me. I shall have the moon and the stars to guide my way. I shall converse with the air and listen to the song of the water. I shall have the trees to give me shelter and so too the caves. And even more than all this, my soul shall be fed by all whom I love, just as if I were nourished by the ravens of the wilderness."

The tears now flowed down her handsome face, wetting the strands of falling hair until they stuck to her skin.

"I had promised myself I would not cry when this moment came. But look at me now. What shall I do without my grizzly bear who came for me from the mountain?"

He stroked his fingers across her wet cheeks.

"May I tell you something, Deborah? May I share a secret with you, something I have not dared to say to you before or even admit to myself?"

"You know you can tell me anything."

"Very well."

Azar paused, the stillness crowding in close as if it were listening. And so too, the silent, witnessing angels.

"I have always spoken to you in truth, my dear friend.

And now, my heart compels me to tell you, that should I have never known my sweet Zara, you are the only other woman I would have wished to be my wife."

There. The word of his heart now uttered. Made real and made known. A bird released from a cage to fly to who knows where.

"I hope my words have not given you offence?"

But the curl of her lips and the luminescence in her eyes spoke otherwise.

"Speak not to me of offence, my dearest friend. For how can there be offence where love resides? And I too shall meet you in kind."

Closer she comes. Even closer than the crowding stillness and the witnessing angels.

"You too must know if I had never met Simeon, you are the only man I would have wished to take as my husband. But this was not meant to be, was it, my love. This was not meant to be."

Again he nodded in silence.

"But please, my fire priest of Asnavant, let us not be sad. Let our last moments together be a time of joy, for your coming has been my salvation. You, who have returned me to my daughter and to my tribe and friends. You have returned my very soul. You, the magi to whom even death bows down. You, who have returned my husband to me. How shall I ever repay my debt?"

"Oh, my dear, dear friend. Speak not of debt. For how can there be debt where love resides? Never, ever can this be. But know this too. That in you, I too have found salvation. I am more than I ever was before."

He stood up with his familiar gusto.

"Look at me, a fat-bottomed phoenix who has taken to flight, all for the blessings of the baker."

Deborah laughed as he waddled around. How good and fitting it was now to laugh together. He sat down once again at her side, his shoulder easing into hers. He fumbled beneath his tunic with trembling hands, feeling for the silver locket, holding it firmly and taking it off. He let it rest for a moment in the palm of his hand, gazing at the shafts of reflected light leaping upwards from its polished surface.

"Please, take this piece of my heart."

He saw astonishment in her eyes.

"But your wife meant this for you only."

"Yes. But now we two have been joined by love. And so bright is Zara's light that the shadows of jealousy flee from her presence. She knows the higher love that will never be confined. She whispers to me in my dreams, that the wife of the stonemason has become like a long-lost sister. She whispers of her gratitude, that you have taken care of her husband in a far distant land. And now she too desires to rest upon your kind heart."

Deborah put out her hands. Azar placed the locket upon them. It radiated with light, as bright as a nugget of gold from the alchemist's cauldron. It rested upon her palms like the ark upon Ararat. He looked at her face shining like a pillar of light. Beneath her noble brow, her eyes shone golden, her heart singing with the sound of weeping fire. Inwardly Azar felt his heart bowing before her. In words from somewhere deep within, he spoke to her as if she were a priestess.

"Please, bestow upon me your light, Deborah of Elnazar. Please grace me with your blessings, baker whose bread is manna from heaven. Have mercy upon this soul, mother of the weaver and wife of the stonemason."

Her eyes never leaving his eyes, she placed the locket around her neck, tears falling from her eyes like a springtime shower, her mouth smiling without any restraint, as bright and as beautiful as the sun at dawn. With tenderness and gratitude, her unbridled heart swelled with love for him. With the care of a mother for her newborn child, she placed her hands upon his cheeks. He shivered and sighed to feel her touch upon his skin. Slowly, slowly, she drew him near. Nearer and nearer, until he felt the heat of her lips upon his own. And then, she kissed him. She kissed him as a lover kisses. She kissed him with the gateway to her heart now fully open, a roaring wind come to sweep him away. Over in a moment, this moment that will last forever. How young she looked to him as she withdrew. As nervous as a fawn before a forest fire. And innocence is her name.

"Forgive me, Azar, for I have been overcome by my feeling for you. Forgive me, for I fear I have taken that which was not meant for me. I pray I have not caused you offence nor risked our friendship."

The taste of her. The taste of her. His body still tingling. His body still burning. The taste of her still in his mouth, upon his tongue and lips. A fragrant flower deep inside. He tried, he tried, to find the words.

"Oh, my sweet Deborah." He paused for a moment, holding the gaze of her beautiful eyes in his own. "Truly you must know this. That there is nothing you could ever steal from me. For all that is mine is yours and so it shall ever be."

He pulled her towards him and held her tight.

"Who is it that shall dare place this glory inside a cage or contain the ocean inside a thimble? Who is it that would dare commit such a blasphemy? Only the unknowing. And should our two hearts decree that they may be bound together, then let it be with such a kiss. For how sweet is the taste of your body. How sweet the taste of your very soul. How sweet the bread of the baker, whose taste is of blessings and salvation."

The dragonfly darts above the still surface of the lake. How quickly it flies. See the effervescent rainbow light upon its wings, skipping this way and that way. Like a dragonfly, a part of her flies into him and a part of him into her. A dragonfly above the silent still waters of their sacred hearts. Oh, that this moment shall never end. End, it never shall. So speaks the voice of the darting dragonfly. Just ride upon my rainbow wings and I shall ever take you here. But now this silent communion must come to end. Splash. A pebble breaking the surface of the listening lake. And upon this surface, there glides a most beautiful swan.

One Stitch Unsewn

"Mother, why do you look so sad?" Panic in the voice of Rebekah now returned from the forest, upon seeing such sadness upon her mother's face. A sadness that had departed since the coming of the fire priest. "Azar, what has happened?"

"Rebekah," said Deborah with surprise. "I did not see you there, my precious. Oh, do not worry. I have been crying because I have been speaking with Azar of what a handsome couple you and Heshel make. These are only the tears of a proud mother."

Though knowing her mother spoke truly, Rebekah knew this was not the whole of the matter. Azar watched his spirit daughter, the cogs of her bright mind turning quickly, gathering up speed in search of understanding. Her eye of blindness shining as bright as torchlight.

"Come, Rebekah, if your mother does not mind, let us two go and sit in the garden. I have something I wish to tell you."

"Of course, Azar. Off you two go and I will prepare some supper for us."

To the garden they walked, hand in hand, sitting themselves in sight of the glistening stone angel. Yet before he had found a moment to utter even one word, Azar found himself swept away by the word of the weaver.

"You are going to leave us, are you not? You are going, I know it. You are returning to Asnavant and I shall never see you again. I shall never hear any more of your wondrous stories or learn more of your craft. You cannot leave. I will not let you. How will we live without you? The sun will turn to darkness and the smiles will depart from my mother's face. She will turn to stone once more. She will return to being only an effigy at my father's side."

Rebekah began to sob. She began to wail. His heart was pierced to hear her thus wailing, wailing like a wild winter wind through the cracks in the door. Wailing like a wounded animal. For a moment, Azar's body remembered hearing such wailing when still a tiny boy, hearing the anguish of the women as they saw their beloved given over to the funeral pyre. Shrieking birds and bleating ewes. Branches splitting, paper ripping, scratching, tearing, a ragged, cutting, desolate chorus of breaking hearts. Way back then, he had been too young to understand. Why did his uncle make his bed upon a tower of wood? Why did he sleep and not wake upon hearing the sound of their bitter tears? Yet awaken, he did not. No refuge from this cacophony of anguish. So loud had been the wailing of the women. So still, silent and stoic, the mute and absent, wilting men. Why should it be so, had asked his yet untutored mind? My heart hurts too and wishes to wail. But even this had not hurt as much as hearing Rebekah crying. Azar felt as if a jagged, burning boulder had become lodged within his throat. He felt her nuzzling deep into his chest, a burrowing fieldmouse, clawing its way to the keep of his heart. Oh, my beloved, I would rather pluck out my eye than cause you any pain. He felt her body convulsing as if in the throes of death. Gone now the spirit of authority that coursed through the veins of the fire priest. Lost and unknowing, stripped, naked, a collapsing tower, to see the tear-drenched face of his spirit daughter he loved so well. He snapped. He broke. He gave in. He wept. Who could have thought this fire could hold so many tears? To hear his sobbing, Rebekah threw her arms around him and held him close. She held him as if she would never let him go.

"Do not cry, my teacher. Do not cry, my second father. I am sorry. Please dry your tears for all shall be well."

She took his hands in hers. Through misty eyes, he looked at her hands, those graceful hands. What wonders, what beauty, would they come to fashion, the master within him could not help but wonder? He felt the stillness of the mountain come upon him.

"What glory this wretched boy from the far mountain has been blessed to behold, for I have seen the spirit of the Shekinah make roost upon these hands."

How noble her young face. How extraordinarily alive, those vision-filled eyes. Rebekah listened. Rebekah gazed at his powerful, knowing hands. How strong yet delicate they were. So roughened, worn and wondrous. Yet the master in her could not help but become entranced by the movement of his ruby-red ring as it traced out marvellous designs upon the skin of the air. All this did not escape Azar's eye.

"Does the ring call to you, daughter of Ariadna?"

Before she could even question why he had named her so, Azar began fumbling to remove the magician's ring.

"What are you doing, Azar?"

"I want you to have it as a parting gift."

"No. Let it remain where the Priest of Isis meant it to be. Can you not see it does not wish to be parted from you?"

"I have never seen more clearly, my dear."

He tugged and tugged, yet the ring would not move. As he did so, he saw the face of the Priest of Isis emerging from within its living ruby-red light. No words, but a look that told him the boy from Asnavant had found his way home. That he had finally arrived at the red mountain of his dreams. Azar felt swept away by love as he watched the golden wings of the ring fluttering in readiness of taking to flight.

"What a true and loyal guide this magic ring has been. How well it has served me. But no, Rebekah, it is not the ring that does not wish to be parted. It knows well that its purpose has found fulfilment. Do you recall I once told you how this ring takes on something of the nature of the one who wears it? It is I who am struggling to leave you. So look kindly upon this magi, ever fated to remain a fool for love."

He began to frantically push and pull it. Never so distant, the laughing clown. Never so far, the enthroned fool, his only sought prize to see a daughter's smiles. Though he could see Rebekah was not yet quite amenable to the spirit of laughter, Azar fell to the floor with a bang and a thud, wrestling with the ring as if fighting a crocodile. As if his very life depended upon it. He turned to look at her. That look. A look full of hope and conspiratorial mischief. How beautiful the light of this childlike soul. And her heart would not withhold him the hint of a smile, thus giving honour and thanks to her great grizzly bear.

"Well," he said, brushing off the dust from his tunic, "I should hardly be surprised it refuses to budge. You would be surprised if you saw the skinny boy to whom the Priest of Isis gifted this ring. By the word of Vata, how shall I ever remove it? It seems even after all these years of striving, I am no further forward with the art of letting go. If only I were a little more like my Zara. But I am that I am. And whether this renders me sufficient or lacking, I swear to you by the light of the holy red mountain, a part of my soul shall ever remain here in Elnazar, for I hold a stubborn heart that refuses to budge. Believe me when I say my word is no simple metaphor. A part of me, which is all of me, shall remain here always, right by your side. And even Rebekah, the weaver, shall lack the power to be rid of this magi."

With these words he kissed the ring with passion, just as the Priest of Isis had once done long ago. Slip, slip, slipping, the ring from his finger. Shine, shine, shining, the glad light of this ruby-red ring. With reverence, he placed the ring upon her finger.

"There. Why, is it not the most perfect fit? Wear me upon your thumb, my daughter, my very soul. May it serve as a light to illuminate your path, you who have been my salvation."

Despite the quiver in her lips and the trembling of her fingers, he must make now complete his heart's unsealed word.

"Yes, my beloved, you have heard me right. My salvation. You have cleansed my secret wound, my far-seeing daughter. You, who have been a mother's comfort and joy. A father's guiding light in the valley of Gehenna. And what of our young carpenter? What songs you have released in him. What craft you have inspired. But this is not the whole of the matter. The mountain mother compels me to tell you of my hidden wound, that you may be brought to full understanding. Are you so willing, Rebekah?"

What need of words when these devoted eyes gave answer?

"Please understand, this is not easy for me to speak of. But speak, I must. You must know my Zara's womb was not fashioned to bear children. I did not blame her for this. No, not even the slightest measure. She has always been whole and beautiful to me. But I still found myself unable to quell my longing to be a father. I knew it should have been sufficient for me to have a wife such as Zara. Sufficient for me to give service to the gods and live the good life of a fire priest. Yet though I tried my utmost to accept my lot, I found myself unable to. I knew many dark and lonely hours. I felt desperate. This feeling tortured me. I felt full of shame. And though I hid this anguish from everyone, even from my Zara, I was not able to hide this from the sight of the holy red mountain. And the mountain felt pity for this blacksmith. It guided him to the home of a baker and stonemason, whose big hearts have allowed me to share in their daughter's love. Such a love has healed me and set me free."

He looked for a moment upon the distant crest of Horeb.

"How shall I ever give sufficient thanks to the holy red mountain?"

"Please, my wondrous, grizzly bear, let us give voice to our gratitude together. Come, let us ride to Mount Horeb, one final time. Just you and me."

He looked upon her, sketching a picture upon the canvas of memory.

"By the gown of Persephone, how can this possibly be, that in little more than a year and a day, this nervous young girl has transformed into this self-assured young woman? Who is the true magi, I cannot help but wonder?"

A sudden sound, the ground vibrating with the thud of heavy hooves.

"Jamil? Oh, please forgive me, my friend. Thank you for your patience. Come, Rebekah, our loyal friend awaits us.

He also has something pressing he wishes to tell you."

They walked to the paddock, Jamil's dark, lustrous eyes fixed upon their every step. And as Rebekah drew closer towards him, Jamil fell down upon his knees.

"Mighty steed, what trick have you learned?"

"This is no trick, Rebekah. He is talking to you."

"I am so sorry, Jamil. Please forgive me my rudeness and my lack of listening."

Though still somewhat offended, as she placed her hand before his face, Jamil could not help but snort softly upon her alabaster skin.

"Thank you for forgiving me."

Jamil rose swiftly, standing tall and proud.

"My spine still tingles to see you. You are truly a magnificent being."

"Listen closer, Rebekah. Listen closer. Hear what Jamil is telling you."

She knew it was not a question of moving her head closer. So she closed her eyes and listened with her heart. This bright light of the Shekinah. And as she did so, she felt as if there were someone mounting upon her back. Running, running, as free as the wind. She saw herself as if from above, riding a white horse with innocent regality.

"He wants to stay with me, does he not?"

"Yes, Rebekah, you have spoken truly."

"First your ring and now Jamil? I cannot take everything that is precious to you. I cannot."

"But you are not taking anything, my Rebekah. You are receiving only that which is gladly given. I am not losing but gaining. This market haggler is content for he has brokered a most favourable price. And though it may seem I am stripped of everything, your love robes me like a king. Who is there that could be a richer man?"

"But without Jamil, how will you find your way home to Asnavant?"

"Ever the practical young woman. How like your mother you are. But do not worry, my Rebekah, for this boy from the mountain shall fare well. I shall go to the house of Sarah and Yitshak where I shall barter for one of their finest steeds. Good. It is agreed. All is as it should be. So, let us make haste. Let us go now together, just you and me. And Jamil, makes three. One final time. Let us ride to the holy red mountain. And today it is you who shall take the reins."

The Watchman's Horn

"Return home?" said Yitshak, unable to conceal the regret in his voice. "And you must leave us so soon?"

"Yes, my friend. I must get my affairs in order with haste and prepare for my journey. I shall ask Gerson to mend my clothes and Uriah to help me stock up on provisions. Though by the grace of Deborah, of bread, cheese and cake, we know I shall not lack. But there is one thing I need that only the mightiest of hunters can provide."

"You only have to name it. Anything, my brother. You need only tell me."

"Anything?" said Azar, a roguish grin rippling across his face. "Well then… perhaps you would not mind if Sarah travelled to Asnavant with me? Her mastery and her unrivalled kinship with horses would be invaluable in tending our herds. What do you say?"

Without warning, Yitshak slapped him firmly upon his back, forcing the wind out from Azar's lungs.

"By the fire of Elijah, another man would feel the wrath of the watchman to dare say such a thing."

"Forgive me, watchman. Forgive me. Please grant me mercy." Azar clasped his hands together in a gesture of pleading. "I am but a poor lost fool who knows not what he says."

"Hmmm... this fool hides something else behind his mask of unknowing. Few are more heedful of their words than the fire priest. You play with words as a child plays with its dolls. You are a conjurer with the power to reverse their meaning, to confound and amaze in equal measure. Yes, a conjurer, I tell you. Yet time has schooled me, that no master of the dark arts are you as once I feared. For who else but Azar could restore smiles to Deborah's face and bring solace to Rebekah and Heshel? Who else could have brought these two together and stoked the holy fire in their bellies?"

"You are sounding more like a poet with each passing day."

"Indeed. Yitshak transformed into a singer? Are there no limits to the scope of your magic? Perhaps I should retire to the mountain and become a teller of stories. Yet I fear I would be unable to put any meat on the table with words as my weapon. So, a butcher and a hunter, I shall remain."

"And what calling is there that surpasses the craft of the protector and provider, a craft no-one undertakes with more art, vigour and devotion than Yitshak, my most formidable of friends."

Yitshak paused for a moment, gazing upon Azar, looking at him, assessing him from head to toe.

"Who would have thought it, that I, Yitshak, would call a Persian my friend and brother? But even I cannot deny the testimony of this heart." He pointed to his chest with a solemn expression. "So tell me now for time is pressing, and you know my impatient nature compels me to action. What is there you need of me?"

"A horse."

"A horse? But why? There is no finer steed than Jamil! What has become of him?"

"Jamil has hatched other plans. My noble steed has chosen to stay with Rebekah."

"Has chosen to stay?" In search of understanding, Yitshak scratched his head and tugged at his beard. "Well, if it is as you say, and who am I to doubt you, then I can only say no horse and rider would make a more fitting match than Rebekah and Jamil. But as for another mount, you know I have no jurisdiction over the horses. That is a matter for Sarah."

"Very well. But before we go to Sarah, let us agree on a fair price."

"A fair price? You wish to pay me? You shall do no such thing. I would not even think of it. No, we will gladly offer you our finest horse."

"Thank you, my dear friend. If only there were a hundred of you, perhaps even far less, we would have an army mighty enough to set this world aright."

"Sarah might not agree with your generous assessment. I think she would say one Yitshak is more than enough."

"Then who am I to query the word of Sarah?"

Time to find this Sarah and to take her counsel. Off they went through the paddock and into the stables. Sarah was busy brushing the mane of a sleek, nimble colt by the name of Roshan, a colt whose coat was peppered with white and black. Azar saw delight in Roshan's eyes as he frolicked and gambled. He saw delight in Sarah's eyes as she tried to brush him, his head bobbing up and down, snorting out hot air towards Sarah as if coaxing her to play.

"Azar. How good to see you. Have you come to assist me? That would be most timely, for see how my children exhaust me." So spoke Sarah, short in stature yet towering with a robust vitality, her hair clipped back, her face round and ruddy and emboldened with freckles, her amber-coloured eyes keen and clear. She brushed off some sawdust from her frock. "What brings you here to my second home? Would you like your mane combed, perhaps?"

Is there no end to her boldness? thought Yitshak, inwardly rejoicing at his wife's earthy nature and childlike abandon. Sarah, so untethered by foolish, manmade law.

"Azar needs our help. I shall leave him to explain his predicament to you. I will be back soon."

No sooner had her husband exited the stables than Sarah turned to Azar, smiling broadly.

"That husband of mine. I do wish he had given me some warning of your coming. I think Yitshak sometimes forgets I remain a proud woman. What a sight I must be, my hair full of dust and stems between my teeth. Even the horse handler would rather be perfumed with flowers than the scent of manure."

She stroked Roshan who whinnied and went racing out, looking to see if Sarah was behind him in chase.

"I am with these brethren so often I think I have taken on something of their nature. I sometimes find myself whinnying to no-one. Maybe one day I will wake to find my feet and hands turned to hooves. Yet, in truth, I would be proud to be as one with these magnificent creatures."

"I understand, Sarah."

"I know it. I have never seen such kinship between man and horse as there is between you and Jamil. And Jamil has told me what a kind master you make."

"I think sometimes it is not me who is the master, but Jamil who holds the reins."

"Perhaps. Jamil has also told me he has chosen to stay with Rebekah. We had a very informative conversation, we two."

Her raised eyebrows caused Azar to laugh.

"That fiend has given away all of my secrets. I shall have to petition Harpocrates to place a spell of silence upon you."

"I think that would greatly please Yitshak. But whilst I still have my tongue, let us decide which horse would best suit you. I think I know just the one. Come, Azar, let us go and see Malka."

They walked a little further through the herd of horses until Malka came into view. Her coat had a lustrous chestnut sheen with a cream-coloured streak along her back. Her ears pricked up to see Sarah coming.

"No horse will serve you with more devotion than Malka. She is swift to learn and has a gentle nature. And of all the horses of the herd, Malka is the most enduring and would be the last to give up. Such a brave heart has my Malka. Would you like to go with Azar, Malka?"

"Mother," a shrill voice suddenly called out from outside the stables. "Who has come to visit us?" In rushed Zakiya, her eyes wide open, her tongue tingling with questions.

"I was just introducing Azar to Malka. But your timing is impeccable. Please, Zakiya, entertain our guest whilst I go and clean myself up and make us some refreshments."

"Yes, mother." Zakiya always loved it when unexpected guests came to her home. But none were more eagerly welcomed than the magi from the mountain.

"Well, well, well. Look who we have here," said Azar with a diamond-bright smile. "Good day, little poppy."

How much she had changed since his first arrival in Elnazar. How she had grown. She now carried herself with an assurance far exceeding her years.

"Oh," she said in feigned alarm, "it is the ghost of Asnavant."

"Zakiya. Please, a little more respect." So spoke Sarah, betrayed by the hint of a playful smile, for well she knew Zakiya loved to bask in the good master's presence. With him, she felt another 'her' deep inside her, a 'her' that was no longer a child. How good it felt to be with Azar. She ran to him and gave him her biggest hug.

"I never really thought you were a hungry ghost."

"Nor did I take you to be one, either." He patted his belly. "And you can see for yourself I am not hungry. Mother Deborah has made sure of that. Now, before your mother leaves us, I have a gift for her."

"A gift?" said Zakiya. "What is it?"

"A gift for me?" said Sarah.

He brought out a golden horseshoe etched with symbols.

"It is beautiful, Azar. But what need have I for one horseshoe? I have no one-legged horse in my stable!"

"Indeed. Indeed. It is just as well this is not the purpose for which it was fashioned. I have made you this charm for the door of your stables, that it might invite health and vitality for all your brethren."

"Thank you, Azar. I shall ask Yitshak to hang it without delay."

With this, Sarah left the stables to attend to her duties. Zakiya looked at Azar with thoughtful eyes.

"Is it true you are leaving?"

"Yes, it is true, Zakiya. It is now time for me to return to Asnavant."

This was not what she wanted to hear. This was not what she wanted to happen.

"But I do not want you to leave." Her mouth started to tremble. Azar's heart sank to see her so, as it always did to see even the slightest trace of anguish in a young one's heart.

"Come, sit by my side for a moment, my young friend. Sit with me so my body may store the memory of your touch and remember you always."

She snuggled up to him. He smelt nice as he had always smelt nice. He smelt like the trees. He smelt like fire and earth, the sea and sky. He smelt of myrrh and frankincense. Of mystery.

"Are we not sometimes called to do things that we would rather not do, yet do, we must?"

"Like cleaning the stables?"

"Yes, like cleaning the stables. And I have been summoned to return home."

"But this is your home."

"Yes, you are correct. I am blessed to call two places my home."

"Then stay at this one."

"Oh, Zakiya. And what of my Zara? She waits for her husband to return. And what of my tribe? They are waiting for their fire priest to once more tend the altar. What would you have me do, my young friend?"

He looked at her with questioning, probing eyes. How strange this man, she thought to herself. What other adult had asked her opinions on such weighty matters? Only Azar. Perhaps she could sway his decision and persuade him to stay. But as she thought of Zara and Azar's distant family, she knew well she could not.

"You must go home."

"Thank you for your considered reply, my lily of the valley, for your word has released me."

Could it really be so, that she, Zakiya, held within her the power to release a magi from the mountain?

"Maybe you are mistaken. Maybe I am not a lily but a little frog?"

Azar laughed at her unexpected turn of words.

"Why do you say so?"

"Well, when I was little, I used to wonder if you could turn me into a frog. A frog who would be the brightest green frog there ever was."

"Would you still like me to?"

"Maybe. I would like to know what it feels like to hop like a frog and to catch flies with my tongue."

"Yes. Me too. But sadly, it is not my craft to turn girls into amphibians. Or anyone, for that matter. Except for perhaps the occasional despot."

"Then what does a magi do? What is the work of a magician?"

"How strange it should be you, young girl, who would ask me that question. Seven times blessed are our children, for they shall see the face of God. What is the craft of the magi, you ask? Why, what else than to transform their own hearts from dust to gold, and then, maybe, help others do the same. But this craft is not needed by you, my Zakiya, for your heart is already as big and as gold as any I have known. Maybe it is you who are the magician, and me who should be asking the questions of you."

"Maybe I am. And if I am, I order you to tell me who you really are."

"What can you possibly mean, my child?" he asked in genuine surprise.

"I think you are really a king in disguise. A king who has come to Elnazar on a secret mission. Sometimes I have even wanted to do this." Her hands reached out to his beard and methodically tugged it. But though she had thought it might, it did not come off in her hands.

"I was so sure that you were wearing a disguise," she said, almost a little disappointed to find out he was not.

"Why, because of my beard?"

"No, it is not the beard that is the disguise."

"Then maybe my clothes or my turban or my dark skin? Maybe I have coated myself in resin from the vine?"

"No, it is not your clothes or your skin. It is something else I cannot work out."

"I am no king, Zakiya. I am Azar, the fire priest. A servant of the Shekinah. Nothing more and nothing less. But are we not all a little in disguise? What of you? I wonder if you see the face of a shining princess beneath the disguise of a young girl? I do. And I know this girl shall one day be a queen."

"Me? A queen? I do not think so."

As she spoke, Azar felt a tingling in the palm of his hand. He clenched his hands together and blew upon them, holding them together as if forming a shell. He moved his hands closer to her, challenging her to try and prise them apart.

"Show me, show me what is in your hands."

"Maybe if you can open my hands, you will find a gift." She tried and tried and tried some more, but still she could not open them. She stopped for a moment.

"Hmmmmmmmm…" she exclaimed, considering her dilemma. She suddenly leapt upon Azar like a wild cat and tickled his belly, forcing him to yield his grasp as he roared with laughter. From his hands fell to the ground the largest of poppies, its bright red petals moist and wet with dew, and shining at its centre, a many-spoked and golden star.

"The poppy queen. *The poppy queen*. You have come back to me. You have returned. It is a miracle. A miracle just for me. Thank you. Thank you."

She placed the biggest kiss upon his cheek and began racing to the door, screaming joyfully all the way. As he returned, Yitshak heard the uproar, only to see Zakiya come flying past him like a shooting star.

"See you later, father. I am off to see my friends."

"Yitshak," said Azar. "My oh my, your daughter is a rare poppy indeed. She is as wise as a rose and just as wild."

"Tell me, Azar, what has happened? Why is she so happy? I feared she would be overcome with grief to say goodbye to you."

"Your daughter is an ocean with great depths within her. Only she had eyes to see through my disguise: that I was a hungry ghost seeking the bread of salvation. She will accomplish great things, Yitshak. Very great things."

"I thank you for your words." Yitshak grabbed Azar and gave him a fierce hug.

"If my arms still function, I have brought you a gift."

Azar reached beneath his tunic and pulled out a sword.

"So, fire priest, you have come to my home with murder on your mind."

"Make ready to meet your maker," bellowed Azar, before roaring with laughter. "To think there was a time I truly feared I would feel the wrath of the butcher's blade."

"You were right to hold such fear though it shames me to say so. Can you ever forgive me for harbouring such vile and unjust feelings towards you, my brother?"

"Forgiveness? Wherefore forgiveness? Have no regrets, Yitshak. Even love must sometimes be a sharp-edged sword. Why else should it be that even the highest angels bear such weapons in their hand? Why do they each wield a fiery sword? No, my own, harbour no such regrets. You are as Michael, a great prince who protects the children of your tribe."

The look in the butcher's eyes said that which his tongue could not find the words for, a look that told of how he would die in battle to protect this brother. All this, the magi saw clearly.

"I must caution you though, for this sword I am gifting you is no ordinary sword."

"It is certainly a beautiful piece of craftsmanship," said Yitshak, first feeling its handle and taking measure of its hold, then running his fingers down its sharp, gleaming blade. "Your work, I would wager?"

"Of course. It is the labour of my heart. For the sake of the butcher has this bear laboured long through the night. Come now, Yitshak, feel its tip. You will find none sharper, I promise you."

Yitshak touched it lightly with his finger. A tiny speck of blood was drawn.

"It is known to our people as a dragon sword. It is a sword that holds within its form, both the spirit of the lightning and the spirit of love. I was once given such a sword by the priestess of our tribe. The daughter of Saenna, the Dragon Lady. She gave it to me to protect my family. And you must know, mighty warrior, the dragon sword is forged to wage battles of the soul."

"Battles of the soul? Then surely you should give it to the rabbi? What do I know of the soul? If you want meat for your table, then come to Yitshak. Should a transgressor of our laws need to be chased away or even slain, then come to Yitshak, whether it be man or beast. No, I am sorry but I cannot accept this gift. Ishmael is the rightful bearer of such a sword."

"Does not our rabbi already bear all the weapons he needs? Please, Yitshak, hold it in your hand, if only for me. Please, for you only has it been conceived."

Yitshak did as Azar asked him. He felt its form nestling upon his hands, sending tingles that danced across his skin.

And though he was not a man of visions, to his utmost surprise and for the briefest of moments, he saw an image of a lamb, nuzzling into the mane of a mighty lion. He struggled to regain a semblance of composure.

"Look," said Azar, "does it not fit perfectly into your hand?"

"Its grip is comfortable, I will grant you that."

"Then hold it, our guardian. Hold it, my brother, with the same passion you protect your wife and daughter. Hold it with the same spirit you watch over all of the children of Elnazar. But know this first, the secret of the dragon sword is to hold it not as if it belongs to you, but as if you belong to it. Hold it thus, always in the service of love and light. And if you do so as I surely know you will, this dragon sword will help you draw down fire from heaven, in service of your people and all that is holy."

Unfamiliar feelings moved in Yitshak's heart. Dim recollections of a life once lived. Sometime other. Somewhere else. His heart felt like molten steel refashioned upon the blacksmith's forge. And so too felt the dragon sword, rejoicing to be reunited with the hand of the watchman.

Hungry Ghosts

"Good day, Jared, do I find you well?"

The pale face of the fisherman glowered in the dim light behind the partially opened door. He growled like an animal, a growl which changed first into mutters, then into sharp, dagger-like words.

"What business brings you here, fire priest?"

"Is Heshel home?"

"He is not."

"Do you know where I might find him?"

"I am not his keeper."

"Then perhaps you could tell me when you expect him home?"

"Who are you to so question me at my own door? We are not in the forest or your workshop now. You are not master here. I already have told you he is not at home. I have matters to attend to. Good day to you, Baal-Azar."

He sounded out the title with sneering contempt.

"Azar, is that you?" the voice of Heshel. "Father, why did you not tell me Azar is here?"

"I thought you were out," he snapped, "not just hiding

from me in your room. Well, it seems you two have found each other. I shall leave you together. I am sure you have important things to discuss and you would not wish me to intrude upon such private matters."

Jared retreated, devoured by the darkness.

"I would invite you in, but as you can see, my father does not welcome guests."

"I understand."

"Let us go to the forest, Azar. I would like to breathe in its fresh air, away from the malady afflicting this house. The atmosphere here oppresses me. The darkness snuffs out my joy. He will not even sanction the burning of candles at night. He says their flickering light disturbs his peace."

"I am sorry, Heshel. I did not realise the extent of how troubled your father has become. Yes, let us go without delay."

They walked together, mostly in silence, until they came before Rafaella's bench.

"I must confess to you, Heshel, it pains me to have become a wedge between a father and his son. I see I have caused great offence to Jared. I have unwittingly stoked up the anger that burns inside him. I will try my utmost to make this right."

"Please do not admonish yourself. You have not come between my father and me. You are not the cause of the distance that has grown between us. The wound has been festering a long time now, ever since the day of my mother's departure. Perhaps even earlier? I cannot say for sure. Your light has only exposed what was already there. And believe me when I say my father needs no help in stoking his anger. You are not to blame for him being barely able to look upon me. Every day he accuses me. He says he sees too much of my mother in me, that the sight of me is like a curse to him."

"It is wrong for a father to speak to his son so."

"Even if he did not speak, I would still see the shame he feels for me. It is written in his eyes. Yet when you look at me, Azar, it is not so. I wish… I wish you would stay with us. Who will I turn to without you?"

Heshel's head hung down. He let out the deepest sigh, his life force leaking.

"As God is my witness, I have tried so hard to make him proud of me. Yet he will only be satisfied if I become a rabbi. Nothing else will satisfy him. But though I have tried my utmost to pursue the path meted out for me, I cannot stifle the call of the forest. I hear it calling me day and night. I feel its fire burning in my blood."

The forest. The forest. How this Heshel loved the forest. Yet how Jared hated the forest and all that was of it.

"Beware the treacherous forest, my only son," Jared would counsel. "Beware of its enchantments. It is infested with demons. Demons so powerful and cunning, that by their craft they once deceived even the wisest of kings. And if Solomon was so deceived, what chance shall the son of a simple fisherman have to resist their call? The same call that caused your mother to betray me. Like you, she spent too much time in the forest. Please, Heshel, I beg you, do not follow her path and become demon-led."

"She was not led by demons. The forest was her home. It was where she came from. Grandfather Yitshak told me the story of how she came to Elnazar."

"Yitshak? Do you choose to believe an unschooled butcher over the word of your father? Lies. Fairy tales. Sweet deceits. He has filled your head with fantasies of what lies in the forest. He speaks like those Davids, filling the children's heads with stories. Trees that talk, angels that sing, golden gateways to heaven in hidden groves. Nonsense.

Blasphemies. Only madness lies that way. Why give heed to these wanderers? They do not even earn their own keep but instead foist themselves upon the gullible who come to feed and clothe them. No, in the dark forest you will find only death and decay and deceiving spirits. The same spirits who call you to the carpenter's path. The spirits who took your mother away from her husband and child."

"You are lying. She was not led astray. I love my mother far more than you."

"Of course you do. She cosseted you. She sheltered you from the realities of life with her fairy tales. All her soft words have only made you weak and ill-prepared for a man's true work. Do not forget that for all her kindness, it was she who abandoned you. But I am still here, labouring to take care of you every day. It is I who remains loyal to you. Is it wrong that I should expect some loyalty in return? No, your mother is not worthy of such blind devotion."

"Please do not say such things, Father. Can you not see you are hurting me?"

"I cannot spare you the pain of the truth."

"Why can you not show me kindness as she did? She loved me just as I am. She did not wish me to be something I am not. She saw I loved to carve wood and sought to nurture my passion. She saw it is only my own true nature."

"Do not be so foolish. You are too young to know what your true nature is. Do you think yourself to be wiser than the rabbi? Such arrogance is the work of the spirits of the forest. They turn your head away from the path God has appointed."

Jared looked at his son with a fleeting, pleading expression.

"Oh, Heshel, can you not see all your talent will be wasted? It pains me to see you wasting your time amongst the trees. Please, listen to me, we have no need of another carpenter. We already have Ebenezar. And believe me when I tell you, your skill falls far short of his mark. Yet Ishmael says you have the mark of a teacher. Should we ignore the word of the rabbi?"

He took Heshel's hands in his.

"How proud it would make me to be the father of a teacher. Perhaps even the rabbi? I, Jared, who am nothing but a fisherman whose name will soon be forgotten. Whose life has amounted to nothing. God alone knows how I have already been shamed by my wife before the eyes of the whole village. But you, my only son, will return honour to my name and respect to our table."

But now, sitting with Azar in the fresh, crisp air at the side of the forest, Heshel felt the full weight of his accumulated grief. He had failed to bring honour to his father's house. He had failed him. This young man whose heart yearned only to be a true and faithful son.

"Does my father speak truly? Have I been deceived by demons? Have I become fairy-led? Is everything I have come to believe, everything I think and feel, nothing more than a sweet deceit?"

"How can I give you answer, Heshel? If I did so, your father might argue I am only further advancing their purpose with you. He already believes me to be in the service of demons. No, I shall not try and persuade you of anything. I will leave persuasion to others who are less sure in their faith. I will leave it to your own heart to decide what is true or otherwise."

"My father is wrong. It is *he* who has become possessed." He stood up and called out in fury as if wanting all the forest to hear his declaration. "How dare he tell me my mother served demons. If my father says this to me just one more time, if he spits out just one more venomous word, I will beat him to the ground."

"Be careful of such anger, my friend. It is not violence that will be a salve to these wounds. Violence will not bring healing nor restore peace to your hearth."

"Forgive me, master."

"There is no need, my apprentice. I am no stranger to such feelings. But an idea came to me in my prayers, an idea I have thought to pursue. As such, I have made your father a parting gift. I wish to try and reach out to him one final time."

"What gift, master?"

"A fishing rod. A rod that will help him attain an even more abundant catch. One that has been fashioned from the wood of the peaceful olive, whose sap flows with the blessed spirit of reconciliation."

"But he will never accept this gift from you, Azar! He does not have eyes to recognise the treasure you are offering him."

Azar placed his hand upon Heshel's shoulder.

"I know, Heshel. I know. But though I am most probably naïve, I still harbour some hope. I will leave it for him anyway. Who knows for sure what the outcome might be. I can only pray there might be an end to this animosity, that he will be restored to being a kind and understanding father. Will you please try and offer it to him on my behalf?"

"I will try. But I fear it will end badly."

"We shall see. Now, please come and collect it. And I shall then spend this night alone in prayer."

"Very well, Baal-Azar."

So Heshel did as asked and brought the rod to his father.

"How dare you bring such an abomination into my home!" Jared howled out in unabated fury. "A gift? He thinks to make me... *a gift*? Can you not see he is mocking me? I shall show you exactly what I think of it."

With a face so contorted with rage that Heshel barely recognised him, Jared snapped the rod upon his knee, whilst all the while staring intently into Heshel's eyes, as if it were his own son he was breaking in two.

"There. It is done. The spell of the demon is now surely broken."

Out of the house stormed Jared, not stopping until he had reached the shore of the lake. There, he hurled the broken parts of the rod as far as he could, watching with grim satisfaction the splash of the water, seeing it swallowed up forever in the lake's deep waters, never, ever, to taunt him again, nor cause him vexation. But though the ripples of the lake soon were calmed, far travelled the waves of Jared's malign intent.

That night there came a sudden and destructive storm. Was it the ripples on the lake that gave rise to the fearsome winds? Was it the waters that gave birth to the vast and monstrously dark clouds, brought into being by a fisherman's fury? Who can say for sure? But as evening fell, the wind grew rapidly in strength and fury. No escape was to be found from the sound of its howling, ripping against roofs and roaring across the treetops, a shrill whistling through every hole, gap and crack. No refuge from the bangs and thuds, the cracking and creaking. The lake churned and frothed in agitation, a wounded animal, pierced by this poisoned arrow hurled into its depths. A rabid wolf with foam upon its lips. The caterwauling, unquiet dead took flight upon the ill wind, desperately seeking to claim possession of all they had lost. Children hid beneath their sheets, quaking with foreboding, trying not to listen to the sound of straining timbers, the weight of ghostly footsteps treading across their bedroom floor. Unseen fingers, tap, tap, tapping upon the windows. Legions of spirits desirous of entry. Demanding admittance. Clamouring. Shrieking.

Amidst the cacophony, Azar sat beside his fireplace in contemplation. *Bang, bang.* The sound of the wind? Surely no visitor would be so foolish as to have set out in the face of such a storm? He went to the door. To his surprise, he found the rabbi waiting.

"Good evening, Azar," he bellowed amidst the roaring gales, the rain fast streaming down his face, one hand holding down his hat. "I hope my coming at this late hour has not disturbed you?"

"Of course not, dear friend. Come in. Come in. You are always welcome. Come in and warm yourself by the fire."

Ishmael smiled. It was a strained smile.

"Oi, yoi, yoi, what a night."

"What brings you out into this storm?"

Ishmael sat down by the fire and leaned towards it. The warmth felt good against his drenched and icy skin.

"This is certainly no common storm. Never have I known a storm quite like it. It is the storm of a lifetime. A wild and wounded, dangerous beast."

Azar could not help but notice the rabbi had not travelled by horse, nor had he brought a torch to light his way.

"How did you get here? Surely you have not walked?"

Ishmael looked slightly puzzled. He knew no-one had brought him here by horseback, nor had he walked. Yet it would not come to him by what means he had travelled. Azar had never seen the rabbi so perplexed and lost for words.

"It is strange to say, but I am truly not sure as to how I came to be here. Perhaps this is a sign of impending age. I only know I was praying for you in my study. And when I opened my eyes, I found myself to be at your door. Yet what is beyond the power of the Most Holy One?"

Azar began to wonder if he was now dreaming, lying asleep in the arms of his chair.

"Well," continued Ishmael, "what we can agree on, is here I seem to be."

"Agreed. And I know such nights can unravel the senses. So, let me prepare some tea to refresh us."

"Thank you. But if you permit me to speak so forwardly before your own hearth, I was thinking of something to add a little more fire to our blood. Would you care to share some wine with me? I have been saving this bottle for a special occasion."

In the rabbi's hands, Azar now saw a silver jug filled with red wine. How puzzling Azar had not noticed this before.

"If you would permit me, I would like to offer up a prayer for your journey."

"Thank you, Rabbi. I am in need of your blessings."

The rabbi reached behind his prayer shawl and placed his right hand upon his breast, drawing out something as if from deep within. For a moment, Azar felt a holy terror. He felt sure Ishmael would pluck out his own still-beating heart. But to his great relief, it was not his heart, but rather a worn and ragged book, elegantly bound in gold and leather.

"It seems the Torah and my heart have become as one." Ishmael thumbed quickly through the pages. "Aaaaaahh…" he exclaimed, then closing his eyes and falling into silence. Azar saw the room turn to yellow parchment. He saw shivers pulsating through Ishmael's body, his fingers teasing through the air. So solemn the look upon his face, yet his every feature framed in ecstasy. In his hands, Azar now saw the stoutest of candles.

"May it be as a light to lost souls upon this unholy night."

Gratefully, Azar received the rabbi's gift.

"Good. It is accomplished. Now, my friend, it would be fitting for us to share some wine. But please forgive my oversight, Azar, for it seems I have brought no cups."

"Do not be concerned. I shall soon remedy this lacking."

Azar knew just what to bring. He went to fetch his finest goblets. But when he returned, two golden cups in hand, the rabbi was gone with only the candle remaining. Perhaps he had gone to take some air? Azar looked all around outside but Ishmael was nowhere to be seen. He returned slowly to his chair to take stock of what had happened. *Bang, bang, bang.* The rabbi returned? But it was not the rabbi. At first glance, Azar could see only the night, the darkness, the raging storm. He wiped the stinging rain from his eyes and slowly, as his eyes became accustomed to the murky light, he saw a form and saw a face. A face that burned with unmitigated malice.

"Jared? What brings you here at this late hour? Is all well?"

"Well? *Well?* No, all is not well. All has not been well since the Persian arrived in Elnazar and stole my son."

Even the storm seemed to cower beside his fury.

"Stolen your son? Please calm yourself, Jared. Surely you know it was Heshel's will to become my apprentice. Come in and take shelter. Let us discuss this matter over a glass of wine."

"*Apprentice*? He is not your apprentice. He is your servant. Your slave. He is the victim of your conjuring. Why did I not send you fleeing long ago? Why did I not prevail upon the rabbi to cast you out?" Jared pulled at his fingers and knuckles until they cracked and buckled beneath the force. "But you have deceived everyone, have you not? Heshel. The rabbi. Yitshak. Deborah. Rebekah. Everyone. You have made them all blind to your treachery. But you have not deceived me. No, you have not deceived me."

"Jared, please listen, it was Heshel's god-given passion that sought me out and nothing else. It is your son's desire to be a carpenter. It is the calling of his heart."

"I will not listen to you. I will not admit you. How dare you tell me it is the calling of his heart to bring shame to his father?"

"What shame does Heshel bring to your house? Is not the builder of the temple most blessed? Did not the carpenter fashion the ark that was your people's salvation?"

"You have brought no blessings but only a curse. The same curse that caused me to lose Rafaella."

"Is there anything I can say to you, Jared, to bring an end to this enmity? Please, come in and sit down with me. Let us talk at my table that we may put it right."

"Put it right? *Put it right?* Be silent, demon. You who have turned my son away from the rabbi's path. I shall not place one foot inside the demon's lair. I know all about you, Persian. I know you to be in league with the accursed forest. Was it not enough it should claim my wife? No, the forest sent you as its messenger to plague me once more. And who is more artful than Azar? Who is more cunning? You have succeeded in turning my son against me. You have whispered to him of the carpenter's path. You are close to winning the battle for his soul."

He opened his mouth unnaturally wide, releasing a scream that chilled Azar to the core.

"That forest. I should have burnt it down long ago. It is the devil's playground. They have all been deceived by it.

But not me, sorcerer. Not me. I alone stand against you and your master."

He took one step menacingly forward.

"I curse you, magi. I curse you, demon. I curse the day you set foot in Elnazar. I curse your craft. I curse your breath. I curse your every step upon your journey home. If I had my way, I would nail you right now to one of your precious trees. But no matter, for as God is my witness, I shall take revenge upon you this night."

Azar saw Jared reach for something beneath his coat.

"No, you shall not leave this place as your master wishes you to. You shall not leave to go and steal the souls of other children. No, Jared, the fisherman, shall bar your way. I shall stand here forever if I have to, but you will not pass. You will not leave Elnazar with Heshel's soul."

"You believe this to be a battle for Heshel's soul? I see no word of mine will persuade you otherwise. So, let us decide this matter by other means. Would it not be proper for this to be settled through the rabbi's arbitration? This is a spiritual matter, is it not, and falls under Ishmael's jurisdiction."

"Why speak of Ishmael? He is not here and has no means to be so."

"Are you so sure of the limits of your rabbi's power? Let us call upon him now. We shall light the candle upon my altar, made by his hand and brought here this very night. A light he has fashioned to guide lost souls. Clearly, the rabbi had foreknowledge of our impasse this night. If Heshel's soul is lost as you claim, then who better than the rabbi to give him hope of salvation. What shall be your answer, Jared?"

"You take me to be a fool. Your every word is a lie. Why would you even offer me the possibility of such hope? What gain for you?"

"I must return home and you threaten to bar my way. I see in your eyes that this is a threat you are determined to fulfil. But one of us must yield and I am equally determined. Perhaps these two equal forces will stand at this threshold forever locked in battle. Is that what you wish? Yet the rabbi's judgement would surely bring this matter to a close. And, if you are as certain as you claim, then you shall have your wish, for we both know the rabbi serves only one master."

"You are trying to trick me. You are trying to claim me as well. There is no such candle."

Jared was silent for a moment. He had little doubt of the rabbi's power. No demon was more cunning than the rabbi of Elnazar. Perhaps the rabbi had seen through the wiles of the magi? Perhaps his wish had come true and Ishmael was ready to cast him out? Perhaps Ishmael had always known Azar's true nature and had only been waiting for the right moment to strike? Yes, cunning was the rabbi. No-one more well versed in the Torah. None more familiar with the secret knowledge. Maybe it was true? Maybe he had gifted Azar this candle on this most violent of nights, that he might finally break the hold of the sorcerer's spell. And arrogant and blind is the demon's nature.

"Show me this candle."

"Come in, Jared," said Azar. "You are welcome to examine it."

"Be silent demon. I will not enter your lair. Bring it here."

Azar brought it before Jared.

"More treachery. I will not make contact with anything that has been corrupted by your touch. Raise it up so I may see more proof of your lies."

Azar did as commanded and raised it high. Jared saw it to be etched with the rabbi's mark.

"Enough of all this. My patience has run out. Light it, devil. Light it and let us bring this matter to a close. Light it. *Light it now. I command you, demon!*"

"As you wish."

Azar returned it to his altar and then lit a taper. As he did so, an icy wind reared up, but he shielded it and drew it towards the wick of the candle. It ignited in a flash that illuminated the room. All went still. All went silent. Azar turned to Jared, but Jared was gone. Gone. Departed. Nowhere to be seen.

Endless Echoes

Strands of morning light streaming in through the window. Spring lambs skipping, contentedly bleating, reflective are the spiders in their now stilled webs. All things shining in this calm and clement dawn, cleansed and polished by the hand of the storm. Streams running quickly, close to overflowing. Languorous clouds, no longer racing. Pebbles and rocks blown to rest in new places. Leaves and petals scattered like confetti, bent-back grasses and shattered timbers. The shrill call of birds seeking their young amidst the fallen, tangled nests. Children running, bellowing and laughing, rummaging through fields littered with snapped-off twigs and broken branches, strewn like fallen soldiers upon the battlefield. Harmony and chaos, destruction and renewal. The strong, steady rhythm of hammer striking nail as the builders labour to make repair. How resourceful, we people. How intrepid and cunning, defiantly, wilfully, clinging on to life in the face of this undiscriminating, elemental fury. Flowers in the cliff face. Proud and upright before the occluded face of the gods. Able and willing to steal fire from the heavens.

Azar sat puffing on his pipe, his brow deeply furrowed. Tonight, tonight, the moment now come. The moon now ready to shine in her fullness. The time to depart and to leave it all behind. To cross the river of no return. But what words to say at this final gathering? What words? How to leave and say goodbye, to give utterance to the butterfly shiver of his funeral pyre heart, that it may be a fitting crowning. That a piece of his spirit would forever remain, singing in their hearts like endless echoes.

He stood up slowly, painfully hauling himself out from his chair. Never before had he felt so old and weary, after this that had been his darkest night. He wiped his tired, bloodshot eyes, his body aching as if having suffered a violent beating. Time to seek the aid of the plant people, the rooted ones. To seek the blessings of the medicine tribe. He took out a pouch containing his last few remaining coffee beans. This special tonic, held in reserve for times of battle when his energies were spent. Slowly, with reverence, he poured all of them out, a little waterfall plummeting into the palm of his hand. There they leapt like salmon from the river, dropping into the gaping mouth of his mortar. Falling like Jonah into the belly of the whale. He ground them into finest powder, armed with the weapon of his trusty pestle, then left them to boil in a pot above the fire. Soon he would be sipping this black elixir, strong, thick and black, imbibing the magic of its vigorous warrior spirit.

Knock, knock. Knock, knock. Who knocks upon my door at this early hour? The hand of the rabbi? The spirit of Jared, once more returned? But no, the opening door reveals neither of these. There stands Deborah, Rebekah and Heshel, as if the dawn had turned to human form. As if his soul had returned.

"What a delightful surprise. Good morning, my dears. Good morning. How good to see you all. Come in.

Come in. What brings you here so early, risen with the woodlarks?"

"To make you breakfast, of course," answered Deborah. "See what we have brought you. Come on, Heshel, place this hamper of offerings before the feet of our fire priest. Just a little bit more. That's it. Good. And now, as for you, take a few steps closer. Come here. Come closer. Do not be shy. Take a peep inside our hamper and see the delicious treats we have brought you. Mmmmmmmm… perhaps a few too many, I may concede? Poor Jamil, it must have been such a heavy burden. And for you as well, Heshel. We are fortunate you both have such broad shoulders."

Rebekah giggled, unable to conceal her pride. Heshel winced slightly, still unaccustomed to receiving such heartfelt compliments.

"Forgive me, Heshel. I did not wish to embarrass you. I am afraid you will have to get used to my doting ways."

"I am grateful for your kindness, mother Deborah. It has been too long since I have received such a mother's words."

Deborah felt the sharp stab of mother love, to see such feeling in those earnest eyes.

"Jamil," roared out Azar, rushing over to hug the neck of the excited stallion. He stroked his mane. They touched foreheads together in fondest greeting.

"My, how strong and healthy you look." Jamil bowed and snorted in agreement, then returned to munching on his well-earned apple.

"Come, mother," said Rebekah, "let us not be cruel and keep our great grizzly bear waiting. His nose has smelt honey. That is not the movement of the mountain you can hear. It is his stomach rumbling."

"Indeed, my dear Rebekah. Indeed. And now, just like the rumbling fire mountain, my stomach too must be appeased. Yet are you three not a most unholy trinity to place such temptation at my door? Zara will barely recognise me when I get home. She will rebuke me for my... excesses. But what am I to do? What am I to do?" He raised his arms in supplication. "Me, just a poor hungry blacksmith, unable to resist your wiles."

"Oh, you poor, helpless blacksmith. Yet this poor helpless blacksmith should know we three do not wish you to resist." So spoke Deborah, in motherly firmness.

"Then show me, if you will, the agents of my demise."

"Very well. Here are some eggs from the house of Sarah. Zakiya was very adamant when she insisted we tell you it was she who picked them."

"She has chosen well and generously," said Azar, peering into the basket.

"Here is some milk and cheese Sarah has made."

"I have never tasted finer. Our horse handler is surely a sorceress. What charms does she use to coax the sheep and goats into such blissful content?"

"Here is some meat from Yitshak," she continued, her head bent down in solemn thankfulness. "The finest cuts from the willing sacrifice, as is our custom. The one oxen desirous of assuming human form. And here is some vintage wine made by the rabbi and some choicest apples picked from his garden."

"We shall feast like wolves and kings. Not even Elijah could be offered finer wine, nor even the Eve, a more wholesome apple."

"Then you had better quickly find yourself a fig tree that you may conceal your coming shame." So chirped in Rebekah, laughing in abandonment, on fire with the spirit of play.

"Rebekah, what is this wanton spirit that now burns inside you? When did you come to have such a brazen tongue? Look at you. I am sure your hair never used to contain so much red?"

She turned to Azar, her face bright with laughter, to see those smiles that could calm a cobra. This face like Elijah, the light of her dearest friend. Miss him. Miss him. For a moment her smiles were tempered by a sadness she quickly tried to conceal. Only laughter this morning. Only songs and smiles.

"Do you have time to take breakfast with us? We know you have much to do. Yet we so wish to make this morning special for you. I know we are being a little greedy, but we want to have you all for ourselves, even if it be for just a moment longer."

"My plans are always happy to bend to the will of the baker, the weaver and the carpenter. Yet has this not already been the most wondrous morning? Is this not the most quiet and pleasant dawn? Who could have imagined such grace after this most violent night? And now my morning has been crowned by your love. What soul in the world could be more fortunate than I? As for insufficient time, why, no matter, for do we not have the aid of our most magnificent and magical stallion? We need only ask and Jamil will magic up some more time with his invisible wings."

Jamil stood up high on two legs as if in agreement, punching the air with his hooves as they turned in circles, the earth vibrating with his deeply resonant braying.

"Then it is agreed," said Deborah, laying the tip of a finger discreetly upon the hem of Azar's kaftan. "Come closer and see, for there is more. Here are some delicious nuts and leaves Heshel has foraged in the forest."

"Thank you, my apprentice, for this food and medicine."

"And we two have brought you some cake, some hamantash, filled with dates and apricots and poppy seeds.

Some bread as well. Come smell this freshly baked kubaneh. There, it is done. Our offerings are complete. So, our magi from the faraway mountain, will you admit these fiends into the sanctum of your kitchen so we may prepare you a feast that you shall never forget?"

"Gladly. Gladly. I grant you admittance. But first, I am afraid there is just one thing upon which I must insist."

"Which is?" asked Rebekah.

"I insist you all first sit down and join me in some coffee. You are just in time. How strange that Jamil always seems to arrive at just the right moment! You truly are a most uncommon creature. Look, I have made a fresh brew from my finest beans, haggled for in the market of Estakhr. Beans so fine they are coveted in the courts of queens and kings. Can you smell their delicious aroma?"

"It smells so good," said Rebekah. "But I hope you will not consider me rude and ungrateful if I decline your kind offer," she said smiling wryly. "You know it makes me insufferable. As frantic as a squirrel. It is true, is not, Heshel?"

"It does make you a little… excited."

"Very well," said Azar, "I shall grant you exemption. I shall instead make you some calming tea, just as you like it. And what of you, Deborah and Heshel?"

"Go on, you old tempter. It makes me feel as if I could vanquish a bull, so you had better be careful."

"As always, my dearest baker."

"Heshel?"

"Yes please, master. I will have a little but perhaps a little watered down."

As they sat contentedly together, sipping tea and coffee and savouring some hamantash, basking in the joy of each other's good company, their conversation soon turned to the night of the storm.

"We are very relieved to find you safe and unharmed," said Rebekah. "That was no usual storm. The air was like… the breath of a demon. The wind was surely the flapping of its wings? I have never before felt such a fury."

Fury? Fury? Heshel's thoughts turned to his father.

"Did my father visit you last night, master? He left before the storm broke and has not returned home since." Never had Azar seen such consternation on his apprentice's face. "I have rarely seen him in such a violent mood. I even feared he had left the house with murder on his mind."

Azar felt his blood chill with the creeping realisation that what he had taken to be no more than the substance of a dream, a spectral visitation, had been the corporeal form of the fisherman out abroad in the storm.

"Your father visited me last night. I had taken it to be a vision but your account has informed me otherwise."

"What was his business with you?"

"He wished to express his displeasure with me."

"I am sorry, master. If I had known I would have come to warn you."

"I know, Heshel. I know."

"Did he say where he was going?"

"No. I am afraid he did not."

"I suspect he has gone to be alone," said Deborah. "It pains me to say it but I believe Jared would have preferred to have been anywhere but Elnazar tonight." She looked at Heshel with maternal concern. "I believe it is for the best."

"Maybe," said Heshel. "I only know his rage burns like a fire in the forest. He has become filled with venom and curses. He curses my mother. He curses his fate. He curses Azar and the day I became his apprentice. Of late, he has shouted at me almost every day like a man possessed. 'Shall you attend the gathering of this deceiver and further shame me? Shall you, my son? Have you asked yourself where your allegiance lies? Your loyalty? Is it not I who have fed you, clothed you and given you shelter? Me. Not this Persian. This thief. Are you not born of my flesh? Of my seed? Yet it seems you would rather betray me, me, your very own father.' This is how he rebukes me. This is the rod with which he beats me. But what am I to do? He must surely know in what remains of his heart, I cannot agree to such a request. I cannot."

He broke and fell into sobbing. Yet quick to move was Rebekah. Quick to break his fall, catching him and holding him close. For ever swift and ready are the arms of love.

"I am so sorry, my apprentice. I know my coming has been a bane upon your father's life. I wish it were otherwise but so it is. Nothing could have been further from my intention. Yet to him, I am no more than a demon at his door. But I will be gone soon enough. And with my leaving, I pray his spirit will no longer be vexed."

Though Azar spoke truly, he felt concern for what the fisherman might do. He had seen before what steps such an anguish could lead a man to take.

"But what if he does return tonight? What then? His anger has taken him far beyond the reach of reason."

"He will not come, Heshel," said Rebekah, her words suffused with authority and knowing.

"No," said Deborah. "Rebekah is right. I just know it. I feel it in my womb. Yet though he may be far away, let us four join together in prayer for your father. Let us pray his wounds may find salve and he will return to us wearing smiles upon his face."

So, with hands held firmly together, they did as Deborah asked. As one, they made heartfelt petition. And when they had released their prayer, they sat around the table ready to feast, to bask one final time in the sunshine of each other's good company. Kin with kin and kind with kind. This spirit family, who would share it all. Nothing withheld. No secrets remaining. No walls, no barriers, just one heart remaining. Four mouths drinking. Four mouths eating, talking and singing. Four fast-flowing rivers, four rivers of blood, flowing as one into the Garden of Great Delight. And when the call of duty summoned them to return from this seventh heaven, they did so gladly and made their goodbyes, leaving the magi with his spirits restored, ready to give himself over to final preparation. Time to walk one last time amidst the heights of the holy red mountain. To sit in prayer in the cave of the spirit eagle, that he may be blessed and set on fire. To bathe in the waters where two rivers meet, that he may be still and cleansed and purified. To comb his hair and beard before the mirror, to anoint his skin with finest, purest jasmine oil, to dress himself in full priestly regalia, in robes as purple as the flowers of a Judas tree. Finally, to place on the crown of his bright ruby-red headdress, scattered with stars of emerald jade, all in readiness to offer the tribe of Elnazar his highest honour.

That night, the moon displayed her most radiant face. Bright so bright, her shining blessings. See how she sails all crowned with stars. Mother moon, how you dance and spiral across the sky. How you move in her belly, you who stand before the golden gateway. You who hold the obsidian mirror. Wise one and weaver, joining all things in the magic of your moonlight webs. Let me run with the pack. Let me roam wild with the wolves. May these eyes see further in your glowing luminescence, my ears hear the night eagle give sermon upon the ancient oak. Oh, what joy that these ears should be filled with the sound of your song, the sound of the contented woman singing. To hear this singing, I would give it all. Yes, would give it all.

Down in the valley, with moonlight streaming in through her window, Deborah sat before the mirror in her blue spring dress. She glanced out through the window. There, outside, the stone angel stood watchful and waiting, bathed in this emerald, crystalline light. Her gaze returned to her reflection as if moved and guided by the touch of some hidden hand. Some higher will. She looked at the lines at the sides of her eyes, the furrows upon her brow. Fields of skin revealing the story of her every lived feeling, ploughed by many years of deep contemplation. She saw the creases at the side of her mouth, her many silver strands of hair, the sorrow written upon her skin. Was this the same face her husband had once loved? The same full lips that he once kissed? This face she thought would never know smiles again. But he had come to find her in fevered sleep. What miracle is this, that those smiles should be restored, resurrected like poppies beneath the touch of spring, returned by him, her dearest friend. Miss you. Miss you. Oh, my darling, shall your leaving cause these smiles to fade and wither, my laughter to end? But swift answer came in this merciful moonlight, come in the sound of her daughter singing. So too in the sound of Heshel, the cedars creaking beneath the weight of his tread upon the floor. She let out the deepest of sighs, but not in sorrow. And as she gazed upon her reflection in the mirror, even Deborah could not deny how uncommonly beautiful she looked this night.

As Rebekah ever so carefully slipped on her ruby-red ring, she felt its heat, its magic coursing through her blood. I shall wear you forever upon my thumb, you who shall ever be my second father. Miss you. Miss you. My great grizzly bear. My midnight sun. My king, now come. Heshel adjusted the hem of his long coat and buttoned his collar, overflowing with feeling for this man, this master, who had never, ever neglected him, nor withheld from him the hidden lore. Zakiya, dressed in her crimson-red dress and polished shoes, so sad to know her grandfather would soon be gone. Stay a while longer, my magic mountain. Sarah hummed to herself in utter content, perfumed in a sweet and flowery scent, content in the knowledge Azar would soon be delivered safely home to his wife upon the back of Malka. For what horse more enduring than her magnificent Malka? What horse more noble, kind and true? Ever the heart of a practical woman. Yitshak paced restlessly around, fully garbed in a warrior's array, wearing a necklace strung with the teeth and claws of wolves and bears, his heart pierced by the quick of the dragon sword for the love of this Persian. The rabbi put on the hoshen, the priestly breastplate, adorned with the twelve precious stones of the tribes of Israel, putting on the knowledge of a thousand years, the skin of his ancestors, calling out to the angels that they may give attendance.

And now, all these tributaries came flowing into the ocean, into the circle of the gathering. All now come together, the tribe of Elnazar. The great hall filled to overflowing with so many tables and so many flowers, with delicious smells and rousing music, the shared stories of the elders, the laughter, sport and chatter of the excited children, as busy as squirrels. Sitting at the high table, Azar watched all this. Yet though he smiled, inside he felt anxious and pensive, waiting, waiting to give forth of his final word. A carpenter with no axe, no blade, no tools. A fisherman without a rod. A weaver without threads. A priest without a spark to light the fire. He looked around this forest of expectant faces. Some old and lined, weathered and seasoned. Ready for the departing. Ready for the returning. Some broken and faded, lost and alone in the vale of despair, worn down with sickness, desirous of healing. The wide opened eyes and ears of these children, the golden gates of their hearts opened and ready to receive. How would he live without sight of their faces? If only he could take them all with him in his pocket, the whole of Elnazar placed inside one of those miraculous glass bottles, one of those marvellous miniatures from the White Palace of Marib. As if a genie had placed the world inside a jar.

His eyes now came to settle upon Zakiya. How beautiful her young face, her eyes filled with so many questions, a million and more. If only he could have a million mouths, that he might give answer to her heart's one remaining question. The question that can never be spoken. Zakiya, Zakiya, daughter of the horse handler, daughter of the hunter. Little Zakiya, my granddaughter found. My poppy of the valley, grown so quickly. My lily of the mountain wearing wisdom's crown. Miss you. Miss you. Oh, that I could remain a little while longer, so I may bear witness to your blossoming. Letting out the deepest of sighs, he turned to Deborah, as if moved, as if guided, by some hidden hand. Some higher will. How sweet the salvation smiles of this never to be broken face. To die with such a sight is no death at all. He saw her dressed with his given necklace, the golden light of his Zara. He saw a shaft of light, a little light leaping, kissing him upon the crest of his brow, between his wide-open eyes. A little bright star. A little star shining and desirous of speaking.

"Receive now, my husband. Receive you the story written upon the torn-out page. The story written in tongues of flame. Its moment now come. Its will to be done. Receive now the story of Yuriko, the lily and the covetous king. Receive and tell well, my most beloved."

He felt it swelling inside him until he felt compelled to release it, he now a gulley through which four rivers flowed.

Yuriko, the Lily and the Covetous King

"There once was a young woman whose name was Yuriko, who lived far away in the abode of the rising sun. Though born in a village and of lowly stock, she possessed a most uncommon beauty. Here, in this village, by the side of a river, little Yuriko came to be very much loved by all. To see her coming would always bring bright smiles to their faces. Yet her beauty was born neither from her delicate frame nor from her kind and gentle, radiant face, though in both of these things, her beauty did not lack. Nor was it born from her hair, long and as black as the sky at night, nor from her eyes that shone like obsidian, her skin as white as a swan, as white as snow, nor her every move and gesture, as filled with grace as a flamingo willow. And of this Yuriko, some said she was a creature come to earth from the highest heavens, from the peaks of Mount Fuji. And there were some who thought, though did not say, that she smiled like Amaterasu, the goddess of the sun. But not even Yuriko herself knew the source of her most uncommon beauty."

Azar looked upon all these faces, so dear to him, quietly listening, still and entranced. He saw a hush rippling out like a pebble in a pond, rippling out this way and that way, spreading out throughout the hall, all falling into silence upon hearing his words. And as each one watched him speak, they felt swept up and taken to another place. Each one feeling as if his eyes were looking into their eyes only, alone together upon the mountain top. This man, this fire, with a million eyes.

"Yes, Yuriko's hair was as black as Yitshak's beard, her spirit no less fierce and brave. Like Sarah, she loved all of the animals and knew their tongue. Like you, Zakiya, she overflowed with curiosity and questions. Like you it was her joy to talk to the little flowers. Like Rebekah, she had eyes that saw far into the great beyond. Like Heshel, she heard the word of the ancient forest. Though unschooled, she was no less wise and learned than our blessed rabbi. Like our baker, there was never a more kindly, tender and generous soul. And like all of you, Yuriko had her favourite of places, for she loved to go and sit by the river that flowed past her village. The River of a Thousand Blossoms. Nothing else was more beautiful to her. Yet though this young woman could hear the voice of almost everything, the word of the river, she could not understand. How she longed to speak with it, this river to whom she poured out her heart. And though it did not give answer, she would always ask the very same question.

"'What is the source of my most uncommon beauty of which other people so often speak? I do not understand. When I look in the mirror, I just see a girl. A girl who is no different from any other girl.'

"Though the river remained silent, Yuriko had the feeling the river was listening, absorbing her every word, carrying her question to who knows where. Sometimes she would bathe naked where the warm waters ran shallow, feeling held by this river that had so captured her heart. But her mother had oft warned her not to do so, for other daughters who had swum there had long since been taken, plucked like grapes from the unwilling vine. Grave danger lurked by the banks of these waters. Yuriko listened with her all, as she always did. But though desirous of being obedient to the will of her parents, she was helpless to resist the call of the river. To try to protect her from own inclination, they refrained from teaching her how to swim. But utterly mysterious and beautiful was the river to Yuriko. There, gazing upon its fast-flowing waters of hyacinth blue, she would feel something stirring deep in her heart, a stirring that she yearned to give voice to.

"One darkest of days, a passing warlord rode by the banks of the river, a warlord who held the power to rule over this territory, to hold the balance of life and death in his hand. And as he rode by, he caught sight of Yuriko. As he watched her, hidden behind a stooping willow, he felt himself become on fire with desire.

"'How beautiful is she,' he exclaimed, with thoughts of claiming her all for his own. 'I have never seen a woman as beautiful as her.' But thoughts came to him of the king that he served, a king desirous of being surrounded by the most beautiful of treasures. 'I shall take her and gift her to our mighty king. In doing so, I shall surely find myself well rewarded for discovering such a rare and precious prize.'

"Yes, the warlord would surely be rewarded with prestige and power, with no lack of beautiful women. So, as according to custom, the warlord went to Yuriko's father to ask his consent. Though he felt a pain far worse than death, Yuriko's father knew he could not refuse the warlord's request, for to do so would bring calamity upon his tribe. With the heaviest of hearts, he felt he had no choice but to acquiesce, and his daughter was taken far from her beloved family to live in the emperor's court. Such was the anguish of her father, he died not long after of a broken heart. And such was the anguish of her mother to lose both husband and daughter, that in her frailty she succumbed to a fever. But not all were sad. No, more than pleased was the emperor with his new and most exquisite possession. More than pleased was the emperor with the eye of the warlord. More than pleased was the warlord with his abundant reward.

"To behold the beauty of this Yuriko, the emperor was utterly amazed and thought to take her for his wife. She would become his seventh wife, the highest of all his unwilling brides. The most precious jewel to adorn his crown. But custom dictated that to do so, he must first wait until she came of age, just as the ancient gods had decreed. In truth, this emperor cared little for custom or the will of the gods, yet he was shrewd and heedful of maintaining appearances before his subjects. And though filled with hunger to know her, he satisfied himself with watching her dance, as it was his pleasure to watch all of the women of court dance. And while he waited, he satisfied his desire by feasting upon these many beauties. Yet even this emperor began to scratch his head, perplexed, wondering what was the source of Yuriko's uncommon beauty, a beauty that somehow set her apart. And this covetous king felt a mighty jealousy growing inside in him, burning out of control like a forest fire.

"'Oh, how she dances, she who shall be my future wife.'

"So jealous was this king, he could not bear that other eyes should look upon her. He henceforth decreed that Yuriko should dance for him and him only, dancing only before the glow of dawn's first light, that not even the sun should be permitted to behold her. She would dance for him only, and should any other be known to dare steal a glimpse, their eyes would be plucked out from their sockets. Such was his envy, Yuriko was forbidden to dance before any living thing. Before the trees or the insects, the animals or the birds, the wind, the mountain or the rushing river. Even the gods, if he had been able to hold such a power.

"Precious little time Yuriko now had for herself. And in those few moments, she would steal out in secret to go and sit by the river.

"'How fortunate am I to have this one blessing remaining, that the palace should rest at the side of the river which flows all the way to my home.'

"There were times she thought to send her parents a message in a bottle. But, as born of lowly stock, she knew not how to write. And the river flowed in the wrong direction. To see her sadness, the mighty river wept, its tears taking the form of a thousand lakes. For the river knew it did not have the power to change the course of its flow. Yet still Yuriko's love for the river knew no limit. By the river, and by the river alone, Yuriko felt herself to be free.

"'Oh, mighty river, if only I were a poet, a musician or an artist, that I could sing and play and paint your glory. But I am a dancer. If only, if only, I could dance for you.'

"Over time, though the very brightest of souls, there were days when Yuriko felt so very sad she would have gladly thrown herself into the rushing waters, giving her life over to the will of the river. Yet she could not do so, for she still clung on to the hope she would someday return home to all she loved. That she would be reunited. Perhaps when she became an old and withered lady, the emperor would discard her and she would be released from her cage. The day when her beauty had faded, when the sight of her had become most displeasing.

"Yet the king was covetous of a different day: the day he would claim Yuriko as his prize and token. For he burned to behold her naked form. Night after night, his one thought and desire, to feast, to gorge upon her unveiled beauty. Fire meeting fire, most beautiful desire. To lay his hands upon her. To court and crown her with his sceptre. To have her kneel in obeisance before his bed. To drink of her sweat and to feed on her flesh. To taste the elixir of her vintage wine waters. To hear her scream out his name to the highest heaven. To sip her blood. Intoxicating. To make her his queen. To make her his concubine. To bind her scent in a bottle and so too, her soul. To own and possess her. Forever and always.

"In such dark spirits, the king impatiently waited. Night after night, ever more sullen and brooding, lustful and vengeful, jealous to take her. His and his only, this most precious bounty. This king, this lord, unused to waiting. And the emperor felt an unsurpassed joy, to see the sun finally set on the eve of his wedding. Yet Yuriko felt the greatest sorrow, for to behold the same sunset was to see her life ending. Beneath a robe of twilight, she slipped out of the palace and to the bank of the river.

"'Oh, mighty river, please answer me this one question, as this may well be my last time in your presence. Why do they say I have an uncommon beauty? And why has such a beauty been as a curse to me? Why has it separated me from all I love? All except you, most holy river, and even that must now come to end. Oh, river, how shall I ever return home? I am lost forever.'

"Yet as she watched the dancing sunlight turn into gold, shimmering on the surface of the silent water, she beheld a most wondrous sight. She saw the dancing light turning into words, words she could not understand.

"'This is the book of many things and of no thing,' spoke the river in a voice that was everything. 'This is a book that holds many answers to many questions. What price would you pay to know these things? What price to read the word of the golden sunlight?'

"Though she knew not why, Yuriko gave swift reply.

"'I will dance for you, river, if this should please you?'

"The river was well pleased and delighted in her answer.

"'You would be willing to give me your all? Then read, Yuriko. Read the golden word now written upon my skin.'

"The time was now late and the sun about to set, its golden rays of light all soon to fade. Yet Yuriko still had time to catch the sight of just one letter, one letter that was sufficient to set alight something deep inside her. And as the sunlight fast faded and the moon began to rise, she was amazed to see a beautiful white lily floating towards her. She ran to the riverside, scooping it up before it flowed past in the river's fast-racing waters. Though she had seen many a lily before, this lily somehow seemed to call to her. This lily that possessed a most uncommon beauty.

"'White lily, white lily, drifting upon the skin of the river. White lily, white lily, so alone and beautiful, carried this way and that way by the will of the water. How wondrous are your many snowy white petals, your stigma and stamen like a golden sun. Who shall be so blessed as to smell your fragrance and taste your sweetest of nectars? Who shall hear your silent song?'

"'Come closer, most fair of flowers,' said the lily. 'Listen. Listen. Far have I travelled, afloat on these waters with grace and ease, desiring to know what awaits me at the end of the river. Desiring to find my way home. Yet it is here to your hand the river has delivered me. If you would only release me that I may flow onwards in my journey, then I shall tell you of all you desire to know.'

"'I promise I will release you, most wondrous lily.'

"'You who are true. You who are faithful. Tell me what would you know, you whose eyes sparkle with kindness and wonder. You, who hold me so gently in the palm of your hand, heedful not to break even one of my petals.'

"'Why are you so alone, my lovely lily? Why so far from home, most delicate blossom?'

"'I am alone for the cause I flowered late in the season. And when the moment came for me to awaken, all of the other lilies had gone. So alone was I, I knew not even what manner of thing I was. But a kind brother bullfrog took pity on me. He spoke to me of my kind, for he had known many water lilies before.

""What is wrong with me that I flowered too late? Where shall I find my family, my brother bullfrog?"

"'But the bullfrog did not hold the knowledge of why the lily had flowered so late, nor did he know where to find the other lilies. He only knew that part of the river. With his quick long tongue, he grabbed a passing fly, a fly that whispered to the bullfrog before it came to meet its end, dying in rapture to behold this lily. The knowledge of the fly now flowed in the bullfrog's blood.

""Maybe the river knows?' said the bullfrog, all puffing up. "Go and ask the river and it will surely help you. It has always helped me. It has always fed me. Just as it fed and helped this little fly that now has become a part of me. Go ask the river, lonely lily, and the river will surely help you."

"'So I did just as the bullfrog said. And then, to me, the marvellous river spoke.'

""""What a thing of beauty you are, my lonely flower. What hand was it that made you? What mind conceived thee? Did the angels attend you at the moment of your unfolding? Come and ride upon my back, my lovely lily."

""""Oh, mighty river, where is it your waters flow and end? For I must find my way to the other lilies."

""""I do not know where I end, nor where I begin. I only know I am a waterfall flowing from the peaks of Mount Fuji and my journey is all the way to the endless ocean."

""""Oh, mighty river, can you take me to where the other lilies have gone?"

""""I cannot, little lily, as I do not know. Many are the things I carry upon my surface, but I am too busy singing deep in prayer to notice where these things have come to end."

"Yuriko now held the fragile lily in her hand. She felt the strangest of feelings, had the strangest of thoughts.

"'How like me is this lonely lily. Just like me, so far away from family and home.'

"'Yes, how alike you two are,' said the watchful river. 'How I wish I could take you both home. But though I do not possess this power, I know of one who does, for I am a river who is one of twins.'

"'Where shall we find your twin, holy river?' asked Yuriko and the lily, as if both one.

"'Come closer to me,' said the River of a Thousand Blossoms. 'Come and look upon me.'

"Closer they looked. And as they thus looked, Yuriko and the lily both saw as if through the same eyes, bright beams of moonlight dancing upon the surface of the river, a bridge of a thousand blossoms. A bridge of light. A bridge that led to a milky river, flowing amidst the endless stars.

"'See my twin, the River of Souls. The river that can take you home.'

"'But how shall we sail upon the waters of the River of Souls? It flows so far away and out of reach.'

"'You must first walk upon the surface of a thousand blossoms.'

"The lily listened and reflected deeply. Who knew better than the lily, the ways of the water? She knew it was not fashioned to bear Yuriko's weight, that though she would float, this Yuriko would drown. And even if she had been able to swim, too powerful was the current of the mighty river. *No, this must not be*, thought the lovely lily. But the lily did not know what next to do. In that moment, she heard the now distant call of the bullfrog, a call that summoned a knowing deep inside.

"'I trust the river,' said Yuriko. 'I have faith in its word. Should the price of our journeying onwards be my death, then so it shall be. Come, lily, let us find our way together to the River of Souls.'

"She took off her vestments so that she could dive naked into the water, holding the lily close and gently in hand. But the lily would not let her, this lily who was now shining with the brightest, pearliest light.

"'No, Yuriko, this is not the way. For now, I see. For now, I see. We must become like the bullfrog and the fly, you and me. We two must now become as one. You must become a part of me, and me of you. Together we shall find our way home upon the River of Souls, for I can float and you can fly.'

"'But I do not know how to fly, my lovely lily. Look at my back. I have no wings.'

"'Not so, my dear blossom, you have wings enough. How high soars your kind and gentle heart. How unrivalled your beauty. See, how radiant are my petals for the sight of you.'

"'Then what must we do, most wondrous lily?'

"'Why, you must eat of me, as brother bullfrog ate of the fly.'

"'But I will kill you, I can do no such thing.'

"'Oh no, you are mistaken,' said the lily. 'I shall not die but will instead be delivered into a greater life. For I see now you are my very own and eternal soul. And happy I am. Yes, how happy I am, that this good river has delivered me here to you. Home at last, to my very own self.'

"As the lily thus spoke, Yuriko shuddered, ecstatic, as if flower petals were unfurling in her hidden heart.

"'I understand,' sang Yuriko, in a joy as high as the peaks of Mount Fuji. 'At last. At last, the eyes of my soul have been opened. I see it is you, wondrous lily, who have always been the source of my most uncommon beauty. You, who are the hidden piece of my soul. Let us two be reunited. Let us be as one. Let us two be whole in this sanctity, our last supper together.'

"Without further hesitation, Yuriko ate of the lily. Her taste was sweet upon her tongue, upon her lips. And as she did so eat, one lone petal fell upon the ground. The next morning, on the day of his wedding, the bride of the emperor was nowhere be found.

"'Where is she? *Where is she?*' screamed out in fury, the covetous king. Every servant in the court was sent to find her, but none could do so. Yet only the warlord thought to go and find her by the river. Yes, he would surely find her there. He had often spied upon this Yuriko, though in disobedience to the emperor's word, for still he lusted after the sight of her. He shuddered, ecstatic, to think of the riches the emperor would bestow upon him. Of what would come of his new elevated position. But by the banks of the river, he found only disappointment. There, he found no prospects of further reward. All he found were Yuriko's robes and, by its side, one lone lily petal. Both of these he returned to the emperor, whose jealousy raged to know he would never lay claim to her body. Such was the violence of his anger towards the treacherous lily, he declared from that time onwards, not even one lily would be allowed to grow in the entirety of his kingdom. And such was the extent of jealousy, he vowed to hunt for Yuriko, even beyond the veil of death. He would track her down, and when he finally came to find her, he would bind her soul and claim her for his own, for all of eternity. His envy transformed into a blood-red dragon that flew across the endless ocean of stars, devouring all things straying into its path. But Yuriko and the lily were never to be found, for they could only be found by the way of love. These two twin stars in the highest heaven, forever free to dance for each and every thing. Floating forever upon the waters of the milky river."

Echoing, echoing, his word treading gently down the corridor of their hearts. His word, a river, upon which these many blossoms gladly sailed. The many candles now started to flicker, as if before a coming presence. All turned to see the door drawing slowly open, a sparkling river of moonlight come flooding in. As their transfixed eyes adjusted to the light, they each began to see what seemed to be the form of a woman of most uncommon beauty, dressed in a robe of stars, as fragrant as a lily. And there were some who thought she was the moon and some, a ghost. There were some who thought she was a star come down to earth. Some, a beautiful young maiden, the kindest of girls with the sweetest of smiles. Others, a handsome woman with the bearing of a queen. An old, even ancient woman, her skin as gnarled and knotted as a cedar, with owl-bright eyes, wearing a gown of wisdom. Yet there was one thing upon which they could all agree: that in her right hand, this woman held a golden book. A book that shone with a dazzling light. And when this woman turned to depart, she beckoned for Azar to follow. This woman he would follow. This shepherdess, this priestess, this girl from the other side of the mountain, come in grace to lead him home. As if all one body, the tribe of Elnazar formed a passageway, a stage curtain parting, two lines of cypresses, all leading to the brightest, golden light. Slowly, silently, Azar glided past, his brethren waving palm leaves. A little wind to blow in his sails.

Outside, how bright the multitudes of stars this night. There, the neck of the snake and the falling eagle, the hen, the hare, the hyena and the wolf. The tortoise and the lion, the horse and the goat. There, Errai, the shepherd, come to guide the flock. There, Meissa, the shining one, come to light the way. The little cloud and the milky road. All are singing, the trees and the mountain, the lake and the river, the wolf and the woodlouse, the owl and the larch. And as he mounted upon Malka, the fire priest turned and smiled one final time, before all too quickly fading out of the sight. Who should dare to break this holy silence? One voice only. The voice of Zakiya. The voice of a red poppy standing still in the field, uttering the one question resounding in all of their hearts.

"Will the King of Salem ever return this way again?"

Thrice Blessed

One night as they lay in bed, Rebekah gazed sadly at her husband.

"Heshel, is it still your desire to be a father?"

"You already know my answer, my love. Your desire is my desire."

More than a score of years had passed since Azar's return to Asnavant, years that had brought much happiness to Rebekah and Heshel. The moons of their courting had been to be reborn in flame. Sweet and fragrant, the springtime of their betrothal; their matrimony, a high summer, a glorious crowning, their spirits bound together in oath and pledge. Always and forever, forever and always, their words spoken beneath the branches of the ageless oak. To see such a happiness brought abundant smiles to many faces, smiling to see the blessed eyes of first love. Seeing all and everything in the gaze of the other. Such contented hearts make of a man and a woman, a king and queen.

Yes, happy were these two. Happy to make their abode in the dwelling at the side of the forest, that had once given shelter to their beloved teacher. This high master of magic, separated now by great distance yet who somehow remained. In each beam and rafter, they still saw the trace of his hand. Sitting together before the hearth, they felt his bright and warming spirit. Drawing water from the well, they heard the whispers of his soul. To work in the forge was to enter the sanctum of his heart. Here, inspired, by the side of this clearing, by the side of this mountain, their craft did come to blossom and bloom. And when mother Deborah would come to break bread and wine as she often did, the floors and ceiling still creaked with laughter, just like the times when these four had once laughed together.

Yet as happy as they were, there came too a secret sorrow, born of Rebekah's longing to be with child. Her desire to weave into substance a being of blood and flesh. What craft higher, she would often wonder? What manner of mother would she come to make? But as days passed to months and months to years, the cradle Heshel had fashioned remained empty, as so too did her womb. No infant form wriggling snugly beneath the quilt she had woven. No child to speak of grandmother Deborah, to rest on her lap beneath the branches of the oak, listening entranced to the David's song. And rumour spread as rumour will, that their weaver could not be with child. Many shared her growing sorrow, though they concealed it beneath a veil of silence. How could it be, they asked themselves, the Most Holy One should withhold the fruit of their union? These two whose dance had blessed the crops?

Sometimes in the long and lonely night, when her heart was hurting and her mind perturbed, Rebekah would slip quietly from bed so as not to disturb her husband. Away to the forest she would wend her way, to sleep beneath the moon that her womb may be quickened. But she did not know, for how could she know, his heart would always sense the ache of her absence. Heshel would suddenly awake from the depths of his dreaming, rising from this ocean like a deep-sea diver, desirous of inhaling the oxygen of her love. Yet, instead, he would find only the outline of her form. The bed still warm. Each time he felt a growing sorrow, the sharp sting of grief lodged deep within his heart, until finally came a night when he felt his heart to be breaking. He ran and ran to the forest of cedars. Running to his brethren. overcome with despair.

"Great trees, my ancient kin and kind. Oh, please help this sad and sorry man. If it is in your power, whisper to me that I may know how to make my love with child. What leaves may I use? What bark must I brew? What must I do? Is there anything this simple carpenter can do to bring joy to his bride?"

To him, the ancient forest did speak.

"Come to me, Heshel, thrice blessed son of the healer. Come to we, Heshel, beloved spouse of the weaver. You who are of we, forever and always. Son and brother. King and kind. Come make your bed here. Come sleep, come rest upon the blissful pillow. Weave you new dreams here. Together. Conjoined. Threaded, entwined, and woven in wedding. The dance of the snake at the eye of the oak. In the forge of Vulcan, let your twin souls be tempered. Refashioned. Reformed. As bright as lightning. As quick as steel. Know the fire of the quickening. May the two be as one, that the one may become three. Tonight. Tonight, this very moment. This night of the Passover. This night set apart. Walk heart in heart through the second gateway."

That night they did know each other like the Adam and the Eve. The mountain had rumbled and so too the sky. Strange visions dreamt by many a child: of an elephant sitting upon a golden throne, singing of the coming of the

Blue Star Spirit. And though some had seen rainbows and some heard a symphony, and though some had smelt the most fragrant of perfumes, only Zakiya had seen Heshel return from the glade. His steps had been brisk and filled with purpose, his face shining like Moses descending from Sinai. Of this, Zakiya told Sarah, who in turn told Yitshak, until rumour spread of what had befallen the carpenter. But there was one thing of which they could all be certain: that with each passing day they felt a growing gladness, to see Rebekah's cheeks flushed with fire, her belly swelling like the hills of Jerusalem.

One late winter's morning, there came a sudden snowstorm. Rebekah lay in bed, her husband, her mother, her midwife beside her.

"Please, can you open the window?" she asked as her mother mopped her brow, as her husband sat stroking the palm of her hand. The rhythms in her body told her the moment had arrived, the ninth moon maiden having come and gone. Heshel went to the window, pulling it slightly ajar. In rushed a cold wind, eager to discover what magic was unfolding. Rebekah sighed to feel it cool her burning blood. She leant to see the snowfall outside, her heart leaping for the sound of their children at play. How strange this joy amidst these waves of pain. She thought of days still yet to come, when the voice of her son would join this merry clamour. Soon now. Soon now. Soon to be holding her babe in her arms, her body braced and ready to give of suckle.

Martha the midwife returned to her side, carrying a pan of newly-boiled water. How reassuring to see her calm yet focused expression, the face of this deliverer, who had given safe passage to many a soul. She watched Martha pour some water into a cup and with it, some oil, filling the room with the odour of eucalyptus, a hint of frankincense and cedar.

Rebekah felt it clearing her lungs, helping her to breathe with greater ease.

"You are doing so well, Rebekah," said Martha. "Have no fear for your child will soon be with us. Gird your limbs for the final push, my dear." Always in her thoughts, the voice of Martha's constant good counsel. "Be as strong yet as subtle as sister willow, who bends in the gale yet never breaks." With such devotion had Martha watched over this daughter of Elnazar. How knowingly she had tended her in both body and soul. Soothing drinks made of many herbs, some bitter, some sweet, all made by the midwife for this mother to be. All manner and kinds of delicious soups, feeding her body that it might be strong and enduring, steadfast yet yielding. So too did Martha feed Rebekah's soul with many a story of many a heroine. Like a second mother, Martha watched over her, ensuring she be restored by calm and rest. This high master of the most ancient craft, teaching Rebekah the mysteries of the breath, just as Rafaella had once done before her.

Humble Martha. Humble enough to embellish her craft with wisdom received from the mouth of a child. A girl from the forest, bringing with her the medicine of the wind and the willow. How fortunate was the weaver to have Martha here at her side. This Martha, who had been as a mother to many. A mother, and more. She had only been seven years of age when it had happened. The night Martha had made her never to be broken pledge, as her mother cried out in the thrall of labour. Terrible to hear her mother's torment. Terrible the anguish etched into her father's face. Those screams of agony on the other side of the door. If only she could have brought an end to her mother's pain. If only she had known what to do. And even worse than her mother's cries, the sound of the silence that followed. Only nothingness, only absence, where should have been the cries of a newborn babe.

"Oh no. Oh no. Where is the baby? What has happened? Please, Most Holy One, may it come soon. No sound? Where is it? Why can I not hear it? Why is it so quiet? Why no cries?"

Unable to contain herself any longer, Martha had done as she had been forbidden to. She had opened the door, filled with fright as to what vision might await her. There, she saw her mother's grief-stricken face as she clutched a small, lifeless form in her arms. Silent, silent, silent screams. A million daggers thrust deep inside her. A mother's face, twisted in torment. Broken, desolate, struck down and alone. Her eyes frozen, unseeing. For though no mortal would dare prise this baby from this mother's unyielding grasp, she had been helpless to stop death from claiming her baby's soul. By her side stood her husband, his head and body hanging limply. Helpless. Despairing.

"Why have you taken him from me?" Martha's mother suddenly screamed, shattering the guilty silence. "*Why?*"

A boy? A brother? So had thought Martha.

That night, when her mother had fallen into sorrowful sleep, as her father gazed vacantly into the fire's fading embers, Martha walked trance-like into the sanctuary of the synagogue. Why she had gone there she was not sure, having been compelled by some inner calling. There upon the altar, as if waiting only for her, the still, dancing light of the eternal candle.

"Come to me," the candle seemed to say. "Come to me, my broken-hearted child. Come to me and I will listen."

There she had howled like a wounded animal and uttered words she did not yet comprehend.

"Help me please, you mighty angel. Help me, Lord Raphael. Help me and I will give my life over to you. I will. I promise. Help me, that I may spare the mothers from this torment."

This young heart spoke truly. But if Raphael heard, he did not say. Yet though she heard no reply, young Martha felt deep within her a most formidable resolve. She would devote her life to this mission, even if to do so meant going against the perceived word of God. In such a darkness, Martha the midwife had been born. And in the days far ahead, she would come to deliver many a child, conceived not in pain but in ease and joy. Yet despite all this, she sensed there was still something lacking in her craft. A lacking she was unable to fathom. Once more she went before the eternal flame, praying as she had once prayed when still but a child.

"Please help me, Lord Raphael. Please grant me your blessings and crown my craft."

But if Raphael heard, he did not say. Until one day amidst her fiftieth year, came Rafaella. It had been in the last days of autumn. All around, this autumn grace. Fallen leaves stacked up high and bright as fire. Autumn grace, see her walk all dressed in russet robes, a glorious glowing before the coming winter chill. And it was in the frosty gloom at the edge of the wolf pit, the hunters first found her. A barefoot waif dressed only in a thin, russet robe, even though the day had been fiercely cold. Her knee-length hair, as red as fire. Keen and spirited, her emerald-green eyes.

"Come here, child. We will not hurt you."

She appeared fearful and shivering, walking forlornly towards them. Yitshak gently draped his coat around her shoulders.

"What is your name, child?"

The girl looked puzzled.

"I do not know. I cannot remember."

"Where have you come from? Where are your parents?"

"I do not know."

"How did you find your way here?"

"I cannot remember. I only recall I was wandering through the forest."

She looked sadly down to her feet, her bright, wild eyes filled with regret.

"I was warned not to stray from the forest. Not to enter the open fields where the Fierce Folk live. But I could not help myself. I thought I heard the sound of wedding bells. They sounded so beautiful. I had to find from whence they had come." She burst into tears. "Are you the Fierce Folk? Are you going to kill me and eat my bones?"

The child saw the look of horror in the stranger's eyes.

"We shall not harm you in any way, my child. Please, hold no fear. We will look after you until we have fathomed how to return you home. I promise you. If I lie, then may the Most Holy One strike me down. Kill you? Why, there would be no refuge to be found from Yitshak's vengeance, should but one hair be harmed on our children's heads. But look. The sky is fast darkening. You must come with us now. Please will you do so? We cannot leave you here, our daughter, all alone and in jeopardy."

The girl looked upon this mighty man, his hair and beard as black as the ravens she knew so well. His eyes held honesty and kindness. Perhaps he was the Raven King, of whom she had heard in the ancient stories? The king who made his castle and his keep in the far distant regions of the wild, wild woods. The Raven King, forever flying between the world of the Fair Kind and the world of the Fierce Folk.

"I will go with you."

Yitshak, with all of a hunter's finely-honed instinct, knew just the people into whose care to place this child. So he rode with her to the house of Martha and Obadiah, the midwife and the shoemaker, who gladly accepted this wild girl as their charge. Just as Yitshak had known they would.

"You are fortunate, my child," said Martha, looking at her bare feet. "My husband happens to be the finest shoemaker in Elnazar. A fine pair of shoes he will fashion for you."

Martha looked intently at the girl.

"Yitshak tells me you have forgotten your name. I can only surmise that you have suffered an almighty shock. But we must call you something. I shall name you, Rafaella, if you will permit me to do so. For surely the mighty archangel has sent you here to Elnazar, in answer to my hidden prayer."

Yitshak was true to his word. But though he laboured over many seasons and searched down many hidden paths, his many years of seeking had not brought him to finding Rafaella's home. Nor had she found herself able to remember. Yet though living with the sorrow of being so far from her kind, Rafaella found happiness with Martha and Obadiah. There, before their hearth, she flourished and prospered. Rafaella, this girl from the forest, who danced and flew in the wind and the woods, her face and hair as bright as a midwinter fire. Her eyes as green as the leaves of a sycamore. Yes, a wild girl was she, a wild child was Rafaella, wild and tender, and no child kinder. A most trusty shepherd to all of the animals, a cup of good cheer to all the children. A light to the living, a light to the dying. Wild Rafaella, wild, untamed and filled with ancient knowing. Kind and fierce, true, loyal and fair. Her smile, a light, a wind from the south, a fragrant spring shower. Rafaella, running with the wolves and singing to stars, she who danced to a different law and different drum, speaking in the tongue of angels. Mad yet none wiser, strange, uncanny, yet none more familiar. Her wide-open eyes seeing as if into another world, as deep as a lake and as wide as a sky. To hear her sing lulled babes in arms to contented sleep, filled the warriors' hearts with fire and passion. Her voice, the melody of a butterfly's wings in flight.

In her school, in her temple, amidst the dark forest depths, to the near-daily wonder of Martha, she unveiled a knowledge most uncommon for one yet so tender in years. Uncommon, even to one aged and ripened by many passing seasons. Wild Rafaella, no wiser teacher, the soul of the vine, both young and ancient. Of the burning blood and the passionate rose, teaching how to see with the eyes of the heart, to listen with skin, to make her mind as the web of the spider, that it may catch many and varied a thing. To touch all things with the wind of breath. From her, Martha learned of many medicines. She taught her to know the spirits of the trees and the spirits of the flowers, even the spirits of the grains and grasses. The spirit of the waterfall and well. She learned where to find these medicines, the proper spirit in which to harvest them, how to prepare and store them and how to finally dispense them. How to make infusions of leaves and flowers, decoctions from roots and bark and twigs. How to make salves and tinctures, how to burn together cedar, juniper and pine needles that malignant spirits may be chased away. She learned how to make oils from wormwood, lavender and jasmine, to rub into an expectant mother's belly and back in the last days before labour. She learned how to make resin from the gum of the galbanum, that a mother may be relieved from pain. Of bark from the willow to ease aching bones and soothe a fever, of placing hawthorn leaves in the cradle to afford the newborn protection. How to make a talisman of pine cones and acorns, that a woman may feel the fertile earth upon her breasts.

"What is the source of your knowledge?" Martha asked her one day. By now, Rafaella had come to remember much more, though still she did not remember her name, her home, nor where lived her kind.

"Our knowledge comes from the trees and the grass. It flows from the burbling brook and the whispering winds, the sermon of the birds upon their pulpit perches. In the stories of the insects and the songs of the fish. But even more than all this, it is taught to us by a holy lady, sometimes unexpectedly met. A woman who carries a book that is bound with leaves and bark, whose pages are spiders' webs upon which are written the secrets of nature's hidden lore."

"Who is this woman?" asked Martha with all the fierceness of a mother wolf, fearing this unknown woman might cause her daughter harm. "Where does she come from?"

"Why, she comes from the forest, of course. As for her name, she has too many to tell. There are some who know her as the Scarlet Lady. There are some who know her as the Emerald Queen. There are some who call her the Lady of the Forest. Some call her the Lady of the Birds. Others know her as the Guardian of the Well, Grandmother Who Stands at the Crossroads. She is mother to the Children of the Hill. The teacher of the Dancers Upon the Mound. But though she has many names, she has one name only. Oh, how I long to reside once more in the keep of her good company."

"Your words alarm me, Rafaella. There are spirits that inhabit the forest whose art is to lure the young ones into their realm. You must be wary now. How can you be sure this knowledge does not come from the rebellious one, that to heed this word is to bring misfortune upon us? Should you not tell the rabbi of these secrets the forest is whispering to you, that he may give of his rule and guidance?"

But even as she spoke, Martha could feel another truth whispering in her heart. Her eyes found swift reply, looking deep into Rafaella's eyes of green fire. She felt chastened by beauty. She felt graced by quietude. She felt her heart bow down as her daughter answered.

"Oh, my mother, you know there is little that escapes the scrutiny of Rabbi's far-seeing eyes. Yet there are some matters that must ever remain a woman's work. A woman's art and a woman's wisdom, known by her and her alone. A knowledge found written in the many mansions of her blessed body. And can it ever truly be transgression, to seek to ease another's pain? No, this can never be. How alike, we two. Have we not both sought guidance from beyond, to give increase and blessings to our craft and vocation? Only you, in the synagogue, and me, in the forest. As for deception, let our souls be at peace, for the heart of the true healer resides far beyond the wiles of the rebellious one. But this, you already know, Martha the midwife. And I understand you have no will to rebuke me, but only to protect me. You harbour only a good mother's intent. So I thank you. I thank you for your vigilance. I thank you for watching over me, as you have watched over me for all the days of my youth. Thank you, my second mother. Thank you, Martha, the thrice blessed."

In the dwelling, now deep in snow, Martha looked carefully upon her charge. This beautiful woman, all glistening with sweat. Her daughter too, for so spoke her heart. She blew upon Rebekah's brow, a cool, soothing wind from the north. The blessing of the grandmothers. She stroked her cheeks and pushed back the hair from her forehead, placing a soft kiss upon Rebekah's crown.

"Soon now. Soon now," sang Martha. As she did so, she glanced over at Heshel and, for a moment, gasped. She felt fire leap inside her. For in his face, she now saw hers. Her face, so missed. Her face, so loved. Rafaella, alive, present, ever-living and unchanging. With tingling fingers, ablaze with inspiration, the midwife stroked unguents upon Rebekah's swollen belly, singing a song the cypress had taught her. More cooling balm she rubbed upon Rebekah's burning brow until finally arrived the moment of becoming. Daubed in crimson, eyes shut fast, his mother's hands the first felt touch upon his head. Warm lips, warm wet kisses upon his cheeks, now safely delivered into the ark of his mother's embrace. His world permeated with the glory of her scent. Once more, the familiar sound of her fast-beating heart. How crisp and clear, the sound of her voice, crying and laughing, speaking, whispering, tender words of welcome. For him. For him, and him only. Only her voice in all the known universe, beckoning him to open mortal eyes for the very first time. She gasped to see those emerald-green eyes, overflowing with amniotic knowing. She gasped to feel the wonder of his smile. For her. For her only. He felt this little wind inside him, filling up his lungs, wailing with the wonder, the wonder of it all.

"This one is given to love," said Martha, though she knew not why.

Outside, the snow had stopped falling and the clouds departed, revealing a moon veiled in a sheen of blue. A rare blue. A royal blue. Occasionally, rarely, when such a blue moon hung across the vast open plains, there would also come, the wildest wind. A searching wind, a restless wind, a wind that would wind through the streets and houses of Elnazar, as if somehow seeking to touch the people that the homestead harboured. As playful as a child, as wily as a weasel. It would race across the fields and rivers to rattle upon the windows of the dreaming children, raking up the hearth fires into a whirl of burning stars, to delight and hearten the villagers gathered all around. A wild wind, carrying upon its back the song of the wolves, the rustling, longing song of the cypress trees, the echoing emptiness of the cradling mountains. Its touch was strong, cool and mischievous, born of the northerly direction. And it was said that any child touched by this wind, would have a little of the wild ever blowing deep within the landscape of their heart. This wind would whisper of nature's hidden things. This wind would carry the call of the wild and of the open road. Claimed to ever be a son or a daughter of the wild, wild wind. Such a wind, Rebekah and Heshel, Martha and Deborah, now all heard.

"Yeshua," spoke the voice of the wind. "Yeshua, Yeshua."

"Thus we must name him," said Heshel. "How true speaks the wind, for his coming has already brought salvation upon its wings."

A Bruised Reed

Early one late spring morning, as Heshel chopped wood and Rebekah gathered herbs, Yeshua let out a sudden cry. Cosy beneath his quilt in contented sleep, a fleeting vision had crept into his dreaming. An unfamiliar presence. A hollow-eyed face with parchment skin, peering into his crib, staring deeply into his eyes as if searching for something. Grimacing and leering, reaching inside him with cold, probing fingers. He felt a shock, a sudden, icy chill. To hear him, the ravens fled the treetops in alarm. The ewes and rams bleated in agitation, chattering to each other in seeming counsel. Yet by the time Rebekah returned, all had been restored to serenity. There, her babe's small form dreaming, safe, warm and still. Stepping forward ever so quietly, her feet unclad, she hovered over him like a dove on the wing. Such feelings she felt. Such feelings. Smiles dancing unbidden upon her lips. Ah, this love, this light, this fathomless well. A belly full of rainbows. An endless ocean. Gently she stroked his softest of cheeks. She knew she should not do so, but she was helpless to resist. Nor could she help but place a kiss upon his brow, or refrain from teasing her finger through one lock of his hair. Such a love would surely bruise the Most Holy One's heart.

But what is this? Peering closer, as the keen eye of a mother is ever wont to do, she saw at his side what seemed to be a large pile of wool. Why had she not seen it before? How strange. She could not remember leaving it there. She surely would not do so? He might place it in his mouth and choke upon it. She looked closer and saw it was not a pile of wool at all, but rather a small spring lamb fast asleep at his side, the two snuggled closely together, Yeshua's hand at rest across its snowy white pelt. Both lamb and baby appeared to smile. Rebekah was astonished to behold such an unexpected sight. How had this little lamb come to be there? Her thoughts turned to the perennial mischief of her own good carpenter.

"Oh, my husband. What a rascal you are to play such a trick on me."

She ran to the forge and summoned Heshel to come immediately and see the uncanny scene, alert all the while to each passing expression on her husband's face. This face she knew so well. This face which would reveal to her its every innermost secret with the utmost ease. In a moment, the puzzle would be solved, the sport of her good husband delightfully exposed. They would soon be laughing together, as they often would. To the scene of the crime she led him like a guilty child, concealing her giggles beneath a mask of alarm. Yet when Heshel stood before his sleeping son, she did not see his pursed lips reluctantly tremble with laughter, nor his bushy eyebrows dance up and down as was his way. Written on his face, she saw only surprise. She saw him struggling to find the words.

"Oh, my Rebekah. This can only be a sign. Come, my love, let us depart. Let we two not break the spell of these holy tidings. Let us leave our two spring lambs to their happy dreams."

Yes, happy dreams and holy tidings. Spells and signs and little miracles. In none of these things was this homestead lacking. In and out of his cradle, Yeshua was as happy as a lamb. In this fertile soil, he grew strong and vital. How he would gurgle with pleasure to see his mother's smiles. To see her beautiful eyes, silent and joyful, for the sight of him only. Those eyes that are everywhere. Those eyes that are everything. Ecstatic was his skin to be cradled in her arms. So too, his heart, to hear the lovely lilt of her turtle dove cooing. Ecstatic, his belly, to feast from her bountiful body. Oh, mother, my mother, sweet mother of mine. Was your name first proclaimed at the birth of all things? A high mountain summit are you. A chalice, a fountain, twin pillars of stone. A lioness, mighty and flaming, vigilantly guarding. A gateway. A garden, through which four rivers flow. An Eden. A paradise, to which I would gladly return. Your body, a temple, wherein I would give of my worship. Your breasts, a well of plenty, where I may drink of your soul's deepest waters. Where I may tread as merry as a pilgrim upon the hills of Jerusalem. Mother, Shekinah, master alchemist are you, creating milk that is manna from your chemical cauldron. A sacred grove that is hidden in the dark forest depths. Your belly, a sanctum. Your heart, a high altar.

To feel such a voluminous ecstasy in so tiny a form, this new mother's heart felt naked and helpless. Naked and helpless, yet never more willing to be so. Cease the folly of your tongue, to proclaim any passion higher, nor any temple more holy. This one mother, feeling as if she were the first mother of all. Ablaze like a seraphim, to feel his tiny fingers firmly gripping her own, his warm head nuzzling into the nape of her neck. The intoxicating fragrance of the flesh of her flesh, feeling unknown places being touched inside her. And when he would wail, she would just rock him gently in the rhythms of a mother's love and knowing. Fear nothing, little lamb, for your mother is here. Safe rest in my arms that so long to hold you, and I will soothe your every tear.

Like a grape upon the vine, this newborn grew. Like a wind, like a river, strange powers ebbed and flowed through his burgeoning form. His cries a little louder, his grasp, a little stronger. So many diverse urges that were yet only one. This inner knowing of blood, bone and marrow, coursing through him, compelling him to arise and take his first faltering steps. How wondrous to stand upright. How tall he felt. How proud to see his mother, crying out loudly and clapping her hands.

"Heshel. Heshel. Come quickly. Come quickly."

The sound of his father's footsteps, thud, thud, thudding as they raced upon the ground, vibrating through the floorboards and into Yeshua's body. The door bursting open to reveal his father's form. The look of surprise written across his face.

"Why, little man, just you look at you. You will soon be standing as tall as an elm. You will be running as quick as the river. How shall I ever catch you?"

How wonderful, Yeshua. How wonderful to see your parents' smiling faces. Smiling for you. Mother sun and father moon. Mother sun, her light radiant and mellow. Warm and wonderful, ever close at hand. Father moon, dark and mysterious as the call of the night, sometimes distant, straying far from the pack. Sometimes hidden, yet always vigilant. Beneath the love of these two, he grew plump, well and strong. Standing turned to walking, then walking to running, begetting days of adventure in the forest and fields. Sometimes soaring, sometimes falling. New wonders waiting around every corner. Curiosity calling like the pipes of Pan. Riddles to solve and games to play. Days of riding high aloft his father's broad shoulders, bouncing up and down, thrown so high he could touch the sky.

"One day I will climb that tree to the very top and then I will see where the bees are going and what they are doing. I will see what the crow sees and from where the wild wind comes."

What joy to hear the sharp wit of the telling crow, the trill of the black-headed bunting, the song and burble of the melodious robin. The cracking of twigs, the whispers of the brush, the tremulous sound of buzzing bees. Intoxicating odours and bouquets of scents, of grasses, of cedars and pine, of oak, cypress and acacia. Brambles and nettles, cones and leaves, mud and puddles, wildflowers and vines, all there for him to play with. Peeping out from the shade and from every corner, rabbits and deer, foxes and weasels, as if the forest had a million eyes. All the forest, Yeshua's playmate. Boulders to climb upon and small stones to throw. Hear them splash. Hear them crash. See the great chunks and piles of warm earth, sometimes teeming, filled with worms. He would scoop up the earth to mould and sculpt, attentive of removing every inconvenienced worm, returning them home as close as he could find.

"Sorry little worm if I have caused you fear. Sorry I have taken you away from your path." So spoke Yeshua, in unuttered words. How gently this son treads upon the earth.

One warm and windless afternoon, Yeshua made ready to make sport of his father. How could he do otherwise, for he was a son of the wild wind? Carefully, thoughtfully, he hatched his plan.

"I will make myself a robe from this mud and those leaves and branches. And then I will conceal myself from my father's sight."

Cunningly camouflaged, he lay in wait for the carpenter, excited and giggling. He pictured his father's shocked face when he would jump out to reveal his hidden presence. His body tingled with anticipation to hear the silence, his father breaking from his labour, no longer chopping upon the rows of wood. His father would soon be coming to check on him. He would feel the weight of his heavy tread vibrating upon the ground, hurrying towards him. Yeshua peeped through the little spy hole he had made, trying to restrain his laughter so as not to reveal his location. He glimpsed Heshel looking all around, realising his son was not where he had left him. He was just about to call out his son's name when he heard an unexpected sound.

"Tawit, tawoo. Tawit, tawoo."

The carpenter was startled to hear such a cry at this hour. Why was an owl singing in the brightness of the day? His face was a mixture of surprise and fierceness. Yeshua watched his eyes darting in all directions, intense, alert, yet filled with bewilderment.

Ha, ha, ha, rippled quietly in Yeshua's belly.

He thought to further confound his father. What a sweet delight. He reached out for a pine cone lying close at hand. He reached out and grabbed it. Heshel saw something moving in the corner of his eye. But when he looked around… nothing. Yeshua waited and waited, ready to take aim. Timing was everything, the key to this art. Ready. Ready. Yeshua knew, at last, the moment had come. Now. *Now*. He hurled the cone with all his might. But the cone did not fly as far as hoped for. Instead, after arcing all too briefly, it slowed down and descended, tap, tap, tapping upon his father's thigh. Heshel turned quickly to see where the cone had come from. No tree above him. No birds in the sky. No squirrels in the branches. What hidden hand had touched him? What power Yeshua felt, veiled behind his cloak of invisibility. He, and he only, the puppet master. And just like the marionettes his father would carve for him, he watched the carpenter dance as he tugged upon imperceptible strings.

"*Tawit tawoo!*" hooted Yeshua, as loud as he could.

Heshel swivelled around, losing his balance as he did so, tumbling into a pile of thick mud, but not before spying small fingers peeping out from amidst the stack of leaves.

"Yeshua?"

He is coming. He is coming. Quick, time to throw off this camouflage and run. Run for your life for the monster is coming. No longer to be as invisible as the wind, but as swift as the wind. Off he ran, as fast as he was able, his father pursuing close behind. Heshel saw his son's face beaming with unbridled delight. Barely could he suppress his laughter. Quickly, quickly, past the trees and across the clearing, all the way to the open meadow. Running, running, his heart beating fast as he struggled to gain speed in his heavy work boots. Running and running beneath the vast open skies. But Heshel would not catch him too quickly. No, he would wait for just the right moment. Yeshua heard the thuds of his father's boots close behind him. Soon, too, his hot breath on the back of his neck. He felt hands grab hold of his waist and scoop him up.

"Got you, little squirrel!"

He squealed with joy to feel his father's embrace, before being put down on the grass. Trying to catch their breath, they lay on their backs and gazed up to the sky. In the distance, even the holy mountain seemed to laugh, the clouds tickling the pate of the old red thunder man. *What manner of miracle is this?* thought Heshel, the door of his heart burst wide open. Ha, ha, ha. He, he, he. Laughing is the wind and so too the forest. Happy is the butterfly at rest upon the leaf. Happy is the stone in the freshly flowing stream. Happy the ant upon the high mountain. Happy the air and the still hidden stars. All laughing, all smiling. All is right with the world. All is as it should be. To die in such laughter is no death at all. No death at all.

Yet as happy as these three were, their carefree days were cut short by the seeds of concern, a day when Rebekah caught words not meant for her hearing. Words not born of cruel intention but from unknowing conjecture, spoken by a few too many careless tongues. How strange, said the villagers, that though now nearly three years of age, Yeshua had not yet spoken one understandable word? What sickness was this that had befallen little Yeshua? What manner of spirit had stolen his tongue? Why was he not like the other children? Why did he look upon the world with those strange, far away eyes? What trade, what craft would he follow? What fate would befall him? What food would he be able to bring to the table? Gradually they named him, Yeshua, the speechless one, though never in earshot of Rebekah or Heshel. And it was said by the villagers, his tongue had been sealed for reasons known only to the Most Holy One.

But they did not know, for how could they know, that this was no malady, no infirmity, no lacking at all. For all this while, Yeshua was listening and speaking. Listening to the sound, the song, of every thing. Listening with his fingertips and toes, with his hair, his skin, his blood and bones, his eyes and his ears, his taste and touch. He heard the choir of angels singing and the blackbird's stories. He saw the knowing worms wriggling upon their way. He smelt the fragrance of the rose, the sweat trickling down the farmer's back as they tilled the field, the smell of his grandmother's freshly baked bread. The scent of death hovering around the dying and the yet still living, as they walked towards the golden gateway. He heard the sound of stones smoothed by streams, of the ringing wood fashioned by his father's axe. Of the soft wool upon the back of a sweet spring lamb. He heard the wise, whispered words of the cold north wind, the mutterings of the mountains, the musings of the lake. He heard the unspoken thoughts of those all around, thoughts that roamed like a shepherdless flock. He felt their feelings upon his skin and within his marrow. No, they did not know, for how could they know that which not even the rabbi knew, that the speechless one had been talking and singing to them for all this time, speaking amidst this ocean of loud unknowing. Why were they silent? Why did they not make reply? So had Yeshua often wondered in words that were not words. How could it be that only his mother and father could hear him? Maybe he was invisible, as invisible as the wind. And, in the crack between the worlds, the pale shadow moved.

The Pale Shadow

He watched the small mouse as it scampered around, darting this way and that way, until abruptly stopping as if having sensed something. Its body became taut, then stiff with alertness. It raised itself on hind legs and peered all around, gazing intensely through pinprick eyes, brushing its whiskers with its fast-moving paws. Though Yeshua had made himself become silent and utterly without motion, he wondered if the mouse had noticed his invisible presence. Eeep… eeep… *eeeeep*. Aah… *aaaaaaaahhh… heh*. A sharp movement above, amidst the high and now glowering branches, ending his musings and snapping the spell, startling both mouse and boy. As if one, their heads turned together, tilting backwards and looking upwards. There, in the shadows, both caught sight of a watchful falcon. Glimmering, gleaming, watching, waiting. Its eyes were fierce, its gaze was focused, the touch of its look was ice and steel. Black burning coals upon a yellow lake. Yeshua had never seen such a bird before. Powerful and proud, a smouldering, crackling fire, no larger than the size of a crow. Before he could inspect further, without even the slightest warning, with no proceeding flap of its wings or shuffle upon its thick, twisted claws, it rapidly descended, diving downwards with its wings tucked in, swooping, hurtling with a terrifying speed, blurring into nothingness, then sweeping the frozen mouse up in its talons. As swift as a stone from the sling of David, so swift that the mouse had no time to feel fear. But this was no clemency, for all too soon the mouse awoke into agony, its nostrils filled with the scent of blood, its eyes filled with a vision of the grasses moving quickly away. High, high into the air, the mouse was lifted. High, high into the air where a mouse should not be. Yeshua felt the fear of the mouse. He felt his body pierced as if by spears. For a moment, the mouse struggled with all its might, trying to escape the falcon's grasp and to cling to life. But all too soon, it knew the bird was far too powerful. To fight it, futile. So instead, in instinct, it gave itself over to death. A sudden death and free from pain. Yet the falcon held a different intent. It would not permit the mouse to die so quickly. It would savour its sport.

It began to paw and pick and play, turning its fierce gaze straight at Yeshua, grinning and salivating, its dark, piercing eyes devoid of all that is known to be mercy. It played with the mouse as if the mouse were Yeshua. A falcon, until for a moment, it was no falcon at all. No longer a falcon, but instead, a shadow, twisting snake-like through the grasses. A shadow that seemed to assume the form of a man, who wore a bright yellow tunic flecked with brown, a jet-black cape draped over his shoulders. How Yeshua knew it was a man he was not sure, yet he knew for sure, that a man it was. A man who was cruel, swift and filled with guile. Man stared at boy, satisfied he had gained the child's undivided attention, before flickering and shifting, transforming himself once more into a bird. A falcon, holding the ravaged yet still moving body. Once more it flapped its mighty wings, flying to land on the earth in front of Yeshua, hitting the ground with a powerful thud, causing the ground itself to move and shake. The boldness in its face revealed it held no fear. There, standing before Yeshua as if before a high altar, with a mocking expression and a grim satisfaction, it spat out the mouse, the air corrupted by the scent of blood made bad and bitter.

"Poor child," spoke the falcon. "Poor, poor boy, what brings you here, all alone with the wolves and the ravens? How frightened you must surely be."

Though afraid, the boy yet found his tongue.

"I am not scared. I like to come here. I like to come to the forest to learn and play."

The falcon stared with questioning eyes, a wry smile seeping through its crooked mouth.

"Oh, we two shall indeed play and learn. In this desire, you shall be satisfied. Yet your words alarm me. Not afraid of the dark forest, you say? Not afraid to find yourself face to face before the forest's most able hunter? Hearken unto me. Do you not hear how the forest is silenced to witness my descent? Do you not feel this stillness upon your skin? How uncommonly brave you must be, dear child. Uncommonly brave. Such bravery I would gladly give employment to. Yet as brave as you seem to be, are you not also, just maybe, a little lacking in discernment? Are you certain that I shall not peck your flesh and taste your blood? That my sharpest of talons will not carve words upon your skin?"

Yeshua had never known of a bird attacking a villager, yet he could feel in his marrow that this bird was not as other birds. The falcon continued, assessing Yeshua all the while in meticulous detail.

"To play and to learn. To learn and play. Can it truly be that your mother has let the forest become your playground?

Say it is not so. But if so it is, though it be a bane unto me, it is my duty to warn you, as I am sworn to watch over all the children who enter my domain. Be heedful you do not become the sport of something other, for there are many who make the dark forest their home. Many inhabitants. Many beings. Many mansions in the depths of this dark forest. Yet I can only surmise you have been born under a fortuitous star, for fate has been most merciful to deliver you unto me."

"Who am I that you should warn me? Why would you do so? You gave the poor mouse no such warning."

"How bold and bright your words, not spoken in mortal tongue. Why, I cannot help but wonder, are you not given to speak as your kindred speak? Are their ways insufficient for you? Is their tongue, perhaps, a little too brutish? Oh, but how easily I am distracted by other such tasty morsels. Why warn you, you inquire? I have taken a liking to you. Nothing more. But consider this, if you will. Perhaps it is your good fortune that our two paths have crossed, for you may find me to be a constant friend to the bold and adventurous. And, if you so desire it, the most wondrous games we two shall play. Have you not already borne witness to the passion I hold for my sport?"

The falcon hopped and danced around in the fashion of a priest making ritual.

"Yes, I speak truly, there is much you could learn from the master of the hunt, if only you be ready and willing to listen. Have you the wisdom to do so, I wonder?"

Yeshua fell silent, uncertain how to make reply.

"So quiet? But tell me now, child, did your parents not teach you politeness?"

"Why do you say so?"

"I have introduced myself. But you have not yet reciprocated in kind. Come now, child, where lies your respect? Where lies your honour for all things? Perhaps these virtues have abandoned you today? Heh, heh, heh."

"Please forgive my rudeness."

"I do so without question. You will find me most forgiving. So, now tell me, what name do you hold? What is your name and where have you come from?"

"My name is Yeshua and I have come from Elnazar."

"Yeshua? Yeshua? Such a grand name. Maybe, Yeshua, you have come here today to save not the mouse, but me." The falcon cackled and crackled. "But tell me, Yeshua, why are you alone here? Has your mother abandoned you?"

"She would never abandon me."

"Indeed. Indeed. I am most glad to hear it. So unlike your grandmother. A fine, devoted mother you must have. Yet 'never' is a long path winding around many unfamiliar corners. Who can determine with full confidence, what shall be deemed to be 'never'?"

Yeshua had never heard anything speak as the falcon spoke. Its word was dizzying as if uttered from the highest of heights.

"Oh, but just listen to me talking. I cannot help myself. You loosen my tongue. Your presence has stirred within me many thoughts and feelings. Some even that are unworthy. Thoughts I pray you may help me dispel."

"What thoughts and feelings?"

"Evil thoughts. Thoughts I feel ashamed to give voice to. Shall you be my confessor? I would accept you as such. Yes, I shall gladly stand beneath your judgement and throw myself upon your mercy. By way of beginning, I confess that I have given admittance to the notion that your mother has been… oh, how shall I put it… has been perhaps a little too… complacent? That she has been found wanting in sound judgement and, in doing so, has put your safety in jeopardy.

Why else would she permit you to play in the dark forest? Surely she must know it is unsafe for one as young as you? No place for youthful innocence to be left alone and unguarded? Alone with me. Can you be sure I am not strong enough to sweep you away? Are you confident that this is not my hidden will? And, if not me, perhaps a passing wolf or bear?"

The falcon volleyed out a sharp cry, turning quickly around as if to check who or what may be stood watching and listening, a worried, guilty expression flashing across its face.

"Such thoughts. Such thoughts. We two must be careful. An ill wind blows through the forest this day. It blasts the trees with the blight of its infernal mutterings. Do you not feel it? I see that you do. All the more reason for me to watch over you. And should I watch over you, you shall not be alone. There are many children, Yeshua, who have found shelter in me and have sought my protection. Yes, they have come to me for I give abode to the lost, to the lonely and the abandoned ones. I provide food for their bellies and make fire for their bones. As for their minds and their souls, that mystery must await the revelation of another day. But though you are neither lost nor abandoned, for you I shall make an exception. You need only ask and you shall gain admittance to our tribe. For, in truth, are you not a little lonely? A little lost and adrift amongst your kind? The best of good company, you could keep with we."

Yeshua felt gripped by its talons, finding it harder to breathe.

"If you are as watchful and seeing as you claim to be, then why do you not know it was my father who brought me here today?"

"Alleluia, the child has truly found his tongue. Do I detect the scent of accusation upon your breath? Poor me, that has been so deceived. Ah, these words, these sweet deceptions. What wiles may lurk beneath these words. I see that you are both clever and cunning. In this, you and me, we are a little alike. But consider this, Yeshua. Pause for a moment, if you will. Think clearly, like a hunter, my accuser and judge. Speak truly now. Did I ever say your mother brought you here? No, I did not, but rather spoke only of abandonment. And many are the ways and means of abandonment. Maybe, just maybe, your mother abandoned you to your father's care on a day when she knew that he had pressing duties to perform?"

The falcon peered at Yeshua with undisguised contempt.

"As for your father, I see he has a quenchless passion. A passion that burns endlessly for his precious trees. A passion for his craft. A passion that seems, and you must forgive me for saying so, to burn even brighter than his love for you."

The falcon saw shock arising in Yeshua's eyes. Its pupils contracted. Its feathers danced with glee.

"Be wary of such a passion, Yeshua, for such a passion may burn brightly yet can also consume. Who is there worthy to bear the fire of this holy sword? But again, I am flying far ahead of the matter at hand, am I not? I cannot help it, for 'tis my nature. As such I have been fashioned by the holy hand. For swift and mercurial is the mind of the falcon, the mind of a hunter, always attentive to finding its next prey. No, I must stop and offer up to you my most sincere apology. How could I have given admittance to such a disingenuous thought? I must again fall beneath your mercy and plead for forgiveness. It must have been the ill wind that whispered, for surely no father holds a deeper love for his offspring than Heshel for Yeshua. Oh, to be blessed with such a father. Yet, if we are to speak in the spirit of truth, as good friends are wont to do, I cannot help but observe that the spirit of betrayal runs deep in your blood. Have mercy on the falcon, both blessed and cursed with the gift of far-seeing. The falcon who knows well the fruit does not fall far from the tree. As for passion, perhaps you should be as wary of this passion as you should be wary of the ways of the dark forest. Such a passion can be every bit as merciless as you take me to be. Such a passion shall not easily brook two masters."

The falcon rocked this way and that way, from side to side and up and down. A steady, measured rocking. Tick tick tock. Tick tick tock. Drip, drip, drip. Drip, drip, drop. Dancing. Pulsating. Mesmerising.

"How well I remember another such passionate father. A father most hallowed to your tribe. A man whose love for his God, for his Lord and Master, far exceeded the scope of any other man." To hear the falcon's advocacy, Yeshua felt a creeping chill, as if he had sipped from a vial of poison. "Yes, I remember when he delivered his first son to the high mountain altar. His precious son. I see you wonder how I should come to remember? Heh, heh, heh. Why, because the master of the hunt was there. A very old bird I must be. But many are the wonders of the forest of Elnazar. And with this holy father, the master of the hunt was well pleased. Such delightful reminiscence. Still, the past is as nothing, for what matters is the now. And such indulgences are not befitting the prince of the forest. Such indulgences shall not keep me fit and lean, nor ready to perform the blessed kill. What matter anyway, whether an insignificant speck such as me should be pleased or otherwise? Of no more import is my pleasure than the pleasure of this small, helpless mouse. Poor mouse. How short its days. What purpose served in its few fleeting moments, spent scampering around for nuts and fruits and twigs?"

"It was content to do so."

"Content? Content? What matter content? What virtue in this content when all may not share in this luxury? Is the ant content to be crushed beneath your heel? The apple to fall from the tree? Content the enemies of your tribe to feel the violence of your father's swords? No, such content is a deceiver. Is the ram not content before the bloody slaughter? So too, the heifer? Content in the fashion that this mouse was content? Precious little protection did this content afford. But be away with such trifles. Let us not be concerned with matters of such little consequence. We have more important things to discuss than the fate of a mouse."

The falcon fell silent, peering with even greater intensity.

"Ah, Yeshua, I see my ways cause you offence. But let me pose you a question. Does not my content hold equal measure? Clearly, it does not. You cannot hide that which is written all over your face. You think my sport cruel, do you not? Consider this though, if you dare, that it is you who plays the part of the unjust and discriminating judge."

Yeshua did not wish to hear its voice any more. His only desire was to run away, but he could not. No more than the mouse was able to.

"Hear my words, young walking one. Hear me loud and hear me clearly. Consider that which I have come to draw to your attention. Perhaps it is you who is errant for being so quick to cast judgement upon me? Let us see. Let us look at this matter with a keen eye not deceived by the glamours of sentiment. If you take me to be cruel, then is it me alone who is cruel? Is not the spider also cruel as it holds the fly captive within its web? Is the snake not cruel when it paralyses with poison, or holds its prey in its vice-like grip? So too the sting of a scorpion or the ravenous lion as it hunts down the deer? What creature more cruel than a cat?

And what of the lack of mercy in your father's spilt rivers of blood? What judgement shall you place upon all these, my confessor? Shall they be condemned to keep me company in the darkness of hell?"

Yeshua felt sick and intoxicated. But still, relentlessly, the falcon pressed on.

"Ask yourself this, young questioning one: what is the nature, the very substance, of that which you deem to be cruel? From what place is its source? From whence came its inception? What hand has fashioned us to be so? Answer me squarely, son of the cedars, are we not all fashioned by the hand of the Most Holy One? If so, then are we not only conforming to our own original nature? Think well, my child, my precious one. Consider this deeply. You might then realise I am in obeisance to my own God-given nature. And, in so doing, I give of my honour and worship."

The falcon flapped its wings and flew in six circles above the treetops, before landing upon the highest branch.

"Any other worship would be but a pale shadow. A blasphemy even. And the prince of the forest is not given to such blasphemies. No, I shall give honour to my creator and rejoice in this gift. I shall take pride in being the master of the hunt, upon whom God has bestowed such prowess. A prowess that is my master's perpetual delight. My master who made me. Me, the mighty falcon."

Once more the falcon flew down to stand before Yeshua.

"As such, I pray it shall one day be with you, Yeshua. You too must be what you are, a bright and blazing thing. Far brighter than my own is the light of your shining. But do not forget, that just as this little mouse is a part of you, so too am I. Not so very different, you and me. Not so very different at all."

"But you have caused pain and suffering to this little mouse. You have caused it to know fear and desolation."

"I gave it honour. I gave it honour by being true to what I am, as it also conformed to its own true nature. Pain and suffering? Fear and desolation? The words of the weak and unfit. We must be strong, you and I, to give honour to the Most High and Holy One. Is not pain and suffering everywhere? There, son of the cedars, standing right before you, behold this rose. Is she not a thing of glory and unsurpassed beauty? Look at her. Regard her closely. Does she not know the sting of grief to feel her beauty fade? To feel her petals wither and die? Listen. Hear well and truly. Just as I, the falcon, hear every sound in my kingdom, for nothing is hidden from my sharpest of hearing. Hear the sound of a mother's lamenting. Hear her cries, to feel her newborn baby snatched away. Hear the sound of the labourer's death throes, lying crushed and broken beneath the fallen rock. The agony and anguish of those afflicted by sickness. Those quivering in terror beneath the soldier's blade. The dying fish upon the rod. The bird's frozen wings in the fierce cold of winter. The fear of the chased and soon to be dying doe. Shall I go on? I see in your eyes you would prefer I did not. But let me ask you, by whose hand has all this come to be so? It was surely not conceived by mine."

Yeshua felt confused. He felt his heart hurting.

"Your heart is hurting because it is weak. It has not been properly fed. Nor has your mind been properly schooled and tutored. Like the body, the soul too needs meat and the sustenance of blood. But I will give you good counsel, if you should so receive it. There is no greater healer than I. And I hold the desire that your heart may be strong. You shall not find fitting counsel in the songs of the Davids. Their song is a blasphemy that fills the children's ears with sweet deceits. No, Yeshua, I shall speak truly to you, for you are worthy of so much more. As true as the voice of the thunder that heralds the coming storm. If all this suffering is born of ill intent, then lay the blame at its source, just as I have lain this mouse at yours. Yet maybe this is only erroneous thinking? For is this not all a part of life? Is this not all a part of the great conception? Does not nature hold both gentleness and violence? Accept things as they are, my chosen one. Take this knowing and grow strong and straight and true. Away with this pity which is nothing but a sickness. Begone, afflicting curse. Look into my eyes and see your true and glorious self, son of the wild wind. Be as you were fashioned to be and not encumbered by fairytales that only make you false and weak. Then maybe one day, you shall understand my mercy and take my blessing, and you too shall be a prince like me."

So spoke this pale shadow, a shadow that could burn brighter than a thousand suns. Yeshua looked at the mouse still before him, panting and struggling for breath. Broken. Yeshua picked it up and held it in his hands. He stroked its head as tears trickled down his cheek, falling upon the clumps of red, matted hair. He stroked it with his hands. He stroked it with his heart until it became stiff and still. The falcon watched all this and let out a shrill, piercing cry and flew away into the darkness of the forest. Yeshua placed the little mouse amidst the tangled, twisted roots of the cedar tree and covered it with leaves, before walking slowly and thoughtfully to where his father still laboured.

Quintessence

Whilst roving in the meadows, Yeshua strayed upon a most remarkable sight. There, flickering and sparkling above the distant treetops, what seemed to be a rainbow-coloured orb of light. What could it possibly be? Perhaps a reflection? Perhaps an illusion? One lost and lonely stray shaft of sunlight? A magical being from a bedtime story? An emissary of the Cloud People? A spirit of the forest? Maybe one of the Fair Kind, desirous of meeting him? He felt a strange longing reverberate inside him. He must get there quickly and unravel this mystery. No moment to dally, lest it too soon depart. Should anyone have spied him hurtling across the wide-open fields, with his long, dark locks and fiery green eyes, his pearly pale skin and delicate stature, they might have taken him to be a sprite from some other world. And the world of this sprite flowed with a mounting excitement, drawing ever closer to the edge of the forest, the orb still remaining as if waiting for him.

At last by the side of a curious cedar, puffing and panting with hands on hips, Yeshua watched the orb hovering above a small pool of water. Hovering like a bird. Hovering like a mist. And in the midst of the still water, upon a glistening black rock, a finger-length crystal emitting dazzling shafts of rainbows. He had seen many different types of rocks and stones before, but never anything quite like this. How had it come to be there? He remembered stories of mermaids, of the Lady of the Lake. Perhaps she had left it there as a gift for him? He reached out and held it in his hot, sticky hands, this fragment of ice that would not melt. He traced his fingers over its cool, sharp edges, whilst strange ephemeral lights danced within its form. And when he moved it, refracted sunlight moved like a great sword of light. What power he had. What games he could play. Yeshua, a wizard with a magic wand, able to conjure bright light into appearance on the bark of distant trees, or even up higher to their leaves and branches. A disgruntled rook took flight from its roost, cawing out in most raucous objection.

"Please forgive me for disturbing you."

But as truly sorry as he was, Yeshua could barely restrain himself from proceeding with his experiments. What next? Oh, look over there. A dark recess inside the trunk of that tree. What treasures might be found hiding inside it? With bated breath, he pointed his wand that it might be illuminated. But no, nothing of interest. No matter. Endless possibilities still awaited. He scanned all around. Ah, what about that log? He shone his light and saw something move, a small woodlouse, scuttling briskly around. It paused, its antennae scanning and probing for danger. The woodlouse, seeming to sense an unfamiliar scrutiny, retreated deeper into the darkness. Satisfied it was safe, it resumed moving around. How lucky was Yeshua. What a blessed day! First the crystal and now this marvellous insect. He had glimpsed its rows of shiny dark grey rings. It was garbed in a suit of armour, as strong and impenetrable as rings of steel. The boy was now fascinated and desired to see more of its wondrous form. Finding just the right position to hold the crystal, he directed the light at the woodlouse as it sought to find refuge. The woodlouse all but froze in the unnatural light, only a slight move of its antennae searching to understand.

"Do not be afraid, woodlouse. I only wish to look upon you." Thus spoke the intention of Yeshua's heart. But to Yeshua's horror, he saw the woodlouse roll over onto its back, its tiny legs kicking in the air as it burned in the light. Yeshua heard it scream. The terrible realisation came that the woodlouse was being scorched. As quick as he could, he hurled the crystal away. But it was too late. Its little legs were no longer flailing but instead grown still, as it went beyond the pain of the blazing light. No more movement of its antennae. Not even a flicker of life. A dreadful knowing crept through Yeshua. He had killed it.

"What have I done? Oh, what have I done?"

He picked up the woodlouse and cradled it in his hands, the tears streaming down his face. He thought to cool it down by blowing upon it, holding on to the desperate hope this would make a difference. But it did not. The life within its body did not return. He must not give up. There must be something he could do? He gathered his tears and let them drop upon the insect, hoping these cool waters would heal and revive it.

"Oh please, please, may you live and be well."

He brushed his wet hair upon it, but to no avail. He cried out to all that was around. He cried out loudly to he knew not what.

"Help me, I beg you. Please reverse the harm I have caused."

But nothing. The trees stood still in silent accusation beneath the now darkening skies. Yeshua slumped to the ground, the woodlouse held in his hands like a babe in a crib. Morning turned to afternoon and still he sat there, lifeless as the corpse in the palm of his hand, until after what had seemed an eternity of bitter silence, he spoke once more to the departed insect.

"I am sorry. I am so sorry."

His sobs echoed past the grief-stricken trees. What could he do to make amends? Nothing. Nothing. Absolutely nothing. Never in his short span of life had he known such sorrow, a sorrow too big for his young heart to hold. But though there were no means by which he could make amends, there yet remained one thing he could do. He would bury the woodlouse. He would lay it to rest, buried in the earth it had so dearly loved. So in a small yet fitting grave, Yeshua buried its mortal remains, still garbed in its suit of armour that had not been as impenetrable as steel. And as he did so, the boy's spirit spoke to the departed woodlouse.

"Please forgive me, woodlouse, for I have taken that which does not belong to me. Because of me, you will never walk again in the forest. I have taken your life and caused you pain, and I can never make this right. Please forgive me. Please hear me, if you can. Please hear my promise. I will never do such a foolish thing again. Never. EVER. Please, tell me if you can, is there anything I can do to make this right?"

He heard a rustling, close behind. He turned his head and saw the falcon, perched upon the withered stump of a tree he had not noticed before, its ferocious eyes staring with violent intensity.

"Not so very different, son of the cedars. Not so very different, you and I."

"Who are you?" cried out Yeshua. "What is your name? What do you want with me?"

"Who am I?" hissed the voice. "*Who am I? Why, I am the king of the world!*"

With this, the falcon was gone. But though departed, Yeshua heard the echo of its words. It was true he was not so very different. For he had taken the woodlouse's life, just as the falcon had once killed the mouse. Before the small grave, he came to know desolation for the very first time. As all this he felt, far away yet very near, the departing spirit of the woodlouse heard a sound. It heard the sound of a mortal one sobbing. It felt waves of deep sorrow and heard heartfelt words, whilst making its sojourn towards the shining beyond. Though its probing antennae were excitedly dancing, perceiving for the first time the radiant forest ahead, it paused on its journey towards this new-found glory. It stopped and turned. It felt sorrow too. It felt what it was to be a mortal one. To be as one of the giants. It moved towards the boy, pulling itself upon its many legs, just as it had always done. Yet now it seemed to walk right through the blades of grass, the jutting stones and fallen leaves. Closer it came until it stood before Yeshua. It looked upon this desolate one. And there, in the sad, still light, in spirit it did sing to the woebegone child.

"How kind are you, son of the soil. How kind you are, that you should grieve for but a small woodlouse such as me. Such as I was. As one who shall not break a bruised reed are you."

Yeshua looked up. He looked up and saw a tiny, shimmering light before him. And as he looked into its uncanny brightness, he thought he saw the form of the woodlouse.

"Be at peace, young walking one. Please. Be at peace now and know this. No pain did I feel. No, no pain at all. For as I entered into the shade of the log, I beheld a wondrous light come upon me. A great light such I had never seen before."

What joy Yeshua felt. Never before a greater joy, to hear, to see, this tiny yet glorious form before him. To hear its softly spoken words.

"Such a beautiful light," continued the woodlouse. "So kind and gentle. I grew still to behold this light which sang to me. It picked me up as if in its palms, but I was not afraid. No, I was not afraid. And then, miracle of miracles, this light spoke to me. Yes, it spoke. It spoke to me of a greater life beyond this forest. A place where I could walk into a new life. A life as a walking one. As one such as you are, but only if I so chose. How could this light have known for such a life I had always prayed? Yes, I had prayed for all the days of my life, praying as it is given for a woodlouse to pray. To be like the giants that sometimes roam through this forest. To be like you, whose joy I could feel spread out as far and wide as the wind. I cannot say why I had this desire. I only knew I felt a yearning deep inside me, greater than the desire to feed upon the delicious feasts this good forest has always so gladly given. I felt thirst and hunger. And I did dream as a woodlouse dreams, to one day become just as you are."

Why would the woodlouse wish to be as he? But he stilled his questioning so he could listen the more to the word of this wondrous vision.

"How could I have known such a day would come? That the prayers of a woodlouse such as me, such as I was, would be heard? Heard and answered. But heard they were, Yeshua, for this day has come. This blessed day. How I raced towards you when I saw you close by. I raced as fast as my small legs could carry me, that I might be near you. That I might feel your joy, as nectar to my soul. I knew I must meet you at the appointed place. And there, glory beyond glory, I saw you change. I saw you transfigured. Oh, such wonder to behold this majesty. I saw you change into a being of light. A light, as if the sun had come to rest upon the earth. As if a door had opened, a door through which soon I would be called to walk. A light that was so bright and burning. But I was not afraid. Only wonder I felt. Wonder that the Most Holy One had heard the prayer of a small woodlouse such as me. Such joy and wonder that I screamed out in not pain, but joy. And happy I am. Yes, happy I am. And now, my deliverer, I must wend my way to that which awaits me."

Endless gratitude Yeshua felt for this spirit that had ceased its journey into the great beyond for a child such as him. The woodlouse walked a few steps away, its form beginning to fade. But then it paused and stopped. It stopped and turned, making ready to utter its final earthly word.

"This you must know, son of the cedars. Hear my word and learn this well. This light is a force that may either heal or hurt. Learn this lesson and my death, which is no death at all, will be a price I would gladly pay. For my antennae which see all, show me you may do great good in this world and in the worlds beyond. That you may shine a greater light. You, who seek the forgiveness of a woodlouse such as me. Such as I was. And, though there is nothing to forgive, I forgive you, son of the wild wind. Truly, I forgive you with my all. And, in my forgiving, you shall know the more of the spirit of forgiveness."

With this, Yeshua saw the woodlouse change into a spark that flew off into the forest. And when he returned home, his mother called out to him, "Yeshua. Where have you been? I was starting to worry you would be caught in the thunderstorm."

He ran to her open arms and she held him tightly. She kissed him on each cheek, her eyes dancing with happiness.

"Yeshua, there has been great rejoicing in Elnazar this day. For whilst you were out playing, a baby has been born. And his name is Zebediah."

Wind Dancer

Yeshua, Yeshua, why do the wind and the river call out your name? Yeshua, Yeshua, as open as an altar, as mysterious as the dark of the midnight hour. As fathomless as the depths of the wild, wild woods. Son of the carpenter, beloved of the weaver, how came your tongue to be silent and sealed? What words are your lips not yet willing to say? What manner of mystery lies behind those brightest of eyes, gazing transfixed as if into some unseen world? Why do you laugh out or weep for no apparent reason? Are you blessed or cursed, touched by the hand of the hosts of heaven, afflicted by malady, by sickness and madness? Why do you love to be so much on your own, shunning the company of your own kind? Why so different, so aloof and unfamiliar? Do you not know that you risk growing up sad and lonely, should you not come to swiftly mend your ways?

Yet for all of their questions, they did not know. No, they did not know, for how could they know, that Yeshua was neither sad nor alone in the depths of the forest. That there in the forest, this child did feel at home. Did feel as one. Cherished times spent roving amidst this magical garden, this temple of mystery, all things his playground, his playmate, his guardian and teacher. What unsurpassed joy to climb the bough of the ancient cedars, pulling himself as high as his strength could take him, so high he could perch beside the cawing crows. Higher and higher with each passing moon, ascending on the rungs of Jacob's ladder. And though he would sometimes come tumbling back down, neither pain nor cuts or bumps and bruises, could dampen his curiosity, nor curb his desire.

One late spring day, brimming over with the promise of soon to be coming summer, Yeshua caught sight of something moving quickly through the brush. He saw bushes start to shudder beneath the weight of some unseen force, branches twisting and bending back. It was surely too big to be a squirrel, a bird or a fox? His skin tingled beneath the scrutiny of this being as it circled around him. It had been known to happen, though only rarely, for a villager to return from the forest daubed in blood spilt from wide-open wounds, pale as ash and weak as sin, a gaze that spoke of unspeakable terror. And though some were favoured by fate to return with tales to tell, others were not blessed with such good fortune, their lives claimed by the dark forest. Their lips forever sealed.

Snap, snap, crack, the sound of twigs splitting all around him. He wanted to cry out for help but stifled his cries, so as not to further alert the stalker to his presence. What was that? A sudden breeze? Something sniffing for his scent? He reasoned that to run would be of no avail, for wolves and bears were fleet of foot. There was only one thing to do that might afford him a chance. He would become so completely still he would disappear from view, just as he had done so many times before. He would become still of body, of thought and feeling, and wait for the threat to pass.

As he thus became silent, he heard the sounds gradually retreating, ever more distant until only quietude remained. A growing conviction arose that the unknown creature had now departed. He breathed in deeply. But all too quickly he found he had made a fatal mistake. The grasses began parting, a vast snake winding towards him. He heard the sound of some creature hissing.

"Please, do not be afraid," came a voice. "I will not hurt you. I promise, I mean you no harm."

With the voice, the movement stopped. Although Yeshua had heard the words clearly, he could not discern from whence they had come.

"May I come closer?"

"Where are you?" called out Yeshua in silent words.

"I am everywhere."

"Everywhere? Then why can I not see you?"

"I am right here before you."

It sounded like the voice of a child. The voice of a boy.

"But I can only see the grass moving. Are you a ghost? The ghost of a child?"

"No, I am not as such," came the immediate reply. Yeshua thought hard, then spoke again.

"Are you a boy who has found a robe of invisibility?"

"No, I am not as such."

"Then what are you?"

"Oh, how I wish you could see me. How I wish it were so. Many times I have seen you. Many times I have watched you play alone, just as I play alone. And though I see you seem content to do so, sometimes when I watch you fall deeply into the silence, I see a different expression come upon your face. What it means, I cannot say. Yet it makes me wonder, could it be that you also sometimes feel a little alone? Alone like me? In such moments, I have wondered if you might care to play with me, even if only for a little while. I wish I had someone to play with. I wish we could play together, you and me."

"I would love to play if only I could see and touch you. But I do not know how. Is there any way you can make yourself visible to me?"

No answer. Just a slight breeze, forlornly tugging upon the hem of his sleeves. With this tugging, a thought occurred to Yeshua. Had not the rabbi once spoken of the hidden power held in a name? The power to call forth the named. To conjure it, to evoke it into manifestation.

"Please, tell me if you will, what is your name?"

Immediately the leaves shook loudly like rattles, a cold, sharp breeze leaping forward and brushing Yeshua's cheeks. He feared he may have given offence and provoked the invisible presence into anger.

"Why do you wish to know that which a mortal cannot comprehend?"

A long silence ensued until eventually, thankfully, it deigned to speak once more.

"Do you not know that by the utterance of my hidden name, you would come to hold me in your power? And my power is far too great for a mortal to harness."

"But I have no thought to hold you in my power."

A dole of turtle doves sang out in testimony.

"I believe you. Truly, I do, for true are you. But then why, I must ask you, do you wish to know that which is beyond the wit of a mortal to understand?"

"I only thought that if you told me your name, then perhaps I would be able to see you. And then we could play together for a little while."

The invisible presence seemed to pause as if deep in consideration.

"If this is truly your heart's desire, then first you must declare your own true name. But think carefully before you do so, for by these means I may come to have power over you."

Whether guarded by innocence or guided by folly, the boy followed an instinct and made swift reply.

"I am Yeshua."

"Yeshua. Yeshua. Why, I have heard that name before. I have heard it sung by the river. I have heard it whispered by the cedars. Yeshua, whom they name to be a son of the cedars. A son of the wild wind. Oft have I wondered, what manner of mortal may bear such a name? I have yearned to meet this son of the wild wind, for he would be my kin and kind. Although a mortal of flesh and bone, yet somehow also a little like me. And now, at last, I have been honoured to meet you. Today, the mystery of Yeshua has been revealed."

The chill of the breeze now turned to warmth.

"Yeshua. Hmmmmmmm… I can see you are well and truly named. And though you are mortal, I smell something other upon your skin. Something which bade me answer you. Something which frees me from fear of transgression. So, young mortal one, you have answered my question. Now, it is only fitting, I meet you in kind. You have asked me to speak to you of that which I am. You have asked me my name and now I shall tell you. Why, I am none but the whispering wind. And Deus is my name."

Yeshua felt his whole body shudder as he heard this name. As if the whole world, no, the whole universe, was speaking to him.

"Deus," spoke Yeshua, with some trepidation, uncertain what would happen if he uttered this name. On hearing his name spoken, Deus spiralled up swiftly and wrapped around Yeshua's body like an airy gown.

"So many times I have watched you, Yeshua. So many times. And yet for all those times, I never knew it was you that the river and the cedars had been speaking of. Long have I searched for you. Long have I wondered in what way we two are alike. You, robed in flesh and me, without skin. But now I see. Yes, now I see. I see something today I have not seen before. Something moving behind the veil of your eyes. Something moving in and out of your lungs. A breath blown into this world, a little wind inside you. A wind housed for a while in this temple of flesh, behind those columns of bones and upon those rivers of blood. And glad I am. Yes, glad I am. So now, little brother, let us make our sport."

"Oh, I would love to, Deus. But I only have until the sun begins to set and then I must make my way home. And as you have told me your secret name, I shall also tell you a secret. In the place that I call home, I am known as Yeshua, the speechless one. To them, I am as invisible as you were to me. As invisible as the wind. And when the children used to call me to play with them, they took my silence for refusal. Now they no longer ask. I am so happy you have asked."

The wind sighed to hear his pain.

"I understand, Yeshua. Your kindred are afraid of that which they do not understand. But let us put such unknowing aside for now. Look, I shall make a picture just for you."

Deus leapt up and sent a huge column of leaves towards the sky, an enormous tree hanging suspended in the air, before releasing them to come tumbling down like snow. Yeshua marvelled to behold such a sight.

"Now," roared the wind, "chase me. *Chase me!*"

The leaves once more were whipped up by the wind, Yeshua chasing them as they danced around the clearing.

Sometimes he would catch one in his hands but Deus would quickly snatch it back. Again and again, until joy and frustration exploded into laughter. Yeshua fell down in exhaustion, his laughter echoing throughout the forest. And Deus laughed too, causing a mighty shaking in the branches of the trees. A horde of rooks fell from their nests, flying around and furiously cawing. But their cawing soon too melted into laughter as they heard the sounds flowing from the clearing beyond. Then, another miracle. Yeshua felt himself lifted from the ground, raised high into the air by an unseen hand. Thus Deus paraded him around, first around the clearing and then through the forest, carrying him like a king upon a throne.

"Hear me, Yeshua. Here me, I who am the north and the south, the east and the west. Hear me now and hear my pledge. Whenever you need me, you only have to call me and I will come, where ever you may be. Just call me by my name and I will answer your summons. I shall ever be your friend and your willing servant."

"Thank you, Deus, with all my heart. But please, I do not wish you to be my servant. I only wish you to be my friend."

"Never mistake service for servitude, my little brother. One is given, the other taken. One a slave, the other free. But who is there anyway who could make a slave of Deus? Who is there, Yeshua, who shall tether the wild, wild wind? Our friendship shall be as free as the wind. What adventures we shall have together, you and me. You will tell me of your world and I shall tell you of mine. I will teach you how such a little wind as you, may walk on water or whip up a storm. And as my parting gift to you, from this day onwards, you shall no longer be the speechless one. For the time has come for this little wind inside to find its mortal voice."

From this day on, Yeshua's tongue came to be mysteriously loosened. To be most miraculously unsealed. Where had once been silence, now poured a waterfall of words, spoken in a voice that was soft, melodious and crystal clear. Rebekah had immediately noticed something different in his gait, in the manner in which he moved, in the smile on his face, the skip in his feet, the shape of his lips and the move of his hips.

"Mother," Yeshua had called out to her. "Mother, where are you?" Mother? Mother? Whose voice is this? Come out from the shadows, my foolish husband. Of such matters is not fitting to make your sport. But she knew. She knew. She knew Heshel did not hide in the shadows.

"Oh, there you are," Yeshua said, his head peeping through the door. Could it really be so? Could this really be happening? It was as if she had awoken into the best of dreams. At first she said nothing, fearful she might scare this beautiful butterfly dream away. What a wonder to hear his very first uttered word, uttered for her and for her only. And then another word and another word more, a roaring river where had been only a silent stream.

"Is that really you, Yeshua?"
"Of course. Who else would it be?"
"Where have you been? What has happened to you?"
"I have been playing with the wind in the forest."
"Come, Yeshua. We must run quickly."

Together they ran and they ran as quick as they could, running to Heshel's workshop, bursting through the door with such force it gave the carpenter a fright.

"Heshel, Heshel. Drop your anvil. End your labour and come to listen to our boy. Quickly, quickly, lest this magic slip away."

And as she spoke, they all heard a wind come whistling through the gaps in the door, through the cracks in the floor, through the slightly opened window, winding down the spout of the chimney stack. All of this, the sport of Deus.

The Sacrifice That Is No Sacrifice

In the clearing at the side of the forest, at the side of the mountain, in the sharp, chill crispness of a late winter's night, the seven cedars stood waiting, listening out for Yeshua's soon to be coming steps. Expectant as brides walking from aisle to altar. Soon now, soon now, the one, the one, who has been writ to come. Come now to this circle that he may return to the temple, that the carpenter may here make good his oath. These seven young cedars, each one grown strong, tall and slender, standing as high as an elephant's head, all bedecked with cone-shaped crowns and leaves of evergreen needles, garbed in robes of dark greyish-brown bark, ready to make ceremony like the oak priests of Albion. Listen, listen, the air tingles rhapsodic with lovers' whispers, reverberating as if bells are pealing, a distant tolling, chiming out upon the borders of sound and silence. Hear now, hear now, the attendant owl cries out in summons, beneath the vastest canopy of watchful stars. For tonight, tonight, has finally come, has come now the eve of his seventh birthday. Tonight the hour to make his bed here, to fall into the dreaming, to traverse the ethers, that his soul may take flight and call out for the vision. That he may walk a while amidst the spirits.

Rebekah gazed at her kindred. This son, this father, her man and boy, two pilgrims ready to set off for the holy of holies. A pair of birds with rainbow feathers. Oh, my heart, my love, my own. May you be safe. May you be well. May you both, this night, know joy and glory. But enough of this, Rebekah. There is work to be done. One last chance to check their readiness. One last opportunity to check through the contents of Heshel's sack. There, there it is, tucked neatly inside, the blanket of hide that shall keep Yeshua warm and snug through the cold of the night, weaved by the spider girl for this very occasion. But what else, Rebekah? What else? Is there something else you have neglected to pack? Something vital that your child might need in the long, lonely night? Be quick, be vigilant, for time is pressing, the hour swiftly passing. She kneaded her chin like freshly blended dough. Sufficient provision to fortify both his body and spirit? Enough bread and water? Even a little red wine to warm his blood and a little cake too, but not too much. The spirits prefer an empty belly. Just enough to give him solace. Just enough that he should feel her close. She thumbed through his attire with meticulous precision: a hat to keep his head warm, thick socks and gloves to warm his feet and hands. For tonight the stars shone so fiercely, she knew the frost would bejewel the world crystalline with its icy fingers, even well in advance of the soon to be coming dawn.

"I think we are just about ready," said Heshel, swinging the sack upon his back and opening the door. Legions of moths came flying in, lunging inwards, joyous and dreamily as if in intoxication, fast towards the light of his leaping lantern. Somewhere, everywhere, in the great expanse of darkness that loomed outside, Rebekah sensed the presence of Ariadna, watching over Yeshua with her million eyes and more.

"See you in the morning, my darling," she said in a faltering, ewe-like voice. And though she wished to say just a few words more, she was unable to do so, her throat now clenched tight with feeling, her lips now sealed.

"See you in the morning, Mother."

She heard excitement and trepidation in the timbre of her little lamb's voice. Heshel looked at Rebekah. How lovely her hands. How strong and nimble her slender fingers. Quintessence of the devoted and dutiful mother. He saw her worries as he always did. How he loved his weaver and always would. Her worry, his worry. Her hurt, his hurt. His heart, her heart. This girl who had once watched him hidden in the shadows, invisible behind the veil of the shady bower, listening out for his soon to be coming steps. Do not fret, my love. Please, hold no fear. Sleep content in the cradle of peace. Be still, those beautiful, anxious eyes. And though he said nothing, his eyes gave testimony to his Rebekah, of how he would watch over their son with every fibre of a father's fierceness.

Once more the urgent cry of the owl cut like a rapier through the veil of silence. No more time for goodbyes. No more kisses. No more waves nor words. Time to depart now, to wend their way across the darkened fields, over the crest of the hill, all the way to the far side of the mysterious forest. Time to let go, Rebekah, to follow the trail of this beautiful calling. For she hears them. She hears them. She hears the sound of the spirits singing. She feels the earth reverberating beneath their coming tread. She feels the softest breeze come close a-dancing, all dove and doe-like, a wind come twisting, arisen from the hem of their moonlight robes. So crisp and fragrant the air this night. Jasmine, frankincense, lotus blossom. Oranges and apples, violet and rose. As if, as if, as if she were walking, as if she were walking through the Garden Where Four Rivers Flow. As if all things were renewed in the light of an ascending sun. As if a new Jerusalem hath come. She felt the hand of her passionate heart slowly letting go in a joyous releasing. In perfect trust. In perfect path. In perfect becoming. In perfect heart. And through the wide-open eye of her spirit, through the soil of her heart, she watched them lift up and fly and soar. So far and high, her man and boy, higher, farther, and ever more distant. Ever more distant, yet never closer. Above the moon, the stars and even farther beyond, floating upon the waters of the milky river. Riding down the good red road, far and high and deep and narrow. And though high, high above, the weaver yet sat right by and betwixt them. And though far, far below, she yet held them as if onto the tail of a kite. Never more firmly, yet never more lax. Her heart in their hearts, their hearts in hers, all three in a tapestry, one stitch unsewn. A woven web. A silver thread. She watched the light of Heshel's lantern ever so gradually fading, a firefly swallowed up by the thirsty darkness. The fire of a wick snuffed out by the night. Off you sail now, my lion and my lamb. Fly where thou wilt, my birds all dressed in rainbow feathers. See you both when morning comes. See you soon, my little angel. One last time Yeshua turned round to see his mother. But the weaver was no longer there to be seen. See you in the dawning, dearest mother of mine.

Onwards, onwards, Heshel and Yeshua now trekked, walking in tandem and gradually picking up the pace, their eyes seeing the more in the violet-black night, the fire of their breath sculpting little clouds in the air. Step by step, walking with sharp and focused, clear intent. Walking towards a little piece of heaven sent. Listen. Listen. Whose thoughts are these whispering out loudly amidst this most silent night? Whose thoughts fill the ethers like birds on the wing? Yeshua, Yeshua, doth the wind give answer. Little Yeshua, giving thought as to what might await him. For never before had he ventured into the forest beyond the threshold of the twilight hour. Would it be as he knew it or would it be something other? Something marvellous and majestic, beyond the scope of imagination? Would he be alone or would he sleep in good company? Would the spirits of the night make their presence known to him? Would Deus be there or did the wind sleep? Or could it be that something evil was there waiting? For still lurking in his mind's darkest recesses, the mocking, leering, savage face of the falcon. What if it was making ready to lay claim upon his soul? He grabbed hold tightly of the carpenter's hand.

"I am frightened, Father."

Heshel stopped and held him. He lifted him up, his weight no more the weight of a feather in the safe harbour of those powerful, work-hardened arms. See him. See him. See the tender shepherd pick up his lamb. Hear him. Hear him, ready now to give utterance to a father's word. With your all now, my son, undivided listen. With your all now listen to a father's testimony, sealed up like a scroll for this very moment. Hear you now the prayer of my heart, released that you shall brook no fear. For you, my child, my precious one. Hold no fear for I shall raise you. I shall hold you. A rock I shall be, that I may always watch over you. So too, a mountain, that I may forever wait. I shall be your fortress and keep, a torch to guide you, even through the abyss of darkest night. A light that wills to weave the way. A circle of fire wrapped all around you and so too, a sword. My bones, a club that I may protect you. My skin, a pelt to keep you warm. My back, a chariot that I may carry you, a mule that would rejoice to bear and serve you. My blood, a drop of wine spilt that you may know no thirst. My body, a loaf of bread that you may eat. My voice to uplift you. My soul to preserve you. My will to protect you. My life for your life, and ever gladly. This sacrifice that is no sacrifice at all.

Yeshua felt the tickle of the carpenter's beard upon his cheek, smelt the scent of fire and cedar upon him. He felt his father's warm breath as if sitting by the roaring hearth fire of home.

"There is no need to be afraid, Yeshua. I shall always be close by. Just call upon me and I shall be right there."

He held the lantern up to his face. He began to snarl, looking as fierce and ferocious as a wild bear. A nearby crow screeched and flew away as if in fright. Yeshua could not help but giggle to see his father so. He knew that any predator would have much to fear from the fury of his father's blade and axe. Yet doubts still lingered, as doubts are often wont to do.

"But what if there are bad spirits in the forest who may wish me harm? Spirits who are not afraid of your weapon? What then, Father?"

"Listen carefully to me, my son. I will tell you what I have not told you before. Here in the forest walks a most powerful spirit."

"What spirit is this, Father?"

"A beautiful lady under whose rule of kindness the forest falls."

"What is her name so that I may call her?"

"It is for this lady alone to tell you her name."

"If she comes and makes appearance, how shall I know it is her and not something else?"

"Have no fear, my son, for your true and gentle heart shall know her."

Heshel saw Yeshua's eyes, still vexed with worry.

"Do not fret. If you need to call out for help, the guardian spirit of your grandmother awaits you. You will see her true form, unveiled to your eyes by the bright light of the dark. But do not call upon her lightly. We must be always heedful as not to disturb the spirits from their prayer. Only if you truly deem the need, you may call out for Rafaella and she will be there. And fierce beyond all measure is a grandmother's love. Far-reaching the seeing of a grandmother's heart."

Little by little, bit by bit, Yeshua felt his muscles shed their load, and peace return to the keep of his belly. He felt himself to be reassured. Beneath the watch of his grandmother, he knew he would be safe. In her, he trusted. With her, his heart did long to be. For well did this Yeshua know his ancestor's stories. And a wild girl was she, a wild child was Rafaella, wild and tender, and no child kinder.

All of this, his father saw.

"Now, do you feel ready to go on, Yeshua? Yes? Are you certain? Good, it is not far now. We are nearly there. Look, over there, can you see them?"

Through the thin veil of fog lit up by the pale green moonlight, the outline of shadowy forms stood looming like giants. A most phantasmagorical sight.

"We have arrived, my son. Welcome. Welcome to the circle of seven cedars, seeded here by my hand at the hour of your conception. And here is the place where we shall make camp." He delved into his sack to pull out seven torches, then knelt upon the earth. "You shall have no fear of wild animals." He scattered some tinder on the ground, igniting it with a spark made from flint and steel. One by one, he lit the torches, carefully forming a circle around the perimeter of the seven cedars, all the while uttering prayers and evocations. "No manner of animal will dare cross this boundary. These torches will burn long through the night and even through into the dawn. There, it is done. Now, take this, Yeshua. You know what to do."

Heshel handed the sack over to Yeshua, his labour finally all done. Nothing left for a father to do. He knew he had reached the threshold over which he must not cross. From here his boy must step into this circle alone. Time to let go of his hand.

"I must go now, Yeshua. But before I go, I wish to tell you just one more thing. I wish to speak to you of a father's pride. A pride no smaller than the mountain or this starry sky. For you, my son, my little Yeshua, now grown so quickly. Perhaps I have not told you this enough? If so, then please grant me forgiveness. Maybe it is a lacking in me that I prefer to speak through the labour of my hands. But truly, no father could be prouder of their child than I am of you. Prouder perhaps than you will ever know. May the hand of the Most Holy One now strike me down should my tongue give false testimony."

He bowed down before his son. How strange! Yeshua had never seen a full-grown man bow down before a child.

"Well, my son, it seems the time has finally come. Time for you to enter the temple. To give yourself over to the vision, just as our ancestors have done before us. The prophets, the dreamers, the scribes and seers. In whatever shape or form it may appear, this vision is for you and for you only. You shall speak of it to no-one. It shall be as a light to follow, even in your darkest hour."

He kissed his son on the forehead with all of a father's blessing, then turned around to leave. As the sound of his father's footsteps faded, Yeshua took a deep breath, making ready to cross the threshold into who knew where. He mustered his courage as best he could, before saying the words he had been schooled in. One deep breath now. Time to speak to the many now gathered and listening.

"I give honour to the circle of seven cedars. I make honour to the seven stars. I pray that you may bestow upon me your blessing, if you should so will it to be, that you may admit me into the school and temple."

To hear his voice, the night seemed to burst into a greater wakefulness, as if its eyes were blinking open. The fish in the lake began to swim in circles and spirals, the mountain rumbled and hummed in prayer. Come now, our child. Come now, the children. Through the slowly passing mist, all tinged with green, Yeshua felt branches coyly reaching out to touch him. He sensed many leaves breathing in of his scent, ecstatic to know him. Thick roots and trunks starting to quiver and sway. An apocalypse, an explosion, of blushing bride beauty. High above the treetops, Yeshua saw a crystal crown descending, seven stars centred with a diadem of royal blue. All things united in a choir-like calling of clamorous questioning.

"Who is there whose heart may bear our crowning?"

He felt their beckoning. He heard their call. Come to me. Come to we. One step closer, a tentative tread. Come return to us. Is this true sight or fancy, this girl with hair of crimson-red, sweetly smiling, rushing by like a river of fire? Echoes of light and lilting laughter. Mutterings and growlings. Something moving upon the ground and in the shadows. What is this? A sight most welcome and unexpected. There before him, the tiny form of an intently watchful woodlouse, proud and noble, if proud and noble a woodlouse could be said to be. The very same woodlouse he once had known, yet now brightly illuminated, lit from inside with an inner glowing. To behold this woodlouse,

Yeshua placed his hands upon his rejoicing heart and smiled. He smiled in joy. He smiled in thanks. Why do the harlot priests never thus smile, but wear instead a scowl upon their cruellest of faces, hid behind the barbed wire walls of their blaspheming altars? But not so, Yeshua. His smiling heart burst into dance and song and salutation, a bright new star now being born. A light, a love, a lamb, a son. As if hath come, Jerusalem.

"How kind are you, woodlouse. How kind are you, woodlouse, that you should wait for one such as me. That you should break your journey, across the bridge between here and there."

At Yeshua's side there now came a hare a-leaping. A leaping hare with pricked up ears and wild, roving eyes, its tremulous whiskers a little lit up by first firefly light. It paused curiously for a moment, then leapt and hopped and ran in spirals, before uncommonly, uncannily, walking ever farther backwards. Here now, hear now, the word of the leaping hare, singing, tracing, backwards returning.

"Here and there and there and thither. There and thither, now and when. Up and down and all around. Within, without, and all about. In and out and up and through. Deep and high, forever, never. There, now and when. Where, then and wither. Become. Become. Here, there and thither."

All of this, the woodlouse saw. Cognisant of having gained Yeshua's full attention, it turned around like an usher, like a priest before the sanctum. And Yeshua now gave voice, no longer in the voice of a child but instead in the eternal tongue of his spirit.

"I shall follow you, woodlouse, in perfect faith. Lead me where you will, guardian of the gate."

The woodlouse walked forward, walking slowly as if in ceremony, behind it there flowing a firefly robe. Through the doorway, the ancient doorway, passing over, passing through, far away from here and there and thither, brushed all the while with angel wing whispers.

"He has come. He has returned. He has come. He has returned. Enter. Enter. Come return to us, our lost yet never forgotten love."

This night is a symphony, a long-forgotten melody. Merrily the unseen birds sing and chortle. Glad is the stream, a melodious lyre. The wind, a viola, that sings and sighs. Drifting like a dream into something familiar and other. Here, so much bigger, vaster than anything expected. A wide-open expanse, a vault peopled with a million stars, stretching out like an aeon. How uncommonly bright the stars this night. Here, as clear as day, no mist at all, he now become a meandering stream. Flow you now unto me, to the centre of this circle, here to lay your bundle down. Come rest upon me, cries out to him the amorous earth. With his receiving skin now on fire and tingling, he unfolded his rug of animal hide and placed his blanket upon it, then sat down and wrapped himself in his thick, soft shawl. It felt so snug and warm. He could smell Rebekah's fragrance upon it. He felt a small friendly tug upon his sleeve, telling him the wind did not sleep.

"Have no fear, young mortal one. Have no fear, our kin and kind. Have no fear, awaited one. Welcome are you here, young son of the earth. Bright soul of the soil. Welcome here, young walking one. Welcome to this circle, son of the cedars. Son of the wild wind."

"May I touch you?" Yeshua asked though he knew not why. A cedar, the tallest cedar of them all, shook its leaves like a priest with a rattle, extending out a branch in invitation. As Yeshua placed his hand upon its trunk, the tree sighed out to feel his touch.

"Lay your head down amongst us in the place of the dreaming. Let your eyes now be sealed that the vision may come. That the eyes of your heart may be now further opened."

Doing as counselled, he laid himself down. His head on a pillow, a pillar of stars. A bridge. A ladder. The blackest of blacks and the whitest white. He falls and he falls. He climbs and he climbs, as if upon the steps of an endless ladder. Still all around him, the familiar sound of crackling torches, until quick, without warning, a flash, a sudden explosion. He could not tell if this explosion of light was from within or without. Yet even these few remaining questions soon came to be stilled, for he saw the cedars shooting out filaments of bright and living light as if a gigantic spider were weaving a web. Shafts of intersecting lines going out into forever. Beams and rafters of a temple, stretching out far into space. Tails up to heaven, and heaven a kite.

He felt them crowding all around him, these seven bright lights, still veiled in mist. He felt fingers upon him, a tender stroking. Seven sisters dancing, each emanating the sweetest of shining star smiles, each one garbed in robes of summer sky, the highest blue. He felt their breath upon his skin, their spring dew fragrance anointing him like the perfume of violets and roses, of sage and cedar, the sharp, fresh scent of the open sea. He heard the sound of delicious laughter and delightful giggles. The sound of their voices, the sound of a fountain, the lullaby rhythm of the first kiss of springtime. The gentle pitter-patter of midnight rain. This heart. This heart. Our blessed, kind and gentle heart. At last. At last. Oh, how we have missed you, you for whom we have waited. Yes, you have come now and most glad are we. Our brother has returned. He who is ever our diadem.

This joy of remembrance. This joy of reunion. As if bathed in the light of a new-risen sun. As if the eight had become as one. As if a new Jerusalem hath come. The touch of fingers gently combing through his hair. The feel of tender kisses upon his cheeks. Circling around him, seven women, majestically beautiful and filled with grace. Their faces, most fair and noble. He felt the wings of his heart unfurl to feel them. He felt his spirit, bowing, flying, crossing over, marching in procession through the pathways and passages of the palace of peace. Coming still closer, with him ever more the willing, each gazed upon Yeshua, their eyes ablaze with a greater life, each one now robed in a colour of the rainbow, their bare feet standing still upon the frosty grass. Standing still yet also somehow moving, gliding. To feel, to feel, this leonine love.

"Behold," said one sister, her voice the sound of wind blowing through the bullrushes. "Behold, my sisters. Behold the light of this little blue star."

"Our little blue star," they all start to rapturously sing. "This little blue star, who is ever and always, a brother to we. And glad are we. Yes, glad are we."

Joy in their eyes. Joy upon their lips. Joy in the movement of their slowly swaying hips. Her hand now came to rest upon his eyes. Her palm, a veiling. She walks him like a blind man through the fires of a golden gateway. He feels a cool marble floor beneath the soles of his feet.

"The vision of this place must wait a while, our little brother, but not for any lacking. Only for the reason that she is not yet here. Yet though not yet here, you, Yeshua, shall be given to enter. You shall be admitted. You shall sit upon the throne."

He felt his skin peeling away like wax from a candle as she seated him upon a throne that was consuming fire.

"Is this death?"

"There is only life here, our brother. Only life is here

in this circle of eternity. And here we shall crown you, our little king."

He felt her standing right behind him, the other sisters too. He heard the sound of angels singing. Please touch me. Please feel me. Please bless me. Please heal me. As if in answer, he felt her place it upon his head. A head which is no head. He felt the touch of her fingers upon his soul, a cool river weaving through flame like Celtic knots. He could not help but reach out a hand to touch her hand, to touch this crowning, reaching out to a hand where a hand was not. He heard their laughter. He felt their love.

"Oh, our brother, it is not that manner of crown. It is not to be touched by mortal flesh, for it has been fashioned from a different substance."

"Then what manner of crown is it and how shall I wear it?"

"You shall wear it as it shall wear you. You shall wear it in the remembering. You shall wear it in the becoming. You shall wear it upon your heart of hearts, for our love for you is an eternal crowning. And glad are we. Yes glad are we, our little brother. Our diadem. How bright, kind and true, the light of your shining. How wondrous your stories. How vital your song. Do you not know the high spirits make pilgrimage from far and wide, just to sit in circle and drink in of your word? Yet even if this you do not yet know, yet still, it is, and shall come to be. So now, Yeshua, returning brother and king that comes, the time has come for you to receive the vision. To see your true self in the obsidian mirror. Time for you to return to the circle with eyes wide open, this final step yours to take alone."

He heard the sound of their footsteps retreating, turning into distant echoes. Echoing down the corridors of silence, as if the beats of his heart were slowly fading.

"Do not leave me," this heart cried out in desperation. "Do not leave me. Please, please, do not leave me. Please stay with me, if only for a little while longer. For how shall I live without the sight of you? I shall miss you more than my heart can bear. Please do not leave me broken and desolate for the lack of your presence." She stopped in her passage. She stopped and turned. She turned and came. She comes. She comes. She comes in glory, comes riding the wind. For mercy is her name. Kindness, her heart. Her thrice-blessed hand now holding his, lightly, fondly, a firm caressing. Sister. Sister. The fires of your love. The scent of your waters. Your fragrance, the taste of the highest, high summer. Your touch, a million deaths and more. And now, he sees her. He sees her coming sharply into view. Grace beyond grace, beauty beyond beauty. Her face is a garden, a roving, warming, untamed wildness and wilderness. Her hair is a forest, an ocean of flame. He beholds the light of her smiling, for the sight of him only. Smiling yet also looking somewhat startled.

"Leave you? Leave you? Why, we could never leave nor abandon you, our little blue light."

"Then please, may I walk with you, if only from time to time. My hallowed sister who is one of seven. Your beauty unrivalled and, so too, your grace. Bless me with your naming that I may call upon you."

He saw her turn to walk away. He heard her footsteps upon the grass and watched the motion of her golden sunlight hair. And as she did so, Yeshua caught the sound of her voice, a wind that whispers, an endless echo.

"I AM. I aaaammm… iiiiii… aaaaaaaaaaaammmmm…"

He wanted to follow. He wanted to follow her, with every fiery fibre of his being. This sister, who did cause each cell to dance and sing. But though he wanted to follow, he knew he could not, for well he knew 'twas not yet his time. Not yet time to be there, in the place that she was. So he stopped and stood, stood still and silent, his feet firm and balanced on the axis of the world. His feet clasped upon the axle of the fast-spinning wheel.

Yet ever-shifting is the vision, as swift as quicksand, dancing and weaving like mist on the moors. Once more he found himself amidst the circle of seven cedars. These seven brethren. These seven priests. And before him he saw the most uncanny vision: a mighty golden eagle, perched upon the head of a beautiful black girl. Her skin was like ebony. Her flesh, as black as midnight sky. So too, her long and lustrous hair. Her lips, ripened pomegranates upon the vine. Her eyes were stars, a million and more, gazing to the heights of the far distant mountain. Her smile, a shining crescent moon. Her smile, the sun for whom his soul did seek. Her perfume sweet and intoxicating. And for him, this girl did flash the sweetest of smiles, familial, enchanting, a diamond-bright light. A smile as bright as the opened ark. Yet the wonder of her presence was but a swift passing moment, her face disappearing behind the mists of the violet veil.

Only now the eagle remained, sitting high upon the branch of the ageless oak. A tree that is always. A tree that is everything. It lilted and shuffled from side to side, as if dancing, as if beckoning, for Yeshua to come closer and look upon it. Thus he did and gasped to do so, feeling fear and wonder in equal measure. Its wings were flecked with feathers of leaping flame, burning with the colours of the dusk and dawn. Its eyes of translucent amber shone with a ferocious knowing. Its blue-tinged beak tipped with mustard yellow, its saffron toes armed with the blackest talons, sharper than the sharpest spear. With a piercing cry it flapped its wings, a fierce wind rising, storming and roaring and hurtling towards Yeshua. A wind that deemed not to strike him down, but only, instead, to gently raise him. The smell of burning sage and cedar filled his nostrils and trickled down to his lungs. The eagle cried out a second time. But now it cried out in the voice of a man, sung in a tongue Yeshua did not understand. Its prayerful tone was deep and resonant. Its undulating cadence, deeply soothing. Somehow he found himself enthroned upon the eagle's back as it trembled in readiness to set off in flight. Ready to hurtle with unimaginable speed and force, far up and high into infinite sky. And as they soared through the clouds, Yeshua heard the sound of children singing from somewhere far below. His young heart rejoiced, giving thanks to the eagle. For this eagle, he felt an endless love. He felt so happy, so free and unfettered.

But amorphous is the dreaming, changing like waves upon the surface of the lake. A shadow was now cast from some source unseen. A creeping, coming darkness, spreading like oil in water, all across the land. Where had once been the sound of children laughing, now was only a dreadful silence, peppered by the clang and clamour of maniacal laughter, expelled by those writhing in the dismal darkness, tormented and pained by deeds once done. He saw the leaves wither and turn to ash. He saw tree trunks grow thin before crumbling to dust. He saw the waters of the lake turn blood-red and the lifeless bodies of animals strewn across the plains. So too, the tribes of insects. The clouds sickened and swooned in a colourless sky, devoid of even but one bird in flight. No longer the fragrance of sage and cedars but instead the rancid odour smell of death, disease and decay.

All this, the great eagle did see, and its heart was stricken with sadness. It cried out loud one final time, unfurling its wings and swooping down, swooping down and flying all around, the burden of the world now upon its back. Higher and higher and higher it flew, the weight of the good earth resting heavily upon it. Higher and higher, beyond the seven worlds with ever-increasing speed, exceeding in swiftness even the pace of Pegasus, nor could the wings of Mercury raise a more mighty wind. And all this while, sitting perched amongst its fiery, golden feathers, Yeshua strained to see all that he could of these different realms. But so fast flew the eagle all was blurred to his sight, everything melting into an ocean of light.

"Oh," sighed Yeshua, "if only I had eyes to see this all."

And then, a voice, as old as a mountain.

"Then see all this through my eyes."

So spoke the phoenix as it soared and winged its way. Seeing as if beyond the edge of the universe, seeing to the core of the smallest of things, Yeshua drank in of the vision in both mind and heart, until after what had seemed a million years and more, the eagle finally came down to rest. Before the wondrous light of a new moon and sun, it lay down its charge, the great darkness dispelled. Gone the dream stealers and legions of shadow dwellers, those who had blighted and withered both root and bough. Gone now. Cast out. Both bound and banished. Fleeing in terror before this light of the living. How his ears rejoiced to hear the tribes sing in one voice yet many, giving of thanks to the rainbow-robed eagle. Giving forth of thanks, each woman and man, each girl and boy, all who had borne witness to the sight of its crossing.

And it was said that some took the eagle for the mightiest of winds. There were some who had taken it for a second sun. Some who had seen a belching, bloodstained dragon. Some, a tribe of angels, casting all things anew.

There were some who quaked in fear to meet their end, in the fast-coming legions of the ravenous one. Some who felt peace, joy and wonder, to see the skies lit up by the coming crystal palace. Yet all became clear, all became apparent, when the eagle passed over one seventh and final time. A vast, soaring eagle, of this no doubt remaining. A vast, soaring eagle, if ever one, there was, wrapping the earth in salve and liniment, enfolding her in robes of wind, causing the blue pearl's heart once more to sing. Seven times flying until all wounds were cleansed. Seven times circling until fading from sight, leaving all hearts bound together in heartfelt pledge. All feet dancing in celebration upon the rapturous earth. For salvation, salvation, salvation is your name.

Far, far away, up and through, beyond and down, in a place that was everywhere, in a place that was nowhere, Yeshua looked once more upon the girl with the long black hair. Entranced was she for the sight of the firebird. And as she thus gazed, he saw a tear fall slowly down her cheek. He heard too the sound of silent sobbing. Her hands clasped together in anguished prayer. Who are you, little girl with the long, black hair? With the blackest skin? More beautiful to me than a forest doe. What is the vision upon which you gaze? The source of your sorrow that my soul would assuage? For him and for him only, there came swift reply. For with her eyes of blackest purple, she saw that broken was the back of the magnificent eagle. Utterly broken. Beyond reach of repair. He followed the trace of her gaze all the way to its source, witnessing for himself the beautiful firebird, releasing of its one final, mortal breath. And in its eyes, Yeshua beheld love itself.

"Yeshua. Yeshua."

But not the voice of the eagle but one more familiar.

"Father?" said Yeshua in a croaky voice and wiping the sleep out from his eyes. "Yeshua." The voice again. The sound of his father. The end of the dreaming. The light of the dawning. The sweet promise and freshness of a brand new day. Return. Return. Return.

This book is printed on paper from sustainable sources managed under the Forest Stewardship Council (FSC) scheme.

It has been printed in the UK to reduce transportation miles and their impact upon the environment.

For every new title that Matador publishes, we plant a tree to offset CO_2, partnering with the More Trees scheme.

For more about how Matador offsets its environmental impact, see www.troubador.co.uk/about/